THE BEGINNING . . . .

Michael's face was close to Tabitha's, and she could feel his hard body pressed full-length against hers. He was looking down at her, his mouth forming unbelievable words.

"You love me, don't you Tabitha?"

"Mike, please—"

She tried to pull herself free of him, placing her hands against his chest and shoving him back. But her resistance crumbled as he folded his arms around her. Then his lips slid down her cheek to her neck, moist, caressing, warm with his desire.

All at once, Tabitha found herself responding, not knowing why, not caring now. She returned kiss for kiss, passionately, trying in wild desperation to please him, to satisfy his needs. And an agonizing thought spun through her mind: *It was never this way with my husband! Never!*

ENTRANCING ROMANCES BY SYLVIE F. SOMMERFIELD

ERIN'S ECSTASY   (656, $2.50)
by Sylvie F. Sommerfield
When English Gregg Cannon rescued Erin from Lecherous
Charles Duggan, he knew he must wed and protect this beautiful
child-woman he desired more than anything he ever wanted
before. When a dangerous voyage calls Gregg away, their love
must be put to the test . . .

TAZIA'S TORMENT   (669, $2.50)
by Sylvie F. Sommerfield
When tempestuous, beautiful Fantasia de Montega danced, men
were hypnotized by her charms. She harbored a secret revenge,
but cruel fate tricked her into loving the very man she'd vowed to
kill!

RAPTURE'S ANGEL   (750, $2.75)
by Sylvie F. Sommerfield
Angelique boarded the *Wayfarer* in a state of shock, just having
witnessed a brutal attack of her best friend. Then she saw
Devon—whose voice was so tender, whose touch was so gentle,
and they both knew they were captives of each others' hearts . . .

REBEL PRIDE   (691, $2.75)
by Sylvie F. Sommerfield
The Jemmisons and the Forresters were happy to wed their
children and thus unite their fortunes and plantations. But when
Holly Jemmison sees handsome but disreputable Adam Gilcrest,
her heart cries out that she has always loved him. She dare not
defy her family, but she dare not deny her heart . . .

*Available wherever paperbacks are sold, or order direct from the
Publisher. Send cover price plus 50¢ per copy for mailing and
handling to Zebra Books, 475 Park Avenue South, New York,
N.Y. 10016. DO NOT SEND CASH.*

MAGNOLIA PLANTATION

BY BEVERLY BUTLER

ZEBRA BOOKS
KENSINGTON PUBLISHING CORP.

ZEBRA BOOKS

are published by

KENSINGTON PUBLISHING CORP.
475 Park Avenue South
New York, N.Y. 10016

Printed in the United States of America

The major characters in this book are fictional and resemble no living persons. Magnolia Manor and the Silver Palace are wholly imaginary, but the city of Natchez and Natchez-under-the-Hill did exist as described. Several historical characters of the time are mentioned, but only in passing—President Andrew Jackson, Johann Sebastian Bach, John Murrell, the Harpe Brothers, Samuel Mason, Virgil Stewart, Joshua Cotton, William Sanders, Albe Dean, Lee Smith, John and William Earle, and Ruel Blake. The yellow fever epidemic (then called malignant fever) did occur frequently during the early part of the nineteenth century, and the attempt to establish an outlaw empire by inciting a slave rebellion is historically accurate.

INTRODUCTION

By the 1830s the white gold called cotton had firmly established itself as King of the South. One of the focal points of its vast empire was Natchez, Mississippi—a city both elegant and ugly, jewel-like and jaded, two disparate cities intricately woven into one.

On the high red-brown bluffs overlooking the broad expanse of the Mississippi River and the alluvial flatlands of Louisiana stood Natchez, a queenly city of sumptuous mansions and presumptuous people. In and around this city, where cotton ruled, the planter families lived in a scented baronial civilization. Here were shadowed streets bordered by magnolia and moss-draped oaks, and elaborate white-pillared homes that reflected the successive cultures of the French, the English, the Spanish, and finally the Americans. Here was an environment of refinement and charm, of high-ceilinged drawing rooms, curved staircases, wide galleries, lush gardens, and stately soirees—all accouterments of a carefully controlled abundance and a way of life that seemed, at least on the surface, to be not only tranquil by unchangeable.

Below the 200-foot bluff, stretched along a soft mile-and-a-half-long shelf of earth at the river's edge, lay Natchez-under-the-Hill. This was a benighted community of jerry-built shacks housing gambling dens, saloons, and bordellos, where a man weary of the river could find anything he wanted at a price he could afford to pay. Keelboats, flatboats, barges—as well as those relatively new trespassers on the scene, the steamboats—bobbed at rickety wharves along the edge of this sordid stretch of land, and the rivermen who plied the muddy waters of the Mississippi filtered through the narrow streets searching for whiskey, song, and women, finding what they sought in abundance.

Between the two cities there existed an uneasy truce. Each needed the other. The proud city on the bluff owed its boundless wealth to the unseemly city that lay at its feet; for Natchez-under-the-Hill was a busy port of call, a gateway through which cotton raised on the bluffs was shipped to markets around the world. For the most part, the wealthy planters who lived on the Hill, insulated against the blatant sin and corruption of the lower city, pretended the cesspool beneath them did not exist. Those who lived or cavorted briefly in Natchez-under-the-Hill were equally content to remain where they had everything their animal instincts demanded, leaving the lace-sleeved "dandies" on the Hill alone.

But occasionally these two intertwined, yet separated cultures met. This is the story of such a meeting.

BOOK I
The Beckoning Bluffs

1

The rain began to fall at midnight, softly. It came first to the silt-laden soil of Louisiana, pelting the rows of half-matured cotton with doubloon-sized drops. Then, having poured its blessings on the arid earth, it skipped across the Mississippi River, stippling the smooth surface of the river where it bent crescent-like before the bluffs of Natchez. The shelf of earth along the deep-banked river—called Natchez-under-the-Hill—became a marshland within minutes, and then the rain climbed the steep bluff to the heights of Natchez proper. For six hours it drenched the land, then stopped abruptly as dawn streaked the eastern sky with saffron and gold, driving the grayness into hasty retreat.

Tabitha Clay lifted the twilled swirls of her ankle-length bombazine skirt and tiptoed cautiously across the spongy morass of Silver Street. It was six o'clock in the morning—an outlandish hour for a young lady of breeding to be about, especially in notorious Natchez-under-the-Hill. The squalid hamlet cuddled beneath the promontory of Natchez proper was known, in this year of 1833, as the most sinful town on the Mississippi—not excluding even the Grand Dame of Sin, New Orleans. For a lady of good reputation to be alone in

Natchez-under at any hour was reason for raised eyebrows, but to be seen on infamous Silver Street at the unexplainable hour of six in the morning was particularly suspect. This was the time when the drunken debauchery of the evening before was coming to a finish, and when those who had participated were emerging from their shadowy dens to gaze once more at the bright miracle of day.

Tabitha was not unaware of this situation. At nineteen (and, she thought, headed for spinsterhood if she did not soon find a man to her liking) she was particularly knowledgeable about conditions in Natchez-under. She had lived for eight years in the flatlands where murder, robbery, and open vice were commonplace, and where everything from hole-in-the-wall dram shops to ornate brothels were not only tolerated but enthusiastically encouraged. Unlike her father, an itinerant preacher who raged with evangelistic fervor against the frightfulness of these conditions, Tabitha did not especially deplore them. She accepted them as a slice of life, did not consider herself capable of changing them, and therefore took the easier course of simply not letting them concern her.

Tabitha even admitted to herself—if, certainly, to no one else—that the dissolute way of life in Natchez-under had its enticing aspects. At the very least the dissipation against which her father preached aroused her curiosity. There were many licentious stories about what went on in the tumbledown shacks along the river. Often the raucous sounds of uncontrolled merriment carried to her own crude cabin on the "outskirts" of town where Silver Street made a stiff climb past an array of liquor and orange shops to the

11

bluff. At such moments her father would leap from his chair in outrage and, standing in the center of the room, proclaim, "In our very backyard exist all the sins of Sodom and Gommorah! I predict that the good Lord will someday destroy this seething place of Hell!" And Tabitha's mother would look up from her knitting—Tabitha could hardly imagine her mother in any pose but knitting or cooking—and say, "Please try to relax, Abijah. We all know it's a place of sin, but the Lord has permitted it to go on now for many years, and I must say He seems reluctant to interfere. We must be patient with Him." This sort of tongue-in-cheek logic rarely made an impression on Tabitha's father. "Doubt not," he'd reply, "that the Lord will wreak His revenge! Some fine day, Rachel, this unholy place will lie in ashes!"

Tabitha would then discreetly retire to her tiny room where she would sit and gaze wistfully out across the low-roofed houses and listen to the discordant noises of the sin her father deplored. It was at these times that Tabitha's rebellious nature was at its strongest. Often she found herself wishing she could spend an evening among the rivermen and their consorts along Silver Street. Not, heaven forbid, as one of them, but as a spectator viewing life. These thoughts she kept to herself, for they embarrassed her at the same time that they intrigued her. Besides, she had no desire to hurt, or incur the wrath of, the staunch disciplinarian who was her father. After all, her sister Ryma had already caused him more woe than he deserved. . . .

Tabitha gazed down Silver Street to the point where it curved toward the river. Over the ages the Mississippi had built an irregular shelf of silty earth a mile and a half long beneath the bluffs that rose two hundred feet to where Natchez stood. The meandering manner in which the three main streets and their intersecting paths gridironed the batture land, along with the unpainted shacks that abounded everywhere, reminded her of a rabbit warren. The three main avenues—Silver, Middle, and Water streets—were each approximately a mile long and ran parallel to the river. At their ends each made sharp turns that terminated at the shoreline. Between these major streets—which were muddy and slippery in wet weather, and dusty in dry—narrow cross-streets and footpaths zigzagged and darted about like furtive animals, dreary streets that smelled of squalor and the green scum that filled their waterholes.

Water Street was so named because it was nearest to the river, the center street was called Middle, and the one nearest the bluffs was Silver. Although there were iniquitous dens of vice on all of them, it was Silver Street which became known, during the first half of the nineteenth century, as the wickedest street in the country. Its reputation was well-deserved. Along its two sides wretched wooden shacks and a scattering of more pretentious buildings housing gambling emporiums, saloons, and whorehouses sprang from the earth like lusty mushrooms. These places operated day and night, filling the air with their bawdy sounds—the tinkling off-key rattle of pianos, the scraping noise of badly played violins, the clink of money and chips at the roulette and faro tables, the merriment of rivermen who had poured ashore to partake of liquor and women before continuing their journeys up or

13

down the Mississippi.

No doubt was left in any visitor's mind but that Natchez-under-the-Hill's most salable commodity was sex. Women of every hue—black, white, and mixed bloods—hung from windows and doorways, beckoning and taunting newly arrived rivermen. At the docks lynx-eyed hawkers told rivermen and travelers of the delights to be found in Natchez-under. Customers, pouring ashore from riverboats were not hard to find. Men trapped on slow-moving vessels for weeks were usually in a prime mood to indulge their fantasies once they poured ashore, and travelers on vacation were always tempted to patronize places they would not be caught dead in at home.

Brawling was almost as popular as drinking and whoring. Every night several dram shops were wrecked by impromptu rioting, and when the morning sun broke upon Natchez-under it invariably revealed a few bodies lying in the streets. Free-for-alls accounted for some of the nightly killings, but not all. Some were coldly premeditated. Many riverside gambling and bawdy houses, perched on pilings above the river, were deliberately equipped for stealthy murder. Unwary visitors were lured into the building, fleeced of their money, and then killed and dumped through trapdoors into the river. What authority existed in Natchez-under turned its head when a dead body was discovered floating downstream. At times the authorities even called the crime an "act of God"—despite knife wounds and other signs of earthly violence.

This, then, was the kind of Cyprian place through which Tabitha had determined to make her way. At

14

the point where Silver Street turned and evaporated into nothingness at the river's edge was a large wooden structure balanced precariously on rickety pilings. This spider-like building was reputed to be the worst—or some said the best—bordello in Natchez-under. Tabitha gazed at it and shuddered. Her heart pounded nervously at the prospect of entering a place of such vile reputation, yet it was imperative that she see Ryma. What, she wondered, would the inside of this place be like? What would be going on? Having a vivid imagination, Tabitha recoiled at the answer to her own questions. She prayed that there would be some kind of anteroom where Ryma could meet her, and that she would not be subjected to the jealous glares of painted women or the calculating glances of uncouth rivermen. Tabitha was, for all her youthful boldness and curiosity, a respectable girl—and promiscuity in any of its baser forms, if not foreign to her nature, was at least foreign to her experience.

As she picked her way through the muddy street—passing the Kentucky Tavern and the Natchez Hotel and notorious Old Bailey's Inn—a door opened in one of the saloons and two keelboatmen stumbled out. Tabitha viewed them askance. One was tall and thin with knobby arms and legs and a prominent Adam's apple; the other, squat and short-legged, resembled a butcher's block. Tabitha deliberately paid them no attention. Still, she was aware of the fact that they were regarding her with frank curiosity and, she thought, a certain perverse admiration.

"Now there's a fancy piece unless I miss my guess!" said the chunky one loudly. "A beauty she is, and built like a keelboat! Bet you could ride her from here

15

to New Awleans and never hit a snag!"

Tabitha felt her face go warm. She quickened her step, and in her heedlessness raced through a puddle and splashed mud and water over the hem of her flared skirt.

"Ain't you had enough yet, Fatty?" demanded the taller man. "I swear to Gawd, you'll wear yo'rself down to a nubbin'!"

The two men laughed obscenely. "I'm a rip-snortin' roarer!" howled the chunky one, going into a typical riverman's boast. "I kin handle me a dozen women a night, and then stand up an' fight any son of a bitch that wants to do me the honor of battle!"

The harsh voices trailed off as Tabitha, less concerned now about mud and water than about errant mankind, sought escape by sloshing across to the other side of the street. She was highly insulted by the remarks, as a proper lady was expected to be—but she did not lose sight of the fact that, had the men not admired her, they would not have made such comments.

Tabitha knew she was pretty. This was a bit of intuitive knowledge that pleased her. She had often looked into the cracked and clouded mirror on her dresser—which she was sure didn't do her justice—and decided that her looks represented an asset she might one day use to her advantage. She was one of those women whose magnolia-white skin seemed never to tan under the treacherous Southern sun. The creamy whiteness was, of course, aided by a predilection Tabitha had for sunbonnets that shaded her face, and also to the frequent application of buttermilk and cucumber poultices which she hated utterly but endured with unflinching bravery. Her hair was ebony-

16

black and pulled into a tight chignon at the back. Her eyes were striking—the deep penetrating color of wild violets—and they peered shyly from an oval-shaped face that abounded in innocence. Still, it was her unique eyes that betrayed her, for they sparkled in a manner that men could interpret only as a lust for life uncommon to women of the day.

Her manners, however, were impeccable, having been imposed on her since childhood by a mother whose stolidity was as immovable as a mountain, and a father who staunchly believed that female interests should be restricted to cooking and sewing, with any observation of the outside world limited to carefully selected books on weekdays and the Bible on Sunday morning. But her feelings were less controllable than her manners, and although she accepted with outward calm her limited station in life, she keenly resented the enforced imprisonment that went with being a woman.

Men, Tabitha ruefully admitted, enjoyed all the advantages of life. They could go to sea, join the army, open up new lands in the west, and lead lives of adventure almost unbelievable to their womenfolk. Women, on the other hand, were restricted by their sex, expected to stay at home, keep house for a man, fill his demanding stomach with nourishing food, submit to whatever erotic notions he entertained abed at night, and silently bear his babies. Tabitha was convinced that such a life was not worth the candle—except, perhaps, under the most advantageous circumstances.

Looking back the way she had come, Tabitha's eyes swept upward to the soaring bluff on top of which the

17

city of Natchez gleamed like a jewel in the sun. The bluff itself was overgrown with wild honeysuckle and grapevines, and its crest was topped with a magnificent sweep of oak. None of the buildings of the town were visible from Tabitha's position, but she had more than once beheld the buildings and had been impressed. All the important people lived on the Hill—wealthy planters, lawyers, doctors, and merchants, those who ruled the city and enjoyed the power that went with money and position. Being the wife of a plantation owner, Tabitha had often thought, would be an experience worthy of her talents. These were the women who lived in stately mansions of great charm and distinction, who circulated in a society of their own making, and who attended dinners and teas and soirees. These were the women who wore flowing dresses imported from foreign lands, who danced the minuet and waltz—and more recently the exciting cotillion—with handsome and polished men. Marriage under such conditions, she thought, would be tolerable. Gnawing envy crept into her eyes again and she vowed, as she had so many times before, that some day she would live on the Hill.

Tabitha had even made a few brief sorties into this realm of the elite with the bold intention of implementing her desires. Chafing under the limitations imposed on her by her ministerial father, she had on occasion climbed the hill to the esplanade, ostensibly to take advantage of the remarkable view it provided of the river. There were always handsomely attired people on the esplanade, including young bachelors who seemed to be more interested in viewing women than the Mississippi. Tabitha was not above putting herself shamelessly on display, but for some time none of the eligible men of Natchez had approached her. And as failure followed failure Tabitha became convinced that she would have to do more to attract men than simply stand there looking out over the Mississippi as if she had never seen it before.

Mulling the matter over in her mind, Tabitha had decided that flirtation was the shortest avenue to success. She was aware that men were men whether they dressed in ruffled shirts and cutaway coats or in the whiskey-stained garb of the river rat. She was also aware that even a decent woman could use sex by inference to gain a desirable end, and the more she thought of it the more determined she became to use her beauty and charm to captivate some elegant gentleman on the Hill. She knew, however, that she had to walk a tightrope between being crudely bold and gently persuasive, and she felt that if she could encourage a man to make the first overture she could handle the development of a romance with skill and cunning.

Then, one day when her father was busy regaling a group of rivermen about their sins, Tabitha scrambled up the incline to the esplanade and almost ran headlong into a man that took her breath away. He was young, handsome, finely dressed — a picture right out of her wildest imagination — and when their eyes met Tabitha did not demurely turn her head. If anything, her stare was bold and inviting, and the man had sauntered toward her in a casual way and said, "It's a lovely view, isn't it?" Unprovocative, innocuous words, but enough to spark a lengthy conversation. . . .

Tabitha tore her eyes away from the Hill with an effort and riveted her gaze on the wicked old building she was about to enter. But her mind remained on the heights. She had dreamed of living on the Hill ever since she had become old enough to have dreams. Some fine day those dreams would come true, she thought, and she would be the grandest lady in all the Natchez country!

2

Racing quickly over the marsh ground, Tabitha approached the wooden structure on the pilings. A gaudy sign with red block letters dangled over the doorway; the place called itself the Silver Palace for no discernible reason since it was neither silver nor a palace. It looked shaky, in fact, as if it teetered on the brink of collapse, and Tabitha recalled that in several instances similar structures had tumbled into the river during nights of rowdy merriment, and that the bodies of rivermen and whores were fished out of the water the next morning, many still locked in sexual embrace.

A ramp ascended from ground level to the door of the building and Tabitha tiptoed up it. Her heart was racing now, for this was a new and frightening experience. To actually enter a bordello—which her devout father described as a "den of iniquity"—was almost beyond her imagination. For one agonizing moment she thought, *What would Father think?* Then she abruptly shoved this disturbing thought out of her mind—a defense mechanism Tabitha habitually employed whenever an unpleasant thought intruded on her conscience—and continued up the ramp.

Tabitha was pleased to find the front door standing

ajar. Had it not been she would have had to pull the rawhide latchstring to enter, a bold action that seemed somehow too deliberate to her. Cautiously she peered inside. The place was dark and uncheerful, illuminated only by a few candles strategically placed to give a modicum of light without invading privacy. The dawning of the day was blotted out by purple draperies at the windows. At a long mahogany bar several rivermen stood, mugs of tafia before them. Their women companions—Tabitha saw that they ranged from white to black—leaned intimately against them. The rest of the barroom was filled with a scattering of small tables and chairs, some occupied by couples, others empty. Somewhere a piano tinkled discordantly, male voices sang bawdy songs and women laughed impishly.

Tabitha retreated hastily from the door. Her ears burned with the crude, earthy lyrics of the song, and her nostrils flared in disgust at the ancient odors of the bordello. Perhaps it had been a mistake to come here after all, even to see Ryma, she thought, and was ready to flee headlong from the place when a strong male voice caused her to hesitate.

"You at the door! What do you want here?"

Tabitha steeled herself to look back into the room. A young man dressed in buckskin breeches and jacket blocked the doorway. Tabitha's alert eyes scanned him quickly, and her instant appraisal was that he looked too clean-cut to be dallying about in a Natchez-under brothel. He was in his mid-twenties, tall, muscular, and, in a rugged backwoods way, reasonably handsome. His eyes were a piercing blue, his square-jawed face closely shaven, and his rust-colored hair billowed back in a giant wave. Although he had the unpolished look of a frontiersman, there was still something about him that suggested a man of manners. But then his slanted grin, and the frank way his eyes traveled over Tabitha's entire body, implied crudity again and fire came into her cheeks. *Heavens,* she thought, *he practically undressed me with one look!*

Before Tabitha could answer he spoke again.

"You don't appear to be the kind of girl that's needed here," he said, the impish grin still cutting across his face. "Of course, I could be wrong. I often am about women."

Tabitha felt shock seep through her, and she fought to regain her lost poise.

"I'll have you know, sir," she said, sounding extremely righteous, "that I'm not here for what you apparently think. I want to see Ryma."

The man's sandy eyebrows arched. He scratched at his chin thoughtfully.

"I'm Mike Long. Dr. Mike Long, to be formal."

Tabitha looked at him with growing distrust. He did not look like a doctor. Her mental image of a doctor was a man in a black frock coat, a Vandyke beard and square spectacles behind which twinkled the wise eyes of a student. This man looked as if he would be more at home in a rough-and-tumble than in a laboratory.

"A doctor in Natchez-under?" she asked, conveying her doubts. "Most reputable doctors live on the Hill."

He smiled at her attempt to lower his prestige with words. Despite herself, Tabitha liked his smile.

"Natchez-under's a splendid place for a doctor," he

said. "Very lucrative. Never a night passes that I don't mend a head or put an eye back in that's been gouged out. Then there are stabbings and shootings too—no end of business!"

Tabitha shuddered. She had to admit that the man's grin was contagious, but still she disliked him. He *was* impertinent.

"If you'll spare me your personal history," she said caustically, "I'd like to see Ryma."

"I'm from Kentucky," said Mike Long, ignoring her request. "Sort of a backwoods doctor. Not much training, pretty stupid, and downright awkward sometimes. But I know how to patch a knife wound or set a broken bone or sometimes even sew an ear back on. Happen to have any wounds you want patched?"

"*May* I see Ryma?" snapped Tabitha in exasperation.

For the first time the young doctor seemed to take cognizance of Tabitha's request. His eyes thinned in puzzlement and he tugged at his chin again.

"What do you want to see Ryma for?"

Tabitha drew in her breath. This man not only provoked her, but something in his bantering manner made her feel common and indecent. Couldn't he see that she wasn't the kind of girl who— Her thoughts halted in mid-flight.

"Ryma," she said stiffly, "happens to be my *sister!*"

Doctor Mike Long accepted this startling information with another elevation of his eyebrows.

"Older sister, no doubt. Ryma's got a few years on her."

"She's five years older than I, if you must know *all* my business," said Tabitha impatiently. "Now, will you let me in?"

"I don't know. Have you an appointment? Ryma's pretty busy, you know. Much in demand."

"Oh, you're loathsome!" said Tabitha in disgust, but the impudent expression on Mike Long's face never changed. He seemed determined to deny Tabitha entrance to the Silver Palace, but he was thwarted when a flash of scarlet moved behind him and a female voice said, "Tabby! For God's sake!"

Tabitha edged past Mike Long, conscious of the closeness of his lean-hard body as she passed. The smell of cheap liquor, sweat, and buckskin clothing assailed her as she entered the room; and she fought off a sudden nausea. She stopped shortly in front of Ryma and only with difficulty suppressed an exclamation of surprise. Tabitha had not seen her sister since she had left home in a raging fit of anger twelve months before, and the change was frightening. Ryma had never worn makeup at home—this being, in Father's opinion, the paint of the devil. Her clothes had always been plain and modest—linsey-woolsey or muslin in somber grays or dark blues—this being, also in Father's opinion, the only proper attire for a decent female. But now Ryma was a gaudy fraud from top to bottom. Her chestnut hair had been dyed a blazing red. Her face was heavily powdered, her lips were a hard red gash, and her exhausting way of life had sewn seams of depravity in her face. She wore a panniered dress that billowed from her wide hips, and Tabitha thought that the color—a garish scarlet—clashed terribly with her fiery hair. The yawning decolletage of her dress made the upper swells of Ryma's full breasts bulge out in swollen globes for the male eye.

Tabitha tried to conceal her dismay, but she doubted her own success. Ryma may have noticed the consternation in her eyes—even Mike Long, she thought with some alarm, may have observed her shock. She attempted to camouflage her surprise by kissing Ryma quickly on her scented cheek but the device lacked artfulness.

"Come with me," said Ryma sharply.

With Tabitha trailing close on her heels like an obedient pup, Ryma led her through a door at the end of the bar. The room they entered was hung with purple draperies similar to those in the bar. The matching carpet was thick, and the room was furnished with comfortable chairs and divans. Three ornamental flambeaux spread a flickering light over the room. Several men lounged in the upholstered chairs, each with a painted woman on his lap. A heavy scent of perfume pervaded the air. Ryma walked quickly through the parlor and through another door. Tabitha, with fluttering heart, followed. She found herself in a tiny anteroom with only a bare table and two chairs.

Ryma closed the door leading to the parlor, motioned for Tabitha to be seated, then sat down herself. Her face was stiff and uncompromising.

"I told you, Tabby, never to come here," she said severely.

"I know. But I had to."

"Is everything all right at home? Is someone sick?"

"Everything's fine, Ryma. I don't come with any sad news."

Ryma leaned back in her chair and regarded her

younger sister with suspicion.

"Then why did you come here? What are you up to?" She waved her hand impatiently as Tabitha began to speak. "No. Don't tell me yet. Let me look at you. You're nineteen, aren't you? You look a little older. That's good at your age." She stood up nervously, paced to a small window overlooking Silver Street. She scanned the street with unseeing eyes, then sat down again, crossing her legs, revealing a silk-clad calf; then, thinking better of it, she uncrossed them again. "I sensed a bit of shock when you first saw me," she said. "What do you think of the way I look?"

"Really, Ryma, I—"

"Oh, don't hedge, honey!" Ryma's lips twisted in a bitter smile. "I came here a year ago, looking something like you do. Wide-eyed and innocent. Now I look like a whore." Her tone became belligerent. "What else did you expect me to look like?"

"Ryma! I'm not here to condemn."

"I thought our dear father may have turned you completely against me." Ryma's voice was edged with cynicism. "How is he—and Mother?"

"They're both fine."

"And Father's still preaching hell-fire and brimstone?"

"Well, if you mean—"

"You know what I mean. Grace at every meal. Bible-reading every night after supper. Silent Sundays. Stirring sermons on the sins of the world—and particularly Natchez-under-the-Hill. God, how I hated it!"

"He's a good man," said Tabitha, feeling the need to defend her father and his beliefs. "He is trying to do good."

"Sure. Wants to live in Natchez-under so he can save a few souls. Goes up and down Silver Street trying to convert drunks and whoremasters and harlots and gamblers." Ryma's upper lip curled in contempt. "Have you ever seen the thick green scum the river washes up along the shore, Tabitha? You wouldn't try to purify it or make anything of it, would you? Well, the human scum the river washes up is the same way—you can't make anything out of it either. Father ought to know he has no chance."

"But if he can convert even one or two," Tabitha said, "he feels it worthwhile."

"For every one or two he converts," said Ryma practically, "five hundred more roll in off the river looking for whiskey and women." She made an intolerant gesture. "And while he's converting a handful of bleary-eyed drunks, he's raising two daughters in the worst hell-hole in the country. It isn't surprising, really, that I ended up a prostitute. I hope you don't."

"You didn't have to take that road, Ryma."

"Oh, God—you sound like Father!" Ryma laughed. "It's just that when I got old enough to be fed up on Father and his religious mania and get out—well, it looked like a logical road and it was certainly nearby." She smiled ruefully. "Oh, hell, I'm not defending myself. . . . Do they ever talk about me at home, Tabby?"

Tabitha shook her head. "Father never mentions your name. Not since he disowned you. He's never got over the hurt, Ryma."

"And Mother?"

"Mother sometimes mentions you, but not often—

and not in Father's presence."

"It's better if they both forget me," said Ryma harshly. She made a truculent gesture with her hand, as if to erase all they had said from some invisible blackboard. "What did you come here for, Tabby?"

Tabitha let her eyes fall to her hands. She was twisting a handkerchief nervously, and Ryma liked the demureness of the gesture.

"I guess it's a little foolish, me coming here," she said slowly. "But—well, there wasn't anywhere else I could go." She looked up suddenly, holding Ryma's eyes with her own. "Ryma, you'll think I'm crazy, but I came here to get a dress."

"A *dress!*"

"Yes. I need a nice dress. A fancy one. A real long-flowing, luxurious one."

"Why did you come to me?"

"Because you have lots of clothes." There was urgency in Tabitha's voice now. She put out her hand and placed it on Ryma's arm imploringly. "You have many beautiful dresses, like the one you have on," she said, ignoring the fact that she thought Ryma's dress was dreadful. "I'm sure you have. I've always heard about the beautiful dresses worn by the women in —in—"

"In my business?" A low chuckle escaped Ryma's throat. "Rumors do get around, don't they? But in the interest of accuracy, women in my business don't need any clothes." She laughed again, as if amused at her own joke. "Oh, I have a wardrobe of half a dozen or so dresses, I guess. I suppose I could find one for you."

"Oh, it would be wonderful if you could," said Tabitha with childlike excitement. "You know I can't ask Father for such a dress. He couldn't afford to buy me one on the Hill, which is where he'd have to buy it. And anyway he doesn't believe that women should dress in such fashion that they look alluring to men."

"I *know* Father." Ryma smiled knowingly. "And, I take it, this is exactly what you have in mind—luring men?"

Tabitha felt her face grow warm. She hated to blush. It was so dreadfully embarrassing.

"I don't want you to think I'm a—"

"Bold woman? No. You hardly qualify, honey. Although I've always suspected that you have certain predatory instincts, well-hidden, of course. Who is this man you're attempting to—uh—lure?"

Tabitha's brow knitted in a frown. "You make it sound so—so physical," she complained. "Anyway, he's a man I met last Sunday. I went up on the Hill, Ryma—you know how I always liked to walk along the old Spanish esplanade. I stopped and looked out over the river—I've always admired the view from the heights—and it was lovely. The sun carved a golden path across it, and on the other side you could see the cotton crops on the Louisiana flatlands."

"You should have been a poet. About this man?"

"Well, he came along and stood near me. For some time he said nothing. But he was something of a flirt, because he kept glancing at me. I wasn't unaware of it, of course."

"What girl is? And besides, wasn't it what you were hoping for?"

"Ryma, for heaven's sake!"

"All right, honey. Go on."

"Well, finally he turned to me and remarked about

30

the view. Then he moved closer and we talked."

"How were you dressed at the time?" asked Ryma calculatingly.

"Not so badly for me," said Tabitha with relief. "I had the same dress on I'm wearing now. It's my only dressy one, you know. But even so I felt rather shabby, because he was so—so exquisite."

"One of the dandies on the Hill, eh?"

"Yes. But very gentlemanly, and very nice. He asked me where I was from, and of course I had to tell him that I lived in Natchez-under. But even then he didn't seem to lose interest, Ryma. In fact, he asked if he could see me again!" This last Tabitha uttered with complete awe.

Ryma regarded her sister under lowered eyelids.

"I suspect he was interested because you *were* from Natchez-under," she said cynically. "When is this momentous second meeting going to occur?"

"Tomorrow—Sunday. And I've got to look right, Ryma. That's why I want so much to borrow one of your dresses. I was all week getting up nerve enough to come here. Please!"

Ryma smiled wryly. "Wearing one of my dresses, you might look like a harlot. They're pretty gaudy."

"But I've got to have one! I can't let him see me in this same dress. Please, Ryma, you've got to help me."

Ryma stood up. She walked to the window and gazed out again at the never-ending chaos below her. The quays, warehouses, and mercantile establishments along the shoreline were humming with activity. A steamboat was docking, which meant that business at the Silver Palace would quicken within the hour. Ryma turned slowly from the window.

"Who is this man?"

"He's a rich cotton planter, Ryma," said Tabitha with excitement. "His name is Nicholas Enright."

Ryma's eyes widened; a low whistle escaped her red lips.

"Nicholas Enright! You're aiming pretty high, aren't you? He's just the wealthiest planter on the Hill, that's all. Owns Magnolia Manor, you know. Has acres of cotton in both Mississippi and in Louisiana, a stable of fine horses, and God knows what else. A Harvard graduate cum laude, very fine breeding, cream of Natchez society, all that sort of thing. Why, the daughters of half the planters on the Hill would like to get their claws on *him!*"

"That's what's so exciting!" Tabitha was quivering all over. "With all the girls he could have, to think he wants to see me again! That makes it all the more satisfying. He asked me to be on the esplanade tomorrow at noon, and he would come by in his barouche and we would go for a ride."

Ryma returned to her chair, sat down tensely on the edge of it.

"You know, Tabby, you're a lot like me. You're frightfully determined to get what you want. Girls aren't supposed to be that way, you know. They're supposed to wait and maybe, if they're lucky, they'll realize some of the nice things in life. If they aren't, they're not expected to complain. But you and I are different. I want money and everything money can get me. You want the same thing. The only difference between us is that we're taking different paths to get what we want—and I'm not so sure but what your path isn't better than mine." She leaned back in the chair, closing her eyes in meditation. "I remember, Tabby, from the time you were a child you said you wanted someday to live on the Hill. It's been an ambition with you—no, a compulsion. It was something you were determined to make come true, although you didn't know just how you would do it. Now, all at once, comes this opportunity. Through sheer accident—or perhaps design on your part—you meet Nicholas Enright. And in him you see your avenue to a better life on the Hill. And Tabby, you'll do anything to get there, won't you?"

"What on earth do you mean, Ryma—*anything*?"

Ryma chuckled. "Don't get me wrong, Tabby. You're not crude, like I am. I just undress and fall into bed, and when it's over I've got money clutched in my hot little hand. You're more subtle. You will sweet-talk Nicholas Enright, and you'll lower your lashes bashfully, and you'll be so damned desirable that Nicholas will go out of his mind. Then he'll ask you to marry him, and maybe you'll even be coy enough to hesitate awhile before saying yes. But you know, right now, that you're going to say yes, don't you?"

Tabitha stared at Ryma in disbelief. She felt as if her entire soul had been stripped bare, as if a door had opened and revealed all her innermost secrets and desires and—yes—her plans.

"Well, I suppose if—"

"No *if* about it, Tabby. You're after him. And let me tell you one thing more. If the sweet-talk and the dropped eyelashes and the coy attitude don't work, you'll seduce him if you have to. Isn't that right, honey? You can tell *me*."

33

Suddenly Tabitha felt confused and embarrassed. She hadn't come here to make a confession, and it wasn't fair of Ryma to force it. Still, she knew Ryma was basically correct in her assumptions. This *was* her chance, and she didn't intend to let it slip away.

"Please give me a dress," she said softly.

A smile twisted Ryma's lips. "And what will Father say when you bring home an outlandish dress with a pinched waist and low bodice?"

"He won't know. He's leaving tonight to go to New Orleans. He'll be gone for several weeks. By that time I should have Nicholas Enright—" She stopped, mortified by what she had intended to say.

"Wrapped around your finger, Tabby?" Ryma said. "I understand perfectly, honey."

3

The squat gorilla-like keelboatman sat in stoic silence as Dr. Michael Long stitched and bandaged the ugly red hole that had once been covered by an ear.

"I came in here for a drink after the fight," he muttered. "I didn't think I'd find no doctor here to sew me up."

"Lucky you did," Mike Long said as he finished the job. "Next time don't pick a fight with somebody you can't lick."

The brawny riverman slowly rose to his feet. "The next time I meet that bastard, he won't chaw off no ear—I swear it."

Promising to pay for the medical aid when he returned from New Orleans with his pay—a convenient pledge Mike Long knew might or might not be kept—the riverman trudged down the ramp to join his fellow crewmen on a keelboat laden with pigs, turkeys, tobacco, corn, and wheat for New Orleans. Mike Long sat down at a small table in the Silver Palace and gazed out the window at the chaotic confusion in the street. A dozen head of cattle had been unloaded from a barge and a planter in a wide-brimmed hat whipped them toward the bluffs. Several pigs ran wild in the street, grunting and poking their leather-like snouts into puddles left by the rain. Carts and drays were everywhere, carrying goods to and from the docks. Half-nude women hung in doorways, calling out to passersby. A parrot, perched on an upper balcony, squawked testily and kept repeating the words he had been taught, "Come in, come in! Whorehouse! Whorehouse!" A few rivermen heeded the parrot's blandishments.

Dr. Mike Long's eyes left the window and returned to the barroom. The place was still dim, with shadows hanging in the corners of the room; it was brightened only in one place where the light of the morning sun cut a golden path through a window and over the sawdust-covered floor. Most of the rivermen had returned to their craft and the dram shop was temporarily deserted. A few of the girls still remained at the bar, but most of them were sleeping off what had been a rigorous night. Mike Long understood that there were twenty-five harlots at the Silver Palace, some reputed to be imported from New Orleans and even Paris because they possessed special whispered-about talents that only men (and a very few women) knew existed. A few were of such tender age that only the perverse instincts of the rivermen could be titillated by them, and others were older and with such wide experience that they were in demand by those men who placed a knowledge of fundamentals higher in their estimations than youthful enthusiasm. Some of the women nursed cuts and bruises which Mike Long had bandaged—a not uncommon lot for women who catered to the brutal whims of the rivermen.

Mike Long had been in Natchez-under-the-Hill for

only three months. He was twenty-eight years old, and for the first eighteen years of his life he had lived in Louisville. His family, poor settlers, had bravely tried to raise six children, but four had died in infancy and an older brother had been killed by an Indian. These misfortunes reduced Mike's family to a heavy-drinking father who frequented the grog shops more than his own home, and an emaciated mother with an incurable case of consumption. When Mike was eighteen his mother coughed up her last blood-splattered sputum and died. Mike's father immediately went on a drinking bout after the funeral, stumbled blindly from a Louisville grog shop into the Ohio River, and disappeared beneath the lapping gray waters.

With nothing left to hold him, Mike Long traveled east, worked and studied, and finally earned a partial medical education at Yale College, where a medical department had been opened in 1810. After two years in school he served as an apprentice to a crotchety old doctor back in Louisville whose medical knowledge was limited but whose dedication knew no bounds. Then, at twenty-seven, Mike Long decided to set out on his own.

Hearing glowing tales of the new cotton frontier opening along the Mississippi—not to mention the delights to be found in a place called Natchez-under-the-Hill—Mike had taken passage on a keelboat and gradually made his way toward his goal. At Natchez-under he rented two cheap rooms and hung out a shingle. The back room of the two served as his living quarters and the front as his office. He was proud of the office, with its medical books and shelves of pharmaceuticals and surgical instruments. It gave him a feeling of confidence, as did his success, which was almost instantaneous. The amount of business that came his way in brawling Natchez-under—for he was the only doctor beneath the bluffs—amazed him even if it failed to satisfy him completely. Mike had a desire someday to set up a practice on the bluffs, or perhaps to associate himself with a rich planter as a plantation slave doctor. In either eventuality, fighting such Southern ailments as dysentery, tetanus, milk sickness, and malignant fever would be better than a steady diet of mending broken heads and smashed faces.

The vision of Tabitha—the creamy skin, black hair, and peculiar violet eyes—kept recurring, and he continually glanced at the door through which she and Ryma had vanished. For some reason he was unable to understand, her presence at the Silver Palace distressed him. She was not a professional woman, of that he was sure. He was equally certain that she was out of place in a house of whores. He had an inexplicable impulse to accompany her home when she left this place, making sure that she traversed in safety the long stretch of Silver Street with its rough array of saloons and assignation houses. He wanted to take her directly to the door of her home, like an errant child, and tell her parents to keep this tender bird caged up, lest she become despoiled. For, despite the fact that she was apparently Ryma's sister—a fact he had considerable difficulty assessing—this girl obviously did not belong on the violent streets of lower Natchez.

At length the door of the tiny room creaked open and Tabitha emerged, carrying a large paper-wrapped bundle under her arm. As Ryma stood grim-faced in the doorway, Tabitha walked with mincing steps across the corner of the barroom toward the door leading to the street. She purposely did not glance in the direction of the bar, because she did not want to see Mike Long if he were still there. But she sensed his presence and the curiosity of his gaze as she walked quickly to the exit.

"Good luck, Tabby," Ryma called. "And please don't come back here."

Mike Long watched until Tabitha left the building, and when Ryma turned back into the parlor he slipped quickly around the end of the bar and followed Tabitha out. He overtook her just as she reached the end of the ramp to the street. For a moment, as she walked along clutching the bundle like a child holding a treasured new toy, she did not see him. With an impulsive gesture he took her by the arm.

"Really!" Her violet eyes flicked up at him and she withdrew her arm with a show of dismay.

"You're too quick, milady," Mike said carelessly. "I didn't get a chance to say goodbye."

"I wasn't aware that it was necessary," said Tabitha coldly.

Mike Long's irritating grin swept crookedly across his rough-hewn face. The amused expression infuriated Tabitha. The man was absolutely insufferable—but he *was* handsome. And the way he looked at a girl—heavens!

"Did you get the job?" Mike asked cagily.

"I don't know what you're talking about."

"The job. Did Ryma sign you on?"

Tabitha's mouth flew open. For the first time Mike Long became aware that the deep violet eyes con-

tained a smoldering, ever-present fire capable of leaping into flame at any given moment.

"You're beastly!" snapped Tabitha. "Utterly
beastly!"

"I'll walk you home," said Mike, ignoring the angry
outburst.

Tabitha stopped. She had no intention of permitting this ill-bred man to accompany her home. It was
obvious from his bold manners that he was no
gentleman—not like Nicholas Enright anyway—and
Tabitha considered that she had taken a sufficient risk
in leaving her home to visit Ryma without returning in
the company of an uncouth and impudent
backwoodsman. She hoped to get home before her
father awakened—for he had spent late hours on the
streets of Natchez-under the evening before spreading
the gospel of the Lord—but if he was awake and saw
her approaching the house with Mike Long there
would be tedious explanations to give.

"You're obviously a man who must be spoken to
with brusqueness," Tabitha said primly, "so I'll try to
accommodate you. I don't care to have you take me
home. I'm perfectly safe, I assure you, and only have
half a mile to walk. Now would you please let me
alone?"

Mike Long glanced up and down Silver Street.
More and more rivermen, with alcohol still in their
stomachs and sex on their one-track minds, were
wending their way back to their crafts. Tabitha was
walking against traffic, away from the quay and along
the bluffs of Natchez proper, and it was highly doubtful to Mike that she could run such a gauntlet of
rivermen and wharf rats in as much safety as she anticipated.

"You're a headstrong girl, and a foolish one," he said. "But I have no wish to impose myself on a lady who values her privacy as much as you apparently do. I'll say good-day."

For a fleeting second she stood and stared at him; then with an angry swish of her bombazine skirt she turned away from him and walked defiantly up Silver Street.

It was less than a minute later that Tabitha had misgivings about her abrupt dismissal of the backwoods doctor. She became acutely aware that the men in the street were regarding her with more than casual interest. A few beckoned her with whistles and calls, but she ignored all of them and looked straight ahead, never changing her rapid pace as her feet flew over the dirt road. On several occasions she even walked through puddles of water without seeing them until she felt the moisture soak through her shoes.

But for a beautiful girl of nineteen to walk the length of Silver Street in Natchez-under-the-Hill without being molested would not only have been an insult to the girl but a black mark on the escutcheon of every riverman in the vicinity. So it was that Tabitha was suddenly confronted with a man whose daring transcended catcalls and whistles. Standing on widespread legs, he blocked her path and forced her to halt.

"If you don't mind, sir—" Tabitha began, and then shuddered as her eyes scanned the figure before her. He was a repulsive man with dark tangled hair that lay in a bird's-nest clump on the top of his rounded head. He wore a patch over one eye, and his other was black and rodent-like. His arms were the muscular bands of a keelboatman accustomed to poling a heavy, almost unmanageable vessel upstream, and his legs were bowed in the shape of an O. His mouth was the most horrible thing about him—an irregular red gash across the lower part of his face which showed crooked, tobacco-stained teeth. His breath was heavy with cheap tafia.

"Well, now, if you ain't a purty parcel!" he said, weaving slightly on his bandy legs. He reached out a grime-encrusted hand to seize her and Tabitha stepped back in sudden shock and tried to walk around him. Deftly, despite his drunkenness, he blocked her path again.

"Please let me pass," Tabitha said, as a sick feeling of fear assailed her.

"You don't figger me for a fool, do you, ma'am? You're as purty a wench as I seen all night, and I ain't aimin' to let you run away without I'm not makin' a try fer ya."

By now Tabitha was thoroughly alarmed. Despite living in Natchez-under, she had never before encountered a situation such as this, and she was not at all sure how to handle it. She decided she had been a fool to venture forth on Silver Street at this particular hour, but it was too late now to fret about her incautiousness. As her thoughts raced, the man lunged toward her, one filthy arm encircling her waist, and she felt the rocklike hardness of his body against her and smelled his sour breath in her face.

Then a new figure loomed suddenly on her right and Tabitha twisted to see who the new intruder might be. Mike Long stood there, the grin of amusement still on his face—and making absolutely no effort to come to her aid!

"Are you in need of help, ma'am?" he asked softly. "Or do you wish to continue on alone?"

Tabitha tried to pull herself free of the drunken keelboatman, but he held her in a grip of iron.

"If you're a gentleman—" she gasped, and Mike's smile broadened.

"With pleasure, milady."

Mike stepped closer and his right fist thudded against the keelboatman's jaw. Like a wounded spider, the tentacles of the keelboatman's arms withdrew, and he stumbled and fell in the middle of the road. Almost at the same time that he struck the blow, Mike Long shoved Tabitha aside, braced his legs in the treacherous mud of the street, and waited for the bull-like charge he knew the keelboatman would make.

The riverman rose slowly to his feet. There was a trickle of blood in the corner of his mouth and he brushed it away with the back of a hairy hand. His one malevolent eye glared at Mike, and he belched copiously before going into a typical frontier boast.

"I'm a ring-tailed roarer and a goddamn water-dog!" he howled, strutting about like a bantam cock. "I'm a salt-river screamer from the Mississip! I kin lick ten times my weight in wildcats and I kin swallow niggers whole, raw or cooked! I kin out-drink, out-fight, and out-fuck any man that's ever set foot in ol' Natchez, and I'm ready to jump down any bastard's throat what wants to say I cain't. I ain't had a fight fer a week, and goddamn if I ain't a-hankerin' to git some of the kinks outa my bones. I kin whip any son of a bitch that wants to stand up and fight me like a man.

43

You wanta see how tough I am to chaw, mister, you step right up. I'm spilin' fer exercise!"

Mike Long simply stood there and surveyed the man, a half-smile playing across his face, his long muscular arms dangling, ready. He noticed for the first time the red turkey feather in the keelboatman's hair, and he knew what it meant. It was a badge of distinction which indicated that this man was an expert in the rough-and-tumble tactics of battling rivermen. He could not have earned his feather without having gouged out eyes, bitten off ears and noses, and in general having raised havoc with other men of his ilk.

Like sparrows attracted to crumbs of bread in the street, other rivermen emerged from the ramshackle buildings and formed a ragged circle around the combatants. Tabitha, crowded now into the circle of onlookers, had speechless horror in her face. She had seen fights before, but only at a distance. In the tough frontier towns along the Mississippi, the rough-and-tumble had become a way of life. There were no rules that governed this form of combat. Hands, arms, heads, knees, elbows, and teeth were legitimate weapons. The object was to reduce your opponent to a helpless and bloodied pulp, thus rendering him unfit for further combat. Any way you could accomplish this desired objective was considered fair. The fight that did not end with an ear bitten off, an eye gouged out, or a groin mutilated, was mild indeed.

In upper Natchez, Tabitha could not help thinking, gentlemen settled their disputes with dueling pistols in an orderly manner. But in lower Natchez complete savagery was the only rule, and to think that such a loathsome sight was about to occur before her very eyes made Tabitha ill.

Whenever a battle took place between a keelboat-man and an outsider, it was not unusual for all keelboatmen present to side with their own kind. Among keelboatmen there was a strange alliance that held them together in sympathetic bond at the same time that it provoked competition among them. Every keelboat and barge coming down the river had its own personal bully who firmly believed he could defeat in battle any other keelboatman alive. This had been good clean fun for years, then had become a more serious matter when steamboats began to ply the Father of Waters. Resenting the clinical white ships, the keelboatman went out of his way to reduce a steamboatman to a quavering mass—for in the development of the steamboat the keelboatmen recognized a threat to their kind of craft and their way of life.

Of course, these river-bred gladiators had ample opportunity to prove their claims of superiority over each other as well as over steamboatmen, for competing crewmen often arranged fights between opposing bullies on which there was always considerable betting. When it came to paying off bets, however, most keelboatmen were something less than good losers. Keelboatmen got along like bull moose in rutting season anyway, and the payoff of bets usually resulted in a full-scale riot that broke up half the riverfront saloons and reduced a considerable number of rivermen to gibbering impotency. Still, despite this severe competition, there was a camaraderie too—for when any keelboatman faced an outsider in battle, his fellow rivermen swarmed to his support like bees to a hive.

Thus it was that Tabitha became immediately aware that the men who formed the circle around the two antagonists were almost to a man backing the ape-like keelboatman against Mike Long.

"Git him, One-Eye!" one man shouted. "Crack his haid open like a watermelon!"

This remark encouraged others so spectacular that Tabitha felt her insides curl into a tight knot of terror.

"Spill his guts, One-Eye!"

"Pluck them eyes outa him and eat 'em fer grapes!"

"Kick him in the balls!"

One staggering riverman decided that Mike Long needed some verbal abuse and cupped grimy hands around his mouth.

"Hey, you, Curly! You sure you ain't bit off more'n you kin chew? One-Eye can lick any man on the Mississip, and I ain't never seen the likes of you that he couldn't break in half and eat for supper!"

Tabitha stood tensely, not wanting to watch, yet fascinated by the savage scene unfolding before her. She felt that it was unladylike to gaze upon such shocking barbarity as was about to occur, yet she could not draw her eyes away—and besides, she had already done several unladylike things this morning and one more wouldn't matter. Quickly she appraised the two antagonists and a sick fear grew for Mike Long. The man they called One-Eye—and he had probably lost his eye in just such a ferocious fight—looked as tough as an old turkey gobbler and virtually impervious to punishment. Mike Long, she had to admit, despite his irritating ways, was considerably more refined. He looked as if he could give an account of himself in an emergency, but never-theless one who would be inclined to fight with certain civilized restraints. One-Eye was a pitiless savage who would do anything to a man to gain his ends.

It did not occur to Tabitha that she was the prize for which the two men fought. In the excitement of the moment, this thought had escaped her. Had she thought of it — and based on her judgment that Mike Long was going to be beaten — she would have fled headlong for her home and the safety of her mother's protective arms and her father's severe inflexibility.

An anticipatory roar went up from the circle of men as One-Eye rushed toward Mike, ape-like arms stretched outward to engulf his victim in a shattering hug. But Mike Long stepped nimbly to one side just before One-Eye reached him, and the keelboatman staggered past him. As he went by Mike delivered a fierce right to the riverman's jaw that straightened him up and dropped him in a ragdoll heap.

Mike stepped back and permitted One-Eye to get up. This gracious action brought another roar, this time of surprise, for the onlookers were not accus-tomed to such gentlemanly tactics. Once you got a man down, you kept him down. While he was helpless on the ground, you kicked him in the head and made sure he didn't get up. Or you kneed him in the groin or gouged out an eye with a hard black-rimmed fingernail.

"I'm a silly son of a bitch if'n I ever seed a fight like this'n," said one man, shaking his head.

By this time One-Eye had struggled to his feet, shaking his body violently like a dog coming in out of the rain. He looked around dully for his opponent and finally located him in the center of the human ring. He plodded forward to do battle again, but this time with more caution. For several minutes the two adversaries circled each other warily, then suddenly they became locked in a titanic, muscle-straining struggle.

In upright position, their feet widespread and braced, they grappled viciously to throw each other. In the straining One-Eye managed to get a foot behind Mike Long. A sudden shove sent Mike backward, the keelboatman on top. Immediately One-Eye took advantage of the situation. His knee buried itself like a battering ram in Mike's groin and Tabitha hid her eyes with her hands. The keelboatman's stubby fingers then went for Mike's eyes and Mike, clutching the keelboatman's wrists, fought with all his strength to keep those clawing fingers from reaching their goal. For long tense seconds the two men strained in this position, One-Eye trying to force his fingernails into the eyeballs of his opponent, Mike battling to keep the vicious human talons away.

Drained of strength by the crushing attack on his groin, Mike felt his arms weakening. But by a superhuman effort he managed to draw his knee up under the barrel chest of the keelboatman, and with a quick movement he catapulted One-Eye into the air.

Mike was on his feet in an instant, determined not to permit One-Eye to again get close enough to grapple him to the ground. Enraged by the escape of his foe, One-Eye charged. Mike stepped deftly aside and rammed his right fist into the pit of the riverman's stomach. Gasping, One-Eye crumpled in an agonized heap on the muddy ground. Mike stooped down and hauled him to his feet almost as one lifts a puppy by the scruff of his neck. A murderous smash to the chin dropped the keelboatman again. Once more Mike picked him up and, straightening him for the clincher, drove a right to the jaw that sent the chunky riverman flying awkwardly into the crowd. This time he did not get up.

For a moment there was a stunned silence. Then the crowd of ruffians began to push and shove as they curiously examined the fallen body of their comrade. One riverman, with a spark of fairness, squinted at One-Eye and said:

"Damn me! Ol' One-Eye got beat fair and square! Least I kin do is buy the winner a drink!"

A tall bewhiskered keelboatman turned on him suddenly, his eyes thinning.

"You go buyin' that fancy bastard a drink, you gotta do it over my daid body, ol' friend."

"I could arrange to oblige ya," said the first man coolly.

It was sufficient to start another conflict. The tall man threw a punch, sympathizers for both men moved in, and in several seconds a full-blown riot had erupted like a mushrooming explosion. Tabitha was brushed aside by a battler and went reeling into the mud, her bundle flying from her arms. An outraged anger seized her as she sat helplessly while the booted feet of the battlers ground the paper-covered bundle into the muck. Then she found herself suddenly scooped up into the arms of Mike Long. Quickly he ran to a safe place in a doorway some distance from the brawl. He sat her down gently.

"My dress!" Tabitha screamed. "I lost my dress!"

"A dress? Is that what you came to the Silver Palace for?"

"Yes!"

A smile slanted across Mike's face. There was too much understanding in the grin and Tabitha wanted to slap it off his face, but didn't.

"A whore's dress," commented Mike wonderingly.

"You're not very careful of your language before a lady!" complained Tabitha. "Besides, Ryma's my sister, and I should think that—"

"I'm sorry. What's so valuable about the dress?"

"I've got to have it!" Tabitha cried furiously, as she saw one of the rioters kick the bundle aside.

"You can't get it now."

"I've got to!" She started toward the brawling men, but Mike caught her arm. He held her close to him and his voice was now one of authority.

"You little fool! You want to be killed by those madmen out there? Look at them!"

Tabitha's eyes flashed toward the maelstrom of men. The brutality appalled her. There were at least twenty men locked in combat. A few lay still on the ground, having been disposed of as worthy opponents. The shouts and noise of the senseless battle roared through Silver Street, and from the buildings came others to join the fray.

Mike did not release his grip on her. She felt herself pressed against his rock-hard body, and she fought against his mastery for a moment before subsiding in exhaustion. As her resistance waned she became uncomfortably conscious that his firm body, straining against hers, was not unpleasant—and for an instant she entertained the unladylike notion of staying in his arms at least until the rioting had ceased. But the female defensiveness that had been bred into her by her strict home environment forbade it.

"Let me go!" she demanded.

"Why? Don't you like it?"

Mike Long was holding Tabitha so tightly that she had difficulty drawing her breath. The clattering noise of battle violated her ears, and the predicament in which she found herself embarrassed her. Being held like a captive bird by an uncouth frontiersman was not exactly what she had bargained for.

"Will you let me go?" she repeated angrily.

"I don't know," drawled Mike. "I haven't had anything like you in my arms for some time, and I'd be less than a man if I released you."

"Really!" she gasped. "You're as bad as—as *he* was!"

Mike Long smiled gently and released his grip. For some reason that she did not quite understand, Tabitha failed to move away from him. There was something protective about him that she liked, at the same time that she abhorred his impertinence. He waved his arm at the rioting rivermen.

"Look what you started," he said.

"I didn't start it!" Tabitha flared, unwilling to admit guilt.

"Oh, but you did, milady. You should have known better than to walk down Silver Street unescorted. Or were you raised in a nunnery where the facts of life escaped you?"

Tabitha's lips went stubbornly thin. What had transpired this morning annoyed her greatly. Everything had turned out badly. She had come for the simple purpose of obtaining a dress so that she might look pretty on the morrow when she met Nicholas Enright. And she had met a sister whose appearance shocked her, a doctor who first insulted her and then rescued her, and had precipitated a brawl of at least twenty men. Not only that, but the beautiful dress Ryma had given her lay now in a puddle, being trampled by the boots of the fighting men.

Everything had ended in disaster.

Tabitha at last backed away from Mike Long. Her violet eyes had brightened, fired by deep anger and intense determination.

"I intend to get that dress!" she said. "I didn't come all the way to the Silver Palace, at considerable embarrassment to myself, for nothing!"

Mike laughted. An infectious laugh, Tabitha thought, but a ridiculing one.

"You may have been embarrassed, but not too embarrassed to do it," he said. "Very well. Stay right here. I'll rescue your precious garment."

He left her standing in the concealment of the doorway and rushed headlong into the milling rioters. Dodging among the battlers, he stooped and picked up the trampled package in his hands, racing back to where Tabitha waited. Breathing heavily, he handed her the mud-smeared bundle.

"There. I hope you're satisfied. I'm sure, when you dress in it, you'll look like the most seductive prostitute in Natchez-under."

"Oh, you *are* a monster!" cried Tabitha.

Mike chuckled. Again Tabitha took note of it: a contagious chuckle but one she was not in the mood right now to appreciate. She was convinced that she hated Mike Long.

"Aren't you going to thank the monster for his services?" Mike asked playfully.

"Thank you," said Tabitha tightly.

"Now I'm going to perform another service," he said. "I'm taking you home."

Determined to salvage at least some self-respect from the mess she had created, Tabitha glared at Mike defiantly.

"I'm perfectly capable of going home myself—"

"Oh, drat it, young woman. You're not capable of any such thing."

"You can't boss me around!"

"I can and I'm going to. Where do you live?" He took her arm firmly and began leading her away like a recalcitrant child.

Suddenly all resistance seeped out of Tabitha. Without interference, she permitted him to steer her toward her house. It was a half-mile to the crude cabin where she dwelt on the outskirts of Natchez-under, not far from the quarter track where planters from the bluffs raced their finest horses during the season. Neither spoke. But as they finally neared her house, Mike looked down at her. Her face had set in severe lines.

"I'm accompanying you right to the door," he warned. "I'm delivering you safely to your parents—or whoever is foolish enough to claim you. I'm telling them to keep a leash on you hereafter, as they would a wayward dog, and—"

"Don't you dare!"

"I am. And by the way, I suspect your family may be surprised to see you in the company of a strange man."

"They certainly will!"

"So don't you think it would be appropriate if I at least knew your name? Didn't Ryma call you—Tabby?"

"Only Ryma calls me that, and I demand that you not assume such familiarity. It's Tabitha Clay—Miss Clay, if you don't mind. And don't you dare come to my home as you threaten."

In a sudden movement she broke free of him, her deep violet eyes alight with fury. On a run she started toward the cabin, but Mike's arm snaked out, his hand fastened in the heavy folds of the skirt's bulging bustle, bringing her up short.

"You force me to employ the most ungentlemanly tactics," he complained mildly. "Now come on, little spitfire—how about acting like a lady for a change? It might be a refreshing experience."

4

Abijah Clay awoke to the realization that the hour was already late. The solitary window in the cabin, a crude three-foot square opening covered with paper soaked in hog's lard to let in the light, already reflected the grayness of morning. Little of the light penetrated the dismal corner in which stood the bed of Abijah and his wife, Rachel, but the greasy whiteness of the paper on the window testified to the fact that daylight had indeed arrived.

It was a rare occasion when Abijah slept late in the morning, but he had experienced a harrowing night in Natchez-under-the-Hill attempting to spread the gospel of the Lord to an inattentive audience, an ordeal that was always tiring. And despite his lean but substantial frame, he was a man who needed his rest. Unbeknownst to him, this was a fact that Tabitha had carefully considered when she had left her residence before six o'clock in the morning to visit Ryma on Silver Street, thinking to reach home again before he awakened. What she had not counted on, however, was the street fight and the delay in her return.

Abijah yawned and looked wistfully at Rachel next to him. She was still asleep, in that completely unfettered way she had of sleeping, barely breathing, hardly moving from dusk to dawn. As he looked at the pale careworn face, the dark hair flecked with the gray so common to pioneer women, he remembered the girl he had married twenty-four years ago. She had been pretty—too pretty, perhaps, for her own good. She had had her choice of many eligible bachelors and probably could have bettered herself by marrying someone more promising than an itinerant preacher. But she had chosen him—for what wondrous reason he was even yet not sure—and she had made him a capable and dependable wife, willing to share the hardships and uncertainties of a traveling man of the gospel, as well as the inevitable ridicule.

Despite a certain cold rigidity in his religious beliefs, Abijah considered himself a warmer personality than his wife. Abijah had been raised in Richmond, Virginia, in a bedlam-torn home of eight children. His parents had died when he was a boy, and he had made his way in the world working at odd jobs. He had never garnered enough money to attend a theological seminary and as a result was not an ordained minister. Yet his intense interest in the Bible—and his burning evangelical desire to improve the world he was living in—had made him as rabid a supporter of the gospel as existed anywhere in the country.

He had met Rachel at a revival meeting outside of Richmond. She was the only daughter of a Gloucester fisherman who, one day, sailed out into the turbulent Atlantic on a fishing boat that never returned. She and her mother had moved to Richmond, apparently in an attempt to forget their tragedy, and it was shortly after her mother's death that Rachel had taken Abijah as her husband. Perhaps it was the prospect of traveling about the country spreading the word of the Lord and preaching the certainty of salvation that had attracted her to him—he did not know. At any rate, she had developed into a loyal and staunch supporter of his work, as well as a devoted wife—with her only faults, Abijah thought, being a cold austerity spawned by her New England background and an annoying tendency sometimes to take lightly the religious matters that weighed so heavily on Abijah's mind.

Abijah remembered the first few years with Rachel. Despite his spiritual preoccupation with the Lord and his works, Abijah had not been above enjoying the pleasures of the flesh. His wife was so beautiful and her form in bed so enticing that he was often beside himself with a raging desire. But Rachel, although she submitted from time to time out of a sense of wifely duty, did not like the act of copulation. He could still remember her words of mild protest.

"I am sometimes appalled at your lust, Abijah," she would say. "For a man who reaches out for divinity, it ill becomes you to engage in such carnality."

"But my dear," he would counter in exasperation, "from such unions more of God's people are created."

"That's *not* what you are thinking of, Abijah!"

Still, she had borne him two daughters, one of whom had caused him considerable grief, the other mild anxiety. Ryma, the older, had been sullen and uncooperative most of her life, and had eventually bolted the family circle to live and work in the shanties of Natchez-under. Abijah had been some months recovering from this shock and had only done so by deciding, at last, that he would ignore the fact that he had ever sired such a daughter and would never mention her name again. Tabitha, now growing into womanhood, was giving him additional cause for concern. She was a curious mixture of coldness and warmth. She had inherited some of the icy practicality of her mother, but she also possessed some of the heated rebelliousness of Ryma. She was habitually unwilling to accept things for what they were, always questioning, always searching, never quite satisfied — and Abijah considered these traits not only distasteful but highly dangerous.

Ryma's defiance of convention had ultimately driven her to the shacks of lower Natchez. Abijah did not think Tabitha would follow her sister's example, for he was certain that, despite her capricious mind, she had more stability than Ryma. Tabitha had an inquisitive nature that simply needed to be held within ladylike bounds. Much to Abijah's regret, she seemed uninterested in the things other women enjoyed — crewelwork or cooking or even water-painting. She did read, however — books carefully selected by Abijah with the goal of improving her knowledge of the world around her — and this reading had sharpened her awareness and improved her intellect. But there was danger, Abijah thought, even in reading, for knowledge seemed to inspire Tabitha to do and say things that disturbed him in a girl so young, gave her an insight into life far beyond her years and in some cases beyond Abijah's own experience. He and Rachel, he felt, must wage a continuous battle to keep Tabitha from going beyond the normal limits imposed by society on any woman who called herself a lady.

Abijah swung his long legs to the floor and sat for a

moment on the edge of the bed. His head itched and he scratched his graying hair. He was only forty-five, but he looked older. His face was lean, drawn, and scarred with the cares of a world that seemed not to understand him. His thin jowls and pointed chin were covered with a black stubble of beard which, in another thirty years, would be made more famous by a man named Abraham Lincoln. The dark beard was sprinkled with gray, like salt spilled on an ebony table, and Abijah calculated that it would not be many more years before his entire beard would be as gray as an ancient mare. Well, so be it. Grayness was, in Abijah's opinion, a sign of maturity, not senility. And he could use all the maturity and wisdom it was his to muster, dealing as he was with the people of Natchez-under-the-Hill—perhaps the most licentious he had yet encountered in all of his travels.

Slowly, with a precision that marked all of his movements, Abijah donned a worn pair of homespun jeans, a doeskin hunting shirt he had purchased in Kentucky, and gnarled shoes that were mud-caked with the soft silt of the Mississippi shoreline. He was not going out to preach this morning—having had quite enough of that the night before when he had waged a losing battle in his attempt to save the souls of dozens of rivermen more interested in complicated women than in simple salvation—and for this reason he did not wear the black tight-fitting suit that was his usual attire as a lay preacher. But during the night, as he lay in bed bemoaning the lack of appreciation shown his efforts of the evening before, a new approach to his usual sermon had occurred to him, and Abijah walked to the crude puncheon table where paper and ink and a leather-bound Bible awaited his hand. The pearl-gray light of the dawn had barely invaded the room and Abijah lit a rush candle on the table and sat down to write in the flickering yellow glow.

His hands were gnarled and calloused, as might be expected of a man who had built his own cabin on the mudflats of Natchez-under. All his life, in fact, he had worked at menial tasks he felt were unbefitting a man of God. But, without money, he had been forced to make his way in the world the hard way, using his meager talent at rough carpentry to pick up odd jobs while Rachel added her ability as a seamstress to augment the family income.

Although he detested all firearms, he had nevertheless learned to fire a pistol, for familiarity with a gun usually meant the difference between life and death in the wilderness areas through which he often passed. He recalled vividly the experience he and his family had suffered on the long Natchez Trace leading from Nashville, Tennessee, to Natchez. The Trace was alive with merciless land pirates who thought nothing of killing travelers for the few cents they might carry in their pockets. They preyed on emigrants moving from the East to establish the new frontier along the Mississippi, and they preyed on rivermen who took cargoes to New Orleans, left their keelboats and barges, and made their way back to the Ohio River via the overland route, their pockets bulging with money from the sale of their produce. One of these criminals had stopped them on the Trace, and it was soon obvious that even the fact that itinerant preachers were known to be mostly penniless would be no protection against the savagery of the robber. Abijah had managed to take advantage of inattention on the part of the pirate and shot him through the head.

It was a sickening experience. He had never before taken a human life, and he felt that God had a right to rain down his wrath upon him for so doing. Still, he had shot the man to save his wife and daughters, for the pirate had obviously been a depraved creature bent on murder. The tragedy had filled him with remorse for the rest of the trip, and even to this day gave him twinges of conscience which he found difficult to shunt aside. In any case, he had managed to guide his family safely to Natchez, and after exploring the town had decided to settle in Natchez-under where he felt the number of souls to be saved on the mudflats greatly exceeded those to be saved on the heights.

Armed with an adz, cant hooks, snaking tongs, and saws, it had taken him two months to build the dreary-looking cabin of felled logs. It was only twenty by sixteen feet, but it was built solidly of logs piled one atop the other and notched and fitted at the corners. At each end wall a firm tree with two of its branches trimmed to form a crotch supported the horizontal ridge-pole, and the roof consisted of bark slabs laid like shingles. The soft clay of the mudflats had been used to chink up the cracks, with a few selected places left unchinked to provide necessary ventilation. The floor was made of puncheons—logs split lengthwise into planks—and this in itself was a luxury since many cabins had floors only of bare earth.

The inside consisted of one large all-purpose room and two curtained-off bedrooms. The large general room served as a kitchen, dining room and living quarters for the family. One wall featured a stone fireplace which supplied the only heat during the chill days of winter. The room was scantily furnished with a large crude table with thick log legs, three split-bottom chairs, a couple of low stools, and a small cabinet—all evidently the untalented work of Abijah. By some very hard labor he had even managed to fashion some wooden bowls and ladles to complement what few kitchen utensils they had carried over the Natchez Trace.

But one of the most remarkable features of the otherwise unrefined cabin was the bookcase that lined the west wall from rafters to floor. This cultural addition seemed out of place in the rough and primitive building, but Abijah had insisted on hauling his books over the perilous Trace. "I want my girls to read good books," he told Rachel, "and if I must give up every other possession I have, I will keep the books."

Abijah loved books. He liked the shape and weight and feel and smell of them—and the contents that could shape a man's mind as surely as a sculptor shapes clay. He considered his books as much a part of him as his arms and legs—more so, since without an arm or leg one could live, without books never.

For eight years Abijah and his family had occupied the narrow confines of this cabin, and while their lives had been restricted by its meager dimensions the entire world was there for the asking in Abijah's precious books. During their formative years both Tabitha and Ryma had made the acquaintance of such writers as Homer, Walter Scott, and Shakespeare. Rachel, who had digested such masterpieces in earlier years, devoted her time to the menial tasks of hoeing and spading a small garden that supplied the family with vegetables. What meat was available she salted, packed in wood ashes until ready for use, and then boiled in water and smoked over an open fire. Life for all of them had been difficult, but Abijah had taught his daughters some of the refinements of life despite their crude environment. Abijah believed that living was an art, and that one cheated oneself if one did not learn the intricacies of this art fully.

For Abijah personally it had been a rewarding life, despite frustrations. There had been those moments—relatively few, he admitted—when his words won over some forsaken soul who had slipped into a life of sin and who recognized the need to escape it. And this made all the physical and mental hardships of his occupation worthwhile. He would go down among the fleshpots of Natchez-under, usually after dark when the tempo of life had quickened along the mudflats, and he would stand on a corner and preach. He had a loud, stentorian voice that carried well above the profane noises issuing from the ramshackle buildings. Sometimes a crowd would gather, listen with veiled respect to his words, and remain discreetly silent. At other times he would be heckled unmercifully by drunken rivermen and their women of the evening. Invariably he would finish his sermon with a plea for all those who wanted salvation to come forth and present themselves, and just as invariably the crowd would then silently slink away.

"Nobody," he said to Rachel one day, "wants to be saved in the eyes of the Lord. None will admit their transgressions. But it is said, *He that covereth his sins shall not prosper; but whoso confesseth and foresaketh them shall have mercy."*

He sat this morning for half an hour at the table, his square steel-rimmed spectacles perched on his thin nose, laboring over his sermon of the night before, thumbing the pages of his Bible for help and inspiration. Despite the fact that he lacked a formal education, words came easily to Abijah. Rachel had often said that he possessed the most prodigious memory of anyone she had ever known, for he could recite passages from Scripture, word for word, on almost any subject that arose. And he managed to put together sermons that were, at least, the best ever heard in Natchez-under.

Perhaps, thought Abijah, they did not equal in worth those delivered by ordained ministers in Natchez proper's vine-encrusted churches, but with the Hill people Abijah was not vitally concerned. They were all elegant humans, well-mannered, Godfearing, the cream of Natchez society, and they would all quite likely go to Heaven without the need of sermons in the first place. But the sinners of Natchez-under were different. They needed help, and Abijah sometimes resented the fact that the well-dressed and successful ministers on the heights did not lower themselves to the level of the mudflats and try to save some souls that desperately needed saving.

Wearying of his writing, Abijah rose and walked slowly to the window covered with the larded paper. He carefully unfastened a corner of it from a protruding nail and peered outside. What he saw brought forth a startled gasp. Tabitha was running toward the cabin and was being slowed by a young man who had a firm grip on her — God forbid — bustle!

Abijah looked twice to make sure, once through the square spectacles, the second time with his own rheumy eyes. Still not wanting to believe what he saw, he scurried toward the bed where his wife still slept.

"Rachel!" he said sternly. "I demand that you get up and go into Tabitha's room and see if she is abed!"

Rachel, awakened from a sound sleep, looked up at her husband with puzzlement.

"What's the matter, Abijah?"

"I looked out the window, Rachel, and I saw Tabitha coming down the road with a man hanging onto her — you will pardon the word, Rachel — her posterior!"

"Abijah! You must be mistaken. Tabitha would not be about at this time of the morning."

"Unless my old eyes are worse than I think, it *is* Tabitha! But make sure she's not abed."

Rachel got up, picked up a robe, wrapped it around her body, and walked into Tabitha's room. She came out at once.

"She's not there."

"Then it *is* Tabitha!" Abijah said it again, face aghast.

"But what is she doing out at this time of morning?"

"That," said Abijah, "is what I intend to find out."

Together they crossed to the window and peered out. Yes, it was Tabitha — dressed very prettily, in fact — and with a young man now walking at her side. Carefully Rachel refastened the greased paper.

"Now, Abijah, we will be calm," she said firmly, trying to ward off a disastrous explosion. "We won't draw conclusions until we hear her story. There must be some compelling reason why Tabitha would venture out at such an ungodly hour, and I intend to hear what she has to say."

But Abijah was beside himself with anxiety, and with Abijah it was a short step between anxiety and outrage.

"She is no lady walking about the streets with a strange man at an unseemly hour, like a tramp from the gutter!" he said in high wrath. "Your daughter, Rachel, has always been rebellious and difficult to control."

"Why is she always *my* daughter when she misbehaves and *your* daughter when she delights us?" demanded Rachel indignantly. "I remind you, Abijah, that you are the father of my child and as such you share the responsibility of raising her."

"I never taught her to tramp the streets with a man before dawn!" intoned Abijah, raising his fist as if he were personally delivering the Sermon on the Mount.

"Nor did I!" retorted Rachel. "Now, Abijah, will you calm down before she comes in that door?"

Abijah subsided slowly, like a flame being systematically smothered to death. But he stood in the middle of the floor, his hands on his hips, his eyes on the door that would, at any moment, swing open on its leather hinges to admit his errant daughter. Rachel busied herself setting three places at the table for breakfast—wondering if she should set four—and was thus innocently occupied when the big log door creaked open and Tabitha peered warily in.

"Good morning, Tabitha. You're up early." Rachel's voice was calm, almost unconcerned, as if this were not an uncommon event. She crossed to the doorway, pretended to see the young man for the first time, and said, "Oh, I see you have a guest."

If this approach was calculated to put Tabitha at ease, what Abijah did quickly destroyed the soothing balm. He was a man who could not tolerate indirectness, and he said the one thing that was on his mind and said it quickly.

"Where have you been, Tabitha? Answer me!"

Tabitha stammered uncertainly, her voice sounding weak and timid. But her mother came forward, standing between Tabitha and her glowering father. "I don't believe, Tabitha, I've had the pleasure of meeting your gentleman friend."

"Oh!" Tabitha flicked a glance at Mike Long. To her dismay there was sly amusement on his face. Damn him, she thought, but she said, "This is Dr. Michael Long—my mother and father." She was grateful that the word "doctor" sounded dignified and imparted at least a modicum of legitimacy to the situation.

"How do you do, Doctor," said Rachel, glancing out of the corner of her eye to see how Abijah was responding. Abijah was simply acknowledging the introduction with a curt nod of his head, but not exhibiting any noticeable warmth.

"I remind you, Daughter, that you have not answered my question," he said severely.

"I'm sorry, Father." Tabitha felt her voice grow stronger. Her mother's heroic effort to smooth the scene had encouraged her. "I just went walking up the road a piece."

"Indeed. At this hour of the morning?"

"I couldn't sleep, Father. You know how I always

enjoy the cool of the morning. Dr. Long was kind enough to accompany me safely home."

"You have not yet answered my question!" insisted Abijah, making a visible effort to control his temper. "I repeat, where *precisely* have you been?"

"Why don't you come in and sit down, Dr. Long?" interposed Rachel helpfully. She glanced at her daughter and the eyes of the two women met briefly. In that meeting there was understanding. Rachel was attempting to reduce Abijah's wrath by inviting a stranger into the house. Abijah sensed what was being done, for he turned abruptly to Mike Long.

"I regret, Dr. Long, that this scene has taken place on your initial visit to our humble home. It is not my intention to embarrass you in any way, but I think you will agree that a man has a right to know why his nineteen-year-old daughter is traipsing brazenly about the streets of Natchez-under-the-Hill so early in the morning."

Mike Long was still holding the package containing the dress. He collapsed lazily into the chair offered by Rachel, then rewarded Abijah with his most winning smile.

"You're quite right, sir. I should feel the same way were I in your position."

Tabitha's violet eyes smoldered. Well, she thought, *he* is a big help! Siding with Father! Damn men anyway, they always stuck together. There was some invisible bond that linked them.

Abijah nodded courteously toward the doctor.

"I can see you are a man of intelligence and sound judgment, and I'm delighted that you share my point of view. It makes my task much less difficult." He turned meaningfully toward Tabitha. "Now, young lady, you may tell me where you have been."

"As I said, Father, just up the road a ways—"

"How *far* up the road?" insisted Abijah, who knew exactly what was up the road.

"Well, I—"

"Perhaps, since my daughter seems to have suffered a lapse of memory," said Abijah scathingly, "you might be able to shed some light on her activities, Dr. Long?"

Mike stretched his long legs, balancing the package on his stiffened knees. He observed a fierce anger afire in Tabitha's luminous eyes. By her expression she was daring him to say a word, but Mike was not one easily swayed by female defiance. He rose slowly and placed the bundle on the table. With a quick movement he tore it open, revealing a rash of scarlet.

"It seems," said Mike easily, "that your daughter needed a dress."

Abijah's eyes went wide. He stared with evident distaste at the billowing scarlet folds before him. He picked it up gingerly, as if it might contaminate his fingers, and let it fall full in front of him. His eyes scanned the low neckline, the brash screaming color of it.

"Where in the name of all that's holy did you get this frightful thing?" he demanded.

Tabitha knew there was no way for her to turn. She might as well admit everything. If she didn't, Mike Long—beast that he was!—would tell the whole story. Perhaps it was better that she tell it, shading it as much as possible, giving it a ring of innocence.

"It's just that I don't have a nice dress, Father," she

said, hurrying her words, trying to get them said faster than he could evaluate them. "And I needed one for—oh, so many things. So I thought, rather than buying one up in Natchez, which would be extremely expensive, I could borrow one from—"

"From *whom?*" roared Abijah.

"From Ryma," said Tabitha meekly.

For a full minute Abijah stared truculently at his younger daughter. He had not uttered Ryma's name since she had left home a year ago to seek her loathsome career in the jerrybuilt shanties. On those rare occasions when her name was mentioned by his good wife or his daughter, he pretended not to hear. But this time he had heard—and everyone knew he had heard—and it came at a moment of crisis when he could not ignore it. Now, instead of speaking directly to Tabitha, he addressed Mike Long.

"I am not certain what your role in this is, Doctor," he said stiffly, "but I at least thank you for accompanying my brash daughter back from the hellhole of Silver Street. Now, if you would excuse my rudeness, I will ask you to leave. I have some important matters to discuss privately with my family."

Mike Long rose to his feet, smiling amiably.

"Of course, I understand, sir." He turned graciously to Rachel. "I'm happy to have met you, Mrs. Clay. And you, Tabitha." He smiled again and walked to the door. His gaze drifted to Tabitha as he closed it behind him, and the last impression she received of him was one of sardonic amusement at her plight.

Tabitha decided, at that precise moment, that she hated Mike Long more than anyone on earth!

But she could not dwell on her hatred of Mike,

since her attention was drawn immediately to the stern form of her father. What she saw terrified her. He stood evenly balanced on widespread feet in the middle of the floor, his face red and mottled with anger. She had rarely seen him quite like this. Only once—when Ryma had walked out of the house after a prolonged and violent argument and had never returned—had there been such towering rage in him. At that time he was white, drained of all color, and there was something of defeat in his manner, something that sorrowed his lean hard face. But this, now, was unreasoning anger, uncontrollable ire, seething all through his gaunt body, reflecting itself in his anguished face, in the fierceness of his eyes, the twitching of his hands at his side.

"So you went to visit Ryma in her house of sin!" he said, and his voice was curiously calm for all his anger.

"Yes, Father." Tabitha nodded quickly, then rushed on with words she hoped might be temporizing. "It was a dreadful experience. I didn't realize what I was doing. I'll not do it again."

The words made no impression. They failed to penetrate the outer wall of her father's rage, and she felt that she could almost see her words bouncing off his forehead, not penetrating to the brain.

"Do not flutter your eyelids in supposed innocence, my daughter," Abijah thundered, "for it is said in Ecclesiasticus that *the whoredom of a woman may be known in her haughty looks and eyelids*. No! I have lost one daughter to the shacks of Natchez-under-the-Hill. I do not intend to lose another. You may tell me, Tabitha, what you need this outrageous dress for.".

Tabitha stood facing him, a few paces away, poised

as if to flee should he make an overt move toward her. Two hours ago she would have died on the spot rather than admit to her father that she had met a strange man on the esplanade above the river, and that she was to meet him again. Now, however, it seemed the lesser of two evils. Much better to admit she had met a gentleman, she thought, than to continue to dwell on her meeting with Ryma in "her house of sin."

"Father, I know you will understand. I'm getting no younger. A girl must think of meeting acceptable gentlemen if she doesn't want to become a maiden woman."

"Yes?"

"Well, I have met the most wonderful gentleman. A very rich and high-bred gentleman who lives on the Hill. It was a—a chance meeting, but he wishes to see me again."

"Why?"

"I suppose—he's interested, Father."

"He's coming here to see you?"

"No, Father. I'm meeting him on the esplanade."

"A departure from accepted convention, to say the least," grumped Abijah. "Why not at your home, as is proper?"

"I don't know. I really don't. Perhaps he's shy. At any rate, the esplanade is a public place. There's certainly no danger of his being indiscreet."

"And you obtained this ungodly dress from Ryma to wear when you meet this supposed gentleman again?"

"Yes, Father."

Abijah made a wry face and Rachel intervened diplomatically.

"There's really nothing wrong with the dress, Abijah," she said. "A trifle brash of color, perhaps, but—"

"You will allow me to handle this, my good wife," Abijah said, cutting her short. His eyes were cold and implacable as he returned his gaze to Tabitha. "Who is this unbelievable gentleman who refuses to call at your home?"

"Mr. Nicholas Enright. Surely you have heard of him."

Abijah had heard of him. Everyone had. The man was one of the wealthiest cotton barons in the South. The sheer importance and quality of the man assuaged Abijah's feelings a bit.

"Well," he said, switching the subject, "regardless of your high-sounding motives in obtaining this lurid garment, you have disobeyed me, Tabitha. I long ago forbade you to walk unaccompanied in Natchez-under, not to mention the esplanade. You have done so anyway."

"But, Father—"

"You have been in a house of harlots, Tabitha. I hope you hated the sight and smell of the place. I hope the stench of sin will be in your nostrils to your dying day, reminding you of your transgression. You have been wayward, and you must seek the Lord's forgiveness. Get down on your knees, Tabitha!"

Tabitha stared uncertainly. Her glance flickered toward her mother, but she found no succor there, for Rachel was studying Abijah's face closely, a slight frown crossing her brow. When Tabitha hesitated, Abijah's sonorous voice filled the room.

"Get down on your kees, as I told you!"

Slowly Tabitha dropped to her knees. She was

frightened and confused, for she knew not what her father planned, but to disobey him would have brought down even greater wrath. As she knelt before him she saw his tall gaunt body trembling as he stood stiff as a rod, his eyes focused on the ceiling of the room, as if God sat in the rafters.

"Repeat after me, Daughter!" he ordered.

"Yes, Father." Her voice was small.

"Our Heavenly Father—"

"Our Heavenly Father—"

"He who would give us everlasting life—"

"He who would give us everlasting life—"

"Cleanse us of our sins and forgive our trespasses—"

"Cleanse us of our sins and forgive our trespasses—"

"Make us, humble as we are before your majesty, worthy of your faith—"

"Make us, humble as we are before your majesty, worthy of your faith—"

"Rescue me from the role of sinner—"

Tabitha's eyes opened wide. Resentment seized her and she dared a comment.

"But I'm not a sinner, Father!"

"Rescue me from the role of sinner—" roared Abijah, shaking both fists in the air.

"Rescue me from the role of sinner—" said Tabitha meekly.

"And bless me with thy Holy Grace—"

"And bless me with thy Holy Grace—"

"This I ask in thy Holy Name."

"This I ask in thy Holy Name."

Tabitha remained on her knees, head bowed, hands clasped. Silence hung like a black shroud over the house as the prayer ended. At last Tabitha glanced up at her father. He stood as rigidly erect as before, but his right hand clutched at his chest just below the left shoulder, his fingernails digging into the doeskin shirt, and his hard-lined face was ashen, his eyes fixed magnetically in space.

"Abijah! Are you all right?" It was Rachel's voice, filled with concern.

He did not answer at once, but finally said, "Yes, Rachel. I am all right."

He moved slowly to a chair and sat down, cautiously, still staring as if hypnotized. Tabitha rose apprehensively to her feet, anxiety in her face.

"Excitement is not good for you," Rachel was saying, as she hovered over him protectively. "Always excitement brings the chest pains."

Abijah forced a smile. He looked tired and drained, as if some vital force had gone out of him with his fervent prayer.

"The pains are receding, good woman," he said. "Do not fear. The Lord will not take me until I finish my work here—and I have quite a bit of work yet to do." His eyes traveled to Tabitha and the lines in his face seemed to deepen as he looked at her. "Your sin saddens me, Tabitha," he said, more gently now.

Tabitha felt a wave of remorse. "I did not intend to sin, Father."

"Perhaps not. But it is said in the Old Testament, *If they sin through ignorance, they are guilty.* You will go to your room, Tabitha, for the rest of the day. Read your Bible. It may prove exceedingly beneficial."

5

Beneath the high-rising loess bluffs of Natchez the Mississippi River widens into a crescent—and almost stops flowing. As if admiring this place of quiescent beauty after a tedious journey from its source in northern Minnesota, the river creates a broad expanse of water as tranquil as an inland lake, and then seems reluctant to leave. There it tarries, in listless idleness, touched by the gold of the sun and hesitant to continue its passage to New Orleans and the Gulf; and the vista created by the river-formed crescent is the reason the Spanish built a magnificent esplanade from which to view it.

Since childhood Tabitha had been racing up the steep incline that led from sunken Natchez-under-the-Hill to the empyreal heights of the Spanish esplanade—usually against the will of her father—where she found the ancient promenade one of the most delightful places on earth. On this Sunday afternoon, with the prospect of Nicholas Enright appearing at any moment in a handsome barouche, it was indeed an earthly heaven.

Still embarrassed by her father's reaction to her adventure in Natchez-under, Tabitha tried to relegate to the back of her mind all disturbing thoughts about the day before. By a considerable amount of hard work and a certain secrecy, she had managed to clean the soiled dress given to her by Ryma, and she wore it now with a piquant charm she knew to be captivating. Her father had left that morning on the *Mississippi Belle* for New Orleans to meet with another preacher and evaluate the progress of the Lord's work among the sinners of the Vieux Carre. Before leaving he had succumbed to the combined blandishments of Tabitha and Rachel, the latter of whom convinced him that there was nothing sinful in Tabitha's rendezvous with Nicholas Enright. Rachel, who was more sympathetic with Tabitha's aims, made an excellent case.

"Mr. Enright is one of the most important men on the Hill," she said persuasively. "That he should even be interested in Tabitha is something of a miracle."

"Why?" snorted Abijah. "Is my daughter not good enough for him to associate with?"

"Well, you know how clannish the planter society is," said Rachel. "They usually cling rather closely to each other. But if Mr. Enright, of all men, is interested in Tabitha—"

"Interested? Do you use the word to imply he may be desiring marriage to our daughter?"

"Nothing is beyond the realm of possibility. But what I am trying to say is that meeting Mr. Enright is an opportunity for Tabitha that she should not miss. She has a chance to better herself, Abijah, to associate with better people than we have here below the Hill. More God-fearing people, Abijah."

The last reference hit Abijah at his weakest point. It set his mind racing over his frustrating career in the cesspool of Natchez-under, tracing the times he had been on the verge of giving up on the job of saving souls that didn't want to be saved, of the times he had secretly thought that his family would be better off in the rarefied atmosphere of Natchez proper. Yes, Tabitha's life would be better if, some day, she moved to the top of the bluffs. This fact he could not logically deny, even though the possibility of such a thing occurring seemed remote and slightly incredible to him.

"Very well, Tabitha," he had said finally. "You may meet your gentleman friend. I exact only one promise from you—that you treat this meeting with circumspection and remain every inch a lady."

Tabitha had promised effusively that she would remain just that and now on the esplanade, she awaited the supreme moment when Nicholas Enright would arrive. Meantime, she enjoyed the view from the bluff. The esplanade, thought Tabitha, actually afforded two views. It not only provided an unparalleled tapestry of the great river below it, but looking eastward one observed the city of Natchez, which contemporary writers had already labeled the "handsomest city in America."

Tabitha, her eyes shaded by her sunbonnet, gazed pensively across the river to the opposite shoreline. Many of the planters who lived on the breeze-swept heights of Natchez owned land on the Louisiana side of the river where the silt-rich soil was ideal for growing cotton, and Tabitha was always favorably impressed by the immaculate whiteness of cotton fields. Nor did she ever tire of looking at the sun-dappled river that curved before the cotton fields, thus providing a panorama of breath-taking beauty. The only jarring note in this symphony of nature was the drab ugliness of man-made Natchez-under-the-Hill. It offered nothing to enhance the scene except a small orange grove close to the rustic log cabin in which she lived—a tiny patch of color splashed against a dreary and depressing background.

Still, Natchez-under, even on the Sabbath, was a teeming, busy place. Although it took frontier-like pride in its evil reputation, the city below the bluffs was a commercial asset of great importance. It lay at the head of waters deep enough for ocean-going navigation, and, being the farthermost southwestern outpost of the United States, it attracted not only river traffic but sailing vessels from all over the world. In 1833, Natchez-under was still observing the slow evolution from the keelboat to the steamboat, and Tabitha could see now the polyglot character of the vessels in port—the forested masts of several ocean-going sailing ships moored at the wharves, the stately charm of the steamboats, and the bobbing and weaving of the lighter keelboats, flatboats, and barges.

Turning, Tabitha looked back at the city of Natchez. She had taken many long exploratory walks through the city—again violating the will of her father—and what she could not now see from her position on the esplanade she could remember vividly. From the esplanade the streets of Natchez fanned east, north, and south, but Main Street ran due east from the bluff. Along this busy thoroughfare were the banks, the mercantile establishments, and other business houses—chief among them the Planter's Bank with its Greek Orthodox facade and fluted Ionic columns of marble, and the shadowed piazzas of the

Parker Hotel. The expensive stores, where plantation ladies delighted in shopping, were also on Main Street, as were the greengrocer's and fruitmonger's stalls; and the haphazard manner in which goods sold by these enterprises spilled out over the sidewalks in colorful profusion created a traffic problem even in those days. Other fine buildings dotted the city—the Parish House of San Salvador, Conti House, the Old Commercial Bank Building, and the steepled First Presbyterian church built just four years ago.

Spreading back from the business section were the residential areas where many successful business men lived. There were tobacco farmers from the Carolinas who had moved to the new frontier in retirement, young lawyers from Eastern colleges, doctors seeking to practice their profession in a new and lucrative land, bankers from New York who sensed financial possibilities in the thriving cotton culture, and young preachers to fill the pulpits of new churches. The city in 1833 contained more than 300 houses and some 2,500 inhabitants. Since history had dictated that Natchez was to be successively ruled by France, England, and Spain before the first American flag was raised in 1798, the city embraced the flavor of each nationality. But the houses retained more of Spanish culture than any other. They were mostly frame, with wide doors and windows to take advantage of the breezes fanning the heights. They boasted such Spanish touches as vaulted corridors, iron grillwork, tiered piazzas, and galleries on which it was customary for ladies and gentlemen to sip mint juleps and planter's punches while basking away the warm hours of the afternoon.

The setting for such congenial living was enhanced by the gracious trees of the South: the black willow, black ash, water maple, pawpaw, cypress, beech, chestnut, and chincapin; and in the spring the chinaberry which spread both a fragrant aroma and inviting shade. Most streets were lined with sweeping oak and glossy magnolia, and winding among the impressive trees were such colorful blooms as night-blooming jasmines, passion flower, lemon verbena, and a tangled profusion of nameless vines.

But even a more unbelievable world existed just outside of Natchez. Deeply worn roads, arched over by spreading oaks to resemble lacy green tunnels, led away from the city and connected with the plantations. Tabitha was familiar with most of the existing plantations in 1833, for she had on one heady occasion ridden past them in open-mouthed awe. There was the many-galleried, Spanish-looking mansion called The Elms, another called Airlee which dated from 1790, Twin Oaks with its considerable grace, Gothic-styled Glenfield, Bontura, Belvidere and Pleasant Hill—all lovely beyond Tabitha's most imaginative dreams. To Tabitha, this was a world apart—genteel and cultured—and her desire to be a part of that world sharpened as she waited on the esplanade for the arrival of Nicholas Enright. Her lips pulled tight with determination and her eyes sparkled and she said to herself, as she had on so many previous occasions, *I will live there some day—I will, I will!*

The bluff on which Tabitha stood was crowned with magnificent oaks of ancient vintage, spreading their leafy branches heavenward like the arms of ministers in prayer. Blue-gray Spanish moss dripped from the boughs, shredding the sunlight and splattering it haphazardly on the ground. The esplanade, or city park, was green and fresh. Its curving drives hummed to the wheels of coaches of every description—barouches, landaus, phaetons, and cabriolets—and rang sharply with the sound of horses' hooves. Couples occupied the green benches or walked along the grassy parkway, enjoying the splendid view of the Mississippi almost as much as they enjoyed themselves. Yes, Tabitha had always loved the esplanade, and she loved it more today than ever before.

The addition of Nicholas Enright to the familiar scene would make the esplanade more meaningful today, and the mere thought of the illustrious gentleman she was to meet caused her to reexamine her own appearance. She looked down at her scarlet dress and decided that, if perhaps a bit showy, it at least gave her a certain distinction. It was a rich silk, billowing out at the hips, with a pinched waistline and a low bodice. Several young women with handsome well-dressed males at their sides strolled along the promenade, and Tabitha glanced enviously in their direction. All of them looked fine, indeed, but not better than she. She observed, with a certain exultant pride, that she was prettier than many of them. Just wait, she thought, until the stately Nicholas Enright arrived—why, they could well be the grandest couple on the esplanade!

Suddenly a negative thought invaded her mind and tarnished the bright expectancy of the moment. What if he did not come? What if, after the flush of their first meeting had worn off, he had decided she was not worth pursuing further? Obviously, he must know many lovely women, and he might conceivably have second thoughts about a slip of a girl from Natchez-under. Still, he had seemed genuinely interested in her at their meeting. He would come, she told herself stubbornly. He would most certainly come.

She had no sooner put the disturbing thought of his possible absence out of her mind when she heard a new sound of wheels grating on the gravel road. She turned slowly, making sure that she did not give the impression of eagerness, and as soon as she saw the handsome barouche, with its dark mahogany finish and its brass accouterments, pulled by two proud iron-gray horses, she knew it could belong to none other than Nicholas Enright. Somehow, it matched his exalted personality—or what little she knew of his personality. It was grand and rich and somewhat pompous, the way Nicholas Enright was, something that stood out from the crowd in bold relief, that was just a touch more impressive than anything around it. It rolled slowly toward her, as if with some malevolent intent, the stately Negro driver in green and gold livery on the high front seat, dangling the reins loosely over the backs of the grays, the clippety-clop of the horses' hooves sounding metallically on the curved road, the even rhythm of the wheels beckoning tunefully. And then it stopped, and Nicholas Enright emerged from the barouche—much, Tabitha thought, like a king descending from his throne.

He was a little late arriving, but Tabitha did not think of that. All she could do was drink in the wonder of him, for he was the most imposing man she had ever beheld. He was over six feet tall, with power-ful shoulders and slim hips, the build of a Greek athlete. She judged him to be in his early thirties, with the calm maturity of a man of his years and his lofty position. He was dressed in the most fashionable mode of the day, with a brown cutaway coat, light fawn-colored trousers, a richly ruffled shirt partially covered by a brocaded creme waistcoat, and a great white silk stock propped under his chin. At his side he carried a riding crop, useless to him at the moment except to lend a certain jauntiness to his appearance.

He stepped down gracefully from the carriage, his black, highly polished boots reflecting the sunlight, and walked a few paces to Tabitha's side. Much to her surprise—for she had not noticed it before—he dragged his right foot slightly as he moved, apparently unable to bend his leg at the knee. It was his only imperfection, but somehow it did not detract from his elegance. Tabitha was virtually hypnotized by his grand appearance, the slightly arrogant half-smile that hovered over his lips, and the dark personal interest reflected in his fierce black eyes as he surveyed her.

She was looking at his pomaded ebony hair, sweeping back from his high forehead, the long black sideburns at his temples, when he said: "Hello, my dear. You look positively ravishing."

He had a low, cultured voice, but his blunt greeting startled her. No man had ever called her by an endearing name before nor complimented her so boldly, and it was a new and stimulating experience for her. Besides, she had never been in the company of such a grand male as Nicholas Enright. The two experiences melded together were almost more than she could bear.

"How do you do, Mr. Enright," she said, and at once knew it sounded stiffly correct and therefore awkward.

Nicholas Enright's smile broadened, or perhaps stiffened. It did not make an impression on Tabitha at the moment, but she recalled later that there was no real warmth in Nicholas Enright's smile at any time, but instead a disturbing unconvincing artifice. It was there on his face, when he wished it to be, yet it seemed like some automatic facial contortion that turned on and off by itself and was not prompted by any feeling within. His hand came out and barely brushed her upper arm as it steered her with polite aloofness to the edge of the esplanade.

"We will begin this delightful adventure by calling each other by given names," he announced practically, and Tabitha noticed with some dismay that he did not ask for permission to call her Tabitha but merely stated inexorably that such was his intention, at the same time ordering her to do likewise. "I am Nicholas; you are Tabitha," he went on. "Getting on a first-name basis is the only proper way to conduct a flirtatious escapade."

Again Nicholas Enright's bantering words upset Tabitha. She was to learn that Nicholas had a perverse talent for using shocking and unexpected expressions, but she knew nothing but surprise now. It was a bold move to meet a man on the esplanade to begin with, but to have him cynically refer to the meeting as a flirtatious escapade annoyed her. Was he trying to cheapen it? Did he have to give it such a name, make her feel as if she were doing something improper? She had little time to analyze her feelings, for he spoke again almost at once.

"It's a romantic view from the bluff, isn't it, Tabitha?"

"Yes, it is—Nicholas."

She had tried the name out, deliberately, and felt a little foolish at using his given name for the first time. But Nicholas seemed not to notice it, accepting it without particular pleasure or awareness as he looked out over the broad vista of water, his finely chiseled profile, bronzed by the sun, turned to give Tabitha the best view. Tabitha bit her lower lip, not knowing what more to say. It was always that way with her, she thought peevishly. At a loss for words at the wrong time. Yet this too seemed to go unnoticed by Nicholas, who seemed content to view the river, his hand resting ever so lightly but with a suggestion of possession on Tabitha's arm.

He had made no mention of her coming here today. He had not thanked her, even though he must have known that a woman does not normally meet a strange man even on the crowded esplanade. He had merely accepted her appearance as a natural development—something that had been arranged in advance and therefore was expected. Despite her excitement over meeting Nicholas, his attitude was disturbing. There was something intolerable about him—a haughty smugness, a towering pride, and a lack of humility that raised subtle doubts about his character.

"I never tire of looking at the river," said Nicholas, not looking at her, speaking as if to someone far off on the horizon. "It has almost human qualities, you know. It is sullen and brooding and nothing can change its pouting face. A steamboat ruffles its surface only momentarily, and then the same brooding face returns." He sighed, as if contemplating his own words and assessing them for wisdom. "But the river is important. Without it, this world of cotton would not exist. Without the river those fiber bolls would never see market. We owe the river everything."

"I used to come here when I was a child," Tabitha said pointlessly, feeling that this trivial information was really of no great consequence and yet saying it because she did not know what else to say. "It's beautiful."

Nicholas Enright turned his majestic head slowly, looking down at her, studying her critically. He shook his head sadly.

"God's doublet, woman!" he said with complete candor. "That bonnet you're wearing is atrocious."

Tabitha's hand went uncertainly to the top of her head. Her eyes were wide at the unexpected comment.

"Oh, I'm sorry," she stammered. "I thought it was quite—"

"And the dress. Positively hideous. Makes you look like a—shall we say—professional woman?"

Tabitha prickled with embarrassment. "I'm—I'm really sorry," she began again, but he put her off with an imperious gesture of his hand.

"Please excuse my bluntness. I dare say the bonnet and the dress would look well on some women. I object only because they hide a certain natural, innocent beauty that you have."

"Oh!" Tabitha felt a crimson blush paint her face, not knowing whether to be embarrassed or pleased. He had managed to turn his shocking criticism into flattery, but why, Tabitha thought angrily, must he give his compliments *backwards?*

"You said last time we met that you were a preacher's daughter, I believe."

Tabitha looked at Nicholas sharply. She had told him nothing of the kind! She distinctly remembered having withheld any mention of her background. But he knew! Obviously, he had been making inquiries. And that might be construed as a favorable indication that he was truly interested in her.

She did not let him know that she had pierced his subterfuge, but simply said, "A lay preacher, but a sincere man of the gospel." She said nothing more, feeling she was in some sort of cat-and-mouse game where she would have to consider carefully every move and every word.

A smile pulled at the corners of Nicholas's mouth, as if wanting to enlarge itself. But he fought away the temptation and scowled instead, his heavy black eyebrows pinching down over his nose to form a V.

"I must say your father has selected an unlikely place to expound the teachings of the Almighty," he said.

Tabitha studied him from beneath demurely lowered eyelashes. Was he making fun of her? Or testing her in some way? It was impossible to say. His face revealed nothing.

"Father hopes that he can do important work in Natchez-under," she said. "He feels there are many souls to be saved there."

Nicholas chuckled, but there was no merriment in it—only a deep cynicism. He slipped a massive gold watch from his waistcoat pocket, wound it with a small gold key, then replaced it. His action was deliberate, a delaying tactic, until he could form precisely the right words.

"I dare say he's right about the number of souls to be saved in the flatlands," he said finally, glancing down his regal nose at the clutter of shacks along the water's edge. "There is probably no more profligate place in the world. And tell me, how many souls has he succeeded in saving?"

"Really! I don't know. I think you're having fun at my expense."

"Nothing of the sort." From an opposite waistcoat pocket he extracted an intricately carved gold snuffbox, opened it gently, took a pinch of the powder, sneezed delicately, and replaced it. He did not look at Tabitha—indeed, he had hardly looked at her with any intensity since his arrival. It was as if he wished to hold himself apart from her, as if he stood at a different level, a higher and more exalted plane. "I'm rather interested in your father's Herculean efforts," he went on. "I should like him to come up on the Hill and save a few souls up here some day. God knows there are some around in need of considerable repair."

"I always imagined," said Tabitha with something of ice in her tone, "that those people living on the Hill were all virtuous and respectable human beings."

"Now you're having fun at *my* expense," replied Nicholas. "I rather suspect that you'll find on the Hill as heterogeneous a collection of thieves, murderers and lechers as anywhere—in grandiose style, of course."

"I don't believe you," said Tabitha.

The smile leaped to his face again, then dissolved.

"Of course you don't. There's been an aura of respectability built up about our plantation culture, you know. Worst of all, the planters themselves believe it. Yet, if we were honest, we would recognize that our hedonistic society spawns a type of sinner well worth your father's ministrations."

She studied him carefully, trying to read the truth in his stiff, immobile face. He was an educated man who chose his words with care, but it was difficult to know whether he believed what he said or was indulging in flights of cynicism and misanthropy merely to shock her. He was obviously a master of the art of tongue-in-cheek repartee, without revealing by the expression on his face whether or not he was completely serious.

Something caught the attention of Nicholas Enright and he suddenly forgot completely about Tabitha and stared with sharpened interest over the parapet. Tabitha followed his gaze. At the old wooden wharf a steamboat had docked, a long stern-wheeler with twin smokestacks rising over white woodwork. The heavy boom of cannon filled the air, for it was customary to thus salute the docking of a steamboat. Already a long line of perhaps fifty slaves were disembarking, and a white man supervising the group of blacks stood nearby waving his arms and gesturing wildly. A contemptuous expression crossed Nicholas's face.

"There's Faunce Manley," he said softly. "Has himself another passel of blacks shipped here from New Orleans. He already has several hundred and if I'm not careful he will supplant me as the largest planter in the Natchez country. He has galling ambition." There was resentment in Nicholas's voice.

"He seems like a very excitable man," said Tabitha, making a point to remember the name, Faunce Manley.

"He's a worried man, my dear."

"Worried?"

"Quite. He's what is known among the planters as a heavy man with the whip. He treats his blacks so harshly that he lives in mortal fear that one of them might hack him to death with an ax at some unguarded moment."

"How dreadful," said Tabitha with sudden repulsion. "I don't believe it necessary to treat slaves so cruelly."

He still did not look at her, but his expression was one of tolerance for an uninformed child.

"One of the first things you must learn, my dear," he said pointedly, "is to never use the word slave. This violates the tender sensibilities of our planter's so-called culture. We call them our blacks, our people, or our hands—but never slaves. The Southerner supports the institution of slavery with a great show of righteousness because it makes him money. But to call the system slavery is anathema to him." There was scorn and ridicule in every word of his explanation, and the fact that Nicholas Enright could speak so disparagingly about his own class of people puzzled Tabitha.

"How many blacks do you own?" she asked.

"I have four hundred. They're good blacks too, hard workers."

"But you do not believe in mistreating them?"

"No. Not for the sadistic pleasure anyway, though

they need the bite of the whip on occasion. One treats them as one must, you see. Since the blacks represent a sizable investment in the cotton business, it's foolhardy to do anything that doesn't extract the greatest amount of work from them. One does not whip a mule unless it stops working. Such are the stern facts of our enlightened feudalistic system."

Tabitha considered this for a long moment. The moral aspects of slavery had not escaped her, for her father detested slavery with such vehemence that he had more than once sermonized upon it at home. But this was the first time she had heard a slave owner comment about it, and the cold implacability of the slave theory made her shudder. You treated a slave as a valuable piece of property that could increase your personal wealth, and therefore you did nothing to interfere with his ability to work unless an urge to sadism dominated your common sense. It was something like caring for your horse, or oiling a wheel of your barouche, so it would continue to serve you.

Such had been Nicholas's explanation, yet Tabitha felt there was something false in his presentation of the facts. There was bitter contempt in his voice, and Tabitha received the definite impression that he, himself, recognized slavery for the inhuman thing it was. Wasn't he, after all, from the East? A man like him could hardly be expected to subscribe completely to the ways of the South. Still, Nicholas kept four hundred slaves. Was it worse to keep slaves if you didn't believe in it, than if you did? Perhaps Nicholas Enright was a man trapped by his times, forced to do things he did not sanction, simply because others did and he had no recourse but to fall in line.

"I shall further expound the planters' theory of slavery so that you can better understand," Nicholas offered, as if reading the confusion in her mind. "The black is a necessary commodity in our cotton culture. Slavery is the only possible arrangement that serves our way of life, else how would you ever plant, cultivate, and harvest your crop? The average black is unintelligent, unskilled, and demands little. He is particularly adaptable to the cyclical routine of the plantation. No intelligent white would sweat in the cotton fields all day as a picker, but since the black is little higher in intellect then the lower animals it is no great burden to him. There are more than two million blacks in this country now, laboring in the fields so that planters like us may live in luxury. Since our 'slavocracy' has grown to such proportions, it follows that the system must be right—don't you think?"

"I think," said Tabitha carefully, "that you do not believe in slavery yourself, even though you own many."

Nicholas acknowledged her astuteness with a nod of his head.

"To some extent you are right," he admitted. "I'm a Northerner. I have the Northerner's dim view of slavery. But you will find, my dear, that I am immensely practical too. I never permit maudlin sentimentality to stand in the way of practicality. In an intellectual sense I may not condone slavery, but in a practical sense I am in favor of it. I will frankly use any means that makes Nicholas Enright richer and more important. Among all men—black or white—Nicholas Enright must stand first."

The words were so chilling, so frighteningly ar-

93

rogant, so devoid of human compassion, that they shocked Tabitha. She did not dare to answer. Her answer might spark a confrontation, and the last thing in the world she wanted to do was to argue with this grand, aristocratic man who was Nicholas Enright, eligible bachelor. Nicholas apparently felt too that the discussion had reached a point of peril for he abruptly changed the subject.

"Come, my dear. We shall go for a drive."

6

On a signal from Nicholas, the solemn driver moved the barouche closer. As they walked toward the approaching carriage Tabitha became acutely aware of the scraping noise made by Nicholas Enright's dragging right foot. The thought of Nicholas being crippled, in even this slight degree, dismayed her. It was terribly unfair that a man of such magnificent build and vast charm should be so handicapped. Yet it did not seem to detract from his physical appeal in the least. She wanted to ask him what had happened to his leg, but she dared not. Perhaps, later, he might mention it himself.

Nicholas opened the door to the barouche as the wheels ground to a stop. He folded Tabitha's small hand in his as he helped her inside, and Tabitha noticed, with some pleasure, that he held it a trifle longer than was absolutely necessary. She sat down, aglow at the rich, luxurious interior of the barouche, the dark red mohair seats and plush silk lining.

"It's gorgeous," she breathed.

Nicholas Enright did not answer. She noticed that he had a pompous way of ignoring unimportant comments, as if he could ill afford to burden his fine mind with trivialities. In fact, Tabitha was becoming more and more aware that there was something quite overbearing about Nicholas Enright. He looked wonderful, he talked well, and was polite when he chose to be; yet there was a magisterial contempt in his manner and voice, as if he sat on some cosmic pedestal and looked down with profound scorn on the rest of the human race. Tabitha could not escape the feeling that he accepted her company as he accepted his slaves, as one to whom he owed no great debt and to whose remarks he would pay attention or not, depending on his whim. He lacked the genteel attentiveness associated with cultured gentlemen, and she felt that he was treating her as nothing very special in his life, despite his slight condescension in holding her hand.

The barouche rolled slowly over the deep-rutted road, rocking gently from side to side like a giant cradle. Nicholas Enright retreated into unsociable silence. He stared fixedly through the swaying window of the carriage, watching the landscape slide by, a large magnolia tree or a black willow occasionally catching his attention, at which time he would cock his head and study the tree with absorbing interest. Then he would lapse again into a strange state of suspension, where he seemed to be floating in a mystical world completely detached from his surroundings.

"The weather is remarkable for this time of year," ventured Tabitha, trying to renew the conversation.

Nicholas glanced at her with an expression that plainly stated her remark was totally inconsequential. He patted her hand as he would a child's.

"People who believe that conversation is the only

form of communication always make appropriate but quite useless comments about the weather, my dear," he rebuked her. "Did it ever occur to you that communication can be accomplished with the mind as well as the mouth? Those who perfect the art of communication with the mind and the soul are a privileged group. Don't you think so?"

The question, Tabitha thought, was specifically designed to test her. And she failed the test miserably. She only half knew what he was talking about, or what kind of answer he expected, and rather than risk making a foolish reply that meant nothing she decided to employ the artifice that has been used by women since the dawn of time—subservience to the male intelligence.

"You're really talking over my little head," she said, smiling her prettiest.

Nicholas's heavy eyebrows pinched together. "No doubt," he said. "I see you will have much to learn."

He took out the snuffbox again, went through the ritual of applying a pinch of the powder to his nose, and sneezed delicately. Then he lapsed into somber silence again, gazing out of the window at the passing scenery.

Tabitha did not dare to break his pensive mood. Chastened, she sat in silence. The barouche swayed like a hammock. Moss-draped oaks swept past the moving window. Somewhere invisible birds chattered like gossiping women. Petulantly, Tabitha considered his remark about her need to learn more. She was afraid to ask him specifically what he meant, yet his comment intrigued her. It sounded in one respect as if he were disappointed in her, and in another as if he had some secret plan for her that required him to assume the task of teaching her those things he found lacking in her education or experience. If the latter was intended, Tabitha thought, it might suggest that he was considering her a possible wife! She felt a slight warmness on her face and she quickly put the thought out of her mind. It was, after all, too incredible to consider—at this point anyway.

They were passing through a heavily wooded sector now, and Tabitha observed that the direction was due south of Natchez. The deeply worn road wound through a shady stretch, enclosed tunnel-like by the road beneath, the vegetation on either side, and a canopy of oak boughs overhead. Tabitha could hear the pleasant whisper of the leaves on the trees as the breeze kissed them fleetingly and fled like a faithless lover. A few insects droned fitfully.

"Where are we going?" she asked finally.

"Does it matter?"

"Well, I just—"

"God's blood, I do believe you're worried!" Nicholas seemed to find high amusement in the situation. "It speaks well of you, my dear, for it labels you a lady. However, I assure you that I am quite the gentleman. My mother raised me to be one, and unfortunately I was too old to change my ingrained habits when I finally realized what enjoyment a man could experience if he wasn't one."

Tabitha looked at him sharply and he seemed vaguely amused at her startled expression.

"I was raised by a rather severe mother," he went on. "She was as insufferably proper as any Bostonian can be—in fact a damned sight more proper than most. I attended Harvard, had a private tutor to help me with such delicate matters as acceptable table manners, took piano lessons from one of the best teachers in the East, was virtually raised on stuffy social events—and, incidentally, learned rather early in life that the accouterments of civilized man are really nothing more than a complicated sham."

"A sham?"

"Of course. Aren't we all frauds? Do you always say what you think, or do you say what you feel is appropriate and will be accepted? Do you always do what you want, or do you do what is socially condoned?"

"I suppose," said Tabitha guardedly, "we all have certain hidden desires that we can't give expression to."

"You say it well," agreed Nicholas. "Hidden desires. Take Faunce Manley, for example. I despise him. I would love to punch him right in the nose—or better yet, cut him down with a colichemarde—but I refrain because it would upset the decorum of our so-called civilized existence."

"But men do fight duels."

"Ah, of course. But only when one has been insulted beyond endurance. Besides, fighting a duel isn't doing what you want to do at all. It's too formalized, too orderly. One would much prefer to kill a man in the heat of argument. Which leads me to another point—we're all potential murderers, you know."

Tabitha did not like the way the conversation was going, but she didn't know how to stop it. All she could think to say was, "Do you really think so?"

"Of course, my dear. I would be perfectly capable

of murder under the proper stimulus, and I don't hesitate in the least to admit it."

Without another word Nicholas Enright again turned to contemplate the scenery gliding past the window, content now, as if he had just won a great and important battle. Tabitha's mind spun in confusion. How strange a man he was! He seemed compelled to say outrageous things, to startle people with numbing thoughts. She watched him as he maintained a moody silence, his fine muscular body swaying gently with the movement of the barouche, an expression of complete serenity on his face, very much like a monarch riding through the countryside knowing that all that met his gaze was unalterably his.

"You haven't told me much about yourself," said Tabitha, unable to endure his silence, "except your severe upbringing in Boston—and that you could be a murderer without much hesitation." She added the last spitefully. "What brought you to the Natchez country?"

Nicholas's handsome face suddenly became stone-like, etched in hard uncompromising lines. Tabitha noticed there was something strange about his black flashing eyes. They were as fierce as a falcon's, yet with a haunting fear in them too.

"My autobiography is not exactly a pleasant one," he said in clipped tones. "But since you have asked for it I shall relate it—and I suspect you'll have to suffer through it. As I mentioned, I was brought up in a severe and straight-laced Boston home by a domineering mother. My father died when I was still an infant. Some sort of congestion of the lungs took him, I am told, although I later grew to suspect that my mother may have been instrumental in driving him to an early grave."

"Goodness!" gasped Tabitha. "What a thing to say!"

He went on as if he had not heard her. "He was a wealthy banker and he left my mother enough money to free her of financial worries. My mother had always dominated the household, and after Father died I assume, although I was only a child, that she became all the more determined to rule what remained of her family with an iron fist—namely, me. Since I was all she had left, it was apparent that she intended to keep me subservient to her at all costs."

Tabitha said nothing. His frankness was somehow disconcerting. He looked now like a man baring his soul, his gaze fixed straight ahead as the words poured forth, his facial muscles stiff and unyielding, his eyes alight with an almost fanatical glow.

"When I was eight years old I fell from an old shed on our property and broke my right leg. Small as I was, I can remember my mother's refusal to get a doctor."

"Refusal?" Tabitha's voice registered astonishment.

"As I said, my dear, Mother was—and is—headstrong. She had some idea that the leg wasn't fractured, or so I thought at the time. She said she would mend it herself. She bound it tightly with bandages, without resetting the bone, and it never knitted properly. That's why I drag one foot behind the other."

"That's terrible," said Tabitha sympathetically.

"It is, isn't it? But it gets more terrible. I went through boyhood with this stiff, rigid leg. It eliminated me from many things. I couldn't keep up with the others in games. I began to stay more and more at home, reading, doing the things my physical deformity would permit. Mother seemed quite content with this situation. As I grew into manhood I found that my deformity eliminated me from other things too. For example, I was apparently repulsive to women."

"Oh, that's not so!"

Nicholas rewarded her with his half-smile and took her hand. Tabitha knew that a lady would have discreetly withdrawn it, but she could not bring herself to do so.

"Thank you, my dear. You don't know how much I appreciate those gentle words." For a moment there was warmth in his voice, but then, as if recognizing it and considering it a weakness, the haughty coldness returned and he looked again into that hazy distance where his eyes seemingly met the past. "At any rate," he went on, "I never married. I am now thirty-three. And as I said before, my mother seems quite content with the situation."

Tabitha regarded him closely. "I don't know that I understand clearly what you mean."

"How could you? You've led a somewhat sheltered life, my dear, under the benevolent influence of a gospel-preaching father. But allow me to go on. As I grew into manhood I realized what I had been missing. I had been sheltered from all people except a few old fossils left over from Mother's early life. I was educated, had developed a certain amount of savoir-faire, but had no one of my age to use it on. I had money, all the fine things in life, except friends. The fine things weren't enough. I decided that I had to expand my horizons, show people of my own time that I was as good as they were, that I could be a success on my own, despite my dragging foot which seemed to bar me from my contemporaries. I began to search around for something to do, something that would build my name and my own personal power so that no one could ever deny my success, so that I could overcome my crippled handicap and emerge better than those who spurned me. Do you understand?"

"Yes. I think so." She kept looking at his dark eyes, fierce, angered, almost anguished.

"Finally," he continued, "word came to New England of the great boom in cotton in the Southern states, of how a man could become wealthy with one or two good crops, how cotton was becoming the king of the South. All a man needed to do was to travel down the Natchez Trace or the Mississippi River, and if he was able to escape death at the hands of land or river pirates, undreamed of riches awaited him. I had heard about the palatial mansions being erected in Natchez by farmers from the East—dirt farmers who had never had anything before, who came from Virginia and Carolina with no refinements of their own, and who were now becoming a part of the new culture—the cotton culture. All this intrigued me and I decided I would also migrate to the South and become the biggest cotton planter of them all."

His voice was bitter now, and there was a hostile wrath in his words that frightened Tabitha. It was becoming clear to Tabitha that Nicholas Enright was a man of complex emotions, a man capable of reaching dizzying heights and descending to abysmal lows. But all this was unpleasant to think about, and Tabitha put it quickly out of her mind. She would not spoil this wonderful moment by entertaining such dismal thoughts now.

"But you already had riches," she said. "You didn't need—"

"I had my father's riches," said Nicholas stiffly. "I had to show people I could be an important man on my own. You see what I mean, Tabitha—do you?" He was insistent, wanting to be understood.

"Yes."

"That was ten years ago. I was twenty-three. I tried to get my mother to agree to my venture, but she would not listen to it. She told me that if I dared leave her she would cut me off from my inheritance. I tossed her threat aside. It didn't matter. I left her, and I made it over the Trace to Natchez."

"And then you became a cotton baron?"

"Not that easily, my dear. I became one in time, but it took me eight long years. I was penniless and I needed capital to become a planter. I started out first in Natchez-under-the-Hill to raise that capital, so that I could buy land and eventually a few blacks." He looked at her keenly. "But I must be boring you."

"Not at all," said Tabitha. "I'm most interested."

"You may lose your interest," he said dryly, "if I tell you how I raised the money to build Magnolia Manor. But I shall risk it. For three years, my dear, I ran a house of ill-fame."

Tabitha made no reply. She felt a tinge of pink creep into her cheeks, but she tried to take Nicholas Enright's pronouncement calmly. After all, she was from Natchez-under-the-Hill. She was aware that such outlandish places existed; in fact, she was uncomfortably familiar with one of them since visiting Ryma.

Still it surprised her that a man of such lofty ambitions should have begun his ascent to wealth and position in a place so lowly. It surprised her even more that he should so callously admit it.

"Do I embarrass you?" Nicholas asked.

"I think not."

"It is not my intention to. So I shall skip lightly over this, shall we say, sordid episode in my career. Suffice it to say that within three years I made enough money from the perverse cravings of rivermen and assorted human derelicts plying the Mississippi to obtain credit, buy a parcel of land, a few blacks, and eventually build Magnolia Manor. Even then I was not immediately accepted by other planters. Southern planters look with distaste on a Northerner invading their domain. But in time the cotton crop began to produce and I enlarged the plantation. I built a stable of fine racing horses, and all the other symbols of the gentry—and even though they hated me, they could not deny my success. And when, at last, I had proven myself beyond doubt, I went back to Boston to get my mother."

"But why?" The words slipped out before Tabitha could stop them.

"Pride, my dear. Masculine pride. I wanted to show her what I had accomplished with my own hands, my own brains, my own wits. I wanted to let her know that I was no longer beholden to her, that she would now be the subordinate member of the family." He shook his head ruefully. "It was the greatest mistake I ever made."

Tabitha said nothing this time. She waited for him to go on. Eventually he did, his voice subdued and tinged with bitterness.

"She first said she would not come," he said. "But even then she was plotting, although I didn't realize it. You see, she couldn't resist the temptation to rule despotically over a Southern mansion in an altogether new and different culture. It was a new challenge for her, and a chance to place me once more under her merciless thumb."

Again Tabitha remained quiet. She was indeed embarrassed at the tale he was unfolding. She did not want to say anything that would anger him or turn him away. Finally he spoke again and there was undisguised hatred in his voice.

"My mother—as you shall perhaps one day find out—is a cruel and domineering despot. She cannot tolerate being second to anyone. It proved a great mistake for me to try to rub her regal nose in what I had accomplished. I thought I could control her, but I was wrong. In two years she has set herself up as queen of Magnolia Manor. She fancies herself above me and above our friends—in fact, she is the queen bee of a giant hive of lesser bees that make up the entire city of Natchez. God's beard, woman, you have no idea what my dear and beloved mother is like!"

He fell quiet again, as if exhausted by the hostility and repugnance he felt. Then, recovering, he turned toward her, placing his hand familiarly on her shoulder.

"I'm going to tell you something else about my mother," he said, his voice still cold and harsh, but more controlled. "It will shock your pretty little ears, my dear, but I'm going to tell you anyway. I am convinced that my mother knew my leg was broken when

I fell from the shed as a boy. I am convinced she knew that her amateurish bandaging would result in the bones not healing properly and would handicap me for the rest of my life. But knowing this, she deliberately did the thing that would assure my handicap — *because she wanted to also assure my subservience to her!*"

"Oh heavens! I can't believe that a mother —"

"*I* can believe it." There was no compromise in his voice. He sat there, staring at her, his jaw rigidly set, his face grim. Tabitha almost shuddered. The man seemed out of control, his eyes burning with an almost demented fire, his facial muscles tightly drawn, etching sharp lines in his proud face, making him look older than he was. Tabitha felt her heart beating rapidly, quickened by the confusion and dismay and fear his words were causing. Why, after all, was he talking to her like this? Why was he revealing to her such personal aspects of his life? They had just met. He did not need to tell her such delicate matters, did not need to drag his tragic early life before her. At first she could not understand his uninhibited loquaciousness, and then all at once she knew. He was confiding in her. This had been boiling and seething inside of him for years and suddenly he had found a good listener, someone to bare his troubles to.

But why her? Why a slip of a girl from Natchez-under-the-Hill? Did he think, because she was the daughter of a man of God, that she would better understand? Was there a kindred spirit between them because he had lived for three years under the Hill?

"It's so hard for me to believe what you say," said Tabitha, hoping to temper his next words.

107

"Is it really?" His voice held amusement, as though he was enjoying the shocking effect of his previous words. "Let me sum it up for you. Visualize, my dear, a domineering mother who wants to make certain her son never leaves her fold. Add to that a fortunate and timely accident and it shouldn't be too difficult to understand. Her actions were simply the age-old methods of a ruthless tyrant. She has always been an autocrat, using people as pawns, manipulating them always to further her own ends—to the extent, you see, of trying to destroy her son to assure her supremacy."

He looked her squarely in the eye as he spoke, his fingers tightening on her shoulder, hurting her, and there was something faintly alarming in his appearance.

"You *don't* believe me, do you? No, of course not!" There was frustration and anger in his voice now—frustration because he knew she doubted his words, anger at his own failure to convince her. He steadied himself with an obvious effort, dropping his hand from her shoulder, gazing again from the window at something far beyond. "Well, my dear, I intend to prove what I've said. If you are willing, I want you to come to Magnolia Manor and stay with us for a month or so. I want you to meet my mother and see for yourself. I want to prove to you I am right."

The blunt, unexpected invitation startled Tabitha and put her on the defensive. The horrible acts Nicholas Enright had accused his mother of seemed almost impossible to her. Now an invitation to spend a month at Magnolia Manor confused and dismayed her. A few minutes ago she would have swooned with delight at an invitation to visit the manor; now she was not sure such a visit would be a pleasure—or even wise.

"Nicholas," she said tentatively, "why should you have to prove anything to me? We've not known each other long enough to—"

"The problem is that *no one* believes me!" Nicholas grated.

"If you say it's true, I believe you," said Tabitha.

"No. No you don't, really. So I must prove it to you. You will come."

Tabitha noticed that it was not a question, but a command. She began to weigh the disadvantages of staying a month at Magnolia Manor against the benefits, but before she could analyze the situation she found herself nodding.

"Of course, if you want me to. And if my father permits."

He settled back in his seat, all at once relaxed, as if a difficult mission had been accomplished, a goal met. "It shall be arranged," he said with complete confidence. "I will have my coachman deliver a proper letter to your parents. In a couple of weeks I will call for you in the carriage. I shall be interested in meeting your parents—particularly that soul-saving father of yours. Do you think he might save mother's soul some day? She badly needs it." He laughed, then, rather loudly for him, more boisterously than was normal, as though sheer bitterness was forcing it out of some unreachable cavern deep in his soul.

Then, stopping abruptly, his face sliding into momentary repose, he said to the driver: "Take us back to the esplanade."

7

The next two weeks were an eternity to Tabitha Clay, but they provided her with an opportunity to think coolly and seriously about Nicholas Enright and what he could mean to her. She was immensely pleased at her unbelievable success in attracting Nicholas Enright in the first place. She had succeeded, quite artfully she thought, in piquing the interest of one of the most eligible bachelors among the Natchez planters. This, in itself, was an accomplishment of considerable stature, since there were planters' daughters by the dozens who, she was aware, would give everything including their honor to realize such a match. He was the catalyst that could make any girl's ambition to live on the Hill come true, and Tabitha was determined to develop her opportunity to its fullest.

Still, some troublesome doubts about Nicholas Enright had crept unbidden into her mind after her second meeting with him. She did not exactly know what to think of him. He was a powerful man, with all the refinement and grace that Tabitha had always associated with the mighty on the Hill. But he possessed a monstrous arrogance, an intolerable pride, and an appalling vanity that made Tabitha wonder if he was capable of loving anyone quite as much as himself.

Obviously, he bore no love for his mother. His rudeness when speaking of her bothered Tabitha. She had been raised to respect her parents, if not always to obey them, and the thought of a mother and son living together under the strained conditions existing at Magnolia Manor was something Tabitha found it difficult to understand. Were she to marry Nicholas some day—and this thought hovered like a predatory bird in the back of her mind—the relationship between her and a woman who intended to be the unopposed queen of her home would be intolerable.

Well, she thought, if she did marry Nicholas something would have to be done about his mother. For the present, however, Tabitha thought it best to put such vexing matters aside and concentrate on winning the total affection of Nicholas. This would be a difficult task in itself, without complicating matters by worrying about later problems with his mother. It was a matter, she decided, of meeting each obstacle as it presented itself, one at a time, coldly, implacably, and with all the cunning she possessed.

Tabitha did not mention the worrisome situation at Magnolia Manor to her mother. She dwelt instead upon Nicholas's handsome profile, his lordly manners, his haughty confidence in himself. She told Rachel how he had determined to win wealth on his own, rather than live on the earnings of his deceased father, and she made this sound like a compliment to his manhood and ambition. She told her how he had sent for his mother after establishing himself as a successful cotton planter, and she made this sound like the admirable efforts of a devoted man. She was sure that her word-picture of Nicholas impressed her mother, and this gave Tabitha support at home that was valuable to her plans. She debated whether or not to inform her parents about Nicholas's invitation to spend a month at the manor, and finally decided not to do so. She was sure that Nicholas would couch his letter in more persuasive language than she was capable of, and she decided to let the letter be delivered as a surprise. Sometimes, she thought, the element of surprise works in one's favor.

At the moment Tabitha was not certain that she loved Nicholas Enright; but this she was quite sure presented no particular problem at the moment. She was certain she could love him in time, and that was all that mattered. If he proposed to her—and she was determined to make this happen—she would not turn him down. This she had already decided. Even so, when the moment of his capitulation came, she must not act too eager. She knew all the artful tactics a girl must employ at a proposal, the dropping of eyelashes, the blushing, the hesitation before total surrender. It was poor strategy for a woman to give a man the feeling that she had been waiting breathlessly for the one heady moment when he would ask her to be his wife, even though she may have waited for years. Men had to feel that they were in control of the situation, that they were asking for a girl's hand in marriage because it had been their decision to do so. This, she thought, would be particularly true in Nicholas's case. His ego would never tolerate the idea that he had been captivated by the wiles of a female, but rather that the woman had submitted to his blandishments. Accepting his proposal would call for finesse and an instinct for timing that came natural to women—and Tabitha was convinced she could handle the matter adroitly when the time came.

Had Tabitha's thoughts been limited to the lofty grandeur of Nicholas Enright she would have perhaps passed a delightful, even though prolonged, two weeks. But much to her dismay—for she truly did not understand this—another thought kept creeping into her mind unwanted, like a footpad lurking in a darkened Natchez-under street. The intruder on her thoughts was Dr. Michael Long.

Several times—even during those precious moments when Tabitha sat alone on the rough puncheon bench outside her log home and dreamed of Nicholas—Mike Long insistently invaded her mind. Her thoughts would be of Nicholas, the proud and vain cavalier, when suddenly the mental image would change to Mike Long, the rugged and unrefined backwoods doctor—and then Tabitha would grow impatient with herself and try to squeeze Mike Long out of her mind. Quite often she did not succeed.

Mike Long, she admitted, was handsome in a robust, rough-hewn way—and just disrespectful enough to be interesting. But the memory of him enraged her. He had violated her privacy and forced himself on her at a most inopportune time. She had resented his crass assumption that she was visiting a house of prostitution to obtain a job, and his infuriating way of suggesting to Tabitha that she really didn't know what life was all about and needed a stable man like himself for protection rankled her. Yet, he *had* rescued her—at considerable risk to himself—from the drunken keelboatman who had accosted her. And, she had to admit, he had handled himself well with her angry father, although always with that maddening grin of amusement at her plight on his lips.

Why his face should continue to impose itself on that of Nicholas Enright's, like two portraits painted one atop the other, Tabitha did not know. There was no comparison between the two men. Nicholas was an important man in Natchez, possessing the cultivated refinement of a gentleman. Mike Long was of little importance anywhere, possessing little refinement and an inclination to boorishness. With Nicholas there was a future for her; with Mike there was nothing. Yet Mike's teasing image continued to intrude on her thinking. And once, infuriated at her own inability to put Mike out of her mind, Tabitha stamped her tiny foot on the ground in exasperation and said to herself, "Mike Long, why don't you go to hell!"

Two weeks after her meeting with Nicholas Enright on the esplanade, an opulent carriage drawn by two prancing bays halted before her home. Tabitha's heart almost stopped, for she knew the carriage could belong only to Nicholas Enright, and she knew what message the driver brought. Trying to hold her excitement tightly within her, Tabitha quickly surveyed the situation. Her father was not yet home from New Orleans. That meant that her mother would read the letter requesting Tabitha's visit to Magnolia Manor first, which would give Tabitha time to win her mother to her side before tackling the matter of Abijah Clay's rigidity. That, she thought, was a break in her favor.

114

Rachel had seen the carriage at the same time and had gone to the door of the cabin. The driver alighted from the vehicle, opened its door and extracted a large flat cardboard box. Stiffly, with the great dignity Negro servants often assumed, he carried the box to the two women.

"Miss Tabitha Clay?" he asked resonantly.

"I'm Tabitha Clay."

The driver handed her the box. His face split into a toothy smile.

"Compliments of Mr. Nicholas Enright, ma'am. I also have a letter for Mr. and Mrs. Abijah Clay."

Rachel reached out her hand. "Abijah Clay is not here, but I am Mrs. Clay. I'll take it."

The driver then climbed back on the carriage and, snapping the thin whip over the backs of the two reddish-brown horses, turned the vehicle around and headed back toward the bluffs.

"Whatever could this be?" asked Tabitha, staring in wonder at the large box in her hands.

"Perhaps both our curiosities would be satisfied if you opened it," suggested Rachel dryly.

Aglow with excitement, Tabitha raced into the house and placed the long flat package on the crude log table. She fumbled awkwardly with the ribbons that bound it, but managed with some effort to get them untied. When she threw back the lid of the box she uttered a delighted squeal.

"A dress!" she cried. "Oh, Mother, he sent me a dress!"

Rachel's eyebrows crawled upward. Quickly Tabitha took the dress from the box and, holding it by the shoulders, let it drop full before her. For a long time she gazed down at it in Cinderella-like wonderment, unable to speak.

It was a pale purple and made of deep rich silk. It had a low boat-shaped neck, large bell sleeves, and the long ankle-length skirt was full and flowing. Around the narrow, pinched-in waist was a darker purple sash. Still in the box was an assortment of crinolines that would make the dress flare outward in bell-like fashion. There was also a matching poke bonnet, a parasol of delicate lavender to complement the dress, a lace scarf for the neck, and—enough to make Tabitha blush—frilled pantalets. There were even purple shoes, and a tiny matching reticule. With the delight of a child, Tabitha swayed around the room with the dress in front of her, the silk rustling like whispering gossips.

"It's beautiful!" she said ecstatically. "It's the most beautiful dress in the world!" Then a sudden thought came to her and her brow furrowed. "Mother, I *can* accept it, can't I?"

"Unmarried women who have met a gentleman only briefly ordinarily do not accept such expensive—and I should say personal—gifts," intoned Rachel, sounding for all the world like Abijah.

"But, Mother, he's no—"

"No gentleman?"

"I mean—well, he's different. I—I don't know how to explain it, really, but Nicholas Enright doesn't seem to be bound by any rules of convention."

"Indeed?" Rachel's eyes widened. "How do you know?"

"Mother, *please* don't be difficult!" said Tabitha impatiently. "I'm sure Nicholas Enright means nothing personal. It's just that he wants me to look nice when I meet Mrs. Enright and—oh, Mother, *can* I keep it?"

Rachel smiled. "Of course, darling. Though how you will explain this indiscretion to your father I don't know."

"I'll think of something. Oh, he must understand!" She looked distraught. "You will help me make him understand, won't you?"

The smile spread across Rachel's careworn face. She loved this irrepressible daughter of hers, even the rebellious spirit which sometimes caused her so much concern.

"Your father," she said thoughtfully, "is a very intelligent man. He is also a man of high principles. Sometimes these towering principles and his intelligence clash, and when they do there is always considerable doubt as to how it will all come out. We shall see if we can persuade his principles to give way to his common sense in this instance."

"Oh, thank you, Mother!" And again Tabitha danced around the room, holding the flowing bombazine dress before her, fancying herself in a fine mansion called Magnolia Manor, with impeccably attired servants drifting by and Nicholas Enright and his mother looking at her, admiring her, knowing, both of them, that she was a delight to have around, that she complemented her surroundings nicely, agreeing that she was what Nicholas Enright needed.

She stopped abruptly, a perplexing thought entering her mind. She looked at Rachel.

"He must have had this dress especially made for me," she said. "But goodness, Mother, how did he know my *measurements?*"

Rachel's eyebrows elevated again. "How *did* he know your measurements, Tabitha? And also,"—pointing to the shoes—"the size of your feet?"

Startled by this mysterious development, Tabitha selected one of the shoes from the box, kicked off the one she was wearing, and fit the new one to her foot. It was exactly the right size!

"I trust," said Rachel meaningfully, "that you didn't *tell* Mr. Enright your measurements."

"Of course not, Mother!"

"Or permit him to—uh—take his own?"

"Mother—for heaven's sake!"

Rachel picked up the dress and admired it anew. The smile still hovered on her lips.

"I must say he has excellent taste. This shade almost matches your rather unusual violet eyes, into which he has obviously gazed quite intently."

"Mother, you're having fun with me."

Rachel made no further point of the matter. Instead she picked up the letter from the table and opened it. Tabitha held her breath as she read it aloud.

2. June, 1833

My dear Mrs. and Mr. Clay:

It is with some trepidation that I take pen in hand to write about your daughter, Tabitha, whom I met on the esplanade on two recent occasions. While these meetings were by chance, and therefore rightfully suspect, still I must assure you that what transpired was fraught with innocence.

118

I am, as you know, a bachelor, and I would be less than honest if I did not admit that I was charmed by your daughter. I would be delighted to have her visit my home, Magnolia Manor, to meet my mother and to sample our way of life. I hope that you will permit her to join me, as I know she is most interested in learning something about plantation living.

If you do not agree to this arrangement, please advise me. Otherwise, I will call for her at noon on Saturday next, and with your permission have her remain at Magnolia Manor—properly chaperoned, of course—for a month. Please accept, too, the small gift I am sending her by messenger. With all respect—

Nicholas Enright

Tabitha surveyed her mother sharply after the letter was read, trying to assess her reaction. Rachel placed the letter on the table without a change of expression.

"Did you know this invitation was coming, Tabitha?" she asked.

Tabitha nodded sheepishly. "I didn't mention it because I thought it was better coming from Nicholas."

Rachel sighed and said. "I rather think that even your father might be impressed with the formality of this request. It sounds virtually innocent."

"It *is*, Mother!" Tabitha was slightly annoyed at the lightness of her mother's attitude. "I can go, can't I?" she asked; then her expression changed quickly to one of determination. "I *intend* to, Mother!"

Rachel laughed. "A team of horses couldn't hold

you back, could they?"

"I think not."

"Then you may go unless your father objects too strongly. And, in this case, I don't think he will. He'll be startled by the gift, no doubt, and he'll shake his head over a girl who accepts such things from a man she barely knows—and he may tell you that you are trodding the path to Hell in little purple shoes—but I think the two of us may be able to persuade him."

"Mother, you're wonderful!" Tabitha threw her arms around her and held her close for a long moment. Rachel did not find the embrace annoying, but she was of old New England stock and not demonstrative, and she finally took Tabitha's arms and put her aside with gentle firmness.

"Come, Tabitha—let's not be maudlin," she said.

"Come help me try on the dress, Mother," Tabitha said in excitement.

The two women went into Tabitha's small curtained-off room. Both were excited, but Rachel restrained her exuberance more successfully. Quickly Tabitha slipped out of the old muslin dress she was wearing and, selecting a corset from a bureau drawer, wrapped it around her waist.

"Lace me tight, Mother!" she said. "I want the smallest waist that ever walked into Magnolia Manor!"

"You're a hussy!" snapped Rachel, but she proceeded to lace the corset, even wrapping the strings around the bedpost in order to pull them tighter. To help the matter along, Tabitha held her breath, drawing in her stomach so that the laces could be pulled to their absolute limit.

"You won't be able to breathe, child!"

"Who wants to breathe?" asked Tabitha gaily, admiring her image in the stained and cracked mirror on the wall.

Her mother could not have known it, but Tabitha possessed thoughts she rarely displayed outwardly, and as she looked into the mirror she decided that she was certainly something that Nicholas Enright, for all his formal stiffness, should passionately desire. She made special note of the fact that the top of her corset lifted her breasts upward, giving them a pointed, almost inviting, appearance. She decided they were very nice breasts indeed — not large, but appropriate to her size, and certainly having a very saucy and pert elevation. With the low boat-shaped neck of the dress revealing just the upper swells, creamy and white, it should be sufficient to make Nicholas Enright pay her a great amount of attention. Her waist was small, too, even without the corset, and after being pinched in would give her the hourglass figure she desired. The thick flaring skirt, toping the luxurious thickness of several crinolines and her pantalets, would take care of the matter of hips, although Tabitha decided her hips were ample in any case. Her legs, too, were shapely and smooth, and she thought it a shame that you could not show you legs. Looking at her legs, she thought, would be Nicholas's privilege later, if he made the right moves and said the right things — and her thoughts skidded to a halt at this dangerous point, for she realized she was again thinking of and even assuming marriage. Nicholas Enright had never, of course, mentioned marriage. But then, a man had to be gently cajoled into mentioning that, and the more Tabitha looked at herself in the mirror the more she thought that her charms were sufficient to make him speak the much-desired words in time.

"After all, there's nothing wrong with me," she said to herself, "and there are several things right."

After the lacings came the pantalets, then the crinolines, one after another in layers, and finally the dress. Tabitha even put on the matching poke bonnet and opened the parasol.

"How do I look, Mother?"

"You look lovely," said Rachel, and meant it.

"I'll need a little pink on the cheeks," Tabitha decided.

"Now, Tabitha! You know how your father deplores any kind of artificiality."

"Oh, fie! I won't *paint* myself. A few geranium petals rubbed on my cheek will turn them pink. I've often done it. And father won't know—he'll just think I'm healthy."

Rachel suppressed a smile. Tabitha often amused her, at the same time that she infuriated Abijah.

"I feel like rushing up to Nicholas Enright and saying, 'Here I am, take me!' Just like that," said Tabitha impulsively.

"Sometimes, Tabitha, you say the most outrageous things," said Rachel sternly. "I suggest you keep a close watch on your tongue when your father returns tomorrow, and permit me to do the talking."

"Yes, Mother." She stood for a moment, before the scarred mirror, admiring herself, cocking her head first to one side, then to the other, striking various poses, tilting the opened parasol over one shoulder, then the other, taking off the bonnet, putting it on again.

"I need the geraniums!" she said suddenly and, whirling, she raced through the front door to the geranium bed in front of the cabin. She was so intent on selecting just the right flower from the bed that she failed to see the figure approaching the house and did not know someone else was nearby until a man's voice came to her as she picked one of the blood-red blooms.

"It'll never work. Geraniums are not the flower to wear with that dress."

"I'm not wearing it, I'm going to redden my cheeks with it!" retorted Tabitha as she swung around. Then her eyes widened and she gasped, "Oh! You!"

Mike Long smiled softly. His keen blue eyes swept her from bonnet to shoes in an appraising glance that made Tabitha feel as if he must be plotting some mischief that involved her body.

"Another dress," he remarked solemnly. "Been to Ryma's again?"

"I have not!"

"Just wondered." His eyes scanned the dress critically. "Looks expensive. Where'd you get it?"

His impertinence irritated her. Tabitha decided she would tell him nothing.

"I *may* have bought it!" she flared.

Mike scratched his sandy hair dubiously, the exasperating smile still on his face.

"Maybe. But I doubt it. Seems likely that you got it from one of two places—Ryma or some admiring swain. And since you have already denied Ryma, I take it a gentleman friend has showered you with this bit of gratitude."

"Gratitude! How dare you!"

"Oh, it's done every day." Mike waved his hands as if to encompass the ends of the earth. "But perhaps I'm wrong. You wouldn't accept such a gift from a man, would you—unless, of course, you had some designs in mind that you wanted to achieve."

Tabitha began to stamp her foot rhythmically on the hard earth, a nervous reaction to Mike's banter. Mike Long, without a doubt, was absolutely incorrigible. He possessed a positive talent for twisting facts to fit his own interpretation of things. And his insolence was intolerable.

"I'll thank you to leave me alone, *Doctor* Long," she said, managing to convey with emphasis her doubts about the genuineness even of his occupation. "What I do is my business—not yours."

"You're right, of course. Only thing is, some people are so impetuous and headstrong that they need the protection of a more stable personality. I was merely offering my services in as subtle a manner as possible because I have an investment in you."

"An investment?"

"Yes. A sore jaw from the keelboatman."

"I'm sorry for the sore jaw," said Tabitha with strained politeness, "and I believe I have already conveyed my thanks for your intervention with the riverman. I don't believe I have need for any more of what you call your services."

"Those who need guidance never think they do," smiled Mike; then, before Tabitha could retort, he added: "I'll see you again. I'm going up on the Hill to find a new job."

Tabitha's interest sharpened despite herself. "Where? What kind of job? You're a doctor, aren't you? Or have you been lying?"

"Yes, I'm a doctor. But I'm a little tired of putting gouged-out eyes back into peoples' heads, so I thought I'd go up on the Hill and either open a new practice or make connections with a plantation owner as a slave doctor. I'd make a good slave doctor, you know, because I have an inherent sympathy for the blacks not normally found in the true Southern gentleman."

Tabitha decided to ignore this insult to the South. She merely nodded her head slightly.

"I wish you luck in establishing yourself," she said primly. "Perhaps association with your betters might improve your manners."

"If it does," said Mike, laughing, "it will destroy my entire personality. Good day."

Without a word Tabitha returned to the house, walked to the mirror, and with anger evident in every motion, began to rub her cheeks briskly with the petals of the geranium. Because she was upset, she put it on too heavily, and Rachel looked with distaste at her daughter and said: "You look like a painted Jezabel!"

In her present mood, Tabitha considered it a compliment.

8

The following day Abijah Clay returned to his home aboard the new steamboat *Southland*, divinely inspired by his brief meeting with his co-religionist in New Orleans. He paced the floor of his tiny cabin for almost an hour, talking about the wonderful work his friend was doing in the sinful Vieux Carre, where things were every bit as frightful as in Natchez-under-the-Hill. All through the diatribe Tabitha impatiently waited, hardly able to contain herself, while her more placid mother sat knitting quietly as she listened to the monotonous drone of Abijah's doomsday voice.

At last he finished and Rachel, in a most casual manner, dropped the letter from Nicholas Enright on the table before him.

"We received an important letter while you were gone, Abijah," she said simply.

Abijah took out his spectacles and perched them carefully on his nose. He read the letter in complete silence, while Tabitha's heart pounded so violently in her breast that she feared he would hear it. When he finished the letter he looked over the top of his glasses at Rachel.

"This Nicholas Enright is a most unconventional person," he remarked. "First he meets my daughter like a skulking schoolboy on the esplanade. Now he requests a rendezvous in the privacy of his home."

"Chaperoned by his mother," added Rachel significantly.

Abijah placed the letter on the table with a gesture that indicated it was slightly repugnant to him.

"It's most irregular," he insisted.

Tabitha could suppress her enthusiasm no longer. Her eyes danced in her head as she pleaded with her father.

"Oh, do let me go, Father! I've never been on a great plantation and it will be a wonderful experience. And I promise to be very proper and—and unapproachable."

Abijah's eyes blinked uncertainly behind the spectacles. "The fact that you evidently harbor the idea that Nicholas Enright might desire to—uh—approach you is somewhat suspect to begin with," he said dryly.

Tabitha mentally cursed herself for having provided him with such an opening. "But my visit to the plantation will be properly chaperoned," she insisted. "His mother will be there, and I dare say I'll even be assigned a personal servant, and—"

Abijah raised his hand for silence.

"Since you are so obviously overwhelmed by this invitation," he said, glancing suspiciously at the letter, "and since it will be adequately chaperoned, and since I trust you to be circumspect at all times, and since I happen to be in a good mood today, I shall permit you to go—*after* I have properly made my views known to Mr. Enright."

It was more than Tabitha had expected. She almost leaped with glee.

"Thank you, Father. Thank you," she said.

It had been much easier than she had anticipated. The thought sped through her mind that perhaps her father, his mind full of his recent trip and the many ideas his friend had given him for better winning the souls of the damned, had understood only the bare words of the letter—not catching the full significance of what the letter implied. If so, Tabitha was not about to enlighten him. Tabitha knew, however, exactly why Nicholas had invited her to the plantation. No man, her feminine mind told her, asked a girl to meet his mother unless he was personally interested in her. Personal interest, Tabitha calculated, implied an eventual proposal. A proposal resulted in marriage. To Tabitha, who had a faculty for believing only what she wanted to believe, it was as simple as that.

She did not show her father the fine dress Nicholas Enright had given her for some time. In fact it was not until the day before Nicholas was to call for her that the opportunity presented itself. Abijah had slowly begun to realize that his daughter was making significant steps toward a society different from that in which he had raised her, but this thought did not suggest to him that wearing apparel might differ along with the society until the last moment. On the Saturday evening prior to Nicholas Enright's arrival, Abijah suddenly looked at Tabitha with concern.

"I presume," he said heavily, "that you plan to wear that outrageous dress you got from—" He broke off, unable even to mention the name of his eldest daughter.

Tabitha glanced at her mother and Rachel nodded. She arose without answering, went into the bedroom, and brought forth the new dress. Rachel reminded Abijah that Nicholas Enright had promised in his letter to send a gift to Tabitha, and explained that the dress was it—and that Tabitha, of course, would wear it on the morrow. Tabitha held the dress in front of her, swaying gently to allow the long skirt to swing back and forth. She was depending on the dress itself to so startle her father that he would overlook the fact that accepting such a gift from a man was not considered the height of propriety—but her scheme failed.

"By the Lord Jehovah!" Abijah cried. "Now he gives my daughter a dress! I swear, the man has gone too far! No, Tabitha, you can't keep it!"

"Oh, Father—"

"It isn't proper for a gentleman to bestow upon a single woman such a personal gift," said Abijah stubbornly.

Tabitha beseeched her mother for help with her eyes. Rachel, showing sudden spirit, put down her knitting with a truculent gesture.

"Now, Abijah! You promised Tabitha she could go to the plantation."

"I did."

"And you object to the dress she borrowed from Ryma."

"I do."

"And you refuse to let her keep this one?"

"Yes."

"Well, Tabitha," she said, turning to her daughter, "it looks as if you will have to visit Mr. Enright naked."

"Rachel!" Abijah exploded. "Your language is

unbecoming!"

"Do you have another solution?" asked Rachel coolly.

Abijah glared helplessly at his wife for a long minute, then finally threw up his hands.

"God forgive me for my weakness," he said, rolling his eyes heavenward, "but I cannot fight the two of you." He stared at the dress again with some distaste, and in an attempt to salvage something from his defeat he said, "It does appear a bit unseemly in the—neck."

"It's a beautiful dress, Father!" said Tabitha. "It would be an insult for me not to wear it after Mr. Enright has been so nice as to—"

"Mr. Enright," said Abijah tonelessly, "is a fine man and one, I am sure, of character. I have heard much in his favor. Had the dress come from any man less important than he, I would not permit you to keep it, despite your mother's persuasive tongue. I must admit I am not in accord with some of the devious methods he has employed in this entire situation. My only solace is that he is a well-known gentleman of high breeding. And, of course, I have my trust in you to counterbalance any unconventional tendencies on the part of this man by being a perfect lady at all times."

"Oh, I will, Father. I've already said I will," said Tabitha impulsively, knowing full well that what constituted a perfect lady was a subject on which she and her father were poles apart. Abijah's eyes narrowed as he drummed on the table top with his gnarled fingers.

"What," he asked slowly, "are the intentions of Nicholas Enright?"

"Intentions?"

"Yes. As you may or may not know, there are different kinds," said Abijah cynically.

"Oh, I'm sure they are honorable, Father."

"Youth is sometimes sure of things they have no reason to be sure of," sighed Abijah. "However, I am inclined to agree that a man of Enright's standing in the community could ill afford to enter on any questionable adventures. Do you like this man, Tabitha?"

"Yes, Father. Very much."

"Do you think you love him?"

"Well, I—I don't know."

"*Could* you love him?"

Tabitha was embarrassed by the pointed questions. She had underestimated her father's sagacity in the matter. Apparently he was aware of the possibilities after all.

"I think I might," she said cautiously.

Abijah considered her reply for several minutes, his fingers playing over the rough-hewn boards of the table, his brow furrowed in thought. He turned to direct his next question to Rachel.

"Perhaps I have not done well by my daughters," he said.

Rachel put down her knitting, sensing that something was troubling him.

"Whatever do you mean?"

"God is a complex entity," Abijah said thoughtfully. "He drives men to admire Him and to spread His word. But perhaps he does not intend that in the spreading of it the man neglect the welfare of his family."

"You have done well by us, Abijah," said Rachel

with fierce loyalty.

Abijah stood up, his gaunt towering frame filling the room. He smiled affectionately at his wife.

"You use the words of a good wife," he said, "and I am humbly thankful. In Ecclesiastes it is said, *Well is he that dwelleth with a wife of understanding*. You have always understood what drives me, but I sometimes think I have not done well by you. In my zeal to spread the gospel among those I felt most needed it, I have raised my family in a hellhole of sin and debauchery. Perhaps that is why I have lost one daughter." He paced the floor with measured steps, tracing a path to the door, back to the table again.

"Tabitha, you have always desired to live on the Hill. Your meeting with Nicholas Enright may prove to be your access to such a life. I do not stand in your way, if such comes to pass. The Hill presents a better way of life. Those who live there are more important to the economy and life of the area—indeed, the entire country—than those who live in the squalor of Natchez-under. The mighty live on the Hill. The men who run Natchez, who play an important role in its existence, who direct its thinking. If you gain a foothold on the Hill, I will feel good about it. I ask only that in seeking this place in the sun you continue to subscribe to those characteristics that make you a good woman, that you hold fast to the honor of being a woman, that you do not lower yourself to gain a purely materialistic end but keep yourself upright in the eyes of the Lord."

Tabitha was impressed by her father's impromptu sermon. She looked at him with sudden new respect. She felt she must make some answer—some important and fulfilling answer—that would reassure a heartsick man.

"I will never dishonor you, Father," she said.

Abijah did not reply. He sat down in a chair and his lean shoulders drooped as if they had been relieved of a heavy burden. But his face remained crisscrossed with worry and he finally turned his gaze toward Rachel.

"Have I wasted my life, Rachel?" he asked dejectedly.

"Of course not. There is nothing more important in life than speaking the words of the Savior."

"I don't deny it," said Abijah. "But I think perhaps it is important to consider whom you speak them to. I find the denizens of the shacks in Natchez-under not wholly receptive to my preachings, you know."

Tabitha kept looking at her father, pained by the sadness in his face. He had questioned the wisdom of the course he was pursuing on other occasions, but he seemed unusually self-deprecatory tonight. It was a rare occasion when he sincerely doubted the need for or the effectiveness of his preachings on Silver Street. But now a powerful doubt gnawed at his mind.

"I have felt that the people of Natchez-under needed me, even though in their childlike ways they did not think so. Yet it is discouraging to stand on a street and deliver the words of the gospel to people who either do not listen or who listen with cynical doubt. At such times I think, 'Why don't I go up on the Hill and preach God's word to those who can understand, who know the value of what He has said, who live lives that reflect His teachings?' And when I think that way I say to myself, 'But the people on the

Hill do not need His words as those below do. Here is where I belong. Among the rabble who have no God, who do not know God, who even reject Him. Here is where I must make headway, plant the seed, nurture it as you nurture a crop of cotton, until it matures into something divine.' So the question becomes, 'Am I right to fight the harder battle, or might I be better off fighting the easier one?' "

"I think you would not be satisfied unless you fought the harder battle," said Rachel.

Abijah's eyes drifted slowly to Tabitha.

"Is Nicholas Enright a church-going man?" he asked.

The question startled Tabitha, and she knitted her brow in thought.

"I don't really know," she admitted.

"You did not think this important enough to find out?"

"It—just never occurred to me, Father."

"Has he discussed religion with you?"

"No."

"If he were a true man of God, the words of the Savior would be always on his lips, " said Abijah simply. "As a cotton planter, he of course owns slaves."

"Yes."

"In the eyes of the Lord, slavery is a sin," said Abijah. "Does he mistreat them?"

"I'm sure he doesn't." Tabitha bit off the words. She was reluctant to get into this area of discussion. How could she explain to her rigid-minded father what Nicholas Enright had said about slaves? His cynical words came back to her now:

"*. . . One treats them as one must. Since the blacks*

134

represent a sizable investment in the cotton business, it's foolhardy to do anything that doesn't extract the greatest amount of work from them. One does not whip a mule unless he stops working."

"Someday," Abijah was saying, "the slaves will be freed, as in all history slaves have always been freed. I do not pretend to know how this will come about, but it will. It is not possible to hold other human beings in bondage forever without fomenting some form of rebellion. Someday the cotton will be harvested by free men, working for wages—not by slaves subject to the whims, caprices and cruelties of the slave master."

And Nicholas Enright's words came again: " . . . *The black is a necessary commodity in our cotton culture. Slavery is the only possible arrangement in our way of life, else how would you ever plant, cultivate, and harvest your crop? The average black is unintelligent, unskilled, and demands little. He is particularly adaptable to the cyclical routine of the plantation."*

"But I digress," said Abijah, smiling kindly. "I have no power to abolish slavery. I'm afraid it is here for a long time to come. And I do not mean to condemn Nicholas Enright. He is a product of the times, a part of the slave culture that has developed in the south. He has been swept up in it and he has no other course to pursue even if he should want to. After all, are we not all swept up in the vortex of history? Am I not, myself, consumed in the wild and barbarous times of the frontier? Nicholas Enright and I are both trapped. And when a man is so trapped he often turns his thoughts away from changing the situation, because it is easier to accept what is. I dare say that Nicholas

Enright has so accepted slavery as a mode of the times that he has rarely questioned its validity or the moral aspects of it. I dare say, too, he sees no great disparity between whipping his slaves into line during the week and worshiping his God in church on Sunday morning. The one does not impinge upon the other."

Tabitha decided it was best to say nothing. She knew that Nicholas accepted slavery because it materially benefited him, and that he had no great trouble compromising the difference between this attitude and his basic Northern view that slavery was morally wrong. He was, as her father had said, simply accepting slavery as a necessity of the times. And then the few contemptuous words Nicholas had spoken on religion came rushing back to her and she knew, all at once, the great gulf that existed between him and her father.

" . . . I dare say he's right about the number of souls to be saved in the flatlands. . . . How many souls has he succeeded in saving? . . . I should like him to come up on the Hill and save a few souls up here some day. . . . God knows there are some around in need of considerable repair."

BOOK II
The Gentle Life

1

Cotton!

The word had become magic. It stirred the souls of men and it tugged mightily at their ambitions, their greed, and their savagery. In the opening years of the nineteenth century, no other word was so often on the lips of men as "cotton." Cotton was the white gold of the emerging South.

The halcyon years of cotton fell between 1830 and 1860. In those exciting and prosperous decades the cotton culture became a way of life for many widely diverse people: the planter who existed in a luxury beyond his wildest dreams; the slave who lived in cypress shacks and spent long days in the shimmering heat of the whitening fields; the factors who handled the financial matters; and the rivermen who carried the precious snow-like burden to New Orleans from where it was shipped to hungry New England and European markets.

The cotton empire had found a natural home along the banks of the Mississippi, where the valley's alluvial soil was more fertile than anywhere else in the nation. The old lands in the east had played out under a policy of vicious and short-sighted cultivation that took everything from the soil and returned nothing.

The broad Mississippi Valley beckoned, and by 1830 the states of Alabama, Mississippi, and Louisiana had become the reigning province of King Cotton. And in these three states King Cotton established his wealthiest baronries.

Men came from everywhere. They poured into the South from the Blue Ridge and Allegheny mountains, from the Atlantic coastal plain, and from the Cumberland and Piedmont plateaus. They were not gentle people. Sons of English and Scotch-Irish colonials, they were rough and often uncouth men who worked the land with gnarled hands and weather-wise minds, who were dirt farmers either with a knowledge of cotton from their previous holdings, or with no knowledge at all. But they came, lured by the rumors of great wealth to be had in the new cotton belt and of riches that stunned belief. They were driven by something in their personalities and in their blood, something that demanded that they own more land than their neighbors, plant more cotton than their neighbors, make more money and build more pretentious houses than their neighbors.

"You can't lose," went the refrain. "The soil is the richest in the world. The river is at your back door to transport your product. You get a passel of slaves, man, and you'll earn back your costs in the first year. After that, profits will soar, as naturally as night follows day. Twenty per cent a year is nothing! Nothing at all! So why do you want to stay in the Carolinas and Virginia anyway? The land there is growing less productive. It's worn out. In the Mississippi Valley there's the best land on earth, enough of it to last a lifetime. Great God, man, here is your chance for riches no other part of the nation can offer!"

Wild rumors of what could be done with cotton titillated their ambitions: Southern farmers were making from 15 to 30 per cent profits . . . each slave could pick seven to eight bales of cotton in a season . . . an acre would average one to two bales . . . and each bale ran about 400 pounds. Figure it out, man . . . cotton sells at from 12 to 15 cents a pound . . . and if you pay $600 apiece for Negro fieldhands, you can pay for two-thirds of them with your first crop, considering that you have any kind of acreage at all . . . and the second crop will pay for the remaining slaves and buy 10 to 15 more . . . and the third year the same . . . and incomes of $40,000 to $50,000 a year are common . . . and how in hell can a man lose?

There was a rhythm to it all, an endless, pitiless, chain-like rhythm: sell cotton to buy Negroes to grow more cotton to buy more Negroes. Over and over again, ad infinitum.

They came to exploit the land, these men, and they did so. For all their humble beginnings, they were proud people, and as their wealth increased they built the fine pillared mansions that became the visible symbols of their success, and they filled these ostentatious homes with fine Chippendale furniture and the best china and silver and all the other accouterments of the hedonistic life. And in the process of building their vast empire they also created a pernicious autocracy, a personal dictatorship, a despotism that gave them unimpeachable sovereignty over acres of white land and hundreds of black people—and they knew little about handling such supreme power. The only answer they had was cruel exploitation of the land and their slaves. And, as in every dictatorship of the elite, frightful excesses became commonplace.

The dirt farmers who assumed this elevated station in life were not the courtly gentleman planters they pretended to be. Many were nothing more than crude savages living in pretentious palaces. They were violent and headstrong and stubborn and often vicious, to each other and to their blacks, for their burning passion was cotton and they loved it more than they loved each other. Still, they were caste-conscious, hugging to their proud bosoms the riches of the era, suspicious of the stranger who tried to encroach on their selfish domain. And they tried to protect their mutual interests by clannish loyalty to each other—and by intermarriage. Any planter's son or daughter who married outside the planter society was always criticized, if not totally ostracized.

The great continental surge to what was then the southwestern United States grew to excessive proportions. By 1830 the cotton empire was at its height, and would remain at its zenith for at least thirty years. As the focal point of this formidable empire, the impressive city on the bluffs overlooking the Mississippi—glorious Natchez—became the showplace of the South. Great homes appeared in the city, and Natchez presented to the world the appearance of a quiet, soft, peaceable city of well-bred and polished inhabitants. In truth, the outer shell barely concealed the inner core. For Natchez was as turbulent and as lusty as any other frontier town.

It merely wore a more exquisite cloak.

2

Magnolia Manor was a proud and noble mansion located a mile south of Natchez, with the white-crested cotton fields that made it possible stretched away at its back and a magnificent view of the Mississippi River winding before it. Despite its lofty location atop the wind-swept bluff, it was barely visible as one approached it over the worn and rutted wagon trail that led from the city. With aged oaks and magnolia to screen it from view, it was jealously tucked away from the eyes of chance intruders as though it desired not to be profaned by the gaze of common humanity.

It had been a long, lazy but quite thrilling ride for Tabitha. Nicholas Enright had called for her in the handsome barouche at exactly noon, drawing the startled attention of everyone within seeing distance. He had treated Tabitha's parents with courtesy, managing a certain pose of magisterial hauteur even as he paid homage to their position as parent of the girl he was taking to his home.

Tabitha's father had maintained a proper if somewhat cold dignity and had refrained from any speculative comments about either the propriety of the arrangements or the power of the Lord, for which

Tabitha was thankful, for she was quite aware that even a minor discussion of such matters could have ruined the entire affair. So all had gone smoothly and Tabitha—wearing the dress Nicholas had given her and carrying a bag containing Ryma's dress, her own "best dress" and other necessary apparel—had entered the barouche with Nicholas. Tabitha had felt like a queen as she became the recipient of stares from her neighbors in the mudflats of Natchez-under, and she settled back in the red mohair seats of the elaborate coach, acutely aware of the presence beside her of the grand and polished man who was Nicholas Enright, dressed flawlessly in a tight black coat and gray trousers, and with an aura of importance about him that no man in Tabitha's life had ever commanded.

She found Nicholas in one of his silent moods, for he said virtually nothing to her. He even acknowledged her gracious thanks for the dress with only a restrained smile and a silent nod of his head. That he should be so aloof on such an important occasion nettled Tabitha, but she dismissed it as simply "his way" and decided not to intrude on his mood. After all, it was necessary that their little escapade get off on the right foot, and she would do nothing to jeopardize their relationship so early in the venture.

As they drew nearer to Magnolia Manor, however, Nicholas became more animated, hunching forward in his seat and pointing out various landmarks along the way. The deep-rutted roadway, over which the barouche rocked gently, was lined with huge and ancient oaks dripping with the gray sponginess of Spanish moss. It wound interminably between the towering trees, some of them encroaching on the road with leafy branches to form an emerald tunnel through which the coach moved. As they approached their destination, the oaks gave way to magnolia grandiflora, spreading upward from the soft soil in a profusion of waxen green leaves and rose-colored flowers, and Tabitha was almost overwhelmed by the thick sweet scent of them. Skirting past bayous and ravines, the road soon was dominated entirely by these lush magnolias, but as if to provide some relief from their wax-like, almost artificial beauty there were vari-colored beds of daintier blooms, a copse of pecan trees alive with their bounty, sweet olive trees, and a profusion of semitropical flowers that hung heavy on brush and bramble.

"Another curve and we shall be there," said Nicholas at last, and there was no mistaking the ring of pride in his voice. "You'll find the view of the river from the knoll quite as entrancing as that from the esplanade, although my favorite view is five hundred acres of cotton seen from the back of the house. Without the cotton, there would be no Magnolia Manor and the river itself would lose its importance."

"I'm sure it is most beautiful from any view," said Tabitha guardedly, noting again Nicholas's emphasis on the importance of his cotton. It was obvious that Nicholas worshiped the white fiber bolls, for they had given him everything—not only riches personally earned but a sense of achievement, of power, that had escaped him in earlier years. The disruptive picture of his mother swept through Tabitha's mind, but she brushed it away impatiently. She wanted nothing to spoil this perfect, heavenly day—and she fervently hoped that her first meeting with Nicholas's despotic mother would not be uncomfortable.

The barouche jounced around the last curve, came out of the forest of magnolias, leaving the sweet fragrance hanging limply in the woods, and emerged into a sun-splashed area free of trees and underbrush. In the center of the clearing stood Magnolia Manor. Tabitha held her breath at sight of it. Its towering white-pillared magnificence was so startling that she could not take in, all at once, its many ramifications or the breathtaking total of it.

"It's lovely!" she exclaimed, her eyes dancing like a delighted child's. "But it would take a month to go through it!"

Nicholas Enright smiled tolerantly. Tabitha experienced again, as she had in the past, a vague uneasiness about his smile. It was a stilted, almost painful smile, as though someone had forced it on his unwilling face. But why think of that now, in the august presence of Magnolia Manor? Impatient with herself, Tabitha put the unpleasant thoughts out of her mind.

Magnolia Manor had an aura of aristocratic pride about it, not unlike that of its owner. It stood like a benevolent white giant on a gently rising crest of land, looking down with haughty aloofness on forest and river and cotton. Constructed mostly of white-washed brick—made on the premises by slave labor, Tabitha later learned—its most significant feature was the great upper story gallery that spread across the front, supported by six stately white Tuscan columns. The very simplicity of the huge columns, unfluted and topped by a modest entablature, lent an austere dignity to the building. Its broad lower veranda was reached by three concrete steps, and the massive main door was uniquely carved and crowned with intricately wrought fanlights. The upper roofed gallery, or belvedere, could be approached at either end of the house by curving stairs made of teak to withstand the dampness of the bayou country. Fronting the imposing mansion was a porte-cochere projecting over the carriage drive that formed a half-circle around the most lovely terraced garden Tabitha had ever beheld.

"All the beams and timbers of the building," offered Nicholas, as the barouche drew nearer, "are held together with wooden pegs—a Spanish touch which was used frequently during the last part of the past century when Spain held dominance over the area. Being from New England, you will find some of the rigid British influence inside—and, of course, even the use of the word manor in its name suggests the feudal days of England. You will also find, particularly in the furnishings, a French motif—since, of course, they were the first settlers in this region with the exception of the Indians. And the facade is typical Greek Revival. So you see, I have neglected nobody."

It was like receiving a history lesson to listen to Nicholas, thought Tabitha. He was well-informed on almost all things, and the fact that he seemed compelled always to impart his knowledge in conversation was probably part of his natural arrogance. Tabitha mentally thanked her father for having insisted on her educating herself. At least, she thought, Nicholas

Enright will not completely outclass me!

"I have seen some of the planters' mansions," said Tabitha, "but never one so beautiful as this."

"Beauty is relative, my dear. What is beauty to one eye is ugliness to another. There is even a certain kind of beauty in Natchez-under-the-Hill, don't you think?"

"I have never thought so."

"Then perhaps you live too close to it to appreciate its many charms," said Nicholas, leaving Tabitha to guess what he might mean.

The barouche had ceased rocking now as the fellies of its wheels ground over the smooth driveway leading to Magnolia Manor, lifting up fine dirt and cascading it down over spokes and hubs in miniature showers. The carriage stopped beneath the porte-cochere and at the exact center of the great veranda, where the three steps led to the main entrance, and the driver descended from his lofty seat and opened the door for Tabitha with staunch dignity. She descended with particular regard to daintiness, touching his proffered hand only with the tips of her fingers, the silk of her dress rustling in hushed conspiratorial tones. Nicholas stepped from the barouche, placing his best foot on the ground and dragging the other from the carriage with some awkwardness. Then, taking Tabitha's arm, he led the way to the door, which, Tabitha observed, swung from solid silver hinges and had a knob and keyplate of the same precious material. An elderly Negro sevant with kinky gray hair and dressed suitably in black trousers and a blood-red jacket, held the door open for their admission.

"Welcome, Miss Tabitha," he said courteously.

Tabitha smiled and nodded. Obviously, Nicholas had carefully coached his servants on her coming!

"This is Toby," said Nicholas obliquely. "You'll find him quite the most accomplished servant in all Natchez."

The black's round face split in a grin. "Thank you, Massa, thank you."

Entering the house, Tabitha found herself in a large high-ceilinged hall which bisected the building from front to back. Immediately upon entering she sensed a vague coldness about the place, almost as if she had stepped from warm sunshine into a dank cave. But when her eyes found the majestic circular staircase with the delicate harplike balustrade that wound gracefully to the second floor, the sheer fragile beauty of it caused her to exclaim with delight.

"I'll show you around first, my dear," said Nicholas softly. "Mother is probably in the music room, and we shall go there last to meet her."

"I'd love to see everything," said Tabitha, almost ecstatic in her happiness. This, she was already thinking, is where I belong. This is what I was made for, and this I must have. . . .

"I suspect that you might first be interested in the original paintings in this hallway," said Nicholas. "At any rate, it would be well for you to acquaint yourself with some of the Old World masters." He let the suggestion dangle a moment and Tabitha was quick to catch the hidden meaning of this pronouncement: He is practically saying that, since I will spend much time with him in the future, I must therefore understand and appreciate his culture. He is also implying that I know nothing of the old masters now, which is an ar-

148

rogant assumption I shall have to correct in time. His remark both encouraged and cut her, but she had no opportunity to reply as Nicholas went on.

"Here is a truly outstanding landscape by Corot, a young thirty-four-year-old French painter in whom I have great confidence," he said, motioning with his hand to a painting near the doorway. "Some people dislike his paintings, considering them dull and lifeless. For my own taste, I enjoy the wispy gray tonality of his work."

Tabitha studied the painting. It was a pastoral landscape, with a huge oak tree at the right, a fast-moving brook through the center of the canvas, with a picnicking family sitting on the ground near the stream. There was something depressing about it, despite its happy subject matter. Perhaps, as Nicholas had said, it was its "wispy gray tonality" that gave it a somber touch, for the painting was done in dull grays and browns with little brightness to it. The foliage of the trees seemed formless and the entire composition monotonous. That Nicholas should predict a great future for this young painter indicated either that he saw something in the Frenchman's work that others did not or that he liked the work simply because others did not.

"On the other side," said Nicholas, moving across the wide hall to a painting on the left, "is a Vigee-Lebrun. Are you acquainted with her work?"

Tabitha thought the question was slyly put. She nodded with as much certainty as she could muster.

"I have heard of her," she lied.

"A remarkable woman and a fine artist," said Nicholas. "Quite a rage in late eighteenth century

France, as you know. In 1783, when she was but twenty-eight years old, she had already won the favor of the court of France, having painted all of the better known court figures." He pointed to the painting, a much brighter picture of an old cobbler working in his shop. "But, as you see, Vigee-Lebrun did not limit her subject matter to court figures only. This is one of her earliest efforts, done when she was but sixteen—a truly remarkable piece of work."

He passed quickly, then, to others. "Here's a mythological painting of Bacchus and Ariadne by Titian, a Venetian who did most of his important work in the early part of the sixteenth century, and one by Correggio, a sixteenth century Italian artist who specialized in humanizing religious figures. And there are many others, as you can see, by Rubens, Van Dyck, Vermeer, and the great Goya, who died just two years ago. But perhaps," he hesitated, looking at Tabitha with only a trace of a smile on his lips, "perhaps you will be most interested in this excellent portrait of my mother by Jacques Louis David. I think it's quite the best Mother ever had done—and when you see her in person I'm sure you will agree, for she has changed little. David was a great portraitist until his death in 1825. He not only painted the physical being but was able to capture the subtlest traits of character in his portraits. This one, I think you will see, brings out something of the tyrannical qualities mother possesses."

Tabitha looked with interest at the large portrait in its heavy goldleaf frame. It was of a woman in her late fifties or early sixties, and Tabitha agreed with Nicholas that it had a distinct quality of hardness and severity. The woman was thin-faced, with high protruding cheekbones, a pointed chin and a firm set to her fine lips. She had sleek ebony hair combed rigidly back, apparently gathered in a tight chignon. Her eyes were as black as her hair, fierce eyes that had a flame buried deep within them, eyes that seemed constantly on the verge of exploding with hatred or anger—yes, eyes very much like those of Nicholas. There was no trace of a smile, nor any indication of happiness in the face, and to say that this was a stern and uncompromising woman would have been putting it in the mildest form possible.

"Is this a —a recent portrait?" asked Tabitha.

"David did it nine years ago. I must say it's a most faithful likeness. She hasn't changed much in the years since. Still as straight and rigid as a beanpole and with about as much warmth."

"Nicholas—the things you say!" Somehow Tabitha could not bring herself to accept the manner in which Nicholas Enright referred to his mother without at least a mild protest. His words, so callously uttered, startled her. Yet she knew that Nicholas was not one to so speak unless he at least believed that there was truth in his statement—and this fact bothered her more than if he had been a congenital liar.

Nicholas, perhaps as a reaction to her rebuke, took out the gold snuffbox and applied a pinch to his nose. The delicate sneeze followed in due course. Then, without a word, he took her arm and led her to a door on the right side of the hall. He opened it and allowed her to look inside. It was a spacious salon, tastefully furnished with comfortable French rosewood furniture that provided the room with a mellow richness. One wall displayed a fresco showing a field of ripening cotton. Across the room, on the outside wall, was a large fireplace with a carved white Carrara marble mantel, on top of which sat intricately fashioned ivory miniatures. Above the mantel an impressive ceiling-high mirror, set in a heavy goldleaf frame, reflected the room in a kaleidoscope of color and shape. But most of all it reflected the huge bronze French chandelier which dripped from the high-vaulted ceiling.

Tabitha stared spellbound at the haughty beauty of the salon, but at the same time a disquieting feeling crept over her. Despite its glorious accouterments, the salon was a lonely room, as if the beauty was there but was idle, standing still, unappreciated and unbeheld. The same feeling of coldness she had experienced upon entering the hallway returned, and she was puzzled by her own reaction. The room looked as if it wanted to be admired and loved, but was instead forsaken.

Tabitha again put her incomprehensible thoughts aside and followed Nicholas into the great dining room behind the salon. It boasted a great mahogany table, satiny sideboards and sturdy chairs, and was big enough to entertain fifty or more guests. The walls were papered with hand-blocked French scenic wallpaper, and the floor was made of black and white marble squares. A large Indian punkah hung indolently over the immense table, as if waiting to stir the air as soon as diners arrived. A sideboard displayed valuable crystal from England.

"You could feed an army in here," Tabitha said,

awed by the magnificence around her.

"I dare say an army would be preferable, sometimes, to the guests we are accustomed to," said Nicholas enigmatically.

Passing through the dining room, Tabitha was led through French doors at the rear of the mansion onto a flagged patio. A hundred feet away was a small, simple brick building, set apart from the house.

"The kitchen," said Nicholas. "I shan't take you there now, although I expect you'll get well-acquainted with it before long. Our servants prepare the meals in the kitchen and run the food along the patio directly to our table on occasions when we have a large number of guests. I might also mention that there are four large bedrooms on the second floor, and a hallway that leads to the upper gallery which circles the house. We shall go up there later, but now I imagine, having viewed her portrait, that you are practically throbbing to meet my mother."

Guiding her with one expert hand on her elbow, Nicholas Enright led Tabitha back into the main hall and through a large oak door into the library and music room. This room was so immense, and the decor so striking, that Tabitha did not immediately notice Nicholas's mother sitting in a large overstuffed chair near the window. Tabitha's first impression was only that she stood within the walls of a room that simply reeked of character and culture. It was the largest room Tabitha had yet seen, rectangular in shape, with three of its oak walls lined with bookshelves. On the shelves was a voluminous collection of books, layers upon layers of them, extending from ceiling to floor, representing such a staggering

153

array of knowledge as to be almost unbelievable.

As she learned later, all the Greek and Roman writers and thinkers were there—Plato, Homer, Sophocles, Euripides, Plutarch, Seneca. The great old English masters and Scottish authors had a section of the bookshelves to themselves—Chaucer, Shakespeare, Pepys, Daniel Defoe, Percy Bysshe Shelley, Sir Walter Scott. And isolated from the rest were the American authors—William Bradford, Cotton Mather, Jonathan Edwards from the earlier days, as well as the most current works of the contemporary writers. Washington Irving's *Tales of a Traveler* and *Bracebridge Hall* were represented; William Cullen Bryant's famous *Thanatopsis,* written when he was but seventeen years old; James Fenimore Cooper's *Last of the Mohicans* and *The Pioneers* graced the shelves; and even the newest writer, an upstart from New England named Edgar Allan Poe who had just written *Tamerland and Other Poems* and who was being touted by some as a budding genius, had his place on the shelves. Every conceivable subject was covered by the vast literary collection—religion, music, art, philosophy, drama, and science leading the intellectual parade of titles.

The fourth wall of the room was the outer one, comprised almost entirely of a large bay window that provided an extensive view of the plantation with its numerous outbuildings, the cypress shacks of the slaves, and the softly undulating fields of cotton. The room was furnished with an uncountable number of large chairs and sofas, deep and comfortable and luxurious, and in the corners were elaborately carved French etageres holding exquisitively fashioned figurines. A cut glass chandelier, reflecting the light of the sun through the window in rainbow-like colors, dangled from the center of the sixteen-foot-high ceiling. Thick red draperies hung from goldleaf cornices at the windows. Against one wall was a small delicately carved rosewood spinet with mother-of-pearl keys, which was the only feminine touch noticeable—although Tabitha was to learn that the spinet was the jealously guarded property of Nicholas who played the piano with comsummate skill.

The woman silhouetted at the window did not move but appeared as inanimate as the furniture and fittings, sitting erect and stiff-backed and blending into the general decor like a statue specifically carved to fit its surroundings. It was probably this rigid immobility that had caused Tabitha to first overlook her presence; then, all at once, she was aware of her. And, like so many other things Tabitha had already noticed in this beautiful and yet strangely disturbing house, Nicholas's mother seemed to bring a chill to a room that was otherwise warm and inviting.

Nicholas guided Tabitha slowly toward his mother, almost in the manner of a subject approaching his queen. As he came closer to her, Nicholas began to employ a noticeable deference of attitude that at first surprised Tabitha until she observed that there was a mocking disdain in his supposed humility. His face was twisted in a cynical smile, as if a carefully veiled contempt was bubbling up from the hidden well of his soul.

"Mother, I want you to meet Tabitha Clay," he said.

Martha Enright did not move. No muscle even so

much as twitched. She stared straight ahead, in Tabitha's direction, her face set in stern inflexible lines, her wide, thin-lipped mouth drooping slightly at the corners. If the portrait had looked harshly severe, the living Martha Enright was expressly so. No painter—even David—could have captured on canvas the uncompromising hostility of the woman. Every age line in her thin hawklike face was severely set as though molded firmly in plaster. Her hair, balled in a chignon just as in the portrait, was straight and black with a few streaks of iron-gray that gave it a metallic hardness. Her eyes did not move, nor even blink. They were black, baleful eyes with heavy brows that hovered over them like storm clouds over twin lakes. In one sitting or a dozen, David could not have caught on canvas the shamelessly wicked glint in those eyes, nor the contemptuous coldness with which she stared at this newcomer to her domain.

"I'm delighted to meet you, Mrs. Enright," Tabitha forced herself to say.

Tabitha was surprised when the wide drooping mouth in the thin face opened up and answering words emerged, for one does not expect a stone statue to talk.

"My son has spoken of you, Tabitha," she said, her voice wretchedly chilly. "I suppose, trusting my son's taste as I do, you are a fitting complement to your present surroundings."

Tabitha did not understand what *that* meant. She glanced quickly at Nicholas. He stood gazing at his mother, the amused half-smile on his face, his body as rigid as a soldier standing at attention before his superior officer, but with his attitude one of quiet disdain rather than respect.

"Well, Nicholas!" snapped the old woman in a waspish tone. *"Tell me what she looks like!"*

Tabitha suppressed a gasp. Suddenly she understood the stony manner in which Martha Enright had been regarding her. She knew, all at once, why the sharp piercing eyes had not moved or blinked, but had stared vacantly ahead. Nicholas's mother was *blind!*

Tabitha's eyes traveled to Nicholas accusingly. Why hadn't he told her? Why had he let her approach this moment with no knowledge that the woman she was to meet could not see her, would never see her? It was a shocking and unforgiveable oversight—if, indeed, it was an oversight. Her look was so reproachful that even Nicholas felt obligated to acknowledge it. He passed his hand before his eyes to indicate by the motion that he mother was blind, and then spoke in soft tones, almost tender, and yet, Tabitha thought, without compassion.

"As I have mentioned, Mother, she is a most beautiful girl. I have more than once described her physically to you, so I need not go further into that. Suffice it to say that she is—and will be—an attractive addition to our home."

Tabitha frowned. His choice of words perplexed her. What did he mean, that she would make an attractive addition to Magnolia Manor? This implied some understanding between mother and son, something they had decided without her knowledge or participation.

Martha Enright's unseeing eyes clung to the spot where Tabitha stood. Tabitha felt like moving to another place, letting her thus stare into space, but she lacked the heartlessness required for such duplicity.

"I understand," said the old woman, "that you come from Natchez-under-the-Hill."

"Yes, Mrs. Enright." Tabitha felt as if she were addressing a royal personage, some great empress out of the past who was no longer alive but mummified.

"Hardly a place of high recommendation," Martha sniffed.

Tabitha studied her carefully. Obviously Martha Enright had decided to be difficult; her comment was likely designed to test Tabitha's temper. Tabitha decided to take the long gamble of answering fire with fire.

"Not all people from Natchez-under are of poor reputation," she said. "And I am told that not all those living high on the bluffs are above reproach."

Martha Enright pursed her lips, as if considering the validity of this statement.

"I suspect there are proper people everywhere," she acknowledged grudgingly. "Still, one must admit that Natchez-under is not the most likely place to find a person of high breeding."

Tabitha looked to Nicholas for help. He was smiling, as if he enjoyed the exchange between his mother and Tabitha. But he came to Tabitha's rescue.

"Tabitha is the daughter of a lay preacher, Mother."

For the first time Martha Enright's stone-like countenance relaxed. The drooping lips curled upward in a slow smile. She turned her head slightly to gaze at the spot from which she had heard her son's voice.

"You must realize, Nicholas, how amusing it is to me that you should recommend this girl by the fact that her father is a preacher—you, an atheist, who never believed in God and who has more than once branded the Bible a collection of fairy tales!"

"Nevertheless, my dear mother"—his voice did not complement the endearing choice of words—"one must admit that the daughter of a man dedicated to religion, however mistakingly, has likely had a stern and disciplined upbringing, for all preachers are inclined to raise their children as puritanically as possible."

"And how puritanical is it possible to be in Natchez-under?" Martha snapped.

Tabitha felt a growing outrage at the way the conversation was proceeding. The bold manner in which they were discussing her appalled and angered her. For a moment she forgot all about her ambition to live on the Hill, and the fact that Nicholas Enright represented her access to such an existence, and her temper warmed the words that now issued from her mouth.

"I don't intend to stand here and be analyzed by the two of you like a slave on the block," she said hotly. "If I am not good enough for your house, I ask that you tell me so immediately so that I can take my departure."

Nicholas's head snapped in her direction. He looked surprised at her outburst. Martha Enright turned her head in the direction of Tabitha's voice, the fierce sightless eyes black in her face.

"Well, well!" she exclaimed. "I must say I like your spirit! It just might be the thing needed to tame my son's disagreeable personality. . . . Come here, my dear, and let me touch you."

It was not a request. It was a command. There was, Tabitha knew, no doubt in Martha Enright's mind but that it would be obeyed. And Tabitha walked toward her, obeying, yet not wanting to, not wanting this strange witch-like woman to touch her, cringing at the thought of such a personal contact. But she stood as the old woman felt her dress, letting her talon-like fingers slip gently over the full skirt.

"Silk," she said. "You bought the dress for her, Nicholas?"

"Does it matter?" Nicholas asked.

The thin body straightened. The cold merciless eyes turned again toward him.

"Never answer my questions with another question," she said severely. "Did you buy the dress?"

"I did."

"I expect it was the proper thing to do under the circumstances," she said. Then she added: "Nicholas, will you pull the draperies? The sun is burning my neck severely."

Tabitha observed that the sun was not shining through the window at all, but Nicholas pulled the draperies across the glistening sheet of glass, and the gathered shadows fell over this strange woman like a burial shroud.

"Tell me, my dear. How did you manage to attract my son in the first place?"

Tabitha fought for an answer. She was beginning to understand Martha Enright better. Despite the compliment to Tabitha's spirit, Martha did not like this intruder in her home, and Tabitha knew she would never tolerate her presence graciously.

"Perhaps your son can answer that question better than I," Tabitha replied evasively.

"Well, son?" The woman's waspish voice was demanding.

"Oh, I'd say it was quite a simple flirtation," Nicholas said easily. "Tabitha made herself as attractive as possible, went to the esplanade, and stood there waiting for a man to notice her. I noticed."

"Nicholas! The way you put it!" Tabitha was distressed at his explanation, but her own fair-mindedness told her that what he said was not entirely untrue. How do you attract a man unless you dress prettily and wait for someone to notice you?

"And you, my son, developed the flirtation?" Martha asked icily.

"I plead guilty to being a man," said Nicholas, "and as such I am normally attracted to a pretty female. Especially one who, in my judgment, was also willing to be—shall we say—approached?" He nodded deferentially to Tabitha as he said the last word, then smiled in amusement at Tabitha's show of displeasure.

"You always showed a tendency to become addle-brained over a pretty face," said Martha scathingly. Then she waved her arm in an imperious gesture. "Well, let that be. Nicholas tells me he invited you to stay a month. I welcome you to Magnolia Manor, and hope that your stay with us will not be too uncomfortable. . . . Nicholas, have Sophie take care of her, will you?"

"I intend to, Mother."

Without another word he gently took Tabitha's arm and guided her into the hall, closing the door to the library. Tabitha turned on him immediately, risking everything with angry words that tumbled from her lips unimpeded.

"For the love of God, Nicholas," she rasped, "why didn't you tell me your mother was blind?"

Nicholas merely shrugged his shoulders.

"It never really occurred to me," he said simply.

3

Sophie turned out to be a large, raw-boned quadroon woman assigned by Nicholas to take care of any needs Tabitha might have. She had bulging lips and broad nostrils to account for the one-fourth Negro blood that was in her, but her skin was almost as creamy as Tabitha's, her hair straight and black, and her dark eyes round and large. The eyes, Tabitha noticed, were always shifting. The woman avoided looking directly at Tabitha when she spoke, but talked to her while pretending to be busy with something else. There was no eye-to-eye contact.

"We have dinner at six," Nicholas told Tabitha as he placed her in the capable hands of the quadroon. "Sophie will aid you with your toilette. Oh, and yes—please ignore Sophie's well-meaning and anxiously given advice and counsel. She'll provide you with an abundance of it, but we know from long experience that the best procedure is to ignore it completely."

Sophie sniffed up her nose at this comment but made no reply. Then, taking Tabitha gently by the arm, she directed her up the impressive circular staircase to the upper floor where a long hallway fed into bedrooms on either side. At one of the front rooms, facing the river, Sophie opened the door and allowed Tabitha to precede her into the room.

To Tabitha's surprise, the bedroom was unlike any of the other rooms she had seen. Every facet of the room possessed a Chinese motif. Tabitha dimly remembered, probably from something she had read in her father's books, that chinoiserie, a style of ornamentation characterized by intricate patterns identified with Chinese art, had been popular in eighteenth-century Europe, but she had never seen an example of it. Everything, including even the big four-poster bed with the canopy over it, was inlaid with Chinese figures and works of art. There was a Chinese Chippendale bookcase with profuse Chinese adornment; an elaborately carved English escritoire with Chinese overtones; a clock with a carved Chinese Mandarin poised at the top. Coming fresh from her examination of the rest of the house, it was like stepping from America's serene Southern atmosphere into ancient, age-old China.

Before Tabitha could comment on the strange room, Sophie inserted her own remarks.

"Ah sure nuff don' know why Mistah Enright evah *dee*-cided to make this heah room look like a Chinese dope den," she said, as if apologizing for her master's idiosyncracies. "Don' make no sense to me!"

Tabitha merely smiled. From the window she could see the Mississippi, sparking yellow and gold under the saffron sun, and beyond the waters the cotton fields of Louisiana—where she understood Nicholas also had property—were whitening under the sun's insistent prodding.

"It's beautiful," said Tabitha with delight.

Sophie took Tabitha's sunbonnet, which she had been carrying in her hands, and placed it on the escritoire.

"It's beootiful only at fust," she said in a dead monotone. "Then that beooty dies deader'n a catfish on a mudbank."

Tabitha looked at the big quadroon with surprise. "Whatever did you mean by that?"

"You'll learn, ma'am," said Sophie mysteriously.

Tabitha felt curiously vexed. She hated people who talked in riddles. Besides, she was thrilled at being in Magnolia Manor, and she resented any cynicism that shattered her dream, whether it came from Nicholas, his mother, or Sophie. There had already been too many disquieting moments, and she resented a mere servant adding to the disarray in her mind.

"Is that what Nicholas Enright meant when he warned me against your advice and counsel?" she demanded sharply.

To her surprise the question brought a soft chuckle to Sophie's lips, and her big eyes rolled mischievously.

"Ma'am, let me tell you somethin'. Mistah Enright tells people that all the time, 'cause he knows that Ah knows what goes on in this place. Ah've been here evah since he's been here—and *she's* been here." Her arm, gesturing, left no doubt as to whom she meant by she. "Ah could tell you a few things 'bout this place—if you'd lissen."

Despite her reluctance, and Nicholas's warning, Tabitha found herself intrigued by Sophie's promising words.

"Tell me," she said, trying not to appear too eager. "I'd like to know everything about Magnolia Manor."

It was all Sophie needed. She went promptly into her speech as if she had been rehearsing it for years and had only been waiting for her moment on stage. It was obvious she enjoyed imparting her knowledge of Magnolia Manor and its occupants to newcomers, for her eyes sparkled with excitement and her lips wore an almost evil smile.

"Ah bet you was mighty impressed the fust time you saw Magnoly Manor, wasn't you? Looks real nice, don't it? You come up in that fine carriage of Mistah Enright's an' you see the house a-sittin' there in the sun, all white like a angel's house—it makes a right good impression. But it's only white on the outside, Miss Tabitha. On the inside it's black, like a funeral's black."

Tabitha regarded Sophie closely. Somehow, in spite of Nicholas's warning, she had a feeling that Sophie knew what she was talking about. She had felt something of what Sophie was hinting at on her entrance into Magnolia Manor. There had been a subtle air of mystery inside the place, heightened perhaps by the obvious tug-of-war between mother and son for dominance in the house. The inside had quite definitely, despite its physical beauty, imparted a feeling of uneasiness to Tabitha.

"Please be more specific, Sophie," she said impatiently.

"Ah'll be as spiffic as you say," responded Sophie with obvious relish. "Fust of all, you take Miss Martha. She ain't right in the haid, Ah've allus said it. Ah was here the fust time she set foot in the place. She could see then, an' you shoulda seen her. Nuthin satisfied her. Beeootiful place it was, but nuthin satisfied her. She had to change everythin' aroun', order new furniture, new decorations, new portiers—them red ones—in the liberry room. An' you know what Ah think, Miss Tabitha?"

"What?"

"Ah think she really didn' dislike things the way they was. She jest had to change 'em to show her *im*-portance. Ah'll tell you one thing right now—she means to be boss-lady 'roun' this place. Make no mistake about it. That son of hers can be mean as hell—pahdon the *ex*pression—when he wants to be. Ah seen him beat slaves an' kick the suhvents aroun', me included. But he talks nice as pie to his mother. He don' know jest how to handle her. He wants to be boss-man here, but she's diggin' a hole right under his feet, like a mole in the groun', an' he don' know how to keep from fallin' in it. Ah'm tellin' you, Miss Tabitha, that woman is a debbil. Ah'm convinced old Satan done crawled inside her an' made his home there. Cause she's mean—downright mean. She figgers to be on top of the heap. Second best ain't no good for her—no, ma'am!"

"So there's a real struggle between mother and son to run Magnolia Manor?" pried Tabitha.

"Struggle, mah foot! They's a fight!"

"When did Mrs. Enright become blind?" asked Tabitha, entranced with Sophie's description of the old lady and the incredible situation at the manor.

"Three years ago, 'bout. Got some *in*fection in her eyes, an' befo' the doctor could stop it, it done blinded her."

"I feel sorry for her," decided Tabitha.

"Ain't no need to, ma'am. She's mo' capable blind

than most people is seein'. She's wurser now. She knows people kin do things now without her seein' it, an' she's even mo' determined now to be the boss an' let nobody git away with nuthin. She jest sits there all day in that liberry an' gives orders to the suhvents an' to the slaves, an' Ah'm tellin' you they's so afeared of her they do's everything she says an' they don' cheat none either jest 'cause she's blind. Why, she's so downright ugly that if a slave eveh made her mad she'd have him drawn and quartered right in front of all the rest of 'em."

"Oh, you're exaggerating."

"You think so, you jest cross her once, then run like hell," advised Sophie.

"Would she really have me drawn and quartered?" Tabitha asked archly.

"Well, now, Miss Tabitha, you'se too pretty to be drawn an' quartered. But Ah reckon she wouldn' be above whuppin' that pretty white hide off'n your back."

Tabitha winced at the thought. She decided she had had quite enough of Martha Enright for one day.

"What about Nicholas?" she asked cautiously.

"Well, now, Mistah Enright is a right fine man in some respecs," said Sophie generously. "But like I tole you, he's got some of his mother's orneriness. They ain't nobody kin tell that man whut to do, cep'n his mother. Mistah Enright come down here to Natchez an' got hisself rich raisin' cotton. Then, after he built Magnoly Manor, he went an' got his mother down here. Ah kin hear him sayin' to me now, 'Ah'm gonna git Mother down here. Ah'm gonna show her what I done down here. Ah've lived too long in her house,

168

now Ah'm gonna make her live in mine.' "

"Is *that* what he said?"

"Them's the words, ma'am. He useta git too much wine in an evenin' an' he'd start talkin' to me, an' maybe sometimes he said more'n he should of—you know how the spirits is with a man's tongue. He useta tell me, 'Ah'm gonna rule this place. Magnoly Manor is where *Ah'm* king. An' when Ah bring Mother down here, she gonna have to knuckle under to what Ah say, because Ah'm the one built this place, on my own, with none of her help. That makes me king, don' it?' An Ah always told him it sure did—an' this made him happy an' he'd go to sleep in his chair all content-like inside. Men are such damn fools, ain't they, ma'am?"

Tabitha ignored the question. "So then what happened when he brought his mother down?" she asked.

"Well, like Ah say, she started runnin' things—not him. It looked to me like Mistah Enright didn' know how to stop her. If she'd a been a man Mistah Enright would have shot her daid with a duelin' pistol. But he couldn' do that to a woman—leastwise his mother—so he kinda gived up, not knowin' what to do. Once, when he had too much wine, he said to me, 'Sophie, why did Ah bring her here?' Ah tole him Ah didn' know, that things looked mighty peaceable befo' he brought her down. An' he said, 'Mighty peaceable, mighty peaceable' an' then he got hisself stupid drunk. Ah tell you it was a sad thing to see, a proud man like Mistah Enright lettin' his mother run him like she did."

"And she's controlled the house ever since?"

"Yes'm."

"Even after going blind?"

"*Specially* after goin' blind."

Tabitha let her eyes scan the room. She walked to the window and looked out. The sky was a brittle blue with a few puffy clouds in bold relief. Each segment of the landscape — the river, flower beds, trees — was etched keenly against the bright canvas of the world.

"It's strange, isn't it, that Mr. Enright would permit his mother to dominate him." Tabitha kept gazing out the window as she spoke. "He seems a dominant personality in his own right, sure of himself, with a sort of cynical and worldly view of life. He's forceful, the kind of man from which leaders are made. But in the presence of his mother he shows complete deference."

It was doubtful if Sophie completely understood Tabitha's musings, but she said, "That woman turns him to mush! You should see him with the other planters, big men with money they is. He lords it all over 'em. An' gits away with it too. They respec' his judgment on crops, an' they ain't none of 'em does much back talk neither. But with his mother — well, if you'll pahdon my blunt talk, ma'am, he ain't wurth piss in a pot!"

"If he's only half a man," Tabitha continued to muse, half to herself, "how do you make him a whole man?"

Sophie surveyed Tabitha shrewdly, round eyes squinted as she appraised the remark.

"Is you fixin' to try to make him a whole man, ma'am?" she asked.

Tabitha flushed hotly as she turned from the window. This woman was more perceptive than she had thought.

"I really hadn't thought about it," she lied.

"Well, Miss Tabitha, Ah knows Mistah Enright tole you not to pay no heed to what Ah say, but Ah'm gonna tell you one mo' thing anyways. You think a good long time befo' you try to change Mistah Enright — 'cause the rest of 'em nevah could do it."

"The *rest* of them?"

"It's been tried befo', ma'am. You's the fourth girl, if Ah may be so bold as to mention it, that's been *in*vited to spend a month at Magnoly Manor."

"The fourth!" cried Tabitha, consternation in her voice.

"Well, now, ma'am, maybe I shouldn' of said nuthin' about that. Thass mah trubble, talkin' too much. Seems like Ah jest git started an' afore Ah knows it mah mouth is goin' too fast fer mah brains to keep up. It's a bad habit, Miss Tabitha, an' Ah'm beggin' your pahdon for sayin' — "

"I wasn't aware," Tabitha cut in sharply, "that Nicholas Enright was trying to form a harem!"

"Oh, now, Miss Tabitha, it ain't quite like that!" Sophie was now alarmed at what her conversation had wrought. "It's jest that Ah figgers Mistah Enright is hankerin' to git married an' he's *in*vitin' ladies here to see Magnoly Manor an' meet his mother. Only Ah guess none of 'em will have him, way it looks."

"But that's ridiculous. Mr. Enright is a fine man — "

"Oh, sooperior, ma'am, sooperior!" Sophie was anxious to please Tabitha now, to agree with everything she said, to avoid a temperamental eruption like she had produced before. "Ah figgers it's because of his mother that they won't have him. Ah really thinks that's why Mistah Enright *in*vites his lady friends to stay a month at Magnolia Manor, so's he kin see how they gits along with his mother. You know whut he done said to me once, Miss Tabitha?"

"When he had too much wine?" snapped Tabitha irritably.

"Yes'm."

"What?"

"He said, 'Ah'll marry the girl that kin handle my mother for a month runnin'.' Thass whut he said."

Tabitha, who had been idly entertaining herself by regarding her figure in a huge goldleaf framed mirror on the wall, suddenly became alert. A predatory gleam flared briefly in her violet eyes; then she dropped her eyelashes demurely.

"Did he say exactly those words?"

"Yes'm. He did."

"You are absolutely sure?"

"Yes'm."

Tabitha crossed to the window again, looked out absently at the gently flowing waters of the Mississippi, not really seeing them now, not sensing their beauty, not caring. This was very enlightening news indeed, but there was a troublesome aspect to Nicholas Enright's statement that he would marry the girl who could handle his mother. She decided that Sophie, who seemed a bubbling fountain of information on all aspects of Magnolia Manor and its occupants, might know the answer.

"What if Mr. Enright found such a girl, Sophie?" she asked carefully. "Would he simply marry her, just like that? Wouldn't he have to love her?"

Sophie's thick lips stretched thin in a smile. A knowing smile, Tabitha thought.

"Well, ma'am," she said, "you wouldn' ask that question if you'd seen some of the girls he's had here. They's all been real charmin' ladies—like yerself, ma'am. The best in Natchez, from the best families. You know they's mo' bachelor men runnin' aroun' in Natchez than they is women to capture 'em—an' Ah guess most any of these women would of give up half their teeth if they coulda' sunk the other half in Mistah Enright. An' as fer Mistah Enright lovin' 'em, like Ah say, any one of 'em woulda been right easy fer a man to love if he'd set his mind to it."

Tabitha felt a flash of jealousy surge through her, then she impatiently thrust the feeling aside. The aura of mystery around Nicholas Enright was now dissolving. What this proud man was doing to her was now more sharply in focus. He was testing her, putting her through a crucible of fire. He would be watching her now, with the cold analytical mind that had made him a success in the cotton business, a great slave holder, a man of means. He would be evaluating her, playing her charm and astuteness against the brazen hate emanating from his mother, watching the effect of each woman on the other. And what he learned would guide his future actions. He would accept or reject her on the basis of her ability to handle Martha Enright, and love would play no part in his decision. What he wanted—much more than a woman to love—was a strong-willed female who could help him to regain his control of Magnolia Manor, who could counteract his mother's colossal determination, fend her off, balance her out, and eventually reduce her to a position of dependence.

Nicholas was literally crying out for help!

It annoyed Tabitha briefly that love was not the keystone to her acceptance as a mate. She was sure, now, that he bore no immediate love for her. But Tabitha was vain enough to believe that he was at least interested, his imagination piqued, his thoughts titillated. She had taken elaborate care, in her dress and her manner, to make this so, and she believed Nicholas would eventually respond to her feminine machinations. As for the present, if Nicholas needed a pawn to checkmate his mother, then she would be one. Her lifelong dream of being a grand lady, a plantation lady, was not going to be shoved aside. She would help Nicholas defeat the old blind witch who stood in his way.

But she would have to be careful. It would not do to underestimate her antagonist. She would have to use every device and stratagem in the book to whip her. It would be suicidal to clash headlong with her, for if she did Martha Enright would see to it that Tabitha's stay at Magnolia Manor was short-lived. No, she must win the old woman over. That was the way to do it. She must agree with everything Martha Enright said, never cross her, flatter her arrogance until the woman, as a result of her own mountainous conceit, would begin to feel that here was a young woman at last who appreciated her, who recognized her wisdom and position. Then, and then only, could Tabitha subtly reverse the trend—making slight unimportant suggestions of her own, gaining small concessions, then eventually larger ones—whittling away at the foundations of the old woman's authority, as termites chew away wood. Finally, Tabitha could begin to assume authority of her own, in small things first, then greater things, until at last she had undermined Martha Enright completely, placed her on the defensive, reduced her to subservience.

Tabitha smiled inwardly as this diabolical scenario took form in her mind. It would be an enormous task and could not be accomplished in the month Nicholas had awarded her. But Tabitha felt she could make sufficient progress in a month to convince Nicholas that she was a willful woman in her own right, who could be trusted to handle the affairs of Magnolia Manor with dispatch and efficiency, thus lessening his need for reliance on his mother. And as for love—well, that could come later.

"You done wanta look at your wahdrobe, ma'am?" asked Sophie, breaking into Tabitha's scheming thoughts abruptly.

Tabitha spun around with an excited froufrou of her silken dress. Her eyes lighted with expectation.

"My wardrobe?"

"Compleements of Mistah Enright," said Sophie. She swung open a small door in a Chinese-adorned armoire near the bed and Tabitha stared in wonderment. Neatly hung on hangers were a dozen expensive dresses, each one more beautiful than the other. There was one of blue silk trimmed with valenciennes lace, a rose-pink tarleton, a diaphanous muslin with ham-shaped sleeves, all with spreading bombazine skirts that filled the armoire with a rich riot of color. There were crinolines and pantalets and matching sunbonnets on the shelf overhead, some spangled with veils, and an entire row of delightful shoes to complement the dresses.

"They're beautiful! I wouldn't know which one to

wear first!" said Tabitha, rushing to the armoire, running her hands over the fine dresses. And again the puzzling and irritating question raced through her mind: How had he known her sizes? Each one looked as if it would fit her perfectly.

"Did Mr. Enright say he liked any particular one?" she asked shrewdly.

"No, ma'am. He jest had 'em made an' when they come he jest hanged 'em away. He didn' say nuthin' about none of 'em." She stopped, saw the slight disappointment in Tabitha's expression, and said, "Ah'm powerful sorry, Miss Tabitha."

"It's quite all right," said Tabitha with forced indifference. "I shall select what I think is appropriate for dinner tonight. But you will help me, won't you, Sophie?"

"Miss Tabitha," said Sophie, with a sudden smile she had not shown before, "fer the nex' month you is my sole 'sponsibility."

4

It was nine o'clock in the evening and darkness had draped a protective black shawl over the white giant that was Magnolia Manor as if to preserve its beauty for the following day. Braving a fresh breeze, Tabitha walked out on the broad and spacious veranda at the front of the house. The moon was full, riding with a quiet majesty in the darkened vault of the sky, shedding its borrowed light in soft phosphorescence over the house and the grounds. Tabitha remembered how, as a child, she had believed the moon to be made of cheese, and that the darker areas were holes in the hogshead. This had been her father's tongue-in-cheek explanation when she had been very little, but she had never forgotten it. And though she knew it was not true, still she felt it was one of the most apt descriptions she had ever heard. Now, at this still moment when the day's activities were done and the world seemed suspended and waiting, like the hands of an old clock that had run down, the moon bore a special significance—for it worked, now, when the world had stopped working, bathing the earth in gentle light, deepening shadows where it did not penetrate, giving deep-dyed color to flowers and shrubs and trees where it touched them, as if it sensed an obligation to hold all things of earth in some sort of breathless suspension until the sun broke from the eastern sky and returned life again to the world.

Tabitha noticed that the magnolias at the edge of the forest, some distance from the drive approaching the manor, were now deep black angular shapes, like mysterious cloaked figures, while the lawn and flower beds in front of the house were splashed in a white light that deepened colors but retained outlines. The breeze rustled the thick hard leaves of the magnolia like a deck of cards being expertly shuffled, and from somewhere came the incessant buzz of insects fussing away the night.

Feeling the coolness of the night air, Tabitha pulled the blue shawl gently around her shoulders. She had chosen the blue silk dress with the Valenciennes lace for dinner—chosen well, she thought, for on several occasions she had caught Nicholas Enright's eyes intently surveying her. On those occasions she had smiled, so that he would know she did not object to his frank appraisal, and Nicholas had acknowledged the smile with a pleasant nod of his head, but spoke no words about her appearance.

The dinner had been an hour of beauty and charm, but marred by an almost unendurable tension. Served by liveried servants, who ran steaming dishes along the flagged patio from the kitchen to the dining room, it had been a delightful and elegant repast. Tabitha was particularly amused by the large white punkah over the table, and at the two small pickaninnies who sat at one end of the immense dining room, in complete silence, pulling the strings that moved the punkah and stirred the heavy atmosphere of the room. And

178

Tabitha had thought, can I ever hope to aspire to such dizzying heights permanently? Will I ever become the mistress of such tasteful luxury as is represented here?

She kept looking across at Martha Enright, amazed at the dexterity with which the blind woman handled everything before her. One would not have known she was blind, except for the fixed stare of her eyes when she raised her head. She dined as she had always dined, with grace and daintiness, never dropping or mislaying a knife or fork, aware at every moment where everything stood. From steaming bouillabaisse through the venison and wild fowl, to the tiny Creole cakes called calas, Martha Enright was the personification of perfection.

Nicholas dined quietly, consuming huge portions of food while at the same time managing to avoid the appearance of gluttony. Tabitha ate small portions, too inwardly excited for even such delectable repast, yet trying desperately to maintain her poise and not show amazement at the elaborate feast.

There was little conversation, but on one occasion Martha Enright looked up, fixing Tabitha with her sightless eyes just as if she were seeing her, and said, "I imagine that you consider our somewhat pretentious manner of dining to be an ostentation that could well be dispensed with," she said harshly, as if daring Tabitha to be argumentative.

Tabitha thought, thank God my father insisted on my education. There were girls in Natchez-under who wouldn't have known what Martha Enright was talking about. But almost to her own surprise, Tabitha had an appropriate answer ready.

179

"Everything's lovely," she said. "And really, one is only ostentatious when one pretends to be something one is not. Isn't that so?"

She glanced at Nicholas and saw an appreciative smile playing about the corners of his thin lips. It was obvious that he enjoyed such verbal exchanges—especially, thought Tabitha, when his mother was bested at them.

"An astute observation," conceded Martha after a moment's thought, then tried to twist it around by adding, "One shouldn't indulge in such vulgar displays of wealth, though, would you say?"

"Not unless one has the breeding and character to go with it," said Tabitha quickly.

Nicholas's smile broadened, and Martha's unseeing eyes sharpened at the remark. She looked shrewdly in the direction of her son.

"Is this young woman of yours trying to flatter me?" she asked. "I must say she shows a talent for it." And for the first time since Tabitha had met Martha Enright the old lady permitted a whimsical smile to spread across her lean face, briefly, like a light touching something and then moving quickly away, for she allowed it to remain on her face only an instant.

"I think you'll like Tabitha, Mother," Nicholas said, and this time he actually tossed a conspiratorial wink toward Tabitha that sent her heart dancing. "I recognized one quality in her from the beginning—not the ability to flatter but complete sincerity in everything she says."

"Humph!" snorted Martha. "The two of you are working against me! And as you must by this time

180

know, Nicholas, I cannot tolerate any conspiracies not of my own making."

With that remark, which was obviously intended to be the closing one, she lapsed into silence for the remainder of the meal.

Now, reviewing the conversation as she stood on the veranda, the lights of the candles and whale oil lamps in the house checkerboarding her figure, Tabitha felt that she had already gained some respect in the devious mind of Martha Enright. She wondered, too, how Nicholas judged her. He had been obviously pleased by her response to his mother's leading questions. But she had not had an opportunity to discuss this point with him, for just as the dinner ended Jed Vale, the overseer, arrived breathlessly.

"I'm sorry to bother you, Mr. Enright," he said, bowing slightly at the waist and twisting his broad-brimmed hat in his gnarled hands, "but one of the younguns is dyin'. I thought you'd want to know."

"Dying?" Nicholas looked startled. "What's the trouble?"

"She's a three-year-old, name of Sarah," said Vale. "We think she's been bitten by a rattler."

Nicholas's brow furrowed, but whether his expression was one of concern or anger at being disturbed Tabitha could not judge.

"God's blood!" he thundered, thumping the table with the palm of his hand. "When did this happen?"

"Two or three hours ago, near as I can judge. The blacks didn't report it at first, I guess figgerin' the snake wasn't no poison one and—"

"Goddamn their thick skulls!" snarled Nicholas. "I swear I sometimes think the Southerners are right about their stupidity. I've told them repeatedly to report any illness or injury at once. The blacks are too damned valuable to take risks with. . . . You are sure the negroling is near death?"

"I'm afraid so."

"I'll go at once." Nicholas stood up.

"You are always so concerned about your people, my son," said Martha Enright shrewishly. "It speaks well of you."

Nicholas did not miss the mild sarcasm in his mother's statement. He stared bleakly at her for a moment and then turned on his heel and left the room without replying. Jed Vale followed in his wake.

"I must say," said Martha Enright after they had left, "that for a boy born in the North, Nicholas has taken to the slave culture with remarkable ease. He loves his blacks in the same manner a Southerner does."

Tabitha looked at the old lady askance. Martha's remarks, she thought, always had hidden meanings—two meanings, really, so that one could choose the meaning desired.

"What exactly do you mean by that, Mrs. Enright?" she asked, trying to force a choice on the old woman.

"Frankly that he bears no love for the Negroes at all," said Martha flatly, "although he makes a great pretense of loving and understanding the Negro, as the Southerners do. Actually, Nicholas's feelings for his blacks are closely akin to the average Southerner's. It is strictly limited by the Negroes' value to him as slaves. This young dying negroling—a delightful word created by Southerners that Nicholas has assumed—is of no particular concern to Nicholas as a person. But as a future hand, raised on the plantation and familiar with its workings, she is most valuable. Therefore he is concerned that he might lose her."

"You truly believe that all Southerners, and Nicholas too, are that cynical and heartless about their blacks?" Tabitha asked with caution, probing for clues to Martha's character as well as Nicholas's, but not wishing to get involved in an argument on abolition.

"I personally have the Northerner's viewpoint that all Southerners are hypocrites," Martha replied. "They talk of their love for the Negro but care little for him except as a slave. They do not consider the Negro their equal in intelligence, nor do they wish any social contact with them. Yet it is all right for a Negro to work in their homes and even serve their food. And although Southern gentlemen believe they are several cuts above the Negro, still they are not above taking a Negro wench to their bedroom."

"You paint a dismal picture of the Southerner," said Tabitha.

"Yes, and that is not all. Do you know the Southern planter lives in mortal fear of his blacks? There have been many uprisings—the worst in 1831 when Nat Turner slaughtered many whites. The planters fear more rebellions, and they employ various ways to ward off such trouble. Some treat their blacks with great kindness, feeling they will not revolt if so treated. Others believe the iron hand of cruelty must be applied relentlessly to keep the blacks in line. I dare say both methods are doomed to failure."

She did not permit Tabitha to comment further on the matter, for she rose suddenly and stood for a moment looking down almost condescendingly at Tabitha.

"Make yourself comfortable until Nicholas appears," she said. "Tell him I have a splitting headache — no doubt caused in part by his false display of concern at the child's plight — and have retired to my room."

"I will tell him," promised Tabitha, and followed behind Martha Enright as she left the room. She watched as the old woman ascended the winding staircase with no difficulty whatever, her long skirts sweeping the steps one by one, rustling as she moved. Not once did she stumble or hesitate. Her outstretched arm, like some infallible guidance system, swept her along unerringly. And once again Tabitha thought how unlike a blind person she was.

Now, walking along the veranda in the soft white light of the moon, Tabitha thought she had learned something from the conversation at dinner. As Sophie had so truly outlined, there was a tense war between mother and son for control of the manor. Each seemed to resent the other. And although this subdued antagonism did not erupt into outright belligerence — at least it had not tonight — still there was an undergrowth of friction that was endless and bitter and subtly savage. She had learned, too, that Nicholas was capable of violent anger, and this discovery intrigued her. He had presented such a cold exterior to her that his fiery anger at the negroling's plight had surprised her. Perhaps, sometime, she might be able to use advantageously Nicholas's propensity for fury. Just how she did not know, but she stored the knowledge of his inclination to anger in the

184

back of her mind for any future use she might make of it; for Tabitha prided herself with a keen understanding of human nature, and the value of using a man's weakness to gain important goals was not lost on her.

As these scheming thoughts flowed through her agile mind—each tucked away in a mental filing cabinet for future use—she became suddenly aware of a scraping noise behind her. Recognizing it as Nicholas's peculiar gait, she turned slightly, her skirts and crinolines whispering provocatively. The moon spread a pale light over his face as he approached her, and Tabitha could see that he was still angry. When he saw her looking at him, however, he erased the ire from his face as a child removes markings from a slate. The smile that replaced the scowl, however, was wavering and somehow unreal.

"You are the only delightful thing in this house," he said gallantly, reaching out and taking her hand in his. "Were it not for the relaxing influence of your company, I would remain infuriated beyond words at the stupidity of my blacks."

"How is the child?"

"She was dead by the time I arrived," said Nicholas simply.

"How awful!"

"Yes. And what provokes me is that death might have been avoided." He looked away from her, out over the hushed landscape toward the river, now almost invisible except for a silvery swath cut by the moon. "Where's Mother?"

"She retired to her room with a headache," said Tabitha.

"Well! Then the evening is not a total loss!"

Tabitha frowned in the darkness. More to lead him into conversation than to express dismay, Tabitha said, "I can't seem to adjust to the way you speak of you mother."

"You will have to," said Nicholas, shrugging. "After all, a man holds no particular love for a woman who has thwarted him—in one manner or another—all his life."

Anger swept his face again and Tabitha thought, half in panic, I've gone too far, said too much. Please, God, don't let me do anything to anger Nicholas Enright! And then she saw the anger, flaring briefly, subside, turning his face into the inscrutable mask it usually was, the stone-like countenance and haunted look that Tabitha found it impossible to read or evaluate.

"You appear to be a rather astute student of human nature, my dear," he said.

"I had never thought so," lied Tabitha, thinking all the time that she *was* such a student.

"You handled Mother this evening at dinner with just the right mixture of flattery and disdain," he said.

Tabitha stiffened. It was one of those backward compliments again, one she could not acknowledge directly.

"You must have misread me," she said. "There was no disdain."

Nicholas looked down at her, smiling. He was still holding her hand, his heavy one caressing hers, enfolding it, like a small butterfly cupped in a thick strangling plant.

"Wasn't there disdain? I thought I detected it. You don't like her, do you?"

"Really, Nicholas, that's such an unfair question. I think she's a remarkable woman, so efficient in spite of her dreadful handicap, and—" She stopped, not knowing why she had been placed in a position of defending Nicholas's mother, uncertain how to proceed.

"I won't insist on a direct answer," said Nicholas. "The fact is that nobody likes Mother. Now, let's change the subject to something more pleasant."

He started to walk along the veranda, still holding her hand, the sound of his foot scraping along the flagstone, his body swaying slightly with the limp.

"What do you think of Magnolia Manor?" he asked.

"I think it's the loveliest home in the world," said Tabitha, delighted that he had retreated from the uncomfortable subject of his mother. "It's so magnificent that it takes my breath away."

"But not too ostentatious?" he asked.

"Of course not," Tabitha said, noticing his employment of the exact word his mother had used.

"Tomorrow I shall show you the out-buildings and the blacks' quarters," Nicholas said. "Perhaps, since tomorrow is Sunday, we might even hear Old Matt preach a sermon. He's a darky with a glib tongue who preaches on Sundays, although he isn't a genuine minister at all.

"That would be wonderful."

"I have other plans too," Nicholas went on, betraying some eagerness. "I will want you to meet some of our so-called friends. I plan a dinner soon. Most of the nearby planters will be invited—that is, those we consider our closest acquaintances. For example, Faunce Manley will be here with his ungainly wife and

187

pimple-faced son."

"The man who mistreats his—uh—blacks?" asked Tabitha, remembering the incident at the esplanade of the arm-waving Manley, landing his latest batch of slaves.

"Yes. He's a frightful bore and a fool and I hate him considerably, but then most of the planter families hate each other in their hearts while they tolerate each other in their minds. It's part of the price you pay for being a member of our celebrated culture—a culture you will find physically opulent and morally spurious." He allowed this statement to simmer in Tabitha's mind for a few seconds, then went on. "There will be old John McRae and his wife, too. Quite a couple there. McRae is close to ninety, a doddering old idiot, and his wife is twenty-eight. And she's a stunning beauty if I ever saw one."

"Heavens! I've never heard of such a thing!"

"No doubt you'll find many things on the Hill you never before heard of. Perhaps I'll invite the d'Ubervilles and the Drews, though I shall be dreadfully bored with both of them. At any rate, you have an experience in store for you, my dear."

"I'll be overwhelmed," said Tabitha, with considerable truth, for she wanted Nicholas to realize that she appreciated everything he was doing for her. But it was the wrong thing to say.

"I would prefer," said Nicholas coldly, "that you not be overwhelmed. You absolutely *must* show poise when you meet these people. I insist on it." His voice was severe, as if on the edge of anger again.

"Of course, Nicholas. I'll do my best."

He surveyed her with some doubt. "So that you will

not be too overwhelmed," he said, "I shall tell you a few basic facts about the so-called cotton culture which has developed here on the Hill—which, perhaps, is not exactly as cultured as you may have imagined it. In the first place, don't permit yourself to be misled by the elegance of the planters' homes or their mode of dress. This aristocratic way of life doesn't necessarily shelter aristocratic people. Most of the planters are Scotch-Irish dirt farmers who have struck it rich in cotton. Despite their fine homes and imported furniture, they are not the cultured gentlemen you might expect—at least, most of them aren't. I happen to come from a genuinely cultured family, and I represent an exception in the sense that I have a few manners and hail from the hated North. Most of these dirt farmers are uneducated and only civilized on the surface—in ways they have been able to assume since becoming wealthy. They're hedonistic, every one of them. They live voluptuously, and sometimes their open display of wealth is downright vulgar. But they have learned to live in fine fashion, demanding the best wines and liquors, the best furnishings for their homes, paintings and other treasures imported from Italy and France and Spain. As a class they are clannish, tending to stick to their own kind, marry within their own tight circle. But they are earthy too, and you'll find that most of them own a few fast horses and a black mistress or two, most of them having heard that black women are more adept at sex than white. Miscegenation—if you will excuse my bringing it up—is not unknown on the plantations."

"Your appraisal of the planters surprises me," said Tabitha, noticing how close his words paralleled those of Martha Enright. "Hasn't it been your aim to be accepted by the planters' society?"

Nicholas smiled. "You have discerned a paradox, haven't you? And you are right. I detest the falsity and shallowness of the planters' way of life, yet my pride demands that I be the greatest among them. I point out this obvious inconsistency only so that you'll be more at ease among these quite frightful people. Also, if you have been entertaining the thought that you might not be able to keep up with the erudite conversation of the planters, you may put your mind at ease. The men have only four topics of conversation — cotton, blacks, politics and horses. The women have two — men and other women. You have an enviable mind, my dear, and I'm quite sure you can best any one of them on any subject."

Tabitha smiled in appreciation at the compliment. "What kind of women belong to these dirt farmers?" she asked.

"Most of them have seen hard work in their time, though to see them now you would never guess it. Some try to put on airs, but those can be spotted rather quickly. And I have no doubt, after listening to you handle my mother, that you can successfully cope with any kittenish wife among the planters of Natchez."

He stopped talking abruptly, gazing out over the moon-splashed landscape in that strange way he had of being attentive at one moment and totally indifferent at the next. He remained silent for several minutes, and at last Tabitha tried to draw him out.

"What are you thinking about?"

Nicholas startled her with the anger in his reply.

"Those damned stupid blacks!" he grated. "I shall have to get a doctor to stay right on the plantation and keep them in good health despite themselves!"

"Oh, I know somebody!" The eager words spilled from Tabitha's mouth before she realized what she was saying.

"Who?"

Tabitha hesitated. Oh, damn, she thought. She had been so anxious to be of help to Nicholas Enright that she had burst out with the news that she was acquainted with a doctor, completely overlooking the fact that she would now be required to identify him and also tell where he could be located. Besides, the last man she wanted anywhere near Magnolia Manor was the insufferable Dr. Mike Long.

"Who is he?" Nicholas asked again.

She could not back down now. She had to tell him.

"His name is Long—Dr. Michael Long."

"A good doctor?"

Tabitha sensed a way out. "Perhaps I was too hasty," she said apologetically. "You would naturally want a man of some reputation. This doctor is only—"

"Only what?"

"A doctor in Natchez-under-the-Hill. A Kentuckian, I believe. Rather a crude man, really."

"Just the kind I would want for the blacks. No man of reputation would confine himself to practicing only among blacks on one plantation. Besides, a crude man might have a better understanding of the blacks, a closer affinity, being not so much their superior as a man of vast experience and knowledge. . . . Where do I find this man?"

"He has his shingle out in Natchez-under."

"He has treated your family?"

"No."

"Then where did you meet him?"

"Oh," Tabitha waved her arm artlessly, "I've just seen his sign on one of the streets."

Nicholas's mouth twisted in amusement. "The streets? Of Natchez-under? I had no idea your acquaintances with those streets was so thorough. Have you been prowling them lately?"

"Oh, Nicholas!" Tabitha managed to convey reproof in her voice. "Do be understanding!"

"I am, my dear."

Tabitha felt limp and weak. What had she done? In her desire to be of help to Nicholas Enright, she had really fouled her own cozy nest. Not only had she aroused his suspicion about her activities on the flatlands, but she had given him the name of a man whose presence at Magnolia Manor would be a personal disaster for her. Oh, it was a huge mess, all right—the first serious mistake she had made since her arrival at Magnolia Manor. She would bite her lip until it bled before she would make another.

She was aware, quite suddenly, that Nicholas was standing closer to her now, looking down into her upturned face. The amused smile still played about his lips, and in the pallid light of the moon his fierce eyes glistened like those of an animal.

"My carnal interests are always aroused by a woman familiar with the streets of Natchez-under," he said.

"Nicholas, for God's sake! Must you make me feel sordid?"

"And of course," he went on, not answering her directly, "you *are* very beautiful."

"Thank you." Tabitha's words were stiff.

She felt his hand move up her arm to her shoulder. She stood with her back pressed against one of the smooth Tuscan columns of the porch, and while he held her shoulder with one hand he touched her face tenderly with the other, still looking down at her, his face so close that she could feel his breath warm upon her forehead. There were a few seconds of mixed hesitancy and fear; then it dissolved into one of triumph. She thought, he's going to kiss me! And I shall let him. I shall permit just enough of a kiss to let him know that I think well of him, but not enough to let him think I am easy. Please, God, she prayed, let me handle this just right. Just right.

He bent his head forward and kissed her softly on the lips, a quick kiss that was fleeting and sweet. But then his hand tightened on her shoulder and his mouth came down on hers, covering it, warm and moist. She felt his body strain against her with a bursting passion, pinning her against the column, his groin pressing hard against the formidable barrier of her multiple crinolines and flowing dress. Expertly his hand brushed her breast, traveled to her hip, and for a moment Tabitha felt complete fright. Then the vision of Nicholas as her husband intruded on the scene, and Tabitha closed her eyes, prepared to accept whatever feeling claimed her as they stood for a long moment, his body crushed against hers, trembling a little with his burning desire. But to her surprise no feeling came to her, nothing at all, and this dismayed and shocked her, for she thought it only natural that she should feel something, that she should experience some thrill, some exultation, and when it did not come she found herself standing statue-like, accepting his embrace, giving nothing in return, not knowing why his fierce trembling body won nothing from hers.

And then, very suddenly, it was over. He shoved her away from him, almost roughly, walking a few steps and leaning against the column next to her, as if exhausted by his fruitless efforts. She saw his body shudder and his hand at his side shook with emotion.

"I think you'd better go to your room," he said hoarsely.

She looked at him, not comprehending how the surging passion that had claimed him could dissipate so quickly. She said, half in guilt, "I hope—I haven't disappointed you."

He rolled his head against the column, gazing at her.

"Disappointed me? God's blood!"

She took a step closer to him, not wanting to offer herself for a second embrace, yet feeling it almost her duty. Perhaps he had sensed her own lack of response; now she felt a need to reassure him, to make amends for her own lack of passion. But he waved her away imperiously. His voice came again, angry, unreasoning.

"Goddamn it, Tabitha, *I said go to your room!*"

The shock of his words shattered her completely. In confusion, Tabitha backed away from him, her eyes fixed on his majestic form. She hesitated to leave abruptly, even under his prodding words, but when she did not go he turned and looked out over the moon-dappled flower beds and his voice came in frigid tones.

"I am not accustomed to being disobeyed. You will

go to your room—*now!*"

She fled, then, choking back a sob, her eyes suddenly brimming. No, she would not cry. She would never let Nicholas see weakness in her. She raced through the hall and up the spiral staircase and slammed the door of her room behind her. For several minutes she sat shaking on the edge of the tester bed. And then she heard the sharp, brash notes of the piano in the library—and she knew it was Nicholas playing. The passage Tabitha recognized—Schubert's *Ave Maria*, but played in violent angry chords that flooded the manor with raucous, blasphemous music.

5

Between the cotton fields and Magnolia Manor were the slave quarters—a long row of crude, whitewashed cypress shacks where those who worked the fields lived, ate, slept and made love, using for these earthy purposes whatever energies they had not dissipated under the implacable southern sun during their long hours of toil.

This morning, with the air still crisp from the coolness of the night, more than a hundred slaves gathered around a large communal shack at the end of the long row of buildings. They sat in a huddled group, on the ground, their dress for the most part somber, although some of the women had colorful kerchiefs wrapped around their heads turban-fashion. On a box before the group an elderly Negro, his face wrinkled and dried from too many days in the sun, his close-cropped hair a patch of fine snow on his black head, stood talking and waving his arms. Perspiration from his exertions poured down his gaunt face, traveling along the paths cut by wrinkles as a river follows its natural course between canyon walls.

Tabitha and Nicholas walked slowly toward the group of slaves kneeling and sitting in the sun. Despite the freshness of the morning, and the fact that a visit to the slave quarters of Magnolia Manor was a new experience for her, Tabitha felt ill at ease. She had not yet recovered from the distressing scene on the veranda the night before. She had spent several sleepless hours trying to evaluate it and had failed utterly. There was no doubt that Nicholas had been passionately attracted to her. He had not only kissed her but had done so in a highly aggressive manner, in the way of the male who is beside himself with desire and means to take what he wants. This part of it Tabitha could understand, but what had followed was inexplicable to her. His curt and angry dismissal, following the embrace, did not make sense to Tabitha. No man, overcome by passion, acted in this manner. Tabitha was enough aware of the male animal to know that, in such a moment, he did one of two things—either he spent his passion on the object of his affections, or, fighting to control himself, he subsided gradually. But to walk away from her, dismiss her in anger, was something completely incomprehensible.

For several hours after going to her room like a chastened child she had tried to fathom his reasons for so violently turning her away. Had she done something to provoke him? Had she, somewhere in the intimacy of the embrace, made a wrong move—a move that frustrated him or drove him to fury? She had cooperated in the embrace and the kiss, although she admitted the experience had not been as exciting as she had expected. Was it possible, then, that he had felt her coolness, sensed her lack of real response, and had reacted in hurt and humiliated anger? She had fallen asleep from sheer exhaustion contemplating these questions.

Sophie had called her early—at Nicholas's demand the quadroon said—and Tabitha had dressed quickly anxious to see Nicholas again and behold his current mood. They had had breakfast together—Martha Enright was still abed—and he had made no comment about the night before. Neither had he shown any continuing anger over the incident. He had been himself—slightly patronizing, peremptorily planning Tabitha's day for her without consulting her as to her wishes, assuming that anything he planned would be accepted without question. Seeing him in his usual guise had lightened Tabitha's worries, but the puzzlement over his actions the night before still rankled within her.

Nicholas stopped some distance from where the slaves had congregated around their "preacher," as if fastidious about closer contact. Old Matt, his lanky arms gyrating in the air, held the blacks spellbound, and few even noticed the approach of the white master and his lady. Old Matt was scolding his "chillun" in a manner that would have appalled most preachers and all congregations but the blacks before him took his words in respectful silence and with bowing deference. The words of Old Matt, flung out like stones from a catapult, reached the ears of Nicholas and Tabitha in the distance.

" . . . An' Ah'm tellin' you, brothers and sisters, that you gotta cast out sin. You gotta throw it out, git rid of it, an' make you'selves clean again. You ain't foolin' me, an' you ain't foolin' the Lord. You's all sinners, an' it's time you git down on your knees an' ask forgiveness, an' then the Lord might forgive you an' He might not. If He thinks youse a real bad sinner, He might tell you, 'Ah can't help you no mo'.' An' if youse such a bad sinner that He says that to you, you's in for it bad. Cause youse gonna go straight to Hell, an' there ain't nobody gonna save you from them fires! But if the Lord smiles on you, an' forgives you your sins, then you can count your lucky stars that youse still in His good graces. . . ."

His arms waved to emphasize his words and rivulets of sweat poured down his creased face. Tabitha watched him in fascination. He was an illiterate Negro, yet he had the gift of standing before an assembly of his equals and rising above them, holding their rapt attention while he threatened them with the wrath of the Lord and the tortures of Hell. And they listened and accepted what he said, for to these simple people Old Matt was believable.

" . . . You ask me, what is Hell?" he went on, although no one had asked him at all. "Ah'll tell you what Hell is, brethren. Ah'll tell you in plain words. It's a place under this here ground you walks on, an' its made up of fire and flames and brimstone, an' it's the God-awfulest hottest place you ever did see, maybe a hunnerd times as hot as them fields out there where youse plants and picks cotton. Old Satan, he's down there with a pitchfork, just waitin' for a chance to torture your soul like it ain't never been tortured befo'. When you gits down there, fust thing he does is give you a bath—in boilin' water. It won't kill you. Nuthin will kill you down there, just torture you, thass all. An' some days you's gonna hafta sit on hot brimstone all day long while your body fries like a hen's egg. An' when old Satan is feelin' extra devilish—like he is most of the time—he'll sit your hide down right in them flames and they'll burn you all day long. . . . Is that the kind of treatment you-all wants? Answer me, sinners!"

"No, no!" wailed the crowd.

"Then you cast out sin, like I done tole you. Throw it out, so it ain't no longer a part of you." He looked at his congregation closely, then began to point with a long thin finger at those he thought were particular culprits. "You, Joe—you cut out the cussin' every time somethin' goes wrong. An', Jesse, you ain't got no cause for gamblin' like you do—gamblin' your clothes away like Ah seen you do it. Cards and dice are the playthings of the Devil. An' Amanda, plain as Ah stand her Ah seen you sneak into Jesse's cabin one night, an' Ah'm tellin' you that fornicatin' with the menfolk ain't no way to git to Heaven!"

"Ah didn't do it, Old Matt, Ah didn't do it!" cried a woman in the crowd.

"Ah seen you, Amanda," insisted Old Matt, "an' Ah'm warnin' you to stay in your own bed at night an' you won't git in no trouble. You got that straight, Amanda?"

"Yes, Ah has."

"An' young Jasper here!" continued Old Matt relentlessly, singling out a tall young Negro about eighteen years old. "You ain't makin' no great impression on the Lord, son, the way you's always lookin' at the girls. Ah knows whut youse thinkin', son, an' you bettah stop it. Becuz thinkin' it is as bad as doin' it, which I don't doubt you might already have done!"

"Ah's innocent, Old Matt!" cried Jasper.

"You aint' no mo' innocent than a stud horse in springtime," said Old Matt with finality, "an' it ain't no good you sayin' you's innocent when me an' the Lord both knows you ain't!"

"It's fantastic," said Tabitha to Nicholas, half embarrassed at Old Matt's blunt accusations.

Nicholas nodded. "He's really quite mild today. You should hear him when he really gets excited." He took her arm carefully, just the tips of his fingers touching her elbow. "This may go on for some hours. . . . Come, I'll show you what makes a plantation."

They took a different path back to the house, one of many that wound gracefully among trees and flowers and helped give Magnolia Manor its character. The number of out-buildings necessary to the existence of a plantation manor surprised Tabitha. There was a huge whitewashed barn that housed a dozen head of fine cattle, the pigpen where tough-snouted hogs rooted in the mud, chicken coops alive with nervously strutting hens and prancing roosters, the smoke house for curing and flavoring of meat and fish, a springhouse built over a cool brook where perishables from the vegetable garden were kept safe from summer heat, a toolhouse where garden implements and other tools were stored, a smithy where ironwork was practiced by two aging Negroes adept at the art and where, Nicholas said, the intricate circular staircase in the manor was fashioned by slave labor. There was a garden house, done of cooling lattice work, where one could sit in the warm afternoon hours and sip an anisette and idle away the hot hours of the day with trivial conversation, and a large rectangular stable where Nicholas kept his horses.

Nicholas led Tabitha down the center aisle of the

stable and pointed with pride to his horses. On the right were half a dozen carriage horses, and about an equal number of heavy-bodied work horses. On the left side as they traversed the stable were twelve race horses which Nicholas used in competition at the quarter track of Natchez-under-the-Hill.

"My horses have won many races down there," he said boastfully. "Old Faunce Manley—damn his soul—has been trying to beat one of my horses for two years and hasn't yet." He chuckled, amused at the situation. "Come, I'll show you Happy Boy. He's my own personal horse, the finest I have."

They moved along the row of sleek shining horses, all carefully curried and groomed, until they came to a tawny strawberry roan stallion. Happy Boy was indeed a magnificent animal, a big raw-boned roan with bulging eyes and a quick alert manner. Nicholas touched him gently with his riding crop and the horse pranced nervously in its stall.

"There, boy, take it easy. We'll go riding soon, old boy. Very soon."

Tabitha was amazed at the tenderness in his tone. It was the first time she had ever heard solicitude in Nicholas's voice. He patted the horse's nose and it nuzzled him. Then he passed on to the next stall.

"This is Lady Belle," said Nicholas. "She will be your horse while you're here. . . . Do you ride, my dear?"

"Yes. I have ridden some," said Tabitha, which was only partially true for she had not ridden in years.

"Good. You'll find Lady Belle very gentle."

Lady Belle was a sleek palomino mare. Her coat was a buff satin, her tail and mane a glistening silvery white. The horse permitted Tabitha to stroke its nose, shying only a little at her touch.

"A beautiful horse," said Tabitha with delight.

They walked on through the stable and Tabitha saw the two grays that had pulled the barouche when Nicholas had called for her at her home. Behind the stables, under a portico, was an assortment of every kind of carriage Tabitha could name—coaches, barouches, phaetons, landaus, landaulettes, cabriolets.

"And now I will show you the kitchen," said Nicholas, and Tabitha could sense the pride with which he was giving her this tour of the plantation, the plantation he had built, alone and unaided, his own personal accomplishment. "As you know, we have the kitchen separated from the main house," Nicholas went on factually. "Wouldn't do to have any connection, for in case of fire the entire manor would go up in flames before the blacks could carry buckets from the river. And some of these cooks are frightfully careless, you know."

The kitchen was a square brick building connected to the manor only by the flagstone patio over which the servants carried hot dishes to the dining room. There were two floors to the building, with the cooking area on the first floor and the servants' quarters above. Several obese Negro women were bustling about the kitchen when Tabitha and Nicholas entered. Each stopped momentarily to greet "Massa Enright" with subservient politeness, and Nicholas acknowledged the greeting with a regal nod of his head.

The focal point of the kitchen was the huge stone fireplace where iron pots dangled on wrought iron legs over open fires. Pots and cranes hung everywhere and in the big fireplace was a spit on which meat could be turned and roasted. Nearby was a clay oven shaped like a beehive, for baking breads and cakes, and in one corner was a butter firkin. Nicholas drew Tabitha's attention to a small table with a faded gray top along one wall.

"A soapstone table," he said. "When fresh game is killed it is cut on this table. The soapstone is always cool and helps to take the body heat out of the animal as it is being cut into pieces."

"You have everything here to prepare a meal for a hundred," remarked Tabitha.

"And we shall—soon," said Nicholas, referring obliquely to the dinner he planned to give for the planter families.

In a far corner of the kitchen a huge Negro was mending the leg of a table. Tabitha's gaze was irresistibly drawn to him, for he was one of the biggest men she had ever seen. Standing over seven feet tall, he had a great muscular body with wide shoulders and arms that were thick and powerful. His face was almost Grecian in its concept. He wore no shirt and Tabitha was acutely aware of the bulging muscles of his glistening ebony body. Noticing her interest in the giant Negro, Nicholas piloted her across the room. The big Negro nodded his handsome head.

"Howdy, Massa," he greeted. Then his eyes flicked toward Tabitha, holding for what was almost an insolent period of time, before his heavy lips broke into a smile and he said, "How do, Miss."

"You're finally mending that ole table, eh, Sam?" said Nicholas amiably.

"Yassuh. Dat ol' table been annoyin' the womenfolk fer weeks and weeks. Ah'm fixin' it so's it won't annoy 'em no mo'.'"

Nicholas nodded, turning slightly to Tabitha. She thought he had a half-amused smile on his lips, though she did not understand why.

"Big Sam's the best carpenter in these parts," he said. "Isn't a thing he can't fix. He not only takes care of all wood work on the plantation, but I have to loan him out to other plantations as well. Old John McRae, who is too old to lift a hammer, has him over at least once a week to take care of things—isn't that right, Sam?"

"Yassuh."

"Miss Clay is taking a tour of the grounds," said Nicholas, suddenly voluble. "She'll be with us for some time. I ask you to place yourself at her disposal if she needs anything."

Big Sam's round eyes shifted toward Tabitha again. There was something about his eyes Tabitha did not like, an insolence or an excessive interest, she was not sure which.

"Yassuh. Ah'll be at your service, Miss. Any time."

As they left the kitchen, Nicholas explained more about Big Sam. "He came to me as a field hand, several years ago. It wasn't long before I realized that his value on the plantation didn't lie in picking cotton. Some of these Negroes—not many, but some—are rather clever, you know. Artisans who can do many skillful things. Some are good carpenters, blacksmiths, curriers, weavers, painters, even musicians. Some drive a carriage well, or serve a table. Some of the women are excellent hairdressers. When you run a plantation, you make the best use of the blacks that you can—and I found that Big Sam was highly talented in two things."

"Carpentry—and what else?" asked Tabitha.

Nicholas smiled. "Carpentry, yes. He can rebuild anything that needs it, and he can even make cabinets—does excellent work of high quality. His other talent—if I may so term it—is studding."

Tabitha glanced at Nicholas inquiringly. His face was bland.

"He has sired a couple dozen healthy negrolings among the younger women," he went on imperturbably. "Does an enviable job."

Tabitha averted her eyes. She had heard of the practice of carefully breeding slaves to produce additional strong specimens, but she had believed it to be an uncommon one. It surprised her that Nicholas Enright, with all his vast dignity and aristocratic demeanor, was also engaged in this animal-like breeding of the blacks.

"Do you mean that he—"

"My dear, it doesn't become you to assume shock. Besides, I observed that you were quite intrigued yourself by his fine black body—"

"How dare you!"

"Oh, but you were!" Nicholas seemed to enjoy baiting her. "He's a marvelous specimen. Enough to tease the imagination of any woman, black or white. There are a dozen or more black wenches, let me assure you, who think a good deal of him!"

"But it's all so vulgar."

"As I explained, one uses his blacks to the best advantage. If you are to run a cotton plantation efficiently, you must take advantage of any talent you discover among your people."

"But it's just like breeding animals!" objected Tabitha, feeling that she must make some point of this to insure her own delicacy.

"Quite so. But then, I have become a Southerner, you know. By force of circumstances, of course. I believe now, just as the true Southerner does, that the average black is not much more than an animal. He's dull and unimaginative, with something of the beast of burden in him. He can work ten times as hard as a white man, but he can't think one-tenth as well. He is much closer allied to the mule than the human, so you work him like a mule."

"You don't really believe that," said Tabitha, sensing in his description of the slave the mockery he always held for things of the South.

"In this business I must believe it or perish. Even the dullest among the blacks are expensive these days—and one can't operate a plantation at a profit by buying new blacks over and over again. You must raise some of your own. Big Sam isn't the only black on the plantation that is used for this purpose, although I suspect that among the females he is the most desired."

"Oh, you're absolutely filthy, the way you put it," flared Tabitha.

"Spoken like a true Southern lady!" Nicholas said banteringly. "You're learning rapidly, my dear. Another week or two in our rarefied culture and I don't doubt that you'll become as coldly regal—and as hypocritical—as any plantation mistress."

Tabitha did not reply. Nicholas was obviously being

sarcastic about plantation life again. He seemed to take a dim view of the southern culture he was now an important part of, and it was difficult, sometimes, to determine if his remarks were serious or frivolous.

They had walked along the flagged patio, then skirted the manor to the front. A huge bougainvillea grew at the corner of the house and momentarily blocked the view of the approaches to the manor. Then, as they walked around it, the magnificent panorama of the terraced garden leaped into view.

In the excitement of her arrival, Tabitha had only briefly glimpsed the flowered magnificence of the huge terrace; now, suddenly, it was a thing of such immense beauty that she wondered why she had not taken cognizance of it before. Nestled in the center of the semicircular drive approaching the house, it fell away in steps from the crest on which the manor stood to the lower road that led off into the oak-shaded approach to the house. The entire garden was bordered with trim boxwood hedges. Inside the hedges was a profusion of flowers that almost took Tabitha's breath away. The well-groomed beds supported a riot of color—vari-colored azaleas, night-blooming jasmines, amaryllis ranging from white to pink to blood-red, lemon verbena with its lemon-scented leaves, drooping white snowdrops, chocolate-colored sweet shrub, and the purplish royalty of bloodleaf. Pink and white crape myrtle lent a pastel background for red oleanders that blazed like the fires of hell. There were fluffy gold acacia, purple mimosa, snow-white lilies and a startling bed of roses, and winding among the blooms were footpaths that descended daintily from the upper terrace to the lower.

"I have never seen anything so lovely," said Tabitha.

Nicholas was looking at her steadily. "I can only reply that you complement the flowers nicely," he said with a sort of stiff gallantry.

The remark pleased Tabitha. Her gaze inadvertently shifted to the sun-splashed veranda of the big manor with its impressive Tuscan columns reaching upward like huge stiff arms, giving the building the Greek Revival look so popular to the times. That was a mistake, for the sight of the veranda destroyed completely the pleasure she felt at Nicholas's compliment. It brought back to mind the peculiar circumstances of the night before, when he had banished her so violently after kissing her in what she felt had been considerable fervency, and caused her to wonder if there was any real sincerity in his flattering words. His dismissal of her, she thought, had been an insult to her and probably an embarrassment to him—and Tabitha knew no other way to erase the memory of the experience from both their minds than to replace it with another of such exquisite and sensual pleasure that the former catastrophe would flee their consciousness. And because she was thinking in such terms, Ryma's words came back to her, hauntingly: *You'll seduce him if you have to. Isn't that right, honey?*

Annoyed at recalling Ryma's prediction, Tabitha tried to rebut her words in her mind. She would *not* seduce him—well, not exactly, anyway. She might offer mild encouragement, but she would be coy about it. She certainly wouldn't offer her body—at least, she didn't think she would. Then, despite such equivocating reflections, she found herself saying: "Let's walk along the road into the woods."

She tried to say it casually, so that it would not appear that she sought a rendezvous, but apparently she was not artful enough, for a brief suspicion flashed in Nicholas's eyes.

"A provocative idea," he agreed. "There's a shady bower near the road where we can sit down and —talk."

The suggestion sounded slightly ominous to Tabitha, but she could not back out now, and they walked through the terraced garden and onto the rutted road that led into the woods. Before they reached the retreat Nicholas had mentioned, Tabitha had lost her nerve. She decided it would be safer to settle the problem verbally rather than physically.

"I want to ask you something, Nicholas," she said.

"Yes?"

"Last night when you kissed me, you grew angry."

She looked up at him to see his jaw harden at her words. He stared ahead, not looking at her, his eyes somber.

"Did I? I'm sure I wasn't angry."

Tabitha, without appearing to initiate the move, managed to be near him as they stopped in the roadway.

"You dismissed me rather abruptly, if I may say so."

"I'm sorry." His voice was frosty, his body rigid as it touched hers.

"I—I want to apologize if I did anything to annoy you," Tabitha said. There. That was perfectly put. She had taken the blame.

He looked down at her for the first time. His big

hand covered hers at his side, and he turned slightly so that they faced each other, standing close together, their bodies touching lightly.

"You did nothing to annoy me, Tabitha."

That was better, she thought. He was warming a bit now, and she would push him just a little further by bringing out of him still another admission.

"I'm sorry if you didn't enjoy the—experience," she said with just a trace of pique in her voice.

"But I did enjoy it, my dear."

Stiffly said. But much, much better. He was coming her way now.

"Then why did you send me to my room like a scolded child?" she asked, deciding to wring the last ounce of penitence from him.

He hesitated a long time before answering. A soft breeze rustled the leaves of the trees. The sun, filtered by the branches, dappled the ground unevenly. Somewhere a bird chirped, calling an inattentive mate. Tabitha waited for his answer, wondering what he would say, and then she saw the irritating smile come into his face—that smile of amusement and contempt she so disliked.

"My dear, you're a fine girl. I even suspect you're a virgin—"

"Of course!"

"I did not want to despoil you," Nicholas said blandly. "I admit to the notion, you know. You aroused every primitive impulse in me last night, and I thought it best to send you away before matters got out of hand. I should dislike very much returning you to your Bible-reading father in a pregnant condition."

"Really, Nicholas, you're so crude sometimes."

Tabitha made a displeased grimace, but she was not totally displeased. She was not so naive as to take Nicholas's explanation without question. There was a taunting tone in his words, a false gallantry. Still, it was possible that Nicholas had experienced certain qualms of conscience. If he had, that meant he respected her, and it seemed obvious to Tabitha that love could not be born unless respect preceded it. What she had construed as a somewhat boorish action the night before might have simply been one dictated by an overwhelming longing for her that Nicholas was fighting to control. She liked to think so anyway, for this meant that she could arouse that feeling again and again until Nichlas was so eager to possess her that marriage became the next logical step.

That she, herself, had failed to experience any such desire Tabitha conveniently stored away in the far recesses of her mind. It was logical to explain her lack of response by clinging to the mores of the day. After all, a lady wasn't supposed to feel the same carnal urges that a man felt. If she did, she was no lady. Such impulses would come at the proper time, on the marriage bed, and Tabitha was certain she could love Nicholas if he asked her to become his wife.

As for Nicholas, she knew, now, exactly what she must do. She would *not* stoop to seduction. Instead, she would permit him just enough liberty to make him crave for more, steadfastly withholding the ultimate pleasure until he had married her. This was the initial step on a difficult road she would have to travel toward acceptance by him and the society of Natchez. It was a goal she knew she would tenaciously pursue even if marriage to Nicholas turned out to be a loveless one. A love-filled marriage was ideal, of course, but marriage it had to be. Being mistress of Magnolia Manor had so burgeoned in importance to her that it was worth the sacrifice of some principles, if necessary, to achieve it.

They started walking again, and this time Nicholas took her hand in his, a gesture that encouraged Tabitha. Within a few minutes they came to a place where heavy brush formed a leafy arbor beside the road—a secluded love nest if Tabitha had ever seen one.

"Let us relax here," Nicholas said.

Tabitha seated herself on the soft bed of grass and Nicholas dropped down beside her. He gazed at her in silence for some time.

"You're a lovely girl," he said with a tenderness uncommon to him.

She let her eyes rise to his.

"Kiss, me, Nicholas," she said deliberately.

There, in the shaded shelter beside the road, his arms enfolded her and their lips met. It was a long, passionate kiss, with neither willing to break it, and Nicholas twisted his mouth against hers until Tabitha responded instinctively with the tip of her tongue between his lips. The kiss and embrace reached bold proportions before Tabitha finally retreated from his ardor.

Gently she disengaged herself from his arms, pleased with herself. It was the proper way to handle it. She had terminated the embrace at the precise moment when its warmth had reached unacceptable dimensions, as a lady should; yet she had been just daring enough to allow him to sample what she held in store for a future occasion. She had done it just right, and Nicholas could not criticize her either for lack of desire or untoward boldness.

But Nicholas was not to be so easily put off. His arms encircled her again and this time she fell back under the weight of him and he pinned her to the earth. His lips sought their target again and his hands played over her body. His breath had quickened, rife with sudden passion.

"Nicholas—no!"

But his lips found hers, his body arched over hers, pressing her against the coolness of the ground. She shuddered like a wounded bird beneath him, and she thought, *Should I fight him off? Should I be outraged? Should I show anger? Should I ask him what he takes me for, a common slut off the streets?* But she found herself unable to say anything, her very breath squeezed out of her as Nicholas lay heavily over her. She felt his entire body trembling in some buried ecstasy that was almost too much for him, and she thought, *I can't permit this. He'll have no respect for me afterward. I must fend him off even at the price of angering and disappointing him.* For Tabitha knew that Nicholas was too proud a man to take in marriage anyone but a virgin, even if he himself deflowered her. She could not allow all her carefully structured plans of marriage to Nicholas to go astray in one wild unreasoning adventure here in the shadowed gloom of the forest.

But she did not have to escape him, for suddenly he gave way, subsiding abruptly and mysteriously as he had the night before, pushing himself painfully to his knees, still looking at her but all at once not desiring her, not needing her.

"God's blood!" he breathed heavily. "Why do you insist on exciting me so?"

She sat up her own breath coming rapidly. What was he saying? Was he blaming her? Was he suggesting she had tried to seduce him, this arrogant man who had so boldly crushed her to the earth? She threw caution to the winds as hurt tones escaped her.

"Damn you, Nicholas! *You* wanted *me!*"

The blunt accusation chastened him. He struggled to his feet, then gave her his hand as he pulled her upright.

"Yes, I suppose I did." He sounded contrite, but there was a light touch to his voice that seemed false and unconvincing. "The fact is, my dear, that you inflame me. But being a gentleman of the highest breeding, I *did* desist, didn't I? Gallant of me, don't you agree?" The last words had a bitter ring, a trace of mockery.

Tabitha's violet eyes smoldered at his sudden pixie-like attitude. She had not liked his clumsy attempt at seduction. But she had been stung even more by his sudden refusal of her charms, even though she had contemplated denying him. Now, to make light of the whole affair irritated her.

"If you lack anything, Nicholas, it certainly isn't arrogance," she snapped. "As for gallantry, I doubt that you know the meaning of the word,"

He simply smiled at her crossness. "Be that as it may, I must sound a warning to you, young lady," he said pompously. "Don't ever provoke me again, as you did just now, or I may forget every gentlemanly manner my beloved mother has bestowed upon me."

"I didn't provoke you!" Tabitha shot back, her resentment at fever pitch.

"You asked me to kiss you."

"Oh, fie!"

Nicholas brushed a few blades of grass from his clothing. He had calmed now, was again composed and outwardly cool.

"A request for a kiss is a provocation," he insisted. "And you're quite adept at provocation—so much so that I wonder where you attained such proficiency."

Tabitha's lips pulled tight. Exasperation had replaced logic in her mind now, momentarily blotting out her vision of a life on the Hill, her ambition to be a grand lady of Natchez.

"You're like all men, Nicholas Enright!" she said vehemently. "You don't know it when you're in love. That's what's the matter with you, Nicholas. You love me!"

She spoke the words maliciously, determined to provoke him into an admission, however grudging. But all he did was smile at her in that unreal, synthetic way he had, as if such childish temper amused him.

"Love you, my dear? You surprise me. One as coldly analytical as you should know that there is no such thing as love."

"No such thing!"

"Of course not. I have an opinion about love which I will someday share with you. Meantime, shall we return to the house? We've been gone a long time and my dear mother may be concerned. She might even ask for an explanation of our waywardness."

6

The quarrel did not endure. By the time they reached the manor Nicholas was again, if not charming, at least civil. He seemed capable of putting aside disagreeable things rapidly, and he did not mention again the confrontation in the forest. Tabitha, her anger slowly dissipating, decided that forgetting the incident was the best thing to do.

The next two weeks passed rapidly for Tabitha. Each day was filled with experiences new and exciting and different. She felt like a naive child being introduced to a strange new world of glamor, where only a few people dwelt in a profusion of luxury and contentment. Craftily, she stowed away the knowledge she gained of plantation life in the recesses of her agile mind, knowing full well that the more she understood Nicholas's world the more valuable she would be to him in his plans to circumvent his mother.

The gulf between mother and son—which Sophie described as "Widah den the Mississip"—became more obvious to Tabitha the longer she stayed. Martha Enright never overlooked an opportunity to place her son in a subordinate position. Every problem of running the manor, however inconsequential, was solved by Martha, and she took particular delight in asking—indeed, commanding—that Nicholas perform small, insignificant and demeaning tasks for her.

Tabitha, too, was a target for Martha Enright's intrigues and manipulations. In subtle ways she managed to convey to Tabitha that *she* was sole mistress of the manse and, as such, would not tolerate interference at any level. Once, when Tabitha became so bold as to offer a suggestion on some minor household problem, Martha bridled and said, "A plantation run by partners never prospers, young lady. There must be one master of each place—or one mistress. Here at Magnolia Manor I am that mistress, and I make all suggestions and decisions. I might also mention to you that Nicholas, although he does not admit it, sorely needs my guidance. He has weaknesses you could not possibly know about."

"The intrigues of the house do not concern me, Mrs. Enright," Tabitha had lied. "I am merely enjoying a vacation here."

"That's as it should be," said Martha.

But the old blind woman's remarks weighed heavily on Tabitha. What weaknesses did she refer to? In most situations—making love excepted—Nicholas seemed a confident, dominating male, arrogant, haughty and proud. Was it possible that this outward show of infallibility covered fatal weaknesses in his makeup? And did he really need his mother's guidance, or was this wishful thinking on the part of Martha Enright? Tabitha had observed a certain deference on Nicholas's part where his mother was concerned; he was always more cautious of speech and manners when his mother was present. But it was not, Tabitha thought, a genuine deference. It was likely that Nicholas was merely playing a sly game, pretending to give his mother her way in all matters, while he carefully maneuvered to take control of Magnolia Manor out of her thin greedy hands. Tabitha decided she would, at the proper moment, discuss this matter more thoroughly with Nicholas, thus cementing her importance to him as an ally.

It was imperative, in fact, that she bring Nicholas closer to her, for the early warmth he had shown toward her had in two weeks' time virtually disappeared. Following the abortive episode in their forested trysting place, his ardor for her had either cooled perceptibly or had been firmly put aside by him, as one places an unwanted object in the back of a drawer. He spent long hours in the music room alone, often playing the piano in the harsh angry tones that signaled dissatisfaction. When he walked beside her now he was extremely careful not to touch her in any way, permitting a distance of at least a foot to separate them. When it was necessary for him to take her arm or help her over a rough spot in the terrain, it was done with the most gentlemanly restraint. His conversation had become less caustic and ridiculing, clinging to subjects that were unquestionably "proper," with never a word about love or the male-female relationship mentioned. Whether all this indicated an actual cooling of his interest in her—which Tabitha dreaded to contemplate because time was now running out on her—or simply a determination on his part to avoid any repetition of their thwarted lovemaking was the big question. And Tabitha had no answer for it.

Still, there was one encouraging area in which

Nicholas continued to show an interest in Tabitha. Although he exhibited a maddening tendency to treat Tabitha as an uninformed child, Nicholas insisted on introducing her to all the amenities of life at the plantation level. There was always an annoying superiority in his method of teaching, but otherwise he seemed sincere in his efforts. The proper dress at soirees and balls, the right silverware to use at the table, the taboo subjects that ladies never spoke about in public, all this was spelled out to Tabitha in almost annoying detail, making her feel that she had no brain of her own. Still, Tabitha appreciated his advice, for he had been born to the grand manner and there were many points of ethics and manners Tabitha came to know for the first time.

"All manners are acquired," he told her once. "Either they are acquired by virtue of the fact that one is born and raised at a certain level of life, or they are acquired later as one reaches that level. As I've mentioned before, many of the planter families are still crude in many ways, but their manners have been polished and their faces washed until they are, today, something they were not a few years ago. Which, if I may say so, emphasizes again the falsity of the planters' social structure."

Tabitha said nothing, but she was aware of the cynicism that crept into his words every time Nicholas mentioned the social life of Natchez. He had been born into a wealthy family steeped in snobbish graces, and he was obviously contemptuous of the Johnny-come-lately planters who only now were pretending to be snobs. Yet, while he considered Natchez society a sham and was secretly amused by it, still he wanted to be accepted and recognized by it. He had called it a paradox, and it was—and his calm acceptance of the paradox he disliked added to the riddle that was Nicholas.

In the cool of early morning or evening hours, Nicholas and Tabitha often went riding. With little practice, Tabitha became an excellent horsewoman. Nicholas, seated grandly in the deeply concave high-pommeled Spanish saddle atop Happy Boy, with his riding crop in his hand, was a regal sight to Tabitha, and when she rode with him on Lady Belle—side-saddle as became a lady of breeding—they made a handsome couple indeed. Often they rode to the esplanade, for they both enjoyed the panoramic view of the river and the feverish activity of the wharves. Tabitha was always thrilled at the sight of one of the beautiful steamboats, white and filigreed and looking for all the world like a floating wedding cake. And Nicholas, watching boats load and unload, inevitably mentioned the importance of cotton to the economy of the country.

When they did not go as far as the esplanade, they rode slowly around the plantation, while Nicholas inspected his blacks and the out-buildings, and it was during these rides that Tabitha came to love Magnolia Manor as she had never loved any home or any land. Particularly, Tabitha loved the grounds around the manse itself. Outside, in the color-splashed gardens or overlooking the whitening cotton fields, there was a feeling of cleanness and brightness and cheer. She learned to love the inside of the manor too, even though she was aware that the house had certain melancholy aspects. Part of this was traceable to the cave-like confines of the big house itself, where the sun never penetrated and shadows clung thick and heavy in the corners of rooms, like huge black bats. But this Tabitha could have easily overlooked if it had not been for the intrigue and suspicion that also hung in every corner — a human-directed darkness that somehow diminished the natural beauty of the house's interior.

"It's lak Ah always said," Sophie offered one day as Tabitha sat at the escritoire making an entry in a diary she was keeping, "this house is made by the debbil. The debbil runs it an' the debbil's gonna have it in the end."

"Why do you stay here, Sophie?" Tabitha asked. "Why don't you run away?"

"Ah wants to find out how it all comes out," said Sophie, stalking indignantly out of the room.

Well, thought Tabitha, it would all come out with Nicholas and her being master and mistress of Magnolia Manor, and Nicholas's scheming mother reduced to a secondary role. At least she would do her best to create this solution. Tabitha was aware that only by the total defeat of Martha Enright could she become a lady of distinction in the social whirl of Natchez. And more and more — since Nicholas was acting like a rational human being now — she was determined to make this dream come true. She would rule Magnolia Manor with Nicholas if it was the last thing she ever did.

Tabitha felt her blood stirring, as it always did when her thoughts fastened on the subject of her own dominance at the manor. She stood up abruptly and walked to the full-length mirror on the wall. She pirouetted gracefully, watching her dress billow from her hips, listening to the whispering of the silks. Yes, she and Nicholas would make an attractive couple at lavish dinners or dancing the simple graceful minuet or the new and intricate cotillion, or even driving down the bustling streets of Natchez in the handsome barouche. They could well set the pace for Natchez's social life, dictate its standards and mold its opinions. She would become known as the most gracious hostess in Natchez's high-nosed society. Her lips set firmly and stubbornly at the thought. Yes, they would all bow down one day to this little girl from Natchez-under-the-Hill!

Already, without her, the Enright name held power and prestige. Tabitha had learned that an invitation to attend a dinner or soiree at the Enrights was already considered one that could not, under any conceivable circumstances, be ignored. Anyone who had either the temerity or the misfortune to turn down an Enright invitation was considered by all others to be virtually out of circulation. Contrariwise, anyone receiving an invitation to an Enright function was at once recognized as a bonafide member of the society's upper echelon. This Tabitha found to be true when Nicholas finally invited five couples to the dinner-party at which he planned to formally introduce Tabitha. The invitations were acknowledged by special messengers dispatched to Magnolia Manor — and in such haste as to appear almost vulgar. Yes, the Faunce Manleys would be there, the John McRaes would attend, the Estabrooks and Drews would be only too happy, and the de'Ubervilles would be overwhelmed. Nicholas smiled smugly as he examined the replies.

"They answer in unseemly haste," he observed. "But then, I told you that the refinements of our social order are mostly false, didn't I? Tonight will be your first view of Natchez social life, my dear — and, although it may dazzle you with its presumptuousness, I suspect it might also surprise you by its vulgarity."

"Vulgarity?"

"Oh, quite. These are frightful people, really. Wait until you meet them!"

Tabitha said nothing, deciding that the derogatory picture Nicholas drew of the people he invited was mostly exaggerated. After all, Tabitha had seen the scum of Natchez-under-the-Hill and she was certain that along side such vermin the grand men and ladies of Natchez proper would be souls of delicacy and propriety. In fact, the prospect of meeting them caused her some trepidation, for she would have to watch her manners, her speech, everything Nicholas had taught her, so that not one thing would suggest that she was ill-bred or lacked poise. This raised a pertinent question in Tabitha's mind and, at a proper moment as they strolled along the veranda fronting the house, she put the question to Nicholas.

"How do you intend to introduce me to these people?"

Nicholas stopped, walking to the edge of the veranda, gazing out over the terraced garden. Slowly he extracted his snuff box from his pocket, inhaled a pinch and sneezed softly. He looked back at her, his face expressionless.

"Are you concerned?"

"Of course. After all, I'm from Natchez-under, and if these people are half the snobs you say they are, they'll look down on me. Oh, Nicholas, I do hope I'll not embarrass you!"

He came toward her. "Embarrass me? Not at all, my dear. I'm inviting them here specifically to meet you. I don't intend to cover up anything in your past, since your past is perfectly satisfactory to me and I see no reason for painting it any different than it is. I'm convinced that if, by chance, any of these great ladies, as you so naively view them, should look down with disdain upon you, you will soon win them over by your charm and grace."

"You flatter me," said Tabitha, not knowing whether he sincerely meant all he was saying.

"In this rare instance, I speak the truth. There are times when I am hardly sincere, as you have no doubt discovered, but in this I am. You have much charm. You possess the poise of any so-called grand lady of my acquaintance. In fact, you are more beautiful than most. In general, my dear, most of our grand ladies are pretty much pigs."

"Nicholas! How you talk!" The protest was artificial. Tabitha was highly elated at his portrait of her. If he really felt she was as he had described her, she was well on the way to winning his respect—if not his affection. She would be extra careful, when she met his guests, that no impropriety of any kind rose to mar the picture he had of her.

"Will you, then, mention that I am from Natchez-under?" she asked, still curious about how he would introduce her to the cream of Natchez society.

"I will likely say, 'This is Tabitha Clay. She's the daughter of a well-respected preacher from Natchez-under-the-Hill. I am proud to say she is the girl I plan to marry.' That should start the gossip mill grinding."

"Marry?" The word exploded on Tabitha's lips. She stood looking at him for a long moment, her heart suddenly racing. He had spoken no word of marriage at any time. In fact, his ardor had cooled so much since the episode in the woods that she doubted her ability to any longer interest him. Now he was looking at her in mild surprise, as though he had expected her to realize his intentions.

"After all, my dear," he said, "isn't that what you've wanted?"

"Wanted?" She felt silly echoing his words, but she could think of nothing else to say.

"Your affection on a couple of rather warm occasions led me to believe that you might accept me as a husband," said Nicholas blandly. "Or did you merely intend to be my mistress?"

"Nicholas! I resent such an implication!" Her voice reflected indignity.

"Look, my dear," said Nicholas patiently, "I supposed all along that we understood each other, but so that there shall be no misunderstanding in the future, I'll recapitulate. I invited you here because I saw in you certain qualities I admired, both physical and mental. I felt that you were an exceptional girl, and that if given the chance could become a wonderfully mature and full woman in our society on the Hill. You have proved my contentions in every way. You have charm and, even more important, you have guts. Is it not quite natural that I should think of you in terms of a wife?"

"But you never mentioned marriage."

Nicholas shrugged as if it did not matter. "Perhaps

not. I'm such a laggard about these things. But my mentioning it now isn't exactly the surprise you are making it out to be, is it, my dear? Isn't it what you intended that I someday say? Isn't it what you've been working toward with all your claws out?"

"Nicholas, that's an insulting way to put it."

"Really?" He laughed shortly. "I don't think so. I think it does you credit. You're a ruthless woman, my dear, with a scheming mind that is permanently anchored to one idea — to become a plantation mistress. And it's that very ruthlessness that wins my admiration. You see, Tabitha, I know you quite well."

She stared at him. Yes, he knew her quite well indeed! And it angered her that he could guess her innermost plans, that he could read her intentions so accurately. It made her even more angry that he was treating them so blandly.

"However," he went on banteringly, "if it rescues your pride for me to propose marriage to you formally, I shall. I believe the proper way is for me to spread a handkerchief on the floor, kneel gently upon it, and ask for your hand — and whatever else goes with it."

Before she could answer he had spread a handkerchief on the veranda steps and was down on one knee before her, making a hideous mockery of the proposal. She felt her body stiffen, and her violet eyes flashed flame. She seethed with such anger and humiliation that she wanted to walk away and leave him kneeling there like a fool, but she held the anger tight within her. This moment called for caution. This was it, the thing she had waited for, the culmination of all her dreams. Nicholas was proposing — albeit in a most outrageous manner — but proposing nonetheless.

All she had to do was say yes, and she would magically become a great lady in much the same manner a caterpillar magically leaves its chrysalis to become a butterfly. She had always felt that when this supreme moment came she would be able to handle it deftly and with ladylike hesitation. But she was not prepared to cope with the way in which Nicholas was making a derisive burlesque of the proposal.

"Please stand up, Nicholas—you make me feel like a fool," she said testily, unable to contain the words. "Besides, I think you may be overlooking one important factor in all this."

"Yes? And what is that?"

"Do you love me?"

There, she had said it. It was something she had to know, and she would force an admission from him. He rose to his feet, looking at her quizzically.

"Does that have anything to do with it, my dear?" he asked.

She stared at him, unable for a moment to comprehend his question.

"It has everything to do with it," she said, and then wondered why she had said it. She had felt the natural resentment of any woman who is taken for granted. She was humiliated to think that she must accept him on his own terms. And she had asked him if he loved her to reassure herself that his proposal was not something he had thought up on the spur of the moment but something she had, by her charm, precipitated.

"I rather think," said Nicholas carefully, "that most men could learn to love you. However, I'm different from most men. And I suspect you are different from most women. Since your overriding aim is not particularly to become my wife, but to become mistress of a plantation—any plantation—would your pride be too great to accept me without love?"

Tabitha shook her head. "I don't understand you, Nicholas," she said. But she *did* understand. Nicholas was right. Deep inside she knew it. She would accept him any way she could get him, so why was she so stupidly insisting on love? Wasn't this—a proposal of marriage—the goal she had been striving toward? Hadn't this been her main target? Now that the elegant Nicholas Enright had proposed marriage, shouldn't she be smart enough to keep her mouth shut? She looked at Nicholas almost pleadingly. "What I mean, Nicholas, is that I think a good marriage must be based on love."

"I don't," said Nicholas bluntly. "I told you that I would one day explain to you my feeling about love, and so I shall. I don't believe in love. It doesn't exist. Love is some ethereal emotion dreamed up by poets—and God's blood, if they don't have people believing it! No, I think a sound marriage must be based on mutual respect and a complete understanding of each other. I respect and understand you, Tabitha. I respect and understand every coldly practical quality you possess, because I am the same way. I respect your ruthlessness and the fact that you have no conscience whatever—and that you will stop at nothing to get what you want."

"I'm sure I don't know what you're trying to say," said Tabitha petulantly.

"Don't you? It's quite simple. You came to the esplanade deliberately to make the acquaintance of a man, didn't you, my innocent?"

"I went to enjoy the view of the river," Tabitha insisted. "I often do."

"Of course. Then, having admired the view, you cast your pretty violet eyes about for an eligible male. I happened along, observed that you were something worth knowing, and put in my bid."

"*You* started the flirtation!" leaped Tabitha, who preferred to think of it that way.

"A matter of opinion, my dear. At any rate, I suspect that you saw in me an opportunity to lift yourself out of the filthy morass of Natchez-under-the-Hill, and I saw in you a girl who, wanting to better her life, would be inclined to ignore propriety a bit—or at least blink at the accepted rules. Which, of course, brings us to a question.

"What?"

"Do *you* love *me?*"

"Why, I—"

"You hesitate, my dear."

"Well, it's rather sudden, Nicholas."

"You see what I mean?" His tone held smug confidence. "You don't love me any more than I love you. Yet I'm sure you wouldn't allow this nebulous factor to ruin an opportunity for you to marry me and become mistress of this great house." He smiled briefly and took her arm. "My dear, I am proposing a marriage of convenience. An opportunistic and loveless marriage of convenience. I need you as mistress of Magnolia Manor and as a foil to my mother's ambitions. Together we can run Magnolia Manor and become the most celebrated couple in all the Natchez country. Separately, neither of us can make it."

230

"But—"

"You need me too," Nicholas pointed out. "You need me to realize your ambition to live on the Hill. The prize for both of us is too great to permit an obscure thing like love to stand in the way of our chances. Under these conditions, can I assume that you accept my gallant proposal?"

Tabitha stiffened. *Damn Nicholas anyway*, she thought. *He rips away all my pride. He makes me feel like a harlot renting myself out for an inducement. But how can I refuse? I simply have to bury what pride I have, push it under the ground, back in my mind, forget it. Maybe I shouldn't insist on love now. I can make him love me later. That was it—later. And whether or not I love him now isn't important either—it's becoming Mrs. Enright that's important; it's being mistress of Magnolia Manor that's important; it's victory over Martha Enright that's important; it's changing my way of life that's important. . . .*

"Despite your cynical view of love, I think there's no doubt that we could love each other in time," she temporized. "After all, we have had such little time together."

"I thought you would rationalize it some way," said Nicholas mildly. He kissed her tenderly on the forehead, his lips barely brushing her smooth skin. As he did so a discordant note struck Tabitha's mind.

"Nicholas."

"Yes?"

"You haven't asked my father."

"That *is* the proper thing to do, isn't it?"

"Of course. You must certainly ask Father for my hand."

Nicholas smiled icily. "As a matter of fact, my dear, I have."

"You have already?"

"Yes."

"Without my knowledge?"

"Oh, God's beard, Tabitha!" Nicholas snapped impatiently. "Quit pretending you're a creature of convention! I dispatched a messenger this morning with a long explanatory letter to your parents, declaring—you'll like this—my undying love for you, and informing them of my desire to give you a life of luxury and ease and make you a grand woman of Natchez. I write such excellent and compelling prose, Tabitha, that I'm sure your father won't be able to resist my blandishments."

Tabitha shook her head wonderingly.

"Nicholas, you've done this all backwards. You should have called on father personally. He's a very proper person, especially where I'm concerned, and—"

"I told him that you and I would call together on the morrow for his answer," said Nicholas smugly. "And, oh, yes—I told him you loved me devotedly. That's all right, isn't it?"

She looked at him in complete amazement. It was impossible to understand Nicholas. Apparently his belief in his own infallibility was so great that he thought it unnecessary to ask anyone's opinion of anything he did.

"But the dinner and the announcement is tonight!" Tabitha pointed out. "Are you so sure of yourself that you'd announce our marriage before you have my father's consent?"

"I am sure of *you*, my dear," said Nicholas coldly. "I know you want this marriage. I am certain that even if your father objected — an unlikely event — you would still marry me, wouldn't you?"

Tabitha gave up. "Sometimes, Nicholas, you can be absolutely insufferable. But to be coldly practical about it, I suppose you are right. As you said, we both profit from such a union, and neither of us is apt to turn it down." She sighed uncomfortably at her own admission of duplicity and turned away from him. "You *have* told your mother, I suppose."

"Of course not." She turned to see his facial muscles contract into hard crevices. "She'd only attempt to ruin it. I plan to announce it at dinner to her and all of our friends. The open announcement, and the element of surprise, will place her at a distinct disadvantage."

"You're diabolical," said Tabitha, not without a slight trace of admiration in her voice.

Nicholas nodded his head in acknowledgement of the compliment. They walked to the end of the veranda, silent for a moment. The day was warm, more pleasant to Tabitha than any she had yet enjoyed at the manor. The sky was a brittle blue, dotted with puffy white clouds that looked like cosmic cotton bolls.

"Another thing," Nicholas said. "The announcement will create quite a stir among the social snobs, you know. I've explained to you that we planters are clannish. We stick together. For years the planter families have married among each other, maintaining a tight group and thus controlling the wealth of the area in a few choice hands. By all tradition, I should marry the daughter of another plantation owner—perish the thought!—to avoid the encroachment of outsiders on our privileged domain. But I find it rather exciting, if not a little vengeful, to marry a girl from outside the socially accepted families of Natchez—for it will raise a lot of snobbish eyebrows, especially among our charming and tigerish women."

"They'll hate me," Tabitha decided.

"I dare say," said Nicholas dryly. "But you shall be able to bear up under it, my dear. After all, you will have achieved your goal, and to hell with all others. Isn't that the way you and I feel about things?"

Tabitha did not answer. But she admitted to herself that Nicholas, for all his bluntness, was right. She wouldn't give a damn about anybody once she was mistress of Magnolia Manor. And she was going to be—she was going to be!

7

There were times when Abijah Clay regretted his decision to preach the gospel in such a dissolute place as Natchez-under-the-Hill. While there was rarely any slackening of his evangelistic zeal, still there were occasions when he doubted his ability to convert to Christ the licentious people that frequented the tumble-down shacks along the river. He was well aware that Natchez-under was no exception among river towns. In every port where keelboats, flatboats and steamboats docked, they vomited forth the dregs of humanity that operated and took passage on them—in New Orleans, Vicksburg, Memphis, and New Madrid as well as Natchez-under-the-Hill. This state of affairs discouraged Abijah, but never totally. He deplored the fact that sin was so extraordinarily popular and his discouragement, like a sensitive barometer reflecting the vicissitudes of the weather, increased or decreased in exact relationship to the amount of shameless dissipation that occurred on the flatlands.

But Abijah Clay was stubborn. He had never admitted that his job was a hopeless one—although he had frequently entertained strong doubts and occasionally expressed them—and he was always willing to go back to the wretched hovels of Silver Street again. He had, over a long period of time, conditioned himself both to inattention and outright abuse, and could stand for hours before a brothel and berate the men who entered. It was only in somber moments of self-evaluation—usually in the early morning hours when Rachel slept peacefully beside him and the cabin was silent—that the doubts emerged like ghastly specters out of a murky swamp. But he always ended by brushing aside the doubts, like sinful intruders on his Christ-like dedication, and going forth once again as a savior among sinners.

It was mid-morning and a blazing sun was already heating the hovels of Natchez-under to oven-like proportions. The night's boisterous gaiety was mostly over, and many of the rivermen had stumbled back to their ships to continue their journeys up or down the river. But the clink of games and raucous sounds of bawdy music still persisted, for the pleasure palaces of Natchez-under never closed. Sin, it had been discovered, was as enticing in burning daylight as in the protective blackness of night, and there were always enough customers around to make it profitable to remain open.

Often, during the day when many of the rivermen were gone, the houses of assignation entertained the more elite gentlemen from Natchez-proper, for it was a truism of the times that, even though the elegant city on the Hill pretended to deplore the squalid conditions along the river, it was not uncommon for young men bent on adventure and pleasure to descend from the heights to enjoy the perverse delights of the mudflats. Should a bachelor of Natchez become beset by physical pressures he was unable to satisfy on the Hill, or should a plantation husband consider his wife entirely too ladylike, there was always a dark-skinned Creole, a quadroon, an octoroon, or—if he proved particular—a Caucasian in Natchez-under at a price. In fact, some of the brothels catered specifically to the "dandies" on the Hill, charging high prices for "imported" girls from New Orleans with talents for perversity not found in the ordinary plantation woman.

Abijah had arrived on Silver Street at daybreak and had already spent several long hours watching bleary-eyed rivermen trudge from the whorehouses and stagger wearily toward their waiting vessels at dockside. He had stood erect, like a pillar of righteousness, amidst a Babel of sin, shouting in his stentorian voice, urging the sinners to repent and give themselves into the hands of the Lord, but none had yet stepped forth to avail themselves of the Lord's benevolent services. Now, with most of the rivermen gone, he saw the "dandies" from the Hill—dressed in light-colored trousers, darker waistcoats, with silk stocks piled luxuriously beneath their chins—filtering down the street and entering their favorite brothels. Abijah wondered how, on a sultry morning such as this one, a man could enjoy intercourse with a whore. He had a mental picture of two sweating bodies locked together, wet in their nakedness, thumping each other ravenously as sweat dampened the bed beneath them—and with disgust he put the mental picture out of his mind. A man of God should not entertain such thoughts; it was bad enough that he had to preach against them.

As he watched the well-dressed men turn into the

brothels he thought, not all men on the Hill partake of this sinfulness. Pray God that Nicholas Enright did not. For he was uncomfortably worried about Tabitha, even though he realized the value of her connection with the Enrights and was well aware of what it meant in improving her life. One does not lightly turn one's daughter over to a strange man, however gentlemanly and refined he might be, without some cause for concern.

One young man in expensive clothing and carrying a walking stick with a jaunty air, headed toward the brothel before which Abijah stood like a religious statue. Abijah decided to attempt one more fling at salvation.

"I beg you not to enter there, young man!" he implored in a quavering voice. "Have some thought of your soul, for God does not take into His Kingdom souls stained with the vile sins of fleshly man. Remember the Psalms, good man, where it says, *Our soul waiteth for the Lord; He is our help and our shield.*"

The man glanced up, scanned Abijah's fervent face, then looked away in embarrassment. But he went into the rickety shack with Abijah's voice, now raised in condemnation, trailing him. "Sinner! Blasphemer! God's wrath will descend on you!"

"Vile and dastardly transgressor," Abijah mumbled to himself, then turned his attention to a group of a dozen rivermen staggering down the street toward the quay.

"You men!" Abijah entreated. "Stop and hear the word of the Lord! Stop and hear about God's Kingdom."

The men stopped, half amused at Abijah's outpourings.

"Which of you," challenged Abijah in a loud voice, "has the courage to be saved?"

The men moved closer. One of them, a grizzly bear of a man with unshaven face and rodent-like eyes, spoke in a voice sodden with liquor.

"If it ain't the preachah! Evah time I gits to Natchez, I sees this Bible-banger. Don't you evah git tired of preachin', preachah?"

"One never tires of expounding the gospel," intoned Abijah. "Come forth, one of you, and be saved!"

"Ain't got no time, preachah," said the ruffian. "I works on the *Mississippi Belle,* and if I don't git mah ass down there soon she'll be churnin' water widout me!" There was drunken laughter from his companions following this spectacular announcement.

"The *Mississippi Belle* can wait, the Lord can't!" shouted Abijah with total sincerity. "Remember, *those that wait upon the Lord, they shall inherit the earth.*"

The talkative member of the group came forward a few steps and squinted one beady eye at Abijah. All at once his face broke into an evil smile.

"Say!" he exclaimed. "Ain't you the preachah has a daughter what's a whore?"

The howl of appreciation that greeted this sally was so loud that it almost drowned out Abijah's angered reply.

"I have no such daughter!" he shouted. "Any daughter who transgresses in the ways of the Lord is not my daughter at all!"

"Ryma—ain't that her name?" pursued the riverman, delighted at having found such a vulnerable chink in Abijah's cloak of righteousness. "A fine piece she is too!"

"The wrath of God upon you!" screamed Abijah, who often reached the point of calling down the wrath of the Almighty when nothing else seemed to work. "May you burn in Hell for eternity!"

This was greeted with cynical laughter and then, tiring of their sport, the group made their way uncertainly toward the quay where the *Mississippi Belle* was moored. Abijah looked after them, his eyes rising to the white steamboat with the gingerbread railings and snowy funnels already belching puffs of smoke. Yes, in a minute the big sidewheel would be churning the water into a froth, and the rivermen would have to hurry to get aboard in time. Abijah decided, with some bitterness, that the impending departure of the *Mississippi Belle* probably did make it impossible for the rivermen to give a few minutes to God.

Shaking his head dolefully at the irreverence and stupidity of God's children, Abijah turned and walked wearily down the street toward his cabin. He had forsaken breakfast this morning for the privilege of serving the Lord, and he hoped that Rachel would have a supply of johnnycake and hot black coffee—and perhaps ham and clabber—to satisfy his physical needs when he returned. He knew she would have something ready, for Rachel's dependability was a staunch pillar of support for him at all times. Often, in the quiet darkness of the night, he gave thanks to God for blessing him with such a woman, for without her silent and patient understanding he was sure he would long ago have lost his way. The knowledge that she supported his cause, however hopeless it must sometimes appear to her, gave him the courage to keep trying.

He was deeply occupied in thought until he drew near the rough log cabin. Then he observed for the first time that a two-wheeled cabriolet, drawn by a spirited gray horse with a flowing silver mane, was standing at his front door. The Negro driver, dressed colorfully in green livery, was handing something to Rachel at the doorway. Then the Negro bowed, got back on the rear of the one-seat cabriolet, snapped the whip over the gray's head, and pulled away. By the time Abijah reached the cabin, Rachel had already read a letter which she held in her hands.

"A message from Tabitha?" asked Abijah eagerly.

"No. From Mr. Enright," said Rachel, her voice low and somewhat somber.

"Is there some trouble?" Abijah asked anxiously.

"No trouble," said Rachel. "In fact, things seem to be going along with exceptional smoothness. Here, you had better read it."

Abijah took the letter. A faint odor of perfume arose from the stationery and he grimaced slightly.

"Scented stationery," he said, as if this might represent a mild form of sin. "I hear it's the latest craze on the Hill. Imported, no doubt, from some heathen nation."

"It's the message that's important," said Rachel practically, and Abijah glanced at her as if considering her comment a form of subtle rebuke. Taking his square spectacles from his pocket, he set them carefully on his long tapering nose and peered down at the letter in his hand.

My dear Mrs. and Mr. Clay:

I am pleased to inform you that your daughter, Tabitha, is in excellent health and, I am sure, enjoying her sojourn at Magnolia Manor. I am, in fact, elated at the manner in which she has adapted to our way of life on the Hill, which I am sure you realize is an accomplishment of considerable importance. Within three short weeks she has become something of a grand lady of the South, true to the storied traditions of all such plantation women. She has learned to handle her own horse—a gentle palomino—riding in the delightful sidesaddle position so becoming to young ladies, and her manners and way of conducting herself among plantation people is indeed a pleasure to behold.

Abijah looked at his wife over the tops of his glasses after reading the opening paragraph.

"He sounds smitten," he said dryly.

"Read on, Abijah, and you'll find how really smitten he is," Rachel advised.

Abijah once more scanned the paper, holding it away from him as if the flowery scent of it was repugnant.

You may have guessed from the above that I have become increasingly fond of Tabitha as I have grown to know and appreciate her. She is a wonderful girl and I think much of her. So much, in fact, that I risk your displeasure in asking you in all humbleness for her hand in marriage.

I say displeasure, although that is perhaps a stronger word than is my intent. I am, as you know, able to offer to your daughter everything that she wants in life—a fine home, money, security, social background, the very best of all things. She will live her life gracefully and in impeccable surroundings and, with her natural charm and her considerable mentality, will, I am sure, become one of the finest ladies in Natchez.

I know that this proposal of marriage will surprise you. But I can truthfully say that I love your daughter most devotedly—and I am flattering myself in believing she feels the same toward me, for she has agreed to take me as a husband upon your consent.

If I have your blessing in this matter, the marriage will take place a week from today, a Saturday, in the salon of Magnolia Manor. I will, of course, inform you later as to the exact hour so that both of you may be present. Your daughter and I will call on you tomorrow for your answer. With all good wishes to your future as a man of God, I remain,

Respectfully,
—Nicholas Enright

Abijah Clay placed the letter gently on the puncheon table and walked without a word to the paper-covered window, taking down the corner of it and looking out with no purpose except to regain his composure. The message had shaken him, even though he admitted to the fact that it was not a surprising development. He was finding it hard to accept because of its suddenness.

Refastening the corner of the greased paper he turned slowly to Rachel.

"It is hard," he said simply.

"Yes."

"But normal, I suppose."

"Yes."

"I will not await their arrival tomorrow," he said at last. "I will go to see Nicholas Enright and my daughter tonight."

Rachel's eyes rose to his. There was concern in them.

"What do you intend to say, Abijah?"

"What can one say? If Tabitha loves this man, and he loves her, then I expect it will be a fine marriage. I guess," he hesitated a long time, "I would favor it."

Rachel smiled, relieved at his conciliatory attitude. She had feared that Abijah would be stiff-necked about the matter.

"She will better herself, Abijah," she said.

"Yes." Abijah's brow furrowed in a worried frown. "I have no right—nay, no desire—to stand in the way of a daughter who wished to escape this stinking hole. I would rather she marry a man of wealth and position on the Hill, even though his way of life and ours differ in material concepts, than to see her become—"

He stopped, unwilling to go on. Rachel dared to complete it.

"You are thinking about Ryma," she said.

He did not lose his temper, as he so often did at the mere mention of Ryma's name. He simply nodded.

"Was it my fault that she became what she has, Rachel?"

She sensed that he was lapsing into one of his moods of self-evaluation, when he doubted the wisdom of his course in life. She stood up, putting her hand on his gaunt shoulder.

"Of course not. Tabitha is going on to a better way of life than she has ever known, because she has the character to accomplish this. Ryma was weak. She took the easy course."

"You are a strong woman, Rachel," said Abijah. "Perhaps she inherited the weakness from me, some flabby thing in my own character." He was remembering, with a lingering embarrassment, his own delight some years ago in the carnal pleasures Rachel's young body had given him. *Abstain from fleshly lusts, which war against the soul*, it was said in Peter—but he had not abstained. He had been married to Rachel, of course, and didn't Corinthians say, *If thou marry, thou hast not sinned?* It was very confusing.

"Stop demeaning yourself, Abijah," Rachel was saying. "Ryma's downfall was imposed on her by her weakness of character and her surroundings. She inherited neither of them."

"I brought her here," said Abijah bitterly.

Rachel decided it was time to be firm. "I say stop assailing yourself! You brought all of us here. Only Ryma fell." She tempered her voice, lowering it. "Do you think you will ever forgive Ryma?"

She saw his jaw set firmly, and the old righteous anger filled his eyes.

"I cannot forgive her!"

"Christ would forgive," Rachel said softly.

Abijah squared his shoulders and looked Rachel in the eye, his whole being severe and uncompromising.

His voice shook when he spoke.

"Although we are fashioned in the image of our Maker and are disciples of Christ, few of us possess the stature of the Lord or His Son. It is my weakness that I cannot forgive."

8

Tabitha stood at the top of the balustraded staircase leading from the second story of Magnolia Manor to the ground floor. She had just spent almost two hours preparing herself, with the bustling help of Sophie, for the dinner party at which her betrothal to Nicholas Enright would be announcèd, and the excitement of getting dressed for the event still glowed within her. She had been assured a dozen times by an admiring Sophie that she was the most beautiful thing "Ah evah helped git dressed," and Tabitha was not so modest that she failed to appreciate the reason for Sophie's opinion. She *was* pretty—as pretty as any plantation lady she had ever seen or imagined—and her proud knowledge of this fact gave her a poise and dignity beyond her years of her experience. She felt, as Nicholas had already told her, that she could hold her own in any company—dominating the males and earning the jealous glances of the females—and this feeling gave her a confidence that might have been missing had she not been so attractive.

She had selected one of the most delightful dresses in the large wardrobe Nicholas had bestowed upon her, an exquisite gown of white satin, fitting snugly over her rounded breasts and pinched in tightly at the waist. From her hips the dress billowed out in a cascade of frills and flounces, draped in U-shaped folds in the front and with a bustle behind, and as she walked the dress and the crinolines beneath whispered intimately to each other, like gossips exchanging unsavory secrets. She did not personally care for the great bell sleeves, although this was the fashion of the day, but she loved the low decolletage—an artifice which she knew her father, if he could see her, would label the work of the Devil.

Throughout the tedious two hours she had suffered alternate feelings of elation and dismay until at last she had her coiffure and toilette just the way she wanted. Tiny scented sachets had been sewn between the folds of Tabitha's petticoats, and about her as she moved through the room was the delicate fragrance of frangipani—an aroma which managed, in Tabitha's opinion, to be distinctly ladylike while at the same time extending a subtle invitation to indiscretion. To lend a final noticeable sparkle to her appearance, she wore a diamond tiara in her high-piled black hair, and long pendant diamond earrings. A diamond necklace dripped from her throat and lay gently upon the upper swells of her breasts. The diamonds, Tabitha knew, would reflect the candlelight of the rooms in most flattering fashion.

Now she was ready to make her entrance, just as Nicholas had planned it—a grand entrance carefully staged to steal attention from his mother and all the guests. Those guests were already in the huge salon, being served glasses of fine imported Madeira by a black servant in faultless livery. Nicholas had insisted that she time her arrival for the maximum effect, sweeping into the salon just a few minutes after the arrival of the last guest.

"I will be standing near the salon door, my dear," he had told her, "and when you appear I shall immediately take your arm and introduce you. I'm sure you will be the recipient of many admiring glances from the men, but whether the women will display one iota of fondness for you I rather doubt."

Tabitha hesitated at the top of the circular staircase. She could hear the conversation and laughter in the salon — the low voices of the men and the higher-pitched and delighted cooing of the women, intermingling in a discordant cacophony of sound. Tabitha descended and crossed the hall, glancing up at the glowering portrait of Martha Enright on the wall. *Fie on that portrait*, thought Tabitha. *When I am married to Nicholas I shall insist that he take it down.* The painting made Tabitha shudder every time she passed it. It was part of what made Magnolia Manor, beautiful as it was, such an eerie place — a condition that Tabitha also intended to rectify once she had the authority invested in her by marriage to Nicholas. No longer would the inside of this gorgeous manor have a dark and depressing atmosphere. Certain changes were going to be made, enough of them anyway to destroy the feeling of mustiness that had crept into the personality of the house.

Well, that was for the future. Right now she had to make an impression on Nicholas's guests. She paused for a moment before entering the room, examining herself hastily to make sure there was no tiny thing about her that would distract from the overall impression she wished to make. Then, placing her fingertips gently on the door, she swept grandly into the room.

In one fleeting instant Tabitha's trained and eager eyes surveyed everyone in the salon. Nicholas was standing near the door as he had promised, a glass of Madeira in his hand, his attire of fawn-colored trousers and ruffled shirt and great waistcoat all immaculate, looking handsome and haughtily aristocratic. She saw the well-attired women in the room in a quick oblique glance, mentally cataloguing the quality of the competition she would be pitted against. She noted that the men were all handsomely dressed, although not one was the equal of Nicholas. Martha Enright sat like a gray statue in one corner of the room, obviously not enjoying the occasion.

Then Nicholas began the introductions—Faunce and Jane Manley, both slightly uncouth in appearance despite expensive attire, John McRae and his lovely young wife Garland, the d'Ubervilles, the Estabrooks, the Drews. Five couples only—those that Nicholas had described cynically as not the "upper crust but certainly the crust" of Natchez society.

"I would have invited more—the Baileys and the Andovers and the Beauregards and the Swansons and the Vales and an endless number—but these five will do for the present," he had said. "Believe me, once they've seen you, your fame will spread throughout Natchez, for nobody talks better or at greater length than the women I have carefully chosen tonight."

To her surprise, Tabitha felt no nervousness. She handled herself well, with the grace required of a high-bred lady, showing just the proper amount of aloofness to the men and a friendliness to the women that was tempered ever so slightly with hauteur. She must, she thought, hold herself apart and above the others, for even though she was not yet mistress of Magnolia Manor she was nevertheless tonight's hostess and was therefore entitled to the homage paid by those fortunate enough to be invited to dinner at one of Natchez's most fabulous plantation homes.

To Faunce Manley she said, "Nicholas has spoken of you many times," a remark noncommittal enough to encompass almost any interpretation, for Tabitha was slightly dismayed at Nicholas's description of Manley's brutality with his blacks.

"I hope," said Manley in a booming voice, throwing out one arm in a wild gesture, "that what Nicholas has told you of me is complimentary—though I doubt it. He and I disagree on practically everything—from President Andrew Jackson to the lowest nigger in the country. I think we shall have to fight a duel some day to settle our many differences." He turned to Nicholas, gesturing with the hand that held his glass of Madeira, almost spilling it. "What would you prefer, my good man, dueling with pistols or colichemardes?"

"I wouldn't duel with you," said Nicholas easily. "I'm much too accomplished with all weapons, and it would sadden me to blow off your head or cut you into ribbons."

Tabitha shuddered, but Nicholas and Manley simply laughed.

"Just disregard their crude conversation," advised Jane Manley bluntly. "It rarely makes sense." She was a tall, dark, heavy-set woman with little beauty. She looked like a typical farmer's wife and in this respect she fit Faunce Manley perfectly. He was red-faced and decidedly extroverted, a crude dirt farmer in fine clothes — and both he and his wife somehow jarred the civility around them and pulled it down to a lower level.

"I'm not an educated man, which is perhaps why my conversation makes so little sense," said Manley, boisterously belaboring the obvious. "I'm a tobacco farmer, turned to cotton — and I never did fancy the kind of living that's been forced on me by my circumstances."

Jane drew in a sharp breath, disgusted at her husband's uncomplimentary appraisal of his background. "Faunce, I do believe you have already had too much Madeira," she said, affecting dismay that this should be so.

Tabitha passed on to the McRaes then, with Nicholas close at her elbow. John McRae, approaching ninety years of age, was a small, wizened man who nevertheless stood as stiff and straight as a soldier at attention. His crystal blue eyes were alert behind square steel-rimmed spectacles and his voice was as strong as any man's in the room, with the possible exception of the strident Manley. But Tabitha's interest was centered mainly on McRae's wife, Garland, who was only twenty-eight. She was the most stunning beauty among the guests, and a woman who could, Tabitha was sure, be severe competition where men were concerned. She was small and possessed that soft delicate complexion that women of the south, despite the severity of the sun, tried so desperately to retain. Her hair was a golden halo, perfectly arranged, with tiny ringlets at the back of her head. Her eyes were a misty blue and her high cheekbones gave her face a heart-shaped look. Her gown was of expensive French lace, flowing in successive waves to the floor, and Tabitha recognized the subtle scent of frangipani—her own scent, Tabitha thought with a slight twinge of jealousy.

Tabitha's instinctive reaction to Garland was one of vague dislike because of her dazzling beauty and one of awe because of her marital connection. What on earth had induced a passionately beautiful woman of Garland's age to marry a decrepit old heap like John McRae? Tabitha was sure that Garland could have any eligible bachelor on the Hill—including Nicholas, she realized with some consternation. Yet she had settled for John McRae, whose advanced age certainly must have brought her problems not normally the experience of a young wife. As far as Tabitha was concerned, only one thing would tempt a woman into such a strange, uncompanionable marriage—money. McRae had plenty of it, owning a plantation home and acreage almost as large as Nicholas's holdings. Tabitha decided that if she had married him for his money, knowing that after his death all his wealth would be hers, she was a despicable opportunist. But then her own unquenchable ambition to live on the Hill flooded her mind, and the similarity of her aspiration to that which she credited to Garland formed a sudden bond that made her appreciate Garland the more.

"May I say, Miss Clay, that Nicholas's choice of women—as of all things—has always been beyond question?" old McRae said with dashing gallantry.

"Thank you," said Tabitha, "and may I add that your own taste in women, Mr. McRae, borders on the spectacular?"

McRae drew himself up like a bantam cock. But, somewhat to Tabitha's surprise, Garland actually blushed. Tabitha placed a hand on her arm, feeling a new closeness to her. "I do it myself," she said, laughing. "I think it becomes a lady."

"You're very kind, Miss Clay," said Garland with genuine relief.

They passed on to the d'Ubervilles, then the Estabrooks and the Drews. Except for Garland, Tabitha disliked the women. She sensed that they looked down on her, either because they had already heard of her poor beginnings or suspected it. The party became a gossip-laden talk-fest, with all the women chattering at one time about their clothes and their furniture and their homes, while the men tended to gather in a group and discuss the last Presidential election or the coming one, their horses and their "niggers." Tabitha kept an ear tuned to catch every part of every conversation, to register in her mind every nuance of every word, storing all of it carefully in the filing cabinet of her mind for whatever use she might later make of it.

"I'm inclined to think," Faunce Manley was saying, "that old Andy Jackson has already reached the end of his rope. There's some dissatisfaction in Washington about him, you know. He's the frontier type, and he's made very few friends among the truly intelligent and refined people."

"Ah, but among the masses he has!" said Nicholas, who seemed always eager to take the opposite view to Manley's. "Really, Faunce, you fail to see the salient point in all this. Former Presidents have been chosen

254

by a learned and aristocratic class of people—doctors, lawyers and, shall I say, planters? Monied people, if you will. But Old Hickory was elected by the common folk. They loved him because he was one of them, rising from poverty by his own energies and determination. Yes, he's a frontiersman, tough as they come and with the manners of a mule skinner—but the people still love him."

"He and his damned spoils system!" shouted Manley, waving his arms violently and not answering Nicholas's argument directly. "Why, do you know that since the foundation of our government only seventy-four men have ever been removed from office. And do you know that Jackson in his first year in office fired two thousand postmasters, clerks, customs officers, and God knows what, just to put in his own men! A damned outrage, if you ask me!"

"To the victor belong the spoils," said Nicholas easily. "I dare say Andy has set a precedent by transferring this old adage of war to the political arena. But enough of politics. Let's talk about something you are more experienced at controlling than national policies—your blacks."

"Don't," said Manley, "get me on that subject."

Nicholas laughed. "Still using the iron fist?"

"You're baiting me, damn it," said Manley resentfully. "Of course I use the iron fist. One must."

"I take exception," put in d'Uberville, a tall graying man with a heavy paunch and a facade of great dignity. "Niggers are a commodity and one is foolish to mistreat them."

Manley knew he was being chided but he could not resist airing his views on a subject so close to his heart.

"Unless you keep those niggers under the whip," he said, "they will someday rebel. Then you'll have another son of a bitch like Nat Turner on your hands!"

"Ah, yes — Nat Turner," drawled Nicholas. "He did spread a bit of terror around, didn't he?"

The minds of each man in the group raced back to that fatal night in August, 1831, when a slave named Nat Turner led a rebellion in Virginia that resulted in twenty-four hours of murder and a wave of terror among plantation owners such as they had never before experienced. There had been unrest among the slaves for six years and Virginia was seething with conspiracies. Nat Turner and a half-dozen followers were among those most restless. On August 21 the men revolted. Attacking the white homesteads, men, women and children were systematically murdered because they wore a white skin. At each plantation the rebels gained new recruits and additional arms — and almost a hundred black men, crazed with a lust for blood and revenge, stalked the land. Stark terror gripped the plantation owners for two long harrowing days; then, finally, the uprising was quelled and Nat Turner was taken prisoner.

"You talk of Turner," said Manley angrily, "as if he was a hero."

Nicholas smiled. "Perhaps he was, to his own people — and maybe to some thinking whites too. Turner rebelled against the whole idea of slavery and the cruelties that go with it. You can't really blame him, can you?"

"You're a hell of a Southerner!" snapped Manley. "You keep coddling those black bastards and you know what will happen? Someone with a persuasive tongue—like your Old Matt, the preacher—will talk them into a revolt. And when they rebel they'll go back to their African savagery and they'll kill you with pickaxes and clubs and they'll rape your wife and daughters. Mark my word!"

"And then," finished Nicholas, "after it's over we who are left will have our revenge on the blacks. Remember what happened to the blacks after they finally captured Turner and executed him? Slave owners, wanting to destroy any ideas the blacks had of another rebellion, descended on them and killed them indiscriminately. Slaves were tortured with fire, they were maimed, their jaws and legs and arms broken, their hamstrings cut—and then their heads were placed on poles and carried down the streets. What kind of savagery do you call that—African?"

"Oh, hell!" snorted Manley. "You shouldn't be a slave holder, Nicholas. No owner of slaves is supposed to see two sides of a question where slavery is concerned. And you always do. You talk like a God-damned abolitionist!"

"Not at all," smiled Nicholas. "I favor slavery because it is advantageous to me. But I recognize its dangers and I have ideas for reducing its perils."

"By treating the blacks with kindness," grunted Manley.

"Precisely."

"You're a fool."

Tabitha heard all of the conversation even as she listened to the chatter of the women and returned bits of conversation of her own. But the voices of the men were shut out abruptly when Jane Manley, arching her eyebrows just enough to be noticeable, said: "And where *do* you come from, Miss Clay?"

Immediately Nicholas, who had apparently been expecting this question and was waiting for it, appeared at Tabitha's side.

"Miss Clay is the daughter of a preacher who has dedicated his life to working in Natchez-under," he said smoothly. "I dare say not many of us can claim such an illustrious father."

Tabitha breathed her relief. *Thank you, Nicholas,* she said to herself. *Beautifully put.*

Jane Manley's eyes widened as she toyed with clumsy fingers at a pearl necklace.

"How interesting!" Her voice was sugary. "A preacher in Natchez-under must be a most difficult job."

"Most jobs are difficult," said Nicholas breezily. "Even running a plantation. And I suspect that if Tabitha's father preached on the Hill he would encounter considerable resistance from the godless pagans that dwell here."

He smiled graciously, rescuing Tabitha from the circle of prying women, leaving them to glance at each other knowingly as he led her across the room to where his mother sat in somber silence.

"You sit apart from our guests," observed Nicholas.

"You know how I detest these affairs," she said. "People milling about, talking in loud voices, displaying their appalling ignorance. I put up with them only because it is expected of us. . . . Is Tabitha with you?"

"I'm here," said Tabitha. "Is there anything I can do for you?"

Martha's fine lips split in a grim smile. She gestured

with one hand.

"You see, Nicholas? The girl is considerate of me. She is willing to be of service to an old blind woman, at a moment that must be delectable to her. However," her voice changed suddenly, becoming colder, "I have servants, Tabitha, who wait on my every whim. I need not separate you from your newly found friends."

Tabitha frowned. She could never be sure, from what Martha Enright said, whether she was winning the old woman to her side or not. And it was an important part of her plan to know.

They drifted around the room, then, stopping for an idle remark here and there, lifting glasses in impromptu toasts to this or that, smiling and being attentive to the guests' wants. And the conversation droned on, bits of it floating about, getting louder as the Madeira warmed the speakers.

" . . . And that bay of mine would have won, too, if that stupid jockey hadn't let himself get boxed in on the rail!"

"Oh, hell, man! Your bay couldn't win in a race with mules."

"Couldn't it, now! A thousand dollars on the next race says you're wrong."

"A bet, my good man, a bet!"

And from the women: " . . . A preacher from Natchez-under! Nicholas always did have a taste in women that was—shall we say—unorthodox?"

"But she's pretty."

"More's the pity."

At last a servant announced dinner and the guests filed into the huge lavishly appointed dining room with its imperial table of carved mahogany, its punkah now being swung slowly by two tiny pickaninnies at one end of the long room, and its hundreds of wax candles alight in their crystal sconces. In the center of the white-linened table was a sparkling epergne reflecting the candlelight in rainbow colors, its compartments piled with fruit, candy and cookies. From each end of the ornamental dish a trail of magnolias, glistening wax-white under the flames of the candles, extended to the ends of the table. On a side table were the cut-glass decanters of wine and brandy, sparkling like large jewels, and as the guests seated themselves servants dressed in spotless livery poured forth the rich liquids into ornate goblets at each setting. Ranging the length of the table were huge mounds of gelatines, salads, and cold meats. The service was the finest china, imported from England, with sterling silver gleaming on the clinically white tablecloth.

The soups and gumbos came first—and for those who wished, the steaming bouillabaisse seasoned with wine—all carried in bright silver tureens in the hands of proud servants who raced from the busy kitchen, along the flagstone patio, to the dining room. Then the wild game appeared—heavily laden platters of venison, turkey, duck, peacock, and breast of guinea, followed at once by chicken and juicy roasts. There were huge serving platters of every conceivable vegetable—tomatoes, lettuce, beans, peas, squash, okra, asparagus, green corn, and artichokes. After that came the desserts of sponge cake and layer cake, sweet potato pie, brioche, and piping-hot Creole rice cakes called calas—a generous abundance that pernitted each guest to indulge himself as he liked.

Over cafe noir and cafe au lait, Nicholas made the announcement for which Tabitha waited with a mixture of delight and dread. He sat at one end of the long heavily laden table, his mother at the opposite end. He waited until the expressions of admiration for the wonderful dinner and the efficiency of its serving had died down. Tabitha noticed that a slight, on-the-bias smile twisted the corners of his lips as he spoke.

"I have an announcement to make which I believe may interest all of you," he said, with just a trace of smugness. "It was primarily to make this announcement, as a matter of fact, that I invited you here tonight. I trust that the ladies present will see that the news reaches the ears of all others not so invited."

There was a tittering at this small joke, and then silence as the people waited graciously for Nicholas to continue. He paused a short time, adding drama to the situation.

"You have all met Miss Tabitha Clay," he said. "Tonight I take pleasure in announcing that we will be married within a week."

For a few seconds a thick, surprised silence hung over the room. Stunned by the suddenness of the announcement, the guests shifted awkwardly in their chairs. Then, recovering from the initial surprise, a few smiles broke out around the table. Tabitha glanced apprehensively at Martha Enright. The old woman's face was an impenetrable mask. She stared straight down the table at her son, a deep-seated fury in her sightless eyes.

Faunce Manley, who was always the first to recover his composure as well as to lose it, leaped to his feet

261

like a jack-in-the-box, holding his brandy glass above his head.

"I propose a toast to the fortunate husband-to-be and the most lovely girl he has chosen for a wife," he thundered in belabored tones. There was a spontaneous murmur of agreement and glasses were raised. Old John McRae, his rheumy eyes glistening wickedly, said, "I heartily recommend marriage, as my own dear wife will attest. And if I can make a success of it at my age, you can do better!"

The brandies were sipped slowly. Tabitha's eyes scanned the table. Martha Enright had not lifted her glass. When the glasses were again lowered, the old woman rose slowly to her feet, standing erect at the end of the table, looking with unseeing eyes toward her son. Tabitha shuddered inwardly as she viewed the lean hawk-like face, the cruel lines in it, the straight hair combed rigidly back, the severe mouth a grim lipless gash across her face. *She's a witch,* Tabitha thought, *a witch, a witch!*

Nicholas glared at his mother, his jaw set grimly, his eyes sharp and alert. Like two fighters facing each other across an open space, they seemed all at once oblivious to the others at the table.

The silence grew to embarrassing length. Someone clicked a glass nervously. Another coughed to break the heavy silence. The servants stood motionless, hardly daring to breathe. The only thing that moved was the punkah overhead, swinging back and forth in respectful muteness, stirring the air languidly.

"Well, mother?" Nicholas's voice was like the ring of a loud bell in the silence of a church. The words seemed to bring Martha Enright back to con-

262

sciousness, as if they had plucked her from some far away place and returned her to the reality of earthly existence.

"I offer my congratulations to you, my son," she said, her voice sepulchral. She turned her head slightly, as if trying to pick out Tabitha among the guests. "And to you, my dear, my profound condolences—*for you know not what you face!*"

She walked stiffly from the room, her hand stretched before her, leaving the chill words hanging in the air like sharp icicles. Nicholas's face was clouded, but he said nothing. Tabitha closed her eyes, not wanting to see the embarrassed guests, not wanting to face inquiring glances, perhaps even secret amusement among the women. And she thought, *The witch, the damned witch! I will get even with her for this embarrassment. I'll reduce her to nothing, Nicholas and I will. I swear it, I'll get even if it takes my last breath!*

"Shall we retire to the salon?" came Nicholas's suave voice.

There was a grateful shuffling of chairs as the guests hastily rose. Tabitha opened her eyes and stood up. Nicholas was behind her, helping her with the chair, leaning close over one shoulder. His voice came, whispering.

"I should give you considerably more than the traditional penny for your thoughts, my dear. They must be murderous."

She glanced at him sharply, annoyed that he could so easily read her mind.

"And your thoughts, what are they?" she demanded.

"Nakedly murderous."

The guests congregated again in the lavish salon and the conversation, hesitant at first, gradually resumed. No one approached either Nicholas or Tabitha with direct congratulations, apparently feeling that Faunce Manley's toast had been sufficient. There was a calculated effort on the part of the guests to keep the conversation on noncontroversial subjects, and at length Garland won approval of all with a suggestion.

"Nicholas, why don't you play the piano for us? You do it so extremely well."

Nicholas made polite objections, but as the other guests insisted he made no effort to deny them. The crowd crossed into the music room and Nicholas sat down at the intricately carved spinet and touched the keys almost lovingly with the tips of his fine fingers. The guests took chairs, waiting for him to begin, all of them knowing he was an accomplished pianist, wanting to hear him. But Tabitha was slightly apprehensive about what he might do. His eyes were bright with a mischievous sparkle, and a smile played coyly along the lines of his mouth. He turned slightly to face his audience.

"In honor of my bride-to-be," he said gallantly, "I shall play Johann Sebastian Bach's *Festival Prelude,* a classic composition which, as you know, has been played with proper tenderness at numerous weddings and therefore seems appropriate to the announcement I made—and which my mother so scurrilously attacked—at dinner."

The guests sat in discomfited silence; fearful of saying the wrong thing, they said nothing. They watched

264

as Nicholas looked down at the keyboard, placing his fingers again on the keys. Then, with crashing suddenness, his fingers pressed down on the first chord of the number he was to play, and the room rang with loud, irreverent notes more suitable to a military march than a wedding composition. He played it through, raucously, thunderingly, profaning it with a belligerent power Tabitha had never before heard given to the work. It was as if he wanted to make sure that his mother, in the quiet of her room, heard it, for he jarred the keys, driving the music from the spinet by main force, reaching a loud bombastic crescendo at the end.

Tabitha saw shock registered on the faces of the guests, amazement that he should play the wedding classic so impiously. When he had finished he turned slowly from the spinet, looking at his guests arrogantly, daring them to comment on the perverted manner in which he had portrayed the hallowed number. No one spoke, but there was a polite pattering of hands.

"I suggest, now, that we all get drunk," Nicholas said.

There were a few soft laughs from those persons preferring to take this last irreverent remark as a joke. Then the group returned to the salon where attentive servants plied the men with brandy and the women with anisette.

Within an hour it became evident that the suggestion was at least being taken seriously by Nicholas himself. He was tossing down brandy with such rapidity that Tabitha would have been annoyed if it were not for the fact that she was desperately trying to keep up with him. The dinner party had not turned out as she had hoped. The announcement of her betrothal to Nicholas should have been a high point of the evening; instead, Martha Enright had turned it into a humiliating and degrading experience. Then, Nicholas's bad taste in desecrating the beloved *Festival Prelude* in such foul manner as to cause it to lose its beauty and meaning, had been inexcusable. Maybe getting drunk was the proper solution to her embarrassments. Maybe she could forget the evening then, forget the shambles it had become, forget that word of this horrible event would spread like wildfire into every plantation for miles around, forget that the rest of Natchez society would secretly revel in her discomfort. She could hear the tongues wagging now. A girl from Natchez-under-the-Hill! What kind of cheap slut had Nicholas chosen, anyway? She *seemed* nice enough, even had a certain amount of poise—but heavens, you would think Nicholas Enright might have had better sense! He certainly won't help his social standing any, but then she's beautiful and I suppose she turned poor Nicholas's head. There's no telling to what low and degrading tactics she may have stooped to get him. After all, men are all the same, you know—and *that* kind of woman would be the first to know it!

Tabitha had never been drunk before. She had rarely even tasted liquor, with the exception of whiskey which her father kept for "medicinal purposes" only. But she had decided to become stupidly drunk now—and to hell with what anybody thought. She switched from anisette to brandy, because there was more fire in the latter. She downed a glass sharply, half-choked, and reached for another. The servant with the tray opened his round eyes wide, but he said nothing. Tabitha smiled and held the glass over her head. Yes, to hell with them! Let the old bitches talk! They were jealous, that's what they were, plain jealous. She had Nicholas Enright, the most eligible and desired bachelor on the Hill, and it was simply more than they could stand. She was going to be the grandest lady of them all, the mistress of Magnolia Manor, and she would have them crawling before her some day. So let them prattle their empty gossip. Every last one of them would come back on their knees, with their wagging tongues stilled, before she was through with them! She knew it—and what was most intolerable to them, *they* knew it!

After several stiff brandies the room became fuzzy to Tabitha. She staggered a little, spilling brandy down the front of her dress. She wiped it off hazily with her hand and reached for another brandy on a passing tray, wondering why the room insisted on whirling around instead of standing still. Nicholas had become more garrulous, more freed of his natural aloofness. The rest of the guests, following the lead of Nicholas and Tabitha—it would have been improper not to!—began drinking heavily too, and the bird-like chatter of the females became more shrill and laughter-filled, and the political arguments of the men more intense and less accurate.

Once Nicholas got Tabitha to one side. His face split in the broadest smile Tabitha had ever seen him manage.

"They hate us, don't they?" His voice reflected pleasure at the thought. "They hate me for marrying outside their exclusive circle, and they hate you for

267

winning me. They'll try to ruin us, but we won't let them, will we? You and I won't let them!"

His eyes looked wild, like an animal's. His words made only a vague impression on Tabitha, for her thinking was becoming fuzzier by the minute. All she said was. "You and me, Nicholas — together!" and squeezed his arm with fierce affection.

Suddenly a wooly-headed servant approached and bowed slightly before Nicholas. Tabitha gazed at the Negro and the ridiculous thought went through her head, *I wonder what it would be like to be black and always bowing to your betters?* She did not try to answer her own question. There seemed to be no answers left in her head. Her turbulent mind was like a rapidly rotating wheel, where thoughts bombarding it were discarded and thrown violently to one side, unable to reach the center where she could consider and weigh them.

"Ah begs you pahdon, Massa," said the servant contritely, "but there is a man at the door insists on seein' you."

Nicholas was obviously nettled. "Tell the fool I'm busy!"

"Ah did, suh. But he is very insistent, suh. He says he's a preachah, come on God's own business."

Tabitha's violet eyes widened. A clear thought had finally pierced the revolving defense of her brain. She looked warily at Nicholas.

"Do you suppose," said Nicholas with a little thickness in his speech, "that it could be your father, so anxious to sanctify our marriage that he came tonight instead of waiting until our visit tomorrow?"

Tabitha felt panic tug at her. She cast her eyes at

the revelry in the room. The guests had drinks poised in hand, several men weaved unsteadily on their feet. Even in her befuddled state she recognized impending disaster.

"Oh, God!" she said. "Let's talk to him in the hall."

But they were too late. Abijah Clay's lean gaunt frame suddenly loomed in the doorway. He had followed the servant in. He stood now like a rigid statue, immovable on the pedestal of his feet. His face was fixed in uncompromising lines, and his zealous eyes scanned the guests critically.

Tabitha thought, *God forbid! He will notice everything! Liquor clutched in the hands of both men and women. Drunken merriment. Loud profane voices. The women in revealing dresses that made an erotic attraction of their bosoms.* She thought of her own low-cut gown, and the enchanting odor of frangipani that clung to her.

"Father!"

She went to him slowly, walking carefully, feeling light and unsteady on her feet, praying, imploring the good Lord that he would not notice she was slightly drunk. He turned his gaze slowly toward her, and his lined face softened briefly.

"Tabitha. It is so nice to see you again."

Nicholas moved forward, dragging his one leg, unsteady too because of the liquor in him. He was smiling, a lopsided smile, cynical, brandy-inspired.

"I fear you made an unnecessary journey," he said heavily. "We would have gladly come to you on the morrow."

"It is perhaps good that I came here," Abijah said. His voice was cold. His keen eyes swept Nicholas from

269

top to toe, missing nothing. They flicked with some repugnance to the brown stain on Nicholas's ruffled shirt-front, made by brandy spilled from an unsteady hand. Then they swept to Tabitha and the similar stain on her dress. He drew himself up, looking over their heads into the salon.

"My dear wife and I received your letter," he said in his clarion voice, and all conversation in the room stopped and eyes became fixed on the spare fleshless figure of this man of God who looked over them and past them as if they did not exist. "I came to give you the hand of my daughter in marriage."

It was as if he had memorized this speech in advance and felt compelled to say it, even as he gazed with concern at the scene before him and even as sudden new doubts invaded his mind.

Guest looked at guest as his voice filled the room. Puzzlement distorted faces. Only Nicholas seemed unmoved by the embarrassing situation. He took Abijah's gnarled hand in his own and shook it warmly.

"I thank you, sir. I'm sure Tabitha—raised as she was in a house of the Lord—is too good for me."

Tabitha almost gagged. Leave it to Nicholas to say the right thing, she thought, even though he didn't believe an iota of it. *House of the Lord . . . too good for me!* What hideous hypocrisy!

"I must say I look with disfavor on this—this Bacchanalian revelry," said Abijah bluntly.

"I apologize," said Nicholas, bowing at the waist. "Perhaps a few of my guests have become more exuberant than is good for them. I must explain to you that you came at a time that is not—shall we say—typical."

Abijah's eyes swept him. He was obviously trying to evaluate the sincerity—or lack of it—in Nicholas's explanation. Before he could reply, however, Nicholas bowed again.

"If I may be so bold," he was saying, "may I offer to you, sir, a bit of brandy—this being a special occasion."

Abijah shook his head. "I do not indulge in drink," he said with proper scorn. "It is the nectar of the Devil." His eyes moved to Tabitha again and she realized to her consternation that she still held a half-filled glass of brandy in her hand.

"Then a lemonade, perhaps," insisted Nicholas, and Tabitha received the distinct impression that he was deriving pleasure from her father's stiff refusal.

"Thank you, no." Abijah's voice was lower now, but not enough lower to escape the eager ears of the guests, some of whom drifted closer. "I have but one request to make of you, sir. The marriage of my daughter to you will, of course, change her way of life. Most of that change, I am sure, will be for the better—despite what I see here now. Yet I know, too, that there is much of crass materialism in the planters' way of life. I ask only that this hedonism not be allowed to impinge on Tabitha's spiritual beliefs. She is devout and believing, and I desire that she continue to stand tall in the eyes of God."

Nicholas nodded respectfully. Tabitha felt there was something of mockery in the motion.

"This is, of course, understood," he said reassuringly. "Life at Magnolia Manor will not be without its spiritual values."

"Very well. Then I shall take my leave." Abijah's

tone was abrupt, as if he had suddenly and with some relief decided he must depart this place of liquor and dressy women and undue merriment. He turned quickly on his heel, like a well-trained soldier, and strode from the house. Tabitha watched him go with a sinking in her heart. When he had left, she turned to Nicholas.

"I hope," she said in a soft voice that did not carry, "that father was not too disturbed by my new way of life."

"I'm sure he's already inured to it," smiled Nicholas. "He's seen so much of the same sort of thing in Natchez-under, you know."

He laughed lightly at his own joke, and a sense of revulsion surged through Tabitha. She was certain that Nicholas had actually enjoyed her father's discomfort.

9

Nicholas and Tabitha were married on July 1, 1833 in the huge glittering salon of Magnolia Manor. It was a quiet, almost secretive marriage. Nicholas had decreed—somewhat imperiously, Tabitha thought—that there would be no guests. "I should dislike to befoul the tenderness of the moment with people I detest," was his way of putting it.

Only Tabitha's mother and father were there, along with Martha Enright and Jed Vale, the overseer, who acted as a witness. A dour Presbyterian minister from Natchez performed the ceremony in an atmosphere that was more grim than cheerful. Abijah Clay stood stern-faced and rigid, as if attending a funeral rather than a wedding. Rachel was carefully formal, making an obvious effort to be precise in every move she made, for she was unaccustomed to the rich surroundings in which she found herself. Martha Enright stood to one side, gazing at the young people before the giant fireplace just as if she could see them, with no expression on her sphinx-like face to belie her feelings. Even as Tabitha repeated the familiar marriage vows, she thought that Martha Enright looked more like the solemn and uncompromising portrait in the hallway than at any other time.

The joyless formality of the wedding persisted through a bleak reception, which consisted of a sumptuous meal and at which Nicholas had graciously decided not to serve liquor. Conversation was embarrassingly limited.

Now it was over and Tabitha lay serenely in a big four-poster bed with a magnificent canopied top and gauze-like drapes in the master bedroom of Magnolia Manor, waiting for Nicholas to come to her. Her tortured mind was troubled with anxiety. Because of his two abrupt dismissals of her during moments of passion, she was not at all certain she could please him. Carefully she ran her hands down her body as if to verify that she was sufficiently endowed with the necessary physical charms, and the feel of her own warmth and softness reassured her. Her lingering doubts would have been less cogent, Tabitha thought, had it not been for a troublesome conversation she had endured with Martha Enright just two days before the wedding.

Nicholas had gone to the stables to inspect his horses and Tabitha stood idly on the gallery of the house, surveying the terraced gardens with their wealth of color. Suddenly she was aware of a movement behind her and turned to see Martha Enright in the doorway.

"I would speak with you, Tabitha."

"Yes." Tabitha was startled. It was uncanny the way this blind woman seemed to know the exact whereabouts of everyone in the house. There was an accusative tone in Martha's voice as she spoke, her words clipped and barbed.

"I do not know what methods you employed to win

my son," she said. "But apparently you have him befuddled enough to desire marriage to you—not an uncommon thing with Nicholas, incidentally. I will make it quite clear at the outset, so there will be no mistaking my feelings, that I believe he is making a mistake by a marriage that is beneath his station in life."

"But, Mrs Enright—"

"Do not interrupt!" Her tone was sharp, brutal. "His announcement of his intention to marry you shocked everyone at the dinner. The news will spread like wildfire throughout the planter families—indeed, already has. I need not remind you that for a man of Nicholas's caliber to select a woman of lower station in life is considered quite scandalous. When a planter like my son—and the name Enright is an important one in Natchez—selects a woman from the mudflats along the river, he brings to this house a sense of—well, I might as well say it—shame."

Tabitha felt outrage surge through her at the bluntness of Martha Enright's remarks. She wanted to strike back, viciously, to tell this hateful old woman what she really thought of her and Magnolia Manor and all the planters she had already met, but she refrained. She said to herself: *I must not anger her. I must not. I must wait for my revenge. First, marry Nicholas at all costs. Then assume control of Magnolia Manor, slowly, by gentle degrees. Yes, that was the best way, the only way.* She looked steadily at Martha, and now a smile, almost of victory, touched the old woman's lips.

"I think you should know that you are overlooking one important facet in this mismarriage," she said stonily. "It will never result in an heir."

Tabitha stared at her. "What do you mean?"

"I mean that Nicholas can never father a child by you—which, in the final analysis, I suppose is a victory for our kind of people."

"I still don't understand," said Tabitha, but she shivered inwardly with a new apprehension, wondering what ominous horror Martha Enright's words portended.

"Then I shall put it to your little-girl mind plainly," said the old woman, a nasty metallic ring to her voice. "Nicholas will never sire a child *because he is impotent!*"

She had walked away, then, a smug smile twisting her cruel mouth, leaving Tabitha standing on the gallery, stunned and unbelieving.

For some moments Tabitha could not absorb the full impact of Martha Enright's words. Nicholas impotent? It seemed incredible. Yet the two occasions when he started to make love to her and had withdrawn seemed to fortify Martha Enright's contentions. Desperately she tried to analyze Nicholas's actions. Certainly he had been aroused on both occasions to a point of passion, but had abruptly put her aside. Why? Could that be impotency? Or was it because he respected her and had fought to control himself before the passion became so unbearable that there was no opportunity to control it. That, she thought, was a logical explanation. It was what she preferred to believe, what she *had* to believe.

Despite Tabitha's stubborn effort to believe only the best, a nagging doubt clawed at her mind for the next two days. Worried and distraught, she finally decided that there was no immediate answer to the question. The answer would emerge in only one way—on the wedding bed.

Now the moment had come. She lay still on the marriage bed, feeling the softness beneath her, aware of her warmth and physical attributes, and she thought with a sudden wildness, *This is the test. Tonight I will prove that there is nothing wrong with Nicholas that I can't repair. I will delight him on this very bed, within the next few minutes. He will surrender to the love I can give him, and I will prove that Martha Enright is nothing more than a meddlesome and vicious old bitch spouting lies!*

Nicholas strode into the room, then, dressed in a silk maroon robe tied around the waist with a sash, tall and proud and with that almost intolerable air of arrogance that made one forget the awkwardness of his gait. He came directly to the side of the bed, looking down at her with a curious smile twisting the corners of his mouth, the half-smile that never seemed to complete itself.

"Mistress of Magnolia Manor," he mused. "You have reached your coveted goal, haven't you?"

Tabitha assumed a childlike pout. "You always make it sound so materialistic," she complained mildly.

He shrugged, sitting down on the edge of the bed. The smile remained fixed.

"I thought we understood each other. You wanted to become mistress of Magnolia Manor, I wanted you as a counterbalance to my mother. We both received what we wanted today—is it not so?"

She looked away, turning her head on the pillow. Her eyes thinned.

"I suppose you're right," she admitted, not wanting

to face the facts but driven by his bold honesty to do so. "But since we are man and wife, Nicholas—no matter how predatory our thinking was prior to our marriage today—we should love each other now. We simply must."

"Why?" Cold cynicism coated the word.

"Because love is a part of marriage."

"God's blood, but you *are* stubborn, aren't you?" Nicholas bounced to his feet, putting his hands on his hips and looking down at her as one looks at a child in a cradle. "Didn't I make it quite clear to you once before that there is no such thing as love—that love is the fictional creation of romanticists?"

"I don't believe it," said Tabitha.

"You will in time. Tonight you are flushed, my dear, with a heady sense of accomplishment. You may even think, at this lofty moment, that you're in love with me. But you're not. You're more in love with being the new mistress of Magnolia Manor than being the new bride of Nicholas Enright. Come now, admit it."

"I won't admit it! I'm sure we will both learn to love each other, if we don't now."

His face hardened and his piercing eyes had the strange haunted look that had so often puzzled Tabitha.

"It is not so much love that is needed," he said somberly, "as mutual protection."

"I simply don't understand you, Nicholas."

"No, I presume you don't." Nicholas sat down on the edge of the bed again, patting her hand as if soothing a small child. "What I am trying to say is that we need to protect each other from the forces

278

that work against us."

"Forces?" Tabitha kept studying his intense eyes.

"Yes, my dear—forces. The forces of this society have always worked against me. They will work against you too. Now that we're married they will work for our destruction. They do not want a northerner to be the greatest planter in Natchez country. They do not want a girl from Natchez-under-the-Hill to be the grandest lady. Oh, they'll work against us, my dear, and we must be alert to defeat them. Just as we must be alert to defeat Mother."

Tabitha stared at him, mystified. Was he talking about the planter families? Were they the forces he spoke about? His serious demeanor, the almost fanatical glow in his eyes, told Tabitha that his thoughts went far deeper than the fear of social competition from Natchez's snobbish society. His mind seemed to be linked to something far more threatening.

"What in heaven's name are you talking about?" was all she could say.

"You shall know in time," said Nicholas enigmatically. Then, quite suddenly, the haunted expression fled from his eyes and his face brightened. "And now, my dear, since you are fired with the thought of our loving each other, perhaps this would be a good time to begin?"

Tabitha felt welcome relief. At last. The moment she had dreaded for two days was now at hand, and she was determined to make a success of it. She would make this arrogant man who did not believe in love succumb to her wiles, even if she had to act like a Natchez-under-the-Hill whore!

But despite her erotic imaginings she played the role of innocent virgin until the last moment, looking up at him with deep violet eyes that expressed absolute purity.

"Yes," she said, with a proper pause. "It is time, Nicholas."

He departed briefly from the bedside, snuffing out the candles in the room until the light fled and darkness crowded in on them. Through the partially opened window the moon invaded, cutting a swath across the floor, leaping like an acrobat across the foot of the bed, and running up the wall as if it were frightened. Tabitha watched Nicholas move slowly toward the big four-poster bed, and suddenly he was next to her, his hands on her bare shoulders, gently pinning her down.

"Tabitha," he said softly, "I must admit it is hard to believe you're my wife."

"Is it?"

"Damned hard. When a man's been a bachelor for as long as I, how can he believe that a few words spoken over a little book can make him married?"

"I occupy your bed tonight," said Tabitha. "That ought to be proof."

He laughed shortly, rearing back his head. "That is no proof at all, my dear, as any woman raised in Natchez-under-the-Hill ought to know. But I doubt that it's wise to bring up such a subject on our wedding night." He was silent for a time, sprawled ungracefully next to her, one leg thrown casually across her body so that its weight was a heaviness that somehow imparted to her a strength and confidence in her own powers that she needed and desired. He kept studying her face, tilting his head as a bird regards a newly found worm, smiling ever so slightly, quietly pleased but not wanting too much to show it. "You know, Tabitha," he said at length, "you're so damned beautiful a man ought to love you. He really ought to."

She looked at him archly. "Even if he doesn't believe in love?" she asked.

He did not answer. He seemed weary of argument now. He lowered his head and his lips sought hers. The kiss was soft and sweet, with a tenderness that surprised and pleased Tabitha, but in gradual stages it became more passionate as he twisted his mouth over hers, forcing her lips apart until he felt the even white teeth and the tip of her tongue on his questing lips. With his lips still clinging to hers he vaulted over her, like some huge panting animal, placing the full weight of his rock-hard body on her. His heavy hand went to her breast, squeezing it almost painfully, and his body began to move rhythmically against hers, applying warm and intimate pressure, relieving it, applying it again.

Tabitha clung to him in a wild unreasoning desperation. She arched her body against him as she imagined a whore would do, letting him know that he had access to any part of her body he desired. She would show him that she was not a reluctant unknowledgeable, inept virgin female, but a warm, passionate, even wanton woman capable of seducing him if *he* showed indecision.

With shameless abandon she kept moving her body seductively against his, inviting his entry. Yes, she would make him love her. First she would make him love her body. There was time later for him to love her as a person, for this would come if he found her body so enticing that he could not endure being away from her.

Nicholas let his lips slide from her eager mouth down her throat to the cleavage between her full breasts. His breath came quickly, with violence, and through it he said, "You're a lascivious little whore, a hot-blooded wench who can drive a man crazy!" And she was not insulted by his remarks but thought, *Yes, that's what I am. That's what I'll be. And he will love me. He will love me.*

And then she closed her eyes, prepared now to endure whatever would follow. His exploring hand, searching, caught the hem of her gown and ripped it savagely the full length of her. She lay naked now beneath his questing body, this great muscular body that now slaved and panted with a lustful yearning the likes of which Tabitha had never before experienced or even conceived. *So Nicholas was impotent? Fie on Martha Enright!*

Nicholas trembled from head to foot as he spread Tabitha's legs, forcing himself against her, seeking an inlet for his passion—just as he had trembled before on the veranda and again on the wooded path near Magnolia Manor. Only this time he was trying to enter her, and there would be no stopping him. Tabitha pulled him closer, helping him to attain his goal. Then, with a suddenness impossible to believe, he changed. A violent shudder passed through him and he pushed himself upright, away from her, fighting off the surging impulse to take her. He was kneeling on the bed now, his nakedness and limpness exposed to her, his face twisted into a sort of helpless agony.

When he realized that she was looking at him in dismay, anger flooded his face. Without warning, he brutally slapped her across the face with the back of his hand. The blow, stinging, rocked her head to one side and fright leaped into Tabitha's eyes. But before she could get away from him he struck her again, this time with the palm of his hand across the opposite cheek.

"Nicholas!" she gasped. "For God's sake—"

Paralyzed with fear, Tabitha tried to struggle from the bed, but Nicholas's strong hands pulled her down, his fingernails digging into her white shoulders so savagely that they drew blood.

"Stay still, Goddamnit!" he said huskily.

She fell back on the bed, looking up at him now with terror-stricken eyes. The anger that had contorted his face was slowly dissipating to be replaced by a lopsided smile that lurked dangerously at the corners of his mouth. His eyes held the same sparkle, the same madness, that had filled them when he had kissed her on the veranda and in the woods.

And the impossible thought tore at Tabitha's brain, *He is enjoying this! He is beating me and he is thrilling to it! Like a man thrills to sexual excitement, Nicholas is being moved to ecstasy by this violent and senseless cruelty!*

And then she found him pulling her bodily from the bed, hauling her to her feet alongside the bed where he held her for a long moment by the shoulders. She tired to struggle free of him, but his hands were like the jaws of a vise on her frail body and she could not move. Then, in one quick movement, his free arm came around in a slashing circle, his hand exploding against her cheek with a bright pain, and Tabitha reeled dizzily across the room, crashing against an ornate escritoire and sending an inkstand and a whale-oil lamp to the floor. Then the blackness moved in, like a great shroud before her eyes, and before she slipped into unconsciousness she heard the unbelievable words come from Nicholas's lips.

"Now, Goddamnit, you know what you've married!"

BOOK III
The Hovering Shadow

1

American slavery had its beginning in the 1660s. It was born in Virginia, where slavery was first legally sanctioned, and it spread like a creeping black disease across the land. Huge broad-shouldered Negroes poured into the country from the West Indies, and later from Africa, and the newly founded "slavocracy" became a hovering shadow over the South. By 1775 slaves comprised two-thirds of the population of the five Southern colonies. By 1830 there were millions of blacks working in the fields, and some 200,000 free Negroes.

The slaves performed a variety of tasks. Mainly they labored in the sun-drenched fields to raise tobacco and rice and sugar, long before cotton became the big cash crop of the South. They were big and heavy with muscle, and they were used for the most menial and back-breaking work; they built roads and worked the mines and cleared the forests and built the houses and cultivated the crops so that America could know expansion. Yet, for the amount of arduous labor they put forth, the slave realized little of the wealth he produced. He was fed and clothed and sheltered by his white masters, but little else. And as in all feudal societies, he was sometimes treated well and sometimes not, depending on the whim of his master.

But the Negro brought to America certain inbred talents that the white man eventually recognized, and in time the whites saw the importance of evaluating their "niggers" and putting them to work where they were most adept. Thus it was that the blacks began to live in the South on three distinct levels.

First came the privileged house servants. For such domestic chores the dominant whites selected the most intelligent Negroes and those thought to be most amenable to civilized living. They were well provided for and enjoyed certain privileges. The men acted as servants or footmen at the big palatial homes. Some drove the fine carriages of their masters. The women raised the white man's children, cooked and washed for him, and kept his house immaculate.

Next came the artisans. Perhaps this group contributed as much to the development of the South as any other, for they were men and women skilled with their hands. There was continuous need on a plantation for carpenters and blacksmiths, and many slaves worked at these tasks. Others were excellent shoemakers, musicians, weavers, barbers, bricklayers, cabinetmakers, caulkers, coopers, cordwainers, distillers, locksmiths, goldsmiths, painters, pipemakers, upholsterers, and tanners. Often Negro hands made the bricks from which the white man's mansion was constructed, and blacksmiths hammered out the intricately wrought iron balustrades and railings. And among the women were skilled seamstresses, dyers, and soapmakers.

But on the lash-scarred backs of the fieldhands depended the real fate of the South. These numbered in the millions and toiled in the fields from sunup to sundown. They were the "lowest order" of Negro, and out of their suffering a prosperous South emerged. From their tedious hours of toil came the cotton that made the white planters rich and the mills of New England and Europe hum with a new and feverish excitement.

The ambition of every slave, of course, was to someday be free, and this single desire created a gulf, a chasm, between the black workers and their white masters. It was a difficult chasm for either the slave or the slave owner to bridge. The cotton barons were reluctant to free too many slaves, for this act would erode the society they had built and cotton production would suffer. On the other hand, offering the slave no hope of eventual freedom created a frightening problem — the possibility of rebellion.

Most slave owners lived in constant fear that the blacks might someday throw off their shackles in a savage uprising. This concern was justified, for the South lived in smoldering ferment. Throughout the slave years the blacks asserted themselves in devious — and sometimes open — ways. They ran away, they employed sabotage, they engaged in work stoppages and slowdowns. Some committed suicide or mutilated themselves to avoid hard work. They struck directly at their masters with arson, and sometimes stealthy murder. Unrest was a continuing phenomenon, and in the more than two centuries that slavery existed in America, two hundred known revolts and conspiracies occurred.

The white planters, for all the grandeur of their mode of life, wore uneasy crowns. To counteract unrest among the blacks, armed men patrolled the roads at night, and state legislatures passed restrictive laws that gradually reduced the Negro to something less than a human being. On almost every plantation there were recurring crises, and many a slave owner sat up all night with a rifle across his knees. Magnolia-skinned plantation ladies had nightmares in which they were being raped by muscular, sweating blacks—and rushed in the middle of the night to the dining room to take a sip of anisette to calm their jangled nerves.

Such was the hovering shadow.

2

The cotton had ripened. The tiny walnut-sized bolls—which in spring had been delicate white flowers, turning yellow and blue as the season advanced, until the blossoms dropped and the squares formed—had burst open like the gates of miniature prisons, and the snowy white fiber had escaped its rigid confinement.

Tabitha stood upon the wide upper gallery of Magnolia Manor, gazing pensively at the whitened fields. The sight reminded her dimly of a childhood winter spent in New England, where her father's travels had taken them, when the snows came and covered the soft earth with a thick blanket of scintillating white. So, too, were the fields of Magnolia Manor covered, except that here the white snowballs would be picked by gnarled black hands, and this valuable snow-like substance would be dumped into great bags and loaded on carts and drays and taken to the gin where the fiber would be separated from the seeds by a machine invented only a few decades ago—in 1793—by a man named Eli Whitney. And from there the precious white gold would be packed in bales and shipped to the hungry mills of the eastern United States, Europe, and even faraway Japan.

Tabitha watched the slaves now, moving slowly over the fields, their colorful kerchiefs on their heads, their hands plucking the bolls like hungry blackbirds, an inexorable army of dusky humans who would denude the fields of their gentle whiteness. And with the slaves in the field was the inevitable overseer, Jed Vale, on horseback, a whip in his hand and a broad-brimmed hat on his head, watching for any laggards among them, encouraging them to pick more, pick more, pick more—for the plantation must prosper if the slaves, or the master, were to survive.

It had been a week since Tabitha's cruel experience on her wedding night. Her face no longer bore the marks Nicholas had left there, and Tabitha had been thankful that Martha Enright's blindness had prevented her from seeing them. Now another worry occupied her mind. She had not seen Nicholas since her wedding night. He had left Magnolia Manor before morning, without announcing his intentions or his destination. Confused and frightened, Tabitha had finally forced herself to approach Martha Enright for help. The old woman was stiff-faced and unyielding.

"Where did he go?" Tabitha demanded. "If you know, tell me."

"I do not know where he went," Martha said coldly. "He left during the night. I advise you not to concern yourself too closely with Nicholas's movements."

"But I'm his wife!" Tabitha answered, eager to impress this point on Martha Enright. "At least he can let me know where he goes."

"You will learn, young lady, that Nicholas will tell you only what he wishes you to know," Martha said.

Then a crafty smile cut her face. "I suspect, my dear, that you and Nicholas had a, shall we say, difficult time last night?"

"I hardly think—" Tabitha began, blood rushing to her face, thankful that Martha Enright could not see her embarrassment.

"Did Nicholas enjoy whatever it was he did to you?" Martha cut in gratingly.

"I refuse to dwell on such matters," Tabitha said.

"Well, I told you he was impotent. Now you know. He has all the natural urges of a man, but he cannot complete the act to which he aspires. His only satisfaction, then, lies in showing his male dominance over a woman in another way—by physically punishing her for his failure."

Tabitha stared at the witch-like face in heartsick disbelief. Martha Enright knew what had happened, or at least had made a shrewd guess! Her mind spun back to her night of terror. After painfully crawling back to her bed, she had lain awake all night alone, for Nicholas had rushed from the room and had not returned. What he had done to her made no sense, and although the frightening thought that Nicholas had obtained satisfaction by beating her had entered her mind, she had dismissed it as too utterly perverse to believe. But Martha knew, and she was saying it in words—plain shocking words that tumbled from her evil lips with almost a lilt of victory that sickened Tabitha further. And what was worse, she knew now that Martha had been correct in her appraisal of her son. She recalled the gleam in his eyes as he had beaten her savagely with his hands. She could still feel the cruel sting of his blows, and she felt relieved that she had emerged from the horrifying experience without permanent injury.

What would years of marriage to Nicholas under such perverse circumstances do to her? The feeling of revulsion that swept her was tinged with a strong sense of having been badly cheated. Through handsome and godlike Nicholas Enright she had realized her ambition to live on the Hill, and now this insane and wicked thing had come along at the moment of achievement to loom as an obstacle in her path. It was something she had not counted on. It was true, she *was* technically mistress of Magnolia Manor now, with all the power and distinction this gave her. But for how long she could continue in this capacity and endure the depraved viciousness of her new husband she did not know.

"I tried to save you from this," Martha was reminding her, not without some pleasure. "I told you about his troubles, as I have told others. Why do you think Nicholas never married before? Because no woman would have him after I told them of his sickness. You ignored the warning."

Tabitha frowned. It was impossible to say whether Martha Enright's actions in warning women away from her son had been altruistic or grossly selfish. But knowing Martha's delight in her own powers, Tabitha was inclined to suspect the latter. The suspicion upset her and she responded with anger.

"You're a mean and despicable old lady!" Tabitha shouted, losing all control of herself. "All your life you've been jealous of your son, wanting to keep other women away from him. You even allowed a broken knee to go unhealed to cripple him and make him

293

unattractive to women and—"

"He told you that old bromide?" cut in Martha sharply. "He's a fool! I never did anything of the sort!"

"—And then you warned women away from him, not because you respected the women but because this was another way to keep your son to yourself!"

"I see he has told you all of his old lies," said Martha easily. "You'll learn not to believe anything he says. He is a sick man. His lies are a part of that sickness. I am sure his actions on your wedding night must have told you something about him."

"You know nothing about that!" Tabitha flared.

"I know everything about my son," Martha said calmly, "and I can accurately judge what transpired last night."

Tabitha was too blinded with anger and frustration to admit anything. Her violet eyes flashed.

"Whatever his problems, I'm glad I married him! He's mine now, and you won't be able to keep him under your thumb any longer! He's mine! Mine!"

"I hope you are pleased," Martha replied. "But I don't envy you. You will find that Nicholas's mind is badly warped. He suffers some sort of persecution mania, in which he believes everyone and everything is against him. That includes me. It includes Faunce Manley. It includes his own blacks— and, in time, it will include you. The story that I crippled him is pure poppycock, the imaginings of his disordered mind. He is not mentally right, my dear young woman, and he is getting worse."

She had walked primly from the room, leaving her terrifying words hanging heavily in the air, crushing Tabitha with their weight and import. Her mind spun with the memory of what Nicholas had said about "forces" on their wedding night: *The forces of this society have always worked against me. They will work against you too. Now that we're married they will be all the more determined. They do not want a Northerner to be the greatest planter in Natchez country. They do not want a girl from Natchez-under-the-Hill to be the grandest lady. Oh, they'll work against us, my dear, and we must be alert to defeat them. Just as we must be alert to defeat Mother.*

The stark horror in the words were for the first time clear to Tabitha. When he had spoken them, she had been puzzled. But now they took on meaning, supported Martha Enright's evaluation of her son. A troubled man, she had called him. A sick man. Something wrong with his mind. Suffering a persecution mania. Believing everyone was opposed to him. Her thoughts traveled fleetingly to the terror of the wedding bed. She shuddered and put her hands to her face. Good Lord in Heaven, what sort of man had she married? A man who beat his wife on her wedding night and whose mind was in some strange, unholy way demented?

Proud, haughty, arrogant Nicholas Enright—mad?

That had been a week ago. Still Nicholas had not returned. Tabitha had personally searched the house and the land, even entering the cypress shacks of the slaves to see if he might be hiding there. His big strawberry roan stallion, Happy Boy, was in the stables, so that wherever he had gone he had likely traveled on foot. In her mind she assessed the possibilities. Perhaps he had been overcome with shame and remorse at his wedding night actions, and was even now stupidly drunk in some Natchez-under tavern. Well, she would not run about from one grogshop to another looking for him—that would not befit a plantation lady. Besides, he may not be in that kind of place at all. He may have gone to New Orleans to see his factor. After all, the cotton was being harvested and financial arrangements with his factor were a necessity. The factor had to know the extent of Nicholas's crop, had to place orders and make arrangements for delivery of cotton to the mills. At one point Tabitha had even considered going to New Orleans, for she had heard that the steamboat *Southern Belle* would dock at Natchez shortly and continue down to New Orleans. She knew that the factors were generally located on Perdido, Poidras and Gravier Streets, and she felt that she would be able to find him if she went. But she discarded this idea too—for it was unseemly that a wife should travel alone aboard a Mississippi steamboat loaded with slick gamblers and uncouth rivermen.

Staying home to continue the subtle battle against Martha Enright's dominance seemed to be the proper thing to do. But Tabitha found that without Nicholas the weapons with which she could fight Martha were dulled. One morning the old woman appeared on the veranda with a trunk packed.

"Where are you going?" Tabitha asked suspiciously.

Martha Enright turned her stone-like countenance toward the sound of Tabitha's voice.

"Since my wayward son shows so little competence as to disappear during the critical time when cotton is being picked, I am taking the *Southern Belle* to New Orleans to make the necessary arrangements with his factor. This, as you should know, is the responsibility of the mistress of a plantation."

Tabitha was vexed by the situation, but she could not stop the old woman. She had to concede that Martha Enright had won a point. Tabitha knew nothing about the intricate business dealings between plantation owner and factor. Martha, by assuming Nicholas's duties in his absence, was pointedly showing Tabitha that she still considered herself the true proprietress of Magnolia Manor. After the old lady had left, Tabitha went to her room and cried in rage. Damn Nicholas anyway! Why did he have to run out when he was so needed? How did he expect her to win dominance of the manor if he did not back her at critical moments?

Stomping about her room in a fury, Tabitha chanced to look out of the window just as a cabriolet approached the house. The carriage was pulled by a prancing gray, urged on by a liveried driver who stood on a tiny platform behind the cabriolet, peering over the rounded top. A woman sat inside the carriage enclosure, but Tabitha could not recognize her from her upper room. Quickly, thinking the arrival of this woman might possibly have some connection with Nicholas's disappearance, Tabitha raced down the spiral staircase and met the cabriolet as it rolled to a stop beneath the massive porte cochere. To her surprise Garland McRae stepped from the carriage. She was dressed in a simple muslin dress and she wore a small poke bonnet, but her radiant beauty was not lessened by her simplicity of attire.

"Garland!" cried Tabitha. "I'm so glad to see you!"

It was true. Garland—astounding wife of a 90-year-old husband—had intrigued Tabitha ever since they had met at the dinner. She had immediately felt a common bond between them, for Garland had been the only woman who had not looked down on Tabitha with mild—but often ill-concealed—contempt. She was, Tabitha had decided, a perfectly lovely creature, and the most genuinely friendly person she had yet come across in Natchez society.

"I thought if I could be of help—" began Garland, and then broke off lamely.

"Help?" said Tabitha, stiffening slightly.

"I'm sorry." Garland was obviously distraught. "I say things so badly at times. But everyone knows—"

Tabitha's eyes narrowed. "You mean about Nicholas?"

"Yes."

It annoyed Tabitha to think that her secrets might be public knowledge.

"How does everyone know?"

"The Negro grapevine," said Garland. "It really works, you know. I suspect that we whites sometimes fail to understand the powers of our blacks. News simply flies between them, even though there is little contact between Negroes on separate plantations. I rather think that news is relayed to the free Negroes by the slaves and goes from plantation to plantation that way."

"And exactly what rumor reached you, Garland?" asked Tabitha, still provoked that her marital troubles could be the open gossip of half of Natchez.

"Only that Nicholas has disappeared. Most people feel that it means nothing, however. Nicholas is a self-sufficient man. He can care for himself. I'm sure no ill has befallen him and that he will return in due time."

Tabitha relaxed. So the rumor involved only Nicholas's disappearance then. Thank God there hadn't been a black face peering through their window when Nicholas had beaten her!

"It's nice of you to be concerned," Tabitha said. "Come in. I've been dreadfully lonely and shall enjoy your company."

They entered the great hall and went into the music room where Tabitha had hot cafe noir served and where they talked for some time of trivial matters. As they conversed Tabitha realized that she was beginning to like Garland McRae very much. She fancied herself a good judge of human nature, and she detected in Garland one of those rare women who is genuinely interested in the troubles of others and anxious to help for the pure sake of helping. There did not seem to be a mean bone in Garland's fine young body, and she exhibited an understanding of human frailty and misery that reached beyond her years. Before long Tabitha was telling Garland about her family and her life — how her father had been raised in a poor family in Virginia, how his parents had died when he was a boy, and how the poverty of the family had made it impossible for him to attend a theological institution. She told how he still felt so strongly about the Bible that he became a traveling lay preacher, with an evangelistic fervor second to no preacher of ordination. Garland sympathized completely with Abijah Clay.

"One who has talent, whether for preaching or writing or painting, has a need to develop it," she said. "It's rather sad when a man of your father's obvious abilities cannot take full advantage of them. My own mother had a great talent for painting, but my father was a Virginia dirt farmer whose sole interest was in raising tobacco. He was convinced that a knowledge of cooking and sewing and how to cure the fever was more important than painting pictures, and she was never encouraged to make anything of her art. When cotton became the staple that would rule the economy of the South, we came to Natchez. My father did well, built a fine home, and at last my mother had the leisure time to apply her art. But it wasn't to be. She died a year after the house was built, of the fever she was supposed to know how to cure. I was only ten years old then."

Tabitha then told the rest of her story, of how the family had braved the perils of the Natchez Trace and settled in Natchez-under-the-Hill which Abijah had seen as a fertile place to spread the teachings of Christ. She did not mention Ryma, but she told with pride of the stolidity of her New England mother, who never complained of hardship or lack of money, or the ridicule that was hers as the wife of a fire-breathing "Bible-banger," so long as her husband was doing the thing he wanted to do and was content that he was making progress at it.

"My background, I can see, will be a severe handicap to me in Natchez society," said Tabitha, testing Garland on this problem that so concerned her.

To her surprise, Garland smiled and shrugged her shoulders.

"It should not be a handicap, although I suspect, as you do, that it will be no help. Many of these so-called fine ladies will look down on you, as I am sure

Nicholas must have told you, and there will be the usual quota of disparaging remarks made. But what these women conveniently forget is that they have not always been elegant ladies themselves. Most of them were the wives of struggling young farmers, and they have struck it rich because of their husbands' efforts, not their own. And I might add that if lowly estate is the criterion for judging the worth of a person, my own must be highly suspect!"

Tabitha sipped delicately of the cafe noir. Her brows arched over the cup.

"I would venture to say that my own husband right at the moment is acting something like an ill-bred boor, rather than a fine gentleman," Tabitha said.

Garland artfully sidestepped any direct answer to the pointed statement.

"My husand and I have known Nicholas for some time," she said. "He has done this thing before, disappearing for a week or two, then returning as though nothing had happened and refusing to even talk about his disappearance."

"But where does he go?"

Garland shrugged again. "Who knows? There are places, as you must certainly know, where men can go."

Tabitha's eyes sharpened. She set her cup down with an angry clatter.

"What do you mean—places?"

Garland laughed. She had a liquid laugh, soft and tinkling and musical.

"There are places a well-bred woman doesn't even mention by name," she said. "But then, I've already confessed to you that I'm not well-bred, coming as I have from a lowly eastern farm. So I'll name them. Whorehouses."

"You're delightful," said Tabitha impulsively.

"All sham," said Garland. "Underneath the fine clothes and acquired manners and studied vocabulary there lies a woman who has known poverty, hard work, sordidness, and yes, even depravity." She raced on as Tabitha's eyebrows lifted at the last word. "But to get back to our subject, you might as well know that I think Nicholas at this moment is probably mercifully drunk in a house of assignation."

It had been the first cruelly blunt statement Garland had made. But instinctively Tabitha knew there was nothing vicious about it. Garland was a woman who possessed the intellectual honesty to speak her mind at all times, and even though Tabitha had contented herself with other milder explanations for Nicholas's disappearance—he had to find another overseer, he was in New Orleans to see his factor, he had to find a doctor for his slaves—she was not unaware of the possibility that, overcome with shame at his incapacity on the marriage bed, he had sought the comfort of a prostitute who would, even while sickened by him, tell him how good he was and what a man he was and flatter his injured ego until he regained enough confidence to return home again.

"I think," said Tabitha carefully, "you're implying that he may have gone down to Natchez-under?"

"It's conveniently located," said Garland easily.

Tabitha made a hopeless gesture, trying to shut unpleasantness from her mind.

"As ladies, it's unseemly to talk about such things," she decided with an attempt at primness.

Garland chuckled. Her bright eyes danced mischievously.

"But of course we're not ladies, are we?" she said. "And we *do* enjoy talking about such deliciously evil things. You know, I have a theory about evil, Tabitha. I am absolutely certain that half the evil of the world would disappear if men were less sexually aggressive, *and* if women were as prim as they pretend to be!"

"Garland! For heaven's sake!"

"It's true," said Garland firmly. "How many women are there in the shacks of the river towns that live a life of sin because men need them—and will pay for them? How many fine plantation ladies, for that matter, have made a bargain with themselves to supply a man his gratification in exchange for a luxurious life in a white-pillared mansion with servants at their beck and call and the best of food and clothing?" Her eyes narrowed, and Tabitha felt acutely uncomfortable, as if she were being personally censured.

"There's hardly a comparison," Tabitha said faintly, remembering Ryma's similar views on this same subject.

"Perhaps not. But I am convinced that women—with a lower sexual urge—would not go astray if it were not for men who persuade them. The woman wants to please the man, and so she surrenders to him. Usually she experiences small gratification herself—indeed, if she is a lady properly married, she isn't *supposed* to feel gratification—yet she may yield again and again until finally she starts telling herself that this is what *she* wants, never realizing that she does not want it at all."

Tabitha scowled. Her brows pinched together over her nose in a perfectly formed V.

"Do you really believe all that?"

"Oh, yes. Although I admit there are exceptions. There are women who are stimulated by the mere touch of a man, by his presence even. These are passionate fiery women who love intensely and hate fiercely, and who live on a level close to the animal. She is, of course, the kind of woman men desire."

"Which means, then, that men are all close to the animal level?"

"Of course!" Garland chuckled again. "Anyway, I guess I didn't come here to engage in a discussion of sex."

"Nor do I care to," laughed Tabitha. "But I *am* glad you came. I want to get to know you better, Garland. You were the only woman at our engagement dinner who I felt was honest and sincere, and that I genuinely liked."

"I'm flattered," said Garland, obviously pleased.

"You needn't be. It's only the opinion of a tawdry girl from Natchez-under, you know."

They both laughed at the quip and from then on they talked like two school girls meeting after a long separation.

"You have probably wondered why I married a man ninety years old," said Garland finally.

"It is not my business," said Tabitha, who had wondered mightily.

"You might as well consider it your business — everyone else in Natchez has," Garland said lightly. "The answer's quite simple. I'm frightfully ambitious."

Tabitha studied Garland, trying to ascertain whether or not she was joking.

"That's rather a severe condemnation of your motives," she said. "Surely, you're not serious."

"Oh, I'm deadly serious. I married old John because of his wealth and what that wealth could do to my life. My husband is a fine old man, but after all, I'm only twenty-eight. It's a frightful mismatch, and don't think I haven't suffered from it."

"Garland. You're so utterly frank."

"But he has given me everything," Garland went on, ignoring the comment. "More than I have ever had in my life. I presume one must pay a price for such a gift."

Tabitha drank the last of her cafe noir and placed the delicate cup on a small teatable.

"You are the kind of person, Garland, who is so charmingly frank that you encourage others to be like you." Tabitha went on. Aping Nicholas's words, wondering why she copied them, yet impelled to do so, she said: "Aren't all marriages—except those swept along by an incredible love that only a few people are capable of—matings of convenience? Take my own—"

"I know. Lowly girl from Natchez-under. Marries the most eligible bachelor among the planters. Now is a respected lady of Natchez, mistress of a great house. And all because you planned it that way!" Garland threw up her hands in mock horror. "Oh, you are a heartless little witch, Tabitha!"

"Now you *are* joking!"

"Of course. I'm really in sympathy with your deviousness. I'm sick to death of the high and mighty women of our cotton culture who place themselves on elaborate pedestals simply because their husbands have made a pile of ill-gotten money! Trying to keep it all in the family by marrying among themselves, each pimple-faced boy carefully coached to propose to another family's simpering little girl. Barring intruders from outside and all that kind of rot. I think it's about time for a few poor conniving wenches like ourselves to disrupt this cozy little arrangement. I marry a ninety-year-old widower who is beside himself with delight because a reasonably attractive twenty-eight-year-old woman will even look at his cracked face—and I marry him because of what he can give me. You, a girl from Natchez-under, marry the city's most coveted bachelor by turning his head—and for the same reason. I say, more power to us!"

Tabitha laughed with delight. Garland was simply wonderful. Here was a woman who talked straight from the shoulder, who was not beset by niceties and subtleties of a culture that decreed that one must talk only in circles and always appear to be what one was not. Tabitha felt a close kinship to Garland, a sort of predatory partnership, and when they parted some time later she promised to visit Garland in the near future. As she watched the cabriolet disappear into the moss-draped tunnel of trees, Tabitha felt for the first time since coming to Magnolia Manor that she had found a true friend.

3

The rambling stables of Magnolia Manor, where Nicholas kept his twenty fine horses, were considerably larger and far better constructed than the crude cabin which Tabitha had called home in Natchez-under-the-Hill. Anxious to escape the loneliness of the manor, Tabitha decided to ride the silver-white palomino Nicholas had assigned to her use. It was the second week of Nicholas's absence and Tabitha felt alone and almost overwhelmed by the emptiness of the great house. In fact, she almost wished that Martha Enright would return from New Orleans, but she did not expect Nicholas's mother for several more days. A ride in the open air, she thought, might restore some sense of balance, some perspective, to her confused and troubled mind.

The palomino Lady Belle had already accommodated herself to Tabitha, and as Tabitha approached the gentle mare's stall the horse nuzzled her affectionately. Tabitha stroked the long smooth nose and spoke softly to the animal. As she did so a ridiculing voice came from behind her.

"If only you were as gentle with men as you are with horses."

Tabitha spun around, her skirts swirling. When she

recognized the speaker she stifled a gasp of surprise. It was Mike Long!

"You!" she said inadequately. "What are you doing here?"

Mike Long's face split into his vexatious grin. It was the same infuriating smile she remembered from their first meeting at the Silver Palace. She scanned his face again—the rugged, chiseled features, the piercing blue eyes and rust-colored hair billowing back from his forehead, the impish angle of his head as he looked at her, the way he fingered his chin thoughtfully before replying.

"I'm the new doctor at Magnolia Manor. It's my job to keep the Master's slaves in good health."

"Who brought you here?" demanded Tabitha, although she knew the question was pointless.

"I understand I was hired because of the graciousness of milady who was so kind as to recommend me." Mike bowed low in mocking homage. The synthetic gesture exasperated Tabitha.

"My husband hired you?"

"At your bequest, yes."

"When?"

"Two weeks ago."

"He didn't tell me."

"Perhaps he thought it of little importance." Mike Long reached for Lady Belle's saddle. "My quarters are above the stables. Not nearly as pretentious as your own, but they are adequate and they fit my personality. . . . Shall I saddle Lady Belle for you?"

"The groom will saddle the horse," said Tabitha stiffly and motioned for Jeff to take charge. She fastened determined eyes on Mike. "Let me inform you that I did not recommend you to my husband," she said tightly. "Your name slipped out in an unguarded conversation, and I regret the mistake. In any case, if you dare to cause me even a mite of trouble by your presence here, *Doctor* Long, I'll—"

She sought to utter some dire threat, but floundered over it. Mike professed complete puzzlement at her belligerence.

"How could a backwoods slave doctor cause any trouble to the eminent Mrs. Enright?" he asked innocently.

Tabitha glared helplessly at him. The man was insufferable. There was a mocking quality to everything he said, a wry note of condescension that irritated her. She was sure he was poking fun at her in the very way he said "Mrs. Enright."

"May I belatedly tender my best wished for a successful marriage?" Mike asked.

"Thank you," clipped Tabitha. "Hurry with the saddle, Jeff."

"I understand the—uh—Master is away," said Mike carefully.

"You needn't call him Master," said Tabitha sharply. "Call him Mr. Enright."

"Of course. I'm beginning to talk like the slaves—or, pardon me, I think Mr. Enright calls them his *people*. How many has he got—in the fields, that is."

Tabitha looked at him uncertainly. As the plantation doctor, he should know this by now. Was he, then, merely trying to bait her? Was he deftly implying that *she* was one of Nicholas Enright's slaves? Even he wouldn't be so indelicate as to suggest such an outrageous thing. And yet, where did men have slaves, if not in the fields?

"I'm sure I don't know the extent of his holdings," said Tabitha curtly. "I pay little attention to the blacks."

"As befits a woman of your fine character," said Mike, bowing again. "Slavery is such a nasty thing to plague one's mind with, don't you think?"

Jeff came with Lady Belle, saddle in place, and Tabitha led the horse out of the stable. Mike Long walked along with her as Jeff returned to his tasks.

"You haven't answered my question, Mrs. Enright," Mike complained.

"I don't know why I speak to you at all!" Tabitha snapped.

"It was about slavery," pursued Mike earnestly. "A woman of such fine sensibilities as yourself must surely have wondered at one time or another about the moral aspects of the institution."

Tabitha frowned with irritation. He seemed bent on provoking an argument and delaying her departure. Was he deliberately criticizing her new way of life, because he wasn't a part of it?

"I take it from your ill-mannered remarks that you stand firmly against slavery?" she asked, deciding to place him on the defensive.

Mike Long smiled. He had nice teeth, thought Tabitha.

"Doesn't your father stand against slavery?"

"I asked *you!*"

"Very well. Yes, I'm opposed to slavery. I don't think it right for one man to own another, the way he owns a horse or a mule or a barn. I think in time this system will fall of its own weight, and when it does the plantation society and all the towering riches will fall with it."

"And what will cause the system to fall?" she asked.

Mike shrugged. He had broad shoulders, Tabitha thought.

"A slave rebellion, perhaps."

"That's ridiculous. You know very well that the blacks can't rebel. They have no leadership, and they lack the intelligence to successfully revolt."

"But there have been rebellions. You have heard of Nat Turner, haven't you?"

"An exception." Tabitha dismissed Turner with a wave of her hand. "In general the Negroes have no stomach for violence. They are docile and pliable."

"Said like a true Southern lady!" chided Mike, grinning in his infuriating way. "Take comfort in your fallacies, my dear, but remember Mike Long's prophetic words when the day comes."

"You're a—a damned abolitionist!" accused Tabitha, at her wits end.

"I'm nothing," replied Mike. "A doctor for a rich man's niggers. Not much better than the slaves themselves. But I have nothing on my conscience and I sleep nights."

Tabitha stamped her foot, eyes flashing. "Oh, fie!" she said. "You're impertinent and I don't know why I put up with you. I ought to have my husband dismiss you."

"Do that," said Mike easily, "if you can find him."

"Oh!" The word exploded with total revulsion. She started to mount Lady Belle and Mike helped to place her in the saddle. She shoved his hands away from her and with a withering look wheeled the horse about and rode off in a haze of hate.

Now she was certain she detested Mike Long more than anybody in the world! Her exasperated fury almost blinded her, and she only subconsciously knew that she had guided the horse down the bridle path toward the slave quarters. By the time she had reached the long row of cypress shacks along the edge of the cotton fields her anger had dissipated slightly, but her mind was still in turmoil. Mike Long, she was sure, had no use for her or the society to which she now belonged. He had been inexcusably impertinent, showing a condescending respect for her new station in life at the same time that he brutally attacked it. He seemed almost amused by the fact that she had become mistress of Magnolia Manor, and such an attitude incensed Tabitha. What bothered her even more was the fact that she permitted him to annoy her at all. Mike Long was nothing, as he himself had said, and she would put him out of her mind. Maybe she *would* have Nicholas dismiss him. It would serve him right.

But she had trouble erasing him entirely from her mind.

Tabitha approached the edge of the cotton fields. It was late afternoon and the colors of the world had deepened with the sinking sun. The snowy fibers of cotton had turned a mouse-gray, and the sun's slanted rays played over and darkened the colors of the kerchiefs worn by the workers. The heat of the day was dissipating, and now a thin breeze moved over the fields to bring a bracing tonic to those who toiled there.

Tabitha sat upon Lady Belle for a long time, gazing out over the broad acres of land that belonged to Nicholas—yes, and to her. Her sudden elevation to mistress of these vast holdings was a cherished dream come true, but the sadistic actions of Nicholas on their wedding night and his subsequent disappearance had turned the dream into a nightmare. She had tried, as was her habit, to relegate her seemingly insoluble troubles to a remote area of her mind and concentrate only on the pleasant aspects of the situation. After all, she lived on the Hill now, among the mighty who ruled the Natchez country, and this fact alone was so eminently satisfying to Tabitha that she was inclined to think that any hardships necessary to maintain her position was worth it. She tried to convince herself that when Nicholas returned everything would be all right again. She was sure she could win, if not his physical love, at least his recognition that she was a helpful companion to his station in life. As for Martha Enright—well, Tabitha knew that she would not have to contend with the old lady for long. She was an elderly woman and she could not live forever. And Mike Long, irritating as he could be, was no major problem; she could have him dismissed at any time she desired. So Tabitha contented herself with the wishful thought that all her problems would in time resolve themselves and she would be the happy mistress of Magnolia Manor and one of the most envied ladies in Natchez.

With such giddy thoughts racing through her head, Tabitha was not aware of the presence of another person until a man's low voice broke her reverie.

"Ma'am, please."

Tabitha looked down from the palomino. It was Big Sam, the huge Negro handyman. Tabitha's alert eyes roved swiftly over the Negro's mammoth black body, the bared chest, the heavy muscular arms, the great head with its flared nostrils and sharp black eyes embedded in white.

"Yes, Sam."

"Beggin' yo' pahdon, ma'am, but Ah wants you to come with me. One of mah babies is dyin'!"

"A baby dying?"

"Yes'm. In dat shack there." He swung his huge arm and pointed toward one of the slave cabins. "Dat woman of mine in there is done everything she knows, an' the baby is a-dyin'."

Tabitha frowned. "Did you call Doctor Long?"

"Yes'm. He's wid her. But sometimes Ah thinks these things need a—a woman's hand."

Tabitha smiled in spite of her mood. "You're very wise, Sam. Take me to her."

Big Sam loped toward the house and Tabitha spurred the palomino to follow. Through her mind ran a single devious thought: *If I can help this baby it will solidify my relations with the blacks. They will like me, a white mistress who would concern herself with a sick baby, and this will be a high card in my hand in the power struggle with Martha Enright*. It pleased her to think that, while Martha had scored a point in dealing with Nicholas's factor, her very absence was now going to work against her and in Tabitha's favor.

At the entrance to the sagging shack Tabitha slid from the saddle. She entered the dark dingy building, fetid with the odor of black bodies. In one corner of the single room, on a thin pallet, sat a young black woman. Next to her lay a small baby, eyes closed as if already dead. Mike Long was already there, squatting next to the child, a bag of medicines at his side.

"Thass the baby there," said Sam unnecessarily.

Tabitha almost gagged at the odor in the room. Sweat, urine, offal. She looked at Sam.

"Is this your wife, Sam?"

"No, ma'am."

"But you said—"

"It's mah baby, ma'am, far as I kin figger. But not mah wife."

Tabitha remembered with some repugnance Nicholas's remark that Big Sam had sired a dozen children among the young slave women, and decided to ask no more questions. She stooped down next to the distressed young mother. The woman's eyes rolled up, frightened by the presence of the mistress of Magnolia Manor in her own crude quarters.

"What's the matter with the baby?" Tabitha asked the girl, ignoring the professional presence of Mike Long.

The girl's eyes rolled in her head, like loose marbles. Her lips fell apart, trembling.

"She's burnin' up, ma'am. She's feverin'. An' she's so still Ah thinks she's gonna die."

At last Tabitha glanced at Mike. "Your diagnosis, Doctor?"

"I haven't yet had the opportunity to make one uninterrupted. If milady will permit—"

"Give me the child!" said Tabitha impatiently. "I'll take her to the manor."

"I doubt that such a move will cure her," Mike said caustically.

"Nevertheless I intend to move this baby to more fitting quarters," said Tabitha levelly. "You may come along. I may have need of your—uh—professional services."

She took up the black bundle quickly and strode out of the evil-smelling shack. The wide-eyed and agitated mother of the child followed her. Big Sam helped her onto the palomino, his big black hands upon her, and as he did so his great somber eyes scanned her body with studied insolence. The thought slid through Tabitha's mind: *Big Sam has had his way with every comely black wench on the plantation, and he had better not start casting covetous eyes at me or I will have him beaten.* Somehow the thought amused her. Have him beaten! She *was* beginning to think like a plantation owner. She was beginning to feel her power. She looked down at the mother of the child.

"Come to the house," she ordered. "What's your name?"

"Emerald."

"Very well. Announce yourself. The servant will send you to me."

"Yes'm."

Tabitha heeled the horse and in an instant was off for the big white mansion, baby cradled in one arm while she expertly held the lines with her free hand. Mike Long slowly mounted his own horse and followed her, remaining at a discreet distance, managing to imply by this act a reluctance to even be near Tabitha. Damn him, anyway, he could be disrespectful in more diverse ways than any man she had ever known!

When she reached the manor she left word with Toby to admit the young mother, Emerald, and strode purposefully to one of the upper bedchambers. By the time Mike arrived, Tabitha had the baby in a clean bed. The tiny black infant in the huge white tester bed looked like a raisin dropped mistakenly on a white linen table cloth.

Mike watched her a moment as she hovered over the child, a smile slanting across his face.

"May I say that, for the mistress of a great plantation, you have made a most noble gesture?" he said acidly.

Tabitha whirled on him. Why was Mike always able to see through her, to dig out her most personal motives, the hidden meanings behind her every action?

"Will you *please* determine what is wrong with this child?" she demanded.

"Oh, I thought perhaps you wanted to do that too."

"Mike Long! This child might be dying!"

Mike shook his head. His piercing eyes scanned the infant critically.

"The child has a slight cold and temperature. I suspect also a touch of the colic. With a little medication, she will be all right."

"You're sure?"

"Yes. I'm sure."

"Good. Will you prescribe then?"

Mike Long nodded. "I will. And when the child gets better, you can take all the credit, Mrs. Enright. There's no denying your cleverness, milady. This will place you high in the esteem of your blacks. They are simple people not given to duplicity and will not suspect your true motives. They'll love you. You will have established yourself in the eyes of the slaves as a sympathetic mistress of the manor."

The truth, coming from Mike, was too much to bear. Tabitha felt sudden hostility. Her violet eyes flashed and her breath came in strained gasps. Her hand reached out to grip a vase of flowers on a small table near the bed, and she would have hurled it at Mike had he not moved quickly, grabbed her arm, and pinned her to him by encircling her waist with his free arm.

"Let me go!" screamed Tabitha, twisting and turning.

Mike's arm tightened instead. "You little bitch! You beautiful tantalizing bitch! You haven't got an honest thought in your head and you've got a heart like the tip of an iceberg. Do you want me to make love to you, or beat the hell out of you?"

"Mike! Let go of me, I say!" Tabitha squirmed helplessly in his iron grip.

"You need some medicine yourself," Mike said, still holding her. "And I'm the doctor who is going to prescribe it."

"Release me, Mike!" railed Tabitha, still struggling. "Oh, damn you!"

"Now, now—let's be a lady! I have a cure for what is ailing you, Mrs. Enright. A warming of the posterior by applicaiton of the hand ought to be most beneficial."

"Mike!"

He fell back into a chair, pulling Tabitha across his knees. While he held her in a rigid grip, he spanked her a half-dozen times like a misbehaving child. The blows stung and Tabitha bit her lip, but struggle as she might she could not get away from him. Just as the last blow descended Emerald walked into the doorway. Her black eyes widened and her mouth went slack.

"Ah declare!" she breathed.

Tabitha struggled to her feet as Mike relaxed his hold. Mortified at what Emerald had seen, she quickly rearranged her dress. Mike was choking with laughter and she turned on him, her eyes sparkling dangerously.

"Prescribe for the child!" she commanded, trying to summon enough authority in her voice. "And as for the prescription given me, my husband will take proper steps."

"He'll dismiss me?" Mike asked through the laughter.

"He might kill you!"

"Formally, of course. A duel in the grand manner?"

"Mr. Enright would not duel a man so far below his level," snapped Tabitha. "But he might cut you to shreds with a whip!"

4

The slave baby was well within a matter of days. While Tabitha admitted to herself that Mike Long's ministrations had cured the child, she was not, as Mike had predicted, above accepting sole credit from the happy mother. The young girl left the manor with the baby in her arms and worship for Tabitha in her eyes.

It was now the third week of Nicholas's absence from the plantation and Tabitha was becoming increasingly apprehensive. She spent most of her days thinking either about him or Mike Long, and resenting both of them. The fact that each had meted out physical punishment to her was nettlesome. More than once she wondered if there was something about her that provoked men to violence. Nicholas's attack on her had been starkly brutal; Mike's had been more humiliating than painful. It occurred to her that if she intended to continue living with Nicholas—assuming, of course, that he returned to her—she would somehow have to make certain that his strange actions on the night of the wedding were not repeated. As for Mike, she was determined to tell Nicholas of the childlike punishment the doctor had imposed on her and ask him to dismiss him. Disposing physically of

Mike and finding some other means to curb Nicholas's bedroom manners now seemed to be the two most important items on her agenda. Even victory over Martha Enright would have to be postponed until she had solved these two critical problems facing her.

Such a delay in strengthening her position as mistress of Magnolia Manor rankled Tabitha. Martha Enright had returned from New Orleans with a victorious announcement that she had made satisfactory commercial arrangements with Nicholas's factor. Then she withdrew to her room and rarely spoke to Tabitha, subtly indicating that Tabitha was of little importance at the manor. What was most galling was that the old lady was correct. Outside of the coup she had achieved with the blacks, Tabitha felt she had made little progress in establishing any kind of personal hegemony. Nicholas should be here now, helping her. He should be at her side. He should be planning soirees and balls and helping her to become the grand lady he always talked about. But only God knew where Nicholas was, or even if he would return. And she would not lower herself to search for him.

On one occasion, as she sat morbidly considering her helpless position, a random thought crossed her mind. Should she return to her parents on the mudflats of Natchez-under? She needed words of comfort and she knew her parents would supply that need willingly and with understanding. But she quickly put the thought out of her mind. It would be too embarrassing to let her parents know of her plight. She must have the grit and determination to play her role at Magnolia Manor without Nicholas, to see this crisis through until Nicholas came to his senses and returned to the plantation.

As she sat on the veranda one day, contemplating her troubles, Tabitha heard the rhythmic clop-clop of a horse's hooves almost a minute before the horse and rider popped into view from the green tunnel of trees. At first she thought the rider might be Nicholas, but then she saw it was a woman riding sidesaddle. Her heart thumped wildly as she recognized the rider.

"My God!" she said. "Ryma!"

Ryma was dressed in a thin muslin with bell-like sleeves and a skirt that flared out over many starched petticoats. Except for the hard lines etched into her face by the rigors of her profession, it is doubtful that a "good woman" would have recognized her for what she was. She drew back on the reins as she approached the porte-cochere and the horse, tossing its head, came to a clattering, dancing stop. In an instant she had dismounted.

"Tabby!"

A moment later she was in Tabitha's arms as the two sisters embraced. Then Ryma stepped back, looking at Tabitha with interest.

"You *are* a true plantation lady," she said in admiration.

"Oh, fie!"

Ryma's brow crisscrossed with sudden worry. Her eyes dropped for a second, then met Tabitha's directly.

"Forgive me for coming here," she said. "I have no desire to embarrass you—"

"What is it, for heaven's sake?" asked Tabitha impatiently.

"It's about your husband. He's at the Silver Palace.

Drunk as a lord. You'd better come and get him."

Tabitha stared bleakly at Ryma. Her lips set tightly, like stretched rubber bands.

"How long has he been there?" she demanded.

Ryma looked uncomfortable. She put out her hand, placing it tenderly on Tabitha's arm.

"Look, honey. You must understand Nicholas Enright. He—"

"How *long*, Ryma?"

Ryma drew in her breath. Her carmined lips parted and the words came reluctantly.

"Since he left you, Tabby."

Outrage flooded Tabitha and her eyes flashed fiercely. She turned and placed her back against one of the unfluted white pillars, defiance in her manner.

"Fie on him! I won't get him! He can rot there!"

Ryma took Tabitha gently by the arm and guided her to a chair. Her attitude had changed abruptly. She was now resolute and unwavering.

"Sit down, Tabby!" she ordered. "I'm going to talk to you, straight from the shoulder. Sister to sister, whether it hurts or not."

Tabitha glanced at Ryma with pouting suspicion. She dropped into a chair listlessly and watched Ryma seat herself across from her. Little sounds became magnified in the silence. Sophie was shuffling about in the hallway. A cooling breeze whispered softly across the pillared porch. From far away she heard the slaves singing as they worked the fields, a palliative that seemed to lighten their labor.

"I don't know precisely why your husband left you, Tabby," Ryma said finally, "but I have an idea. I'm giving it to you straight—I think he came to the Silver

Palace for about the same reasons he usually comes."

"Usually!"

"Yes. Honey, let me tell you something. I knew Nicholas Enright before you ever met him. He has made frequent trips to the Silver Palace over the last several years, sometimes spending days there, sometimes weeks."

"What for?" demanded Tabitha petulantly.

"Tabby, don't be naive. What does any man go to the Silver Palace for?"

Tabitha scanned her sister through narrowing eyes. The words came out with difficulty.

"I know, Ryma. But he's—" She stopped, unable to say it.

"Impotent?" Ryma shrugged her shoulders. "I know. He confided in me."

Tabitha gazed at her sister with indignant amazement. The pieces were falling into place, jarringly. Nicholas had frequently visited the Silver Palace. . . . Ryma had known him for some time. . . . She had become his confidante in intimate matters, knew even his most personal failings. It seemed incredible.

"I don't understand, Ryma. Why would he confide such a thing to you?"

"It is a perversion of man that he usually confides less in his wife than in his mistress," said Ryma softly.

Tabitha was shocked. Apparently she didn't understand men as well as she thought!

"Hear me out, Tabby, before you make any judgments," Ryma said with a sudden note of authority in her voice. "You're my sister and you've married well, and I would do nothing to ruin your new life. So will you listen to me?"

Tabitha nodded dumbly and Ryma went on.

"All right. To begin with, Nicholas *owns* the Silver Palace."

"Owns it?" It was a foolish echo, but Tabitha could think of no better words.

"Yes. He always has. It's where he first made the money to build this." Ryma swept her hand to encompass Magnolia Manor.

"He told me he had an unsavory beginning," said Tabitha with some primness, "but I didn't know he still operated that—that place."

"Well, he does. And he makes a great deal of money out of it too. He has often told me that cotton made him a great man, but that prostitution made him rich."

"Damn him! He never told *me* that!" Tabitha was incensed that her sister seemed to know more about Nicholas than she did.

"The Silver Palace has always been a second home to Nicholas," Ryma continued. "That's where I first met him."

Tabitha stiffened at the words. *Met!* In a house of prostitution her own sister and her husband had *met!* What a mild and innocent word to describe what had actually taken place! But that had been before her marriage to Nicholas, Tabitha hedged. Yes, she would hear Ryma out.

"I'm not going to spare you, honey," Ryma said. "I was his—his favorite. He asked for me each time he came back. He told me at the beginning that he was impotent, that no woman could do anything for him. Well, he was a challenge to me, I guess. And I was able to meet the challenge. I was good for him. After that he said that I was the only woman he had ever met capable of making him feel like a man. Ever since—when he was troubled, when a crop failed, when he had difficulties with his mother, when his needs dictated—he would come to me for solace."

Tabitha sat in stunned silence, unable to speak. She was not exactly surprised that Nicholas would have a mistress. But the fact that his mistress was her own sister shocked her violently and made it more repugnant. Ryma shook her head slowly.

"I'm sorry, Tabby."

Tabitha sighed. "Why didn't you tell me all this before?"

"I couldn't. There was no point."

"You should have. When I came to you for that dress I told you I had met Nicholas Enright. Why didn't you tell me then that you—you—"

"Tabby, listen to me. Nicholas Enright came to me one day and told me of his troubles with his mother, how she insisted on ruling Magnolia Manor, taking everything away from him that he had built. He said he could not fight her alone, that he needed the help of a strong-willed woman who could handle his mother only as one woman can handle another. He said he was sick of the mealy-mouthed gentlewomen—his words—on the Hill. He said he needed a woman with as much fire and determination as his mother to counterbalance her at first and then, later, to run her."

"Ryma! He didn't ask you—"

"To marry him?" Ryma laughed delightedly. "Of course not. A man never asks his mistress to marry him. A mistress and a wife are two separate things. I can see that your practical education has been neglected, Tabby. Anyway, I told him I knew such a girl. I told him I knew a girl with an overwhelming determination to live on the Hill, to become an important lady—a girl that would be more than a match for his mother, however domineering she might be."

"Ryma!"

"I recommended you pretty highly, Tabby," Ryma finished.

Tabitha's mind reeled. Ryma, her own sister, mistress to Nicholas, had recommended her as a wife? It was impossible to believe, and yet—Tabitha suddenly remembered the little things Nicholas had known about her. He had known that her father was an itinerant lay preacher, and she had suspected him of inquiring about her. He had known her body measurements, what she wore. Now it was clear. Ryma had given him all the information he had gathered about her!

"I feel like a black slave that has been looked over, discussed, and judged as to worthiness," said Tabitha witheringly. "Did he *pay* for me too? How much did I bring on the market?"

Ryma smiled tolerantly. "It's not that bad. Nicholas was immediately interested, and it was only after I had aroused his interest that I told him you were my sister. He laughed. He thought it was a fine joke. He said, 'Justice always triumphs. If I marry your sister I not only obtain a woman, by your own judgment, capable of handling my mother, but I shock the crinolines right off of all the perfumed ladies on the Hill by not selecting one of *them!* He was highly pleased, Tabby."

"It sounds just like him!" said Tabitha, still bitter.

"He wanted to go at once to meet you. But I cautioned him against going to your home unannounced—you know how Father is. I told him that you went almost every Sunday to the esplanade. I described you. I told him about your peculiar violet eyes, and I even knew what dress you would wear because you had only one that was suitable. I told him I thought that a chance meeting would be better—that you were not above a casual flirtation—and that later he could approach Father and Mother."

"You, Ryma, are a conniving, underhanded, matchmaking witch!" said Tabitha, but there was now more appreciation than anger in her voice.

"Well," said Ryma, smoothing the ruffles of her dress with her hand, "now you know. Will you come with me now and get Nicholas?"

Tabitha assumed her most hurt pouting expression. There were still aspects of this situation that disturbed her, and still enough pride left in her to resist running after Nicholas.

"Have you been—entertaining him?" she demanded.

"Tabby, honey, do try to understand. I'm his mistress. I will remain so until he has no further use for me, which is the fate of all mistresses. You can bring about that condition by properly handling Nicholas yourself."

"I tried! God knows I tried!"

The high pitch of Tabitha's voice—almost hysterical—caused Ryma's eyes to narrow.

"Did he beat you?"

Tabitha could not answer vocally. She simply nodded. Ryma's face hardened.

"I'm sorry, Tabby. He can be such a brutal bastard at times. I suppose I should have warned you, but I didn't think he would mistreat his wife." She stood up, looking down at Tabitha, subdued now. "Look, honey. I understand Nicholas. He's a man who desperately needs love. He doesn't think so, but it's true. His arrogance stems from the fact that he's lonesome, that he needs acceptance and has never really had it. Tabby, he's basically a weak man whose arrogance is a cover-up for his feelings of inadequacy. I can tell you things you must do to make him feel like a man."

Tabitha looked at Ryma with distaste. "Some Godawful perversion, you mean?"

"That's your word, not mine. No. You take my advice and you can help Nicholas become a confident and more satisfied man."

Tabitha looked at her sister with suspicion. "All right," she said. "Tell me what to do."

"First of all," Ryma said, "you must understand Nicholas is incapable of completing a normal sex act. But he needs closeness to a woman, and there are things you can do that delight him and satisfy him in his own way." She went on to explain, in embarrassing detail, the devices that Tabitha could employ— long, teasing foreplay, caresses and kisses over his entire body, manual manipulation, and the moist stimulation of fellatio—the age-old tactics of the prostitute. Tabitha reacted with disgust.

"I couldn't do that! It's against my nature."

Ryma shrugged. "It's your decision," she said. "Anyway, Tabby, will you come with me and take him home?"

"Yes." Tabitha saw Sophie in the hallway and beckoned to her. "Go down to the stable, Sophie, and tell Jeff to send up Lady Belle. Oh, yes, and Happy Boy too. Both saddled."

"Yes'm." Sophie was off for the stables, her skirts flying around her legs. Minutes later Jeff arrived, leading the palomino and the big strawberry roan. He helped both women to mount, with Tabitha taking the reins of the roan in her hand, towing the horse behind Lady Belle.

The trip was neither long nor particularly hazardous, except for a rather steep descent from the bluff to the mudflats which Tabitha had never negotiated on horseback. Ryma led the way down squalid Silver Street. There were hoots and calls from men in the doorways of dram shops, saloons, and bordellos. Tabitha thought that Silver Street had certainly not changed in her brief absence. Ignoring the comments of male passersby, they went directly to the Silver Palace, dismounted and tethered the horses at the hitching rail.

"Where will he be?" asked Tabitha, feeling a nervousness tugging inside of her.

"He *won't* be with another woman while I'm gone," said Ryma dryly. "Likely he'll be in the waiting room. He drinks alone much of the time."

Ryma walked boldly into the weathered building with Tabitha trailing somewhat timidly behind her. Tabitha kept close to her sister, for she felt a modicum of protection in her presence. Despite having been here once—a most frightful experience she preferred to forget—she loathed the place and found no comfort in entering it. As before, the saloon was dark and dismal, as if a shroud had been draped over it to hide its impiety from the outside world. A few sinister figures lurked at the bar, behind which the obese bartender washed glasses, and one or two tables were occupied by couples more interested in each other than the mugs of tafia before them.

Ryma turned with an impertinent swish of her skirts, walked through the bar and into the waiting room where Tabitha and she had met before. They found him there, alone, sitting morosely in the cheerless room, huddled over a bottle on a small table. He sat staring bleakly, not moving his head when they entered, apparently unaware of them, his gaze fixed on some vague point in space. He was dressed in light trousers but he had discarded his cutaway coat which lay over a nearby chair. He had a heavy growth of beard on his face. His eyes were red-rimmed with weariness, and from one corner of his mouth saliva dripped unheeded.

"Nicholas!" Ryma shook him hard. "I've brought Tabitha."

His head wobbled precariously on his shoulders, as if in danger of falling off. He turned slowly, trying to focus his eyes on the two women. He blinked drowsily, the effort bringing pain to his face.

"Leave me alone!" His voice was whiskey-raw.

"I said I've brought Tabitha," repeated Ryma.

He squinted at the two women again. This time a flicker of understanding crossed his face.

"Take her 'way! She shouldn' be in a place like this!" he said thickly. "Shouldn'a brought her here, Ryma. This is a whorehouse, an' she's a bride—a *virgin* bride!" He chuckled inanely at his little joke.

"She's come to take you home, Nicholas," said Ryma.

Nicholas straightened up, as if insulted. He wiped the back of his hand across his wet mouth.

"I'll go home when I'm Goddman good an' ready. Take her 'way!"

"Nicholas!" said Tabitha urgently. "I've got your horse outside. We've been worried about you. Come with me now."

Nicholas turned his brooding eyes on Tabitha. His face split suddenly into an imbecilic grin.

"Want a son of a bitch like me at home, do you? Well, now that's real compliment'ry. Didn' know you gave a damn, my dear."

"I'm your wife!" reminded Tabitha, trying to control rising anger.

"Oh, yes. Wife. I *did* marry you, didn' I? Shocked half the female pop'lation of Natchez right outa their pantaloons when I married you. Girl from Natchez-under, no breeding, no education, not one of our favored girls. Gave 'em quite a start, didn' we?"

"Is that what you married me for?" Tabitha could not help hurling forth the challenge.

"That—an' other things. Gave my dear mother a start too, didn' we? 'Nother woman in the house. God's blood, I bet she hates you!"

Tabitha glanced warily at Ryma, then moved closer and put her hand on Nicholas's sagging shoulder.

"Nicholas. Stop talking now. You're not making sense and—"

"I'm makin' too damned much sense for you to stomach, my dear," he interrupted. "Marriage of convenience. That's all—convenience. Now I'm stuck with a wife who demands love, an' you're stuck with a husband who doesn' believe in it. We made a lousy mess of it, didn' we?"

"Nicholas! You've got to come home now. We have to start making our life together."

He looked up bird-like, his head cocked to one side in the manner of a robin regarding a newly found worm.

"Life together? God's doublet, woman, you talk like we're normal people. Life together, my ass! What do you want me home for? Want your dear husband to make love to you again? Great lover, that's me! Nicholas Enright, great lover! Want me home so I can beat the hell outa you again? That what you want?"

Tabitha's face flushed red. "Nicholas, for heaven's sake! Just come along quietly. I have Happy Boy outside."

He sat there a moment, staring blankly at the bottle on the table. Then, dizzily, he staggered to his feet. The table tipped and the bottle of whiskey rolled along the top and crashed to the floor. He stood swaying uncertainly for a moment. He started to take a step forward and fell awkwardly against the wall. His body crashed against a tiny metal lever protruding from the wall.

"Watch out!" cried Ryma in alarm.

The lever moved under Nicholas's hand. There was a groaning sound, as if unoiled gears were meshing, and suddenly a trap door opened in the floor, inches from where Nicholas was standing. Tabitha looked down into the murky depths in amazement. The trap door opened above the river, and Tabitha could see the dark muddy water below.

Tabitha recalled again the purpose of the trap door

and her flesh crawled. She had heard that some of the brothels and grog shops set on pilings over the river were equipped with these hideous devices. Unwary visitors who dared to flash money in a Natchez-under dive would be lured to a room above the river and mercilessly murdered. After the thugs had relieved the victim of his money, they would drop him through the trap door into the river. Several days later a body would be found floating down the river, several miles from the scene of the crime.

Nicholas stared momentarily at the opened door near his feet. Then he belched loudly and grinned.

"Excellent place for disposing of one's enemies," he said slurringly. "Maybe some day I'll invite old Faunce Manley here. Drop him right in the Goddamned river, the old son of a bitch!"

"Nicholas!"

"Never could get Mother here, though," he said, chuckling. "Too aristocratic, Mother. Wouldn't step inside a whorehouse. Wouldn't even breathe the stinking air of a whorehouse." He reached out impetuously and grasped Tabitha's shoulder. "Not a bit like you, my dear. There's no place you wouldn't go, is there?"

Tabitha ignored the question. Ryma pushed the lever and the yawning chasm at their feet groaned again and closed. Tabitha tugged at his arm.

"Come home, Nicholas," she implored. "You're needed at the plantation."

Nicholas made an elaborate and mocking bow, almost pitching forward on his face.

"Needed! That's what I wanta be—needed. Nobody's ever needed me for anything. Everybody's always tried to get rid of me, do 'way with me—Mother, my so-called friends, everybody!" He lurched to one side, as though the force of his words threw him off balance. His eyes glowed fanatically as he looked at Tabitha. "Maybe I never told you. You're my wife an' you should know. I've heard many voices in my time, but they never said they needed me."

"Voices?" A sudden chill ran through Tabitha. He had heard voices? It didn't make sense. But then, she temporized, he's drunk. That would explain such meaningless mouthings.

"At night," Nicholas said, "the voices come."

"Whose voices?"

"Who knows? My enemies, all speaking at once."

Tabitha glanced at Ryma. Ryma shrugged.

"Come on home, Nicholas," Tabitha said again, not knowing what else to say.

"All right. I'll come home. Can't fight my enemies sittin' here, can I?" His mind seemed to drift off, then struggle back. "I'll come back an' see if you can make a man outa me, like your sister does. That's it. Sisters ought to be able to do iden—identical things. Ryma, tell Tabitha what to do to make a man outa me."

Ryma and Tabitha were both leading him now, out the door and into the clouded bar. Tabitha was thankful for the gloom of the barroom, for it hid her shame like a protective shawl over her face. Outside they stood for a moment beside the two horses.

"Can you mount Happy Boy?" asked Tabitha doubtfully.

"I can mount any damned horse that ever walked on four legs," said Nicholas boastfully. He put his left foot into the stirrup and vaulted upward. He almost fell off the other side of the horse, but regained his balance, sat up ramrod stiff, and looked down at Tabitha as if expecting applause. Slowly, leading the roan, Tabitha rode with her drunken husband through the seamy streets of Natchez-under-the-Hill, until finally the road rose sharply toward the bluffs and ultimately to Magnolia Manor. She breathed a sigh of relief that her father was not on the streets at the moment, for to explain such a scene to Abijah Clay would have been an impossibility.

5

The morning sunlight, penetrating the opened portieres in a diagonal shaft, awakened Tabitha. There was a blessed few seconds of tranquil peace before her mind began to stir, and then the memories, haunting and agonizing, began to flood back. She remembered, then, every harrowing detail of the preceding day. The long uneasy journey from Natchez-under to Magnolia Manor, during which Nicholas twice almost tumbled from his horse. The incredible experience of getting her husband to bed in a guest room, helped by a solicitous Sophie who cluck-clucked like an old hen saying, "The Massa jest don' know which end is up, thassall, an' even if he knew he wouldn' care!" She recalled, too, the tense scene with Martha Enright, when she told her that her son was home in a drunken condition, at which the old lady sniffed and said, "*He* wants to boss the plantation. *He* wants the top hand. He's not fit, I tell you, not fit!" And finally Tabitha remembered her escape to her own room where she spend a restless night, alternately embarrassed at her memory of entering the Silver Palace and bringing forth her husband, and concerned at what he would say to her when he sobered.

Well, there was no use delaying the inevitable. The

sun was already high, and Tabitha guessed it must be mid-morning. With a feline grace she slipped out of bed, threw off her night garment and got into pantaloons and several petticoats. She put on a white muslin dress with a lavender sash around the waist, which she thought matched her eyes rather well, then took particular care of her toilette. She wanted to look attractive to Nicholas this morning—not that he deserved it, she thought petulantly. She was not certain what his reaction to her boldness in taking him bodily from the Silver Palace might be. He might be angry, in which case a pretty wife might at least reduce the sharpness of his tongue. And even if he was apologetic—a remote possibility—her perfect toilette should at least aid her cause.

Ready at last, Tabitha drew her breath in tightly and descended the delicate winding staircase to the hall. It was not until she had reached the bottom step that she was aware that Nicholas was playing the piano in the music room. This time it was Beethoven, and played with less violence than most of Nicholas's renditions. When she entered the room he stopped abruptly and stood up. He was impeccably dressed in fawn-colored trousers topped by a white ruffled shirt with a thick tan stock under his chin. Tabitha noticed at once the unbearably smug smile on his freshly shaven face.

What, she thought, do I say to him? Do I immediately turn shrewish and scold him about his absence from home? Or do I ignore it completely, as if it had never happened, as if it were something a man was privileged to do and that a wife had no business questioning? But while these questions bounced through her mind, Nicholas opened the conversation.

"You look exceptionally beautiful this morning, my dear," he said, inclining his head slightly. "One would hardly believe that beneath your delicate exterior there lurks the brazen gut of a Roman legionary."

Tabitha halted in her tracks. A compliment followed by a condemnation. Typical of him.

"I accept your compliment, Nicholas," she said cooly, "although the latter portion of it seemed rather meaningless."

"Not meaningless at all, my dear," said Nicholas, rubbing his hands together and smiling over them. "It took considerable fortitude for you to come down to Natchez-under and haul your drunken husband home. I am forced to admire you. Had you not come, I dare say I may have stayed there forever."

Tabitha crossed the room to the large bay window and gazed out over the almost denuded cotton field.

"You might have had the courtesy to let your wife know where you were. No one had any idea where you had gone."

"Exactly as I wished. You will learn, my dear, that I am a man of rash actions. At any moment I may decide to go to New Orleans or Vicksburg—or Natchez-under. I don't always bother to tell people, since I consider it solely my own business."

"Isn't it your wife's business?"

"Rarely. In our case particularly—since our marriage is strictly a business arrangement—I do not consider that the bonds of normal matrimony tie me so tightly that I cannot move."

"But Nicholas!" Tabitha whirled toward him, alarmed as she always was at his evaluation of their marriage. "We must try to make our marriage more than just a convenience or a business arrangement. If we try, we can learn to love each other."

There was no softening in his face, no understanding.

"You are well acquainted with my opinion of love," he said. "It may take you some time to adjust to it, but you will have to. A loveless marriage might kill some women, but I am sure that if you have at your fingertips all the advantages of our high-level society, you will find it tolerable."

Tabitha threw up her hands in a hopeless gesture. She was weary of arguing about the subject of love. She knew that his ideas about love were ingrained, and there was no sense badgering him in an effort to change his mind. He simply would not do it.

"You could at least give it a try," was all she would say.

He shook his head. Taking her by the shoulders and holding her at arm's length, he said: "I pride myself in being a strong man. I tolerate no weaknesses whatever. Love is a weakness and I will not bow to it."

Before Tabitha could conjure up a reply to this strange assertion, a door creaked unexpectedly and Martha Enright entered the room. Her face was as grim and uncompromising as always—like mother like son, Tabitha thought—and her sightless eyes unerringly riveted on the exact spot where Nicholas and Tabitha stood.

"It is you, is it not, Nicholas?" Her voice was rasping.

"Yes."

"I imagine that I do not have to remind you that

you left the plantation at a critical time?"

"It is my plantation," said Nicholas boldly. "I have an overseer to handle matters. I leave when I choose."

Martha Enright managed to convey her contempt for Nicholas's answer by a sniff of her nose.

"Your actions, my son, were nevertheless inexcusable," she said. "I found it necessary for me to travel to New Orleans to make arrangements with your factor. If you continue your irresponsible behavior I will find it necessary as mistress of this plantation to—"

"My dear mother!" Nicholas cut her off. "I remind you that I am married now. My wife is now mistress of this plantation by legal right. I supposed you understood this."

It was a bold statement. Tabitha closed her eyes, expecting at least a frosty denial of her rights by Martha. But there was instead a long silence. The house was hushed. Somewhere upstairs Tabitha could hear Sophie's footsteps, echoing. At last Martha spoke, her words coming in clipped, tight tones.

"I am not unaware of Tabitha's legal rights," she said. "But I am distinctly aware that her experience in handling the multitude of decisions necessary to the proper running of a plantation is virtually nil. When you are on one of your drunken orgies, I am the only one here with enough knowledge to keep this place operating."

She did not wait for a reply, but swept grandly from the room. Tabitha looked apprehensively at Nicholas. His face was mottled with rage, but he said nothing. The stern rigidity of his jaw, the falcon-like fierceness of his eyes, almost made Tabitha shudder. At such

341

moments she was sure that Nicholas was capable of anything—including murder.

"Don't let her words upset you," Tabitha cautioned. "She is quite right, you know. It will take time for me to gain sufficient experience to take over the decisions to be made on the plantation. And I must not appear to fight your mother, Nicholas, but must win my way—our way—in a gradual manner."

His face slowly drained of its color and he looked down at her. The hard uncompromising lines in his face softened.

"Precisely why I married you, my dear—because I needed badly someone who could destroy my mother by degrees, thereby making it unnecessary for me to take rash action. Like matricide!"

Tabitha felt a tremble go through her at that last horrible word. She decided quickly that it was time to change the subject. Realizing she must say something that would have the power to pull Nicholas's mind completely away from his troubles with his mother, she decided to be as sensational as possible.

"Nicholas," she said, "while you were gone something occurred that was frightfully embarrassing to me. I want you to dismiss Doctor Long."

The blunt statement had its desired effect. Nicholas looked at her with a new interest.

"Dismiss him? What in God's name for?"

"He's impertinent!"

"Really?"

"And he insulted me!"

Nicholas's eyebrows arched. He moved to the spinet, sat down and let his fingers roam gently over the mother-of-pearl keys in a running glissando.

"He's a good doctor. I need him." His voice was as soft as the chords he played.

"But he insulted me!"

The fingers stopped with a loud crushing tone. He got up.

"Insulted you?" Instead of being angry, he seemed amused. "The man must be a genius. I would have thought it impossible."

Tabitha felt anger building up in her. Nicholas could make her more irate than any man in the world—except, perhaps, Mike Long. She drew herself up.

"Perhaps if I tell you what he did to your wife you might give the matter more consideration," she snapped. Then she poured out the tale of the sick slave child, and how she had taken the baby to a guest room and how Mike Long had prescribed for it. Nicholas nodded approvingly.

"A touching story," he said, "although I realize, of course, that you were less interested in the recovery of the child than with the impression you were making on the blacks. A rather obvious move, my dear, but I congratulate you nonetheless."

"Nicholas! Now *you're* insulting me! I was very concerned about the baby, even if you and Mike Long don't believe it."

Nicholas's face assumed that taunting expression of amusement.

"So Mike saw through your little subterfuge too? I told you it was obvious. It's something we must guard against."

"What?"

"Your ill-considered actions. While they may be

343

diabolically clever and have a delightful Machiavellian twist that I appreciate, still they are too transparent. You must make more subtle advances, my dear, so they are not so readily apparent to people like your fine doctor."

"But—"

"Anyway, what happened after Mike Long tossed his uncalled-for accusation at you?"

"I tried to throw a vase at him."

"Really?" Nicholas chuckled. "How was your aim?"

"I never threw it. He caught my arm and stopped me!"

Nicholas, much to Tabitha's disgust, seemed highly amused at the story. Tabitha had the feeling that her grim saga was not having the telling influence on Nicholas she had envisioned.

"Then what happened?"

Tabitha looked Nicholas squarely in the eye. Her lips became thin lines.

"He—he spanked me!"

For a moment Nicholas stared at her in disbelief. Then a trace of a smile lifted the corners of his lips.

"He—*what?*"

"Oh, it was most humiliating. He actually spanked me!" Tears began to swim in Tabitha's eyes.

She had expected to see a violent and perhaps even jealous reaction from Nicholas. After all, no man will idly stand by and have another spank his wife! But to her chagrin he only laughed—laughed, in fact, in a way she had never heard him laugh before. It was a loud raucous laugh that echoed in the big room, a laugh of complete merriment that stung and hurt Tabitha.

"God's blood!" ejaculated Nicholas finally. "This Long has qualities I was unaware of. . . . So he really spanked you!"

"He did!"

"Across the knees on your bare bottom?"

"Not on my bare bottom!"

"But across the knees, like a spoiled child?"

"Yes!" She fairly screamed the word, upset that Nicholas should regard this most embarrassing situation with such apparent delight. He laughed again, wholeheartedly, with higher amusement than he had ever revealed to her. Finally the spasms of laughter died down and he spoke to her in bantering tones.

"Well, my dear, I dare say you had it coming!"

"Is that all you can say?" flared Tabitha. "I tell you it was most humiliating and I demand that you get rid of him!" She was hot-eyed and furious now, angry enough to make demands, and she decided to add ridicule to her abuse. "In fact, if you were any kind of man, you'd challenge him to a duel for the insult he has levied at your wife!"

This sally only brought another laugh from Nicholas. "My good woman, you're like all the rest. Women love to have men fight duels over them. Must do a great deal for their egos to see two men duel to the death for them. However, I shan't give you this uplifting pleasure, my dear. Mike Long is a good doctor and comes highly recommended—from my own dear wife, incidentally. I need him on the plantation. I should be doing myself a disservice to either fight him in a duel—which, of course, I would win—or dismiss him from his job."

"Don't you ever think of anything but your own interests?" said Tabitha heatedly.

"Never, my dear. When a man has been persecuted by everyone from his mother down, he builds a wall of resistance to all blandishments. Besides, who am I to interfere with a doctor's prescription? In your case, Doctor Long thought a good spanking was a proper antidote. He prescribed it, and he administered it. A doctor's duty, my dear — I feel he would have been derelict not to have prescribed the medicine he felt would be the most help to you. I must remember to thank him."

He laughed again with hearty amusement and stalked from the room, leaving Tabitha in a state of shock and rage at his inexplicable attitude. She sat for fully half an hour, feeling suddenly small and insignificant. The story of Mike's abuse had done nothing for her, but had had the reverse result of making her look foolish and childlike. Nicholas's reaction to her story had not been at all what she'd expected. That he would blandly — even good-humoredly — accept the insult Mike Long had leveled against her and do nothing about it was incredible to Tabitha. Yet, as she thought about it, it was not so unbelievable at all. Nicholas sorely needed Mike on the plantation to keep the slaves in good health and working. Therefore, as long as Mike had such high value to him, Nicholas would not dismiss him — even if he insulted his wife! The plantation, and the power he derived from it, came first with Nicholas Enright.

6

After her anger cooled, Tabitha on sudden impulse left the house and headed for the stables. She had decided to ride Lady Belle. It was always a relaxing experience to ride through the forest, under the suffused light seeping through the towering oaks and shredded by Spanish moss, and at this moment it seemed a proper medicine for her wounded ego. She would ride to the esplanade and gaze out over the placid waters of the Mississippi, she thought, depending on this favorite scenic spot to make her forget the problems that plagued her.

While she stood waiting for Jeff to saddle Lady Belle, Mike Long loomed in the doorway. Tabitha cursed inwardly her bad luck. If there was anyone in the entire world she did not want to see right now, it was Mike Long.

"I find it convenient to live above the stables," he said, "since I can always see you when you come from the manor. . . . Milady would ride?"

Tabitha looked at him insolently, then withdrew her gaze.

"Hurry with the horse, Jeff," she said crisply.

"Milady is looking beautiful this morning," Mike continued.

Tabitha decided, as she had before, that she despised the doctor. She resented his insistence on speaking to her when she had tried to turn him away. Still, she found it difficult to resist a compliment. She favored him with an answer this time, but a sharp one.

"Will you please stop calling me *milady?*"

"I do so only with the respect due the mistress of a great house," Mike said smoothly.

Tabitha glared at him. He was being deliberately obsequious. His more-than-proper manner annoyed her. She knew that he was slyly poking fun at her, ridiculing her, telling her indirectly that he didn't believe her to be the great lady she pretended.

"The Master has Happy Boy out near the cotton fields," Mike went on. "I must say he seemed in a good mood. Complimented me on something I don't quite understand, in fact. What he called my scientific approach to medicine for females."

"Oh, damn!" Tabitha exploded. "He's impossible!"

Mike Long pulled at his chin thoughtfully. His blue eyes scanned Tabitha with interest.

"You seem distraught. As a doctor I find it pointed to ask what ails you, Tabitha."

"It hardly behooves a slave doctor to inquire," said Tabitha haughtily.

Mike laughed. "I remind milady of her own small beginnings," he said, then added quickly, "But I apologize. Such impertinence is uncalled for."

"Thank you," said Tabitha. Suddenly her brow furrowed in thought. She glanced at Mike Long with a calculating expression. "Do you have anything to do at the moment?"

"Nothing at all. There seems to be no illness among the blacks and no babies are due. Does milady wish something?"

"I'd like you to ride with me," said Tabitha impulsively.

Mike's eyebrows raised inquiringly, but he bowed with a graciousness that covered his surprise.

"A great honor."

"Quit prating about it being an honor and get a horse saddled!" snapped Tabitha peevishly.

As Mike instructed the groom to saddle a second horse, Tabitha had sudden misgivings about her request. What on earth had induced her to ask Mike Long to ride with her? She could not logically account for making such a request; it was as if something inside of her had slipped out of control, as if her lips had spoken words her brain did not want uttered. Mike Long had infuriated and embarrassed her, and yet she had asked him to accompany her. It did not make sense, and she wondered at her own lack of logic. There was the fact, of course, that Mike Long was an attractive man in a rugged sort of way. She had been aware of his masculine appeal for some time. At various intervals during Nicholas's recent absence she had found herself thinking of Mike Long. This fact never ceased to amaze her. She did not know how to explain it, and it was perhaps some deep-seated psychological quirk in her mind which she did not understand that had led her to invite him on a ride. Perhaps, if she could keep her temper and talk rationally to him—a difficult task with Mike Long!—she might discover what it was about him that so intrigued her despite her dislike for him. Was there ever a woman, Tabitha thought, with two more ag-gravating men in her life?

Mike Long helped Tabitha to mount Lady Belle, his hand lingering on her longer, she thought, than was necessary. Mounting a gray stallion, he turned slightly in the saddle and said: "Where to, milady?"

"Nowhere, unless you stop saying milady!"

"Very well, Mrs. Enright. Where?"

"Let's ride to the esplanade."

"The Master will not complain?"

"Why should he?" The three words were devas-tating. They implied not only her disrespect for Nicholas but were a plain implication that Nicholas would never consider a mere slave doctor as any kind of competition for his wife's interest.

They rode off in silence, cutting across the field to the circular path fronting the manor, spurring their mounts along the gravel road, past the colorful flower beds and into the tunnel of magnolias and oaks that led away from the plantation toward the city of Natchez. The horses' hooves beat a rhythmic clippity-clop and the delicate chirping of birds floated song-like on the morning air. The sun, shredded by the moss-draped trees, dappled the pathway with a filigreed pattern. Tabitha felt a tranquility here on the pathway that she never experienced at the manor and for a while she did not speak, reluctant to disturb the soft whisperings of the forest. But at last Tabitha glanced at Mike Long obliquely.

"Do you like your job on the plantation?" she asked.

"I'm fond of the blacks."

"Do you like your *job?*" repeated Tabitha with em-phasis.

He turned his head toward her. A smile was fresh on his face and Tabitha thought, *He has a pleasant smile when he cares to use it, much more pleasant than Nicholas's half-smile.*

"How could one not like working for a woman of such elegance and charm as yourself?"

"Oh, fie!" Tabitha tossed her head. "For once, let's dispense with the synthetic compliments. You didn't think me so charming the other day when you—you—"

"Spanked you?" Mike laughed outright. "I must apologize for that. I had no right. Even though I'm convinced you deserved it."

Tabitha fought to control herself. She had determined to talk sincerely and logically with Mike Long, and was resolved to let nothing he said irritate her. She wanted to find out more about Mike, everything she could about him, and anger would not help.

"You're a riddle, Doctor," she said calculatingly. "I don't understand you at all."

Mike turned away and looked straight ahead, over the graceful arch of his stallion's neck at the road winding silently through the moss-draped oaks.

"Sometimes I don't understand myself," he said more seriously. "I react to people in various ways. You seem to bring out either the best or worst in me, depending on my mood at the moment—and yours."

Tabitha considered this comment carefully.

"Since we seem to be airing our views in complete honesty," she said, "I must tell you that you can be most irritating at times."

Mike laughed again. "It's one of my charms."

"Perhaps it is at that," agreed Tabitha.

They lapsed into prolonged silence and the horses, close together, traversed the narrow road until it widened at the approach to the esplanade. The music of the horses' hooves sharpened as they left the soft loess soil for the hardened road and in seconds they reached the railed edge of the esplanade. Mike dismounted and helped Tabitha slip to the ground. They stood for some time looking out over the broad vista before them. A dense mist lay over the river, like tired clouds sleeping on the water's surface.

"There's something unchanging about the river," Mike said at last. "Man changes, and his works along the river change, but the river itself never does. It doesn't struggle and strive to make itself something it isn't, as man does. It knows its own majesty and its own strength and is content—and I imagine it must secretly laugh at man's feeble efforts to be something he is not."

She looked at him sharply. For a moment she was not sure what he meant. Then she decided that he might be commenting upon her own attempt to be a grand lady of Natchez when, in his opinion, she was not. She chose to ignore this interpretation, however.

"You're something of a philosopher," she said.

He remained silent. The saffron sun dangled like an idle ball of fire in the vaulted sky, greedily sucking up the gray mist from the river. Where the Mississippi broadened and swept into a wide scimitar beneath the bluff, its waters reflected the sun, giving them a golden glow. Tabitha noticed a change in the cotton fields on the Louisiana side; the whiteness was gone and the plants looked barren. Below she could see her own small cabin, and looking down on it now she felt with some headiness the drastic change she had made in her life. Silver Street, Middle Street and Water Street, all interlaced with meandering crossroads, lay in a crazy-quilt pattern below her, and her eyes inadvertently traveled over the rows of hovels to the rickety Silver Palace, standing like a stiff-legged spider on its pilings at the river's edge.

Near the Silver palace a steamboat was nuzzling the quay like a woman snuggling up to her lover. Steamboats were always a thrilling sight to Tabitha. The great gingerbreaded whiteness of them was unbelievable to her, for it seemed that such intricate delicateness belonged only in a fairyland. All steamboats looked the same, and yet they were different. There were always the twin smokestacks with filigree trimming at the tops, the huge paddlewheel that churned the water to a froth, ample decks for produce and animals, another for passengers. Usually the steamboats were heavily laden, and most of the time their cargo was cotton. Some could carry up to 6,000 bales piled in tiers up to the hurricane deck, and when they were thus loaded they sat low in the water and looked like huge white mountains floating downstream.

Only once had Tabitha boarded a steamboat, and it had been one of the thrills of her life. She remembered yet the unbelievable luxury of it: thick spongy carpets, plush draperies, glistening chandeliers . . . dining rooms, saloons, barber shops, women's cabins, card rooms . . . planters sipping their punches and talking about cotton . . . fine ladies on the white stairways.

Still, Tabitha was somewhat afraid of the steamboats. The life of a steamboat was calculated to be only a few years, and many of them ended their days in fiery violence. There were many boiler explosions on the river these days, with much loss of life and many injuries, and that anything as beautiful and serene as a steamboat could be ripped by explosion and fire seemed incredible to her. Right now the huge sidewheel of the docking steamboat was turning, lifting up the yellowish water of the river and cascading it down again, until the captain ordered the boat slowed. Then the wheel stopped, the agitated water receded, and the big steamboat moved on its own momentum until it was dangerously close to the dock. Suddenly, on command of the captain, the wheel reversed and the water boiled up again, and the magnificent vessel came to a gentle halt alongside the crude quay. On shore cannon boomed—as they always did when a steamboat arrived—and the thundering noise made the earth shudder as if it had suddenly awakened from a long sleep.

"Why did you ask me to ride with you?" asked Mike suddenly.

"I don't really know."

"Could the mistress of Magnolia Manor be lonesome?"

"I don't know what you mean by that. I like someone to talk to, if that is what is meant." Her voice showed slight irritation again and she added with searing malice, "At times, even you will do."

"I recall that you were going to have your husband dismiss me."

Tabitha looked away. Her lips framed a pout.

"I changed my mind," she said.

"Or he refused—which?"

She resented his talent for seeing through her lies and she turned on him.

"Are you calling me a liar?"

"Milady, you are a congenital liar," laughed Mike. "As a doctor, I can spot symptoms."

Tabitha did not reply. They walked along the esplanade railing for a few moments, watching the ornate carriages come and go, some stopping as their well-dressed passengers alighted to view the panoramic scene, others slowly driving by, usually with an elegantly dressed couple inside peering out. They talked little during the walk and managed to avoid controversial matters, and at last they returned to their horses and mounted again. On the way back to the manor, in the cool shadows of the oak-lined road, Mike turned part way in his saddle and regarded Tabitha with the most serious expression she had ever beheld on his face.

"Tabitha," he said, "I don't want you to take offense at what I'm about to ask. But as a doctor I am concerned about Nicholas Enright. Has he treated you well?"

Tabitha started. She tried to determine what had prompted the question. Had he heard rumors? Was the story of their wedding night common gossip on the plantation? She could tell nothing from his face. It had the doctor's unrevealing mask.

"Yes, of course." What else, she thought, could she say?

"I'm glad," he said, "although I am concerned that your marriage may be a difficult one."

Tabitha started to protest, but he waved her down.

"Please. I'm talking now as a professional man. I

have known men like Mr. Enright. Some of them are totally incapable of loving anybody but themselves. They sometimes are cruel. I hope, in Nicholas Enright's case, I am wrong."

Tabitha's poise was shaken by his words, but she tried to cover up her concern. That Mike Long had been astute enough to evaluate Nicholas, and had voiced the very fears that she herself felt so strongly, frightened her. Suddenly she felt a need to defend Nicholas.

"Nicholas is often arrogant and cold," she admitted. "But I'm sure he could not be cruel to me." What a lie! Why was she saying this?

Mike studied her closely, a frown gathering on his brow. Tabitha felt that she was being medically diagnosed.

"What does Nicholas fear?" he asked.

"I don't know what you mean."

"I detect in his manners and his words that he feels persecuted, that everyone is working against him. This is not a healthy situation, Tabitha."

Tabitha felt increasingly distressed at the trend of the conversation but at the same time she welcomed it. Nicholas's strange actions had frightened her, and she had wanted badly to talk to someone about them. Momentarily she forgot her deep-seated dislike for Mike Long. Suddenly she wanted to consult with him about Nicholas, as one does with any doctor.

"Mike, will you help me?"

"I will try."

"I want to tell you everything about Nicholas, and I want you to listen strictly on a professional basis. I'm asking for advice."

"I understand."

She drew in her breath as if in preparation for an ordeal. When she spoke her voice seemed too loud for the quiet of the forest and she lowered it lest it sound on the edge of hysteria.

"As you say, Nicholas does seem to have a feeling of persecution. I think it stems from the actions of his mother when he was a small boy." She told him, then, of the injury he had suffered to his leg and how he accused his mother of not having the bones set.

"What would be his mother's reason for doing that?"

"Nicholas's mother wanted to keep her son with her as long as she lived. She took this means of assuring herself that he would grow up crippled and unwanted by the opposite sex."

"It sounds hard to believe."

"I know. But Mrs. Enright is a tough and cynical old woman. If you saw her, talked to her, you could believe it of her. At any rate, Nicholas has felt ever since that everything—life, the world—was against him. He seems to fear many things. He thinks his mother is out to defeat him in everything he wants in life. He believes other plantation owners dislike him and want to see him destroyed. He is afraid, too, of a slave rebellion, which is why he treats his slaves kindly. He told me after our marriage that we would have to fight to maintain our position in Natchez, that everyone would be out to get us."

"How does he appear when he talks this way?"

"He has a haunted look in his eyes."

"Anything more?"

"Well, I recently went to Natchez-under to bring

him home. He was drunk, so perhaps that explains it. But he kept telling me he had heard voices plotting against him."

Mike Long's face was set in deep lines of concern. He stared for some time into space, saying nothing.

"Is there something wrong with him, Mike?" Tabitha asked anxiously. "Something seriously wrong?"

Mike hunched his shoulders. "I would not be a very good doctor if I made a prognosis without thoroughly examining the patient, would I?" he asked. "However, the symptoms you outline give me cause for concern. Do you want to know what I think is wrong?"

"Yes."

"Well, let me begin this way. When Nicholas came to me in Natchez-under to hire me as a doctor for the blacks, he mentioned to me his fear of a revolt. He told me he wanted me to act not only as a doctor, but as a spy."

"A spy!"

"Yes. He wanted me to report to him any sign of a revolt among his people." He smiled wanly, and they rode for a moment, listening to the soft clop-clop of the horses' hooves on the sponge-like soil. "The request intrigued me, and I agreed to come with him because I wanted to study him as much as the slaves."

Tabitha drew in her breath. It did not sound good, not good at all.

"Another thing he told me," said Mike, "was that he would hire me if I promised not to become like the rest of them. He was indefinite when I asked him exactly who 'they' were, but he said that many people were out to destroy him, and if I didn't join his enemies we would get along fine. I observed the look in his eyes that you described as haunted, Tabitha, and I was worried—for not only him but for you."

"For God's sake, Mike! Tell me! What's wrong with him?"

"Have you ever heard of paranoia, Tabitha?" Mike asked.

"No."

"It isn't a generally known term, but after my meeting with Nicholas I went to my books and looked it up. The ancient Greeks used the term to describe a distraught or distracted mind. The term fell into disuse until the Middle Ages when it became synonymous with any type of insanity."

"Oh, Mike! You don't think—"

"A doctor named Heinroth in 1818 classed the paranoias as disorders of thinking. I would say that a persecution mania, which I have seen a few times, falls in that class."

Tabitha looked at him with genuine horror in her eyes. She shook her head slowly in disbelief.

"Are you trying to say that Nicholas is insane?"

"No." He shook his head. "Not in the sense that people become crazed and violent and unmanageable. But there are several stages of paranoia, and Nicholas shows signs of going through them. First, the individual affected becomes thoroughly wrapped up in himself, extremely self-centered, unable to think of anyone but himself and his own good. This can take the form of an overbearing arrogance."

Tabitha's eyes widened. She nodded slowly.

"Arrogance—yes."

"Eventually he becomes suspicious of other people. Because he feels so strongly his own importance, he thinks others are out to undo him. He is suspicious and misinterprets remarks he overhears. If a person so much as leaves the room at the moment he appears, he thinks it has some special significance, that everything and every action is aimed personally at him. Do you understand?"

"I think so."

"So finally he believes there is some gigantic plot against him. And hallucinations of hearing, such as voices plotting against him, is a common symptom."

Tabitha felt her insides knot together. What Mike Long was saying fit Nicholas perfectly. God in Heaven, what sort of man had she married?

"I don't want to frighten you further," said Mike kindly, "but I must tell you at least this. The true sufferer of a persecution mania eventually suspects that his food is poisoned, that people are placing poisonous vapors in the air, or that there is some monstrous organized society carrying out activities against him. Everything, no matter how small or unimportant, has a special meaning to him—is directed against him."

Tabitha could feel her heart pounding crazily. This was worse than she had dared to think. She wanted to tell Mike about Nicholas's violence on their wedding night, but she could not bring herself to do so. Instead she said: "Mike. If—if Nicholas is truly suffering this way, what will finally happen?"

"It's hard to say. He might retreat from life, lock himself in a room, stuff paper in the door cracks to ward off poisonous vapors, sleep with a gun in his bed. Or he might flee to a completely new environment, to escape his supposed tormentors. In some cases he might become dangerous and attack those he believes are his persecutors. One doesn't know."

"Is—is there any cure?"

"I know of nothing," said Mike softly. "Please, Tabitha, forgive me if I've frightened you. But I have worried about this since meeting Nicholas. I felt you ought to know what the possibilities are. I don't say, at this point and without the aid of a thorough examination, that Nicholas is paranoiac. I know that he shows some of the symptoms. That is all. We will have to watch him closely. And be aware, Tabitha, that I am at your service any time of day or night if you need me." He lowered his gaze and said, "It was one of the reasons I took this job, Tabitha—to help you if I could."

She looked at him, and all at once there was new respect for him. Respect that transcended all the petty little irritations that had marked their acquaintance up until now.

"Thank you." Her voice was small.

"I want to ask you something else, Tabitha," he said. "Not as a doctor this time, but as a man. Do you love Nicholas Enright?"

"Of course I do!" The words shot automatically from Tabitha's mouth, without thought behind them, because they were words she knew she must say.

"Your answer was too quick," commented Mike, the banter returning to his voice. "Do you love Nicholas Enright, or do you love what he stands for?"

Suddenly she found herself on the defensive again.

"I appreciate what you've told me about Nicholas," she said, "but you have no right to question me about our relationship."

Mike Long did not answer. Instead he reached out quickly, before she could divine his intentions, and with his free arm took her about the waist. His strength pulled her toward him at the same time that the horses nudged against each other, flank to flank. Before she realized what was happening, his mouth pressed against hers. His lips were warm, moist and questing, and Tabitha felt her own lips almost bruised against her teeth by the violence of his kiss. She put her hands against his chest, wanting to shove him away, but the feeling came again, the same sensation she had experienced when he had held her tight against him during the riot in Natchez-under, the feeling she had never savored with Nicholas—and she did not want to stop him. For several seconds her desires and her conscience fought each other, then at last he broke the embrace himself, and his eyes, deep now and serious, scanned her face.

She pulled away from him, her own eyes afire with pretended anger, but it amazed her to realize that she was not really angry at all. Nevertheless, she kicked at her horse's flank as Mike let go of the reins.

"You're an insufferable beast!" she fired at him, knowing that a protest was in order, and then the horse, startled by the heel of her shoe in his flank, dug in its hooves and broke into a trot. Mike watched the palomino go, kicking up dirt with its beating hooves as it trotted toward Magnolia Manor. Tabitha felt a curious bewilderment take hold of her—a painful embarrassment not only at Mike's precipitous action but because she felt a personal guilt in tolerating as much of it as she had. After all, his behavior had been atrocious, and even though she was not as irate as she had pretended to be, she felt a need to punish him for the liberties he had assumed. Yes, she thought wildly, he would have to go. She would again implore Nicholas to dismiss him. Mike Long was too dangerous to have around, too dangerous because Tabitha was afraid to trust either him or herself.

Even as the cool breeze stirred by her trotting palomino's motion fanned her face, her lips still burned with the fever of Mike's kiss and her entire body was tingling and trembling from the experience. She knew instinctively that she had no right to feel this agonizing thrill. She was angry at herself because she could not put it aside, and defensively she transferred her anger to Mike. So maybe he was a good doctor for the slaves. Maybe he had told her the truth about Nicholas too, and maybe he had even been concerned for her welfare and safety, as he had said. Still, he was something of a cad, for no gentleman kissed a married lady forcibly in the sheltered depths of a forest.

She rode Lady Belle straight to the stable and turned the horse over to Jeff. Then she walked quickly to the house. Before she entered she heard Nicholas at the spinet. He was playing softly, something melodious and sweet which she did not recognize. He looked up when she entered, his fingers bringing the melody to an end.

"What's the matter?" he asked. "You seem distraught."

She wanted to tell him about Mike, but she held back. She needed to think the problem through before confronting Nicholas with her complaint, and besides she feared that Nicholas might only laugh at her as he had before. The hilarity Nicholas had exhibited when she had told him of Mike's indiscretion in spanking her was still too fresh in her mind to permit her to lodge another complaint about the backwoods doctor.

"I had a hard ride, that's all," she lied quickly.

"Does one good sometimes to ride a horse hard and forget all else," Nicholas agreed. "So few women have the feeling for horses that men do. It's a satisfactory comradeship." His face clouded suddenly. He arose, crossed to where she had collapsed into a chair, and looked down on her. "My dear, I have something to speak to you about. I suppose a true gentleman would offer proper apologies for such actions as those occurring on our wedding night. However, since I do not claim to be a gentleman, I shall refrain from any maudlin statements by simply saying that now you know what I am like."

Tabitha stared at him in surprise, for up to now he had said nothing about the horror of their wedding night.

"It's all right, Nicholas," was all she could think to say.

He smiled, perhaps in grim recollection at the distress he had caused her.

"Maybe you should have heeded Mother's warning."

"Nicholas—"

"Oh, I know she told you about my—shortcomings. It's a favorite topic of hers. However, it pleases me to know that in you, Tabitha, she collided head-on with an entirely new reaction to her dire warnings. You were determined to be a plantation owner's wife, whatever the cost, and Mother's warning that I was impotent wasn't strong enough to deter you from your path—isn't that so? I dare say my incapacity as a lover will not unduly pain you. You now have everything else you wanted—power, prestige, position. I suspect all this will adequately compensate for lack of a sex life."

"You make me sound so predatory, Nicholas," Tabitha objected.

"Yes. That is the word, isn't it?"

"Besides," she continued primly, "you needn't worry about our problems abed hampering our marriage. You know very well that sex isn't as important to a woman as to a man."

Nicholas laughed shortly, throwing his head back in high amusement.

"You *are* rapidly becoming an elegant lady, aren't you? Our great ladies traditionally ignore such tawdry things as sex—most of them believing that if they pay no attention to it, it will somehow go away. They take the viewpoint that the carnal desires are only for men—not highly bred women. I suspect that's why so many planters keep a convenient Negress on the scene or a willing mulatto in town."

"Oh, fie!" Tabitha said petulantly. "What's so good about a black wench anyway?"

"Ask Faunce Manley some time. He should be able to tell you in quite lecherous detail," chuckled Nicholas. "However, we stray from the subject. You will tolerate my—uh—shortcomings, won't you?"

"Of course, Nicholas." She reached up and took his hand. She unaccountably felt a sudden fondness for him. She realized how difficult it must be for Nicholas, proud and haughty, to say such things, and she knew that his jesting manner was designed to cover up what must be a total embarrassment for him.

"I have decided on arrangements," he said with a peremptory note in his voice. "From now on you will continue to occupy the master bedroom. I will use the guest room. It is better that way."

"But, Nicholas—"

"It is better," he repeated. "If it is not done this way, you will be subjected to other experiences like that of your wedding night. I don't want it to happen. I need you, and I cannot lose you."

She looked at him in amazement. He was refusing to share her bed—not, Tabitha was shrewd enough to guess, because of any true concern for her welfare, but because of his own interests. He had said, "I need you." With these words he had managed to convey the fact that, needing her as a foil to his mother, he did not want to jeopardize their relationship needlessly in the bedchamber. The analysis disturbed her and she spoke resentfully.

"Nicholas, when are you going to learn to love me for my own sake instead of as a weapon against your mother?"

His face reddened under her words. Angrily, his fists clenched at his sides.

"Goddamn it, Tabitha, quit prating about love! I told you once there is no such thing!" He paced the floor for a moment, defying her to reply. After a minute his face drained of color and he slowly returned to normal. "There is other news I have for you," he said, changing the subject abruptly. "The cotton is almost all picked. I will be leaving in a week for New Orleans aboard the *Creole*. John McRae and Faunce Manley will be going with me. I shall check with my factor on Mother's arrangements. I also intend to buy a few more blacks. I'll be gone a week, perhaps ten days. During my absence, you may have some difficulty with Mother."

"I will do my best to avoid an open break with her, Nicholas," Tabitha replied. "But I do feel that I must stand up for our rights."

The use of the word "our" did not escape Nicholas. He started to smile, and Tabitha thought he might go all the way this time, but it froze on his face. He leaned down and kissed her lightly on the forehead.

"I have great confidence in you," he said, "if for no other reason than the fact that you are so damned ruthless."

Tabitha smiled. Despite his sarcastic way of putting it, there now seemed to be a meeting of minds. Her heart was almost singing. Nicholas had come as close to tenderness in his fleeting kiss upon her forehead as he had ever come, and Tabitha hoped that this was the beginning of a change in his attitude toward her. For a moment she could think of nothing else except how grand and wonderful her life would be if Nicholas could look upon her as something else than a wife of convenience. If not love, she would settle for respect. And then her thoughts of such bliss were rudely shattered as the shadow of what Mike Long had told her crossed her mind.

Paranoia!

And, to compound her problem, Mike Long's kiss was still unaccountably hot on her lips and in her memory.

7

The week before Nicholas left for New Orleans with
old John McRae and Faunce Manley proved to be one
of the most pleasant yet spent at Magnolia Manor.
Nicholas, for some unfathomable reason of his own,
seemed determined to please Tabitha. They took advantage of the warmest days of early October to go for
long rides through the shaded woods, sometimes in the
handsome barouche and on other occasions on
horseback, taking with them a picnic lunch and
spreading it upon the soft ground, enjoying to the
fullest the still-warm sun and capricious winds of the
heights. During these sojourns, Tabitha studied
Nicholas closely for any hint that he was changing.
His attitude toward her had softened appreciably, yet
she was not sure if this was genuine or a deliberately
calculated plan with some mysterious motive behind
it. He smiled oftener, though never fully, and his
heart seemed lighter than it had been since she had
first met him. He took an interest in smaller things,
where the little unimportant matters of life had never
before won his attention. Once they picked wild-
flowers together with the spontaneous joy of young
children; another time they rode into the city and
dined at a fashionable restaurant; and often they rode

to the esplanade and gazed down on the soft-flowing river below them. On Sunday they even attended the First Presbyterian Church, and Tabitha was surprised at the number of people who made it a point to greet Nicholas and his new bride.

Tabitha suspected that his kindness was meant to atone for his crude actions on their wedding night, and that Nicholas expected her to understand this without the need of his explaining his feelings in embarrassing words. But, despite many moments of cheerfulness, he never really lost his seriousness, nor his haughty manners, nor the cold reserve in which he held their relationship.

Once, in a thoughtful mood, he said: "You and I, Tabitha. We're going to win out over Mother. Before I found you, I never thought so. A man has no weapons to fight a woman's subtleties.. He can physically punish another man, but a woman must be defeated by another woman. You have fought the battle well so far, my dear."

"I wish no such battle was necessary," said Tabitha truthfully. "I wish she would accept me."

"She will never accept any threat to her personal domain. Mother couldn't live if she was not the dominant personality. She would wither inside and die."

Then Tabitha deftly changed the subject, so that he would not dwell on his troubles, for she did not want to spoil the magic of his mood. She was encouraged, too, that he made no further reference to being persecuted or hearing voices, and she thought that perhaps her presence and his liking for her had eased his mind and dimmed his fears. It was possible that Mike Long's dire prognosis was incorrect, and that all

369

Nicholas needed was the knowledge that he was wanted to make his fears vanish.

At the same time that she was making such progress with Nicholas, Tabitha was adding another strong card to her hand. She was rapidly winning the affection of the blacks on the plantation. Since her experience with Emerald's baby, the blacks almost fawned at her feet. They loved her dearly, wanting to talk to her as she walked among them, looking at her with admiration in their black, white-lined eyes. On several occasions Nicholas remarked about it.

"They love you, my dear. That gives you a strong hand, because they despise Mother. They will work more willingly if they think they are working for you. We must get across to them that you are the true mistress of Magnolia Manor. If they love you, it will reflect in the work they do in the fields, and the plantation will prosper. They are valuable allies in our battle." The businesslike, pragmatic outlook again, thought Tabitha, but wasn't she as guilty as Nicholas?

Despite Nicholas's softening feelings for her, he still did not sleep with Tabitha at night. He clung to his plan to use the guest room, protecting her against his devious and erotic nature. And, much to her surprise, the separation did not particularly distress Tabitha. She was willing, at least for the moment, to accept a loveless marriage for the purpose of cementing her position as mistress of the manor. Perhaps on some future day she might be able to win his love, but right now she was content to let this phase of their partnership remain dormant until the marriage ship was on even keel.

Meanwhile, Tabitha had deftly hardened her approach to Martha Enright. She no longer showered the old woman with extravagant compliments. She felt it necessary now to assert herself, demand her rights—always in a nice but firm manner—and let Martha Enright know that she intended to protect her newly won position on the plantation. On several occasions when she strongly asserted herself, she was surprised to find that Martha remained docile. But she did not like the alertness of the old woman's face and there was no fathoming her mind at all. Tabitha was constantly on guard against her.

Tabitha found, too, that she was gaining the respect—if not the love—of some of the other planters' wives. Nicholas made it a point to call with her at neighboring plantations, and those she had not before met treated her the new bride with the courtesy due her. But Tabitha was not fooled by their blandishments. They had no true feeling of closeness to her. It was simply that Magnolia Manor was one of the biggest and wealthiest plantations in Natchez, and in the status-conscious society of the planters no one ignored its owner, Nicholas Enright. To be invited to an Enright soiree was the apex of social achievement; to be omitted, the depths of disgrace. And because Magnolia Manor weighed so heavily in the minds of Natchez ladies the aura of respect also fell upon the new mistress of the house.

Among her fast-growing circle of acquaintances, Tabitha found that Garland McRae was by far the best and most genuine. The attractive young woman and her aged husband drew closer to Nicholas and Tabitha than any of the others, and they spent many evenings together at both Magnolia Manor and the

McRae menage, which was called Bellaire. The men would discuss politics in heated but friendly tones, or get into an argument about the best ways to produce cotton, while the women would discuss the slippery vagaries of social conduct and the wifely problems of plantation life—for it fell to the women to supervise household servants, the kitchen, the cellars, the dairies, and the sewing rooms. During these discussions Martha Enright would sit statue-like, resenting the fact that Tabitha thought these concerns to be hers, and finally she would retire to her room when the resentment became unbearable. Tabitha always had a feeling of victory when she left.

At the opposite end of the social spectrum, in Tabitha's mind, were the Manleys. Faunce and Jane Manley made the biggest show of liking her, and for that reason Tabitha was convinced they despised her. Their false pretenses were amateurishly transparent. Faunce never missed an opportunity to loudly compliment Tabitha in front of others, and the falsity of his comments was so blatantly obvious that they fooled no one. Jane was more discreet, but Tabitha knew the woman harbored a feeling of contempt for her that was almost unbearable.

Nevertheless, when Nicholas, Faunce Manley, and John McRae departed for New Orleans, the three wives rode together to the esplanade to see them off. Tabitha would have accompanied Nicholas to the dock, but Jane Manley demurred. As a lady of Natchez, she explained, she felt it inelegant to travel to the dock area, which—as Garland and Tabitha must know—was overrun with profane men and questionable women, thus managing to convey a slight contempt for Tabitha's origins. At this propriety Tabitha almost retched—as she was sure Garland did—but they complied with Jane's wishes. As a result they saw their husbands board the *Creole* only from a distance, and saw the water churn white as the big sidewheel revolved and the steamboat moved cautiously into the depth of the river channel. Then the women returned to Magnolia Manor where Sophie served tea and cafe noir with small sugar cakes and brioche. And like women everywhere they discussed their absent husbands.

"I heartily dislike Faunce going to New Orleans," said Jane Manley in half-shocked tones. "Although I realize it is necessary for business purposes, it's such a degrading place."

Tabitha's interest quickened. Just as she knew much about the sin of Natchez-under, so she had heard of the awful debauchery of New Orleans.

"If all I've heard of the Vieux Carre is true, it must be a terrible place," she agreed, mentally resenting Jane's pretensions of ladylike alarm.

Garland chuckled. "You and your young husbands! If you had married a man as old as John, you'd have nothing to worry about!"

"Garland! You shock me," said Tabitha in a delicious tone of voice that plainly indicated she was not shocked at all.

"It's really quite simple," said Garland. "John has long since passed the age of certain—uh—desires. But you know how young men are. Like eager stallions."

"And unfortunately there are plenty of mares to accommodate them in New Orleans," sniffed Jane.

Garland's eyes narrowed and a knowing expression

crossed her oval face.

"It works both ways," she said. "Did it ever occur to you that there are, as well, plenty of young men willing to accommodate a lonesome woman left alone on a plantation?"

"Shame on you, Garland," scolded Jane. "Such thoughts should not even enter the head of a married woman!"

Garland chuckled again at the little sensation her remark had caused.

"Perhaps I shouldn't think of such things. But then I have a different problem than you do. My old man is too old to—shall I say—satisfy my requirements. My lonesomeness is therefore continuous, whether or not he is home. When he leaves, I must say my opportunity for satisfaction is greater—if, of course, I choose to make use of it."

Jane Manley humphed to show her disgust at the trend the conversation was taking. Then she leaned forward in a confidential pose.

"Do you suppose," she asked, "that our husbands have ever attended a quadroon ball?"

Garland laughed. She seemed in the merriest of moods.

"Why, of course they have! Why shouldn't they? They're alone in a strange city. They're away from their wives. Why not?"

"Garland! The light manner in which you treat such matters can be very disquieting!" said Jane sharply. "I personally would not want Faunce to attend such a ball."

Tabitha had never heard of a quadroon ball and she made a helpless gesture.

"I'm afraid I'm dreadfully ignorant of such things, but what is a quadroon ball?"

Jane Manley tossed a suspicious glance at Tabitha, implying that any girl from Natchez-under must have heard of quadroon balls.

"You are the innocent thing, aren't you?" she said scathingly.

"Which only goes to prove that innocence can thrive anywhere—even in Natchez-under," said Garland helpfully.

"Thank you," said Tabitha. "And now, about a quadroon ball. Since you seem to be so knowing about it, Jane, suppose you tell me what it is."

Jane sniffed slightly under the implication now in Tabitha's voice. When she spoke it was in the tone of a mother telling her child a simple fact of life.

"My good woman, I *will* explain. The quadroon balls—sometimes called the Bals du Cordon Bleu—are an attraction to half the gentry in New Orleans and for plantation owners from miles around. The girls at these affairs are all mixed bloods, but all of them very gorgeous, they tell me. Real wenches for a designing man, to put it bluntly."

"It sounds like a brothel," said Tabitha.

"Yes, but with a difference. As the young men of New Orleans drift around the dance floor with their quadroon or mulatto partners, the mothers of the girls sit around the edges of the floor. If a man decides he wants his partner as a mistress, he must go to the mother and ask permission."

"Heavens! Isn't that highly embarrassing for all concerned?"

"Not at all. The mothers are anxious for their

daughters to make a good match, just as they would be in marriage. These quadroons and mulattoes are taught almost from birth that their one important job on earth is to please men. The only stipulation is that each mother tries to make sure that her daughter is taken by a man of wealth and distinction and worth."

"It sounds unbelievable," said Tabitha.

"What happens is this—the man informs the mother that he wishes her daughter as a mistress. The mother then will haggle over financial arrangements. Usually she demands that her daughter be kept in a luxurious apartment, well-fed, well-clothed, and that any children resulting from the union will be amply cared for and educated. If the man is willing to go to this expense, then his mistress will remain devoted and as true to him as if the union was sanctified by a marriage ceremony. The only difference is that she will not have him all the time. He will visit her only on those occasions when he is able to escape from his trusting wife."

Tabitha shook her head. Miscegenation had never quite made sense to her.

"And the men, do they really enjoy these women?"

Jane laughed cynically. "I am not an eavesdropper, but I happened to overhear my husband and some other planters talking in our stable about the quadroons' lascivious talents. What they said was fit to be said only in a stable, believe me, and could not be repeated by a lady!"

"How awful!" said Garland, but Tabitha looked at her quickly and caught a wicked glitter in her eye that belied her expression of shock. "Men are really beasts, aren't they?"

"I'll tell you this much," said Jane, eager to divulge some of the conversation she had heard even if it couldn't be repeated by a lady. "I heard a couple of planters say that the quadroons had forgotten more about the art of love than plantation white women ever knew. Now that's something to think about, ladies!"

Tabitha was hardly incensed by Jane's statement, but she felt obliged to say, "Do men expect their wives to act like harlots?"

Garland laughed delightedly. "Yes! Of course they do! And that's precisely where we wives fail. We don't gratify our men as completely as a whore would!"

"You're a fine one to talk," Jane snorted. "In your case, your husband is beyond the point of such desires."

"Yes, of course," said Garland mischievously. "But being unable to perform as he did in earlier years, he has substituted other methods still in his power. I would be derelict in my duties if I viewed his methods as the feeble efforts of an old man and did not try to help him."

"Shocking!" Jane's voice was filled with righteousness, and they dropped the subject.

When the two women left, Tabitha retired to her room and seated herself at the escritoire. She took the quill from the inkhorn and proceeded to write a letter to Nicholas. It would have to be written now, for it would follow on the next steamboat going downriver, and mail service was slow and cumbersome. But her hand poised over the paper and she could think of nothing to write. Only one question kept nagging at her mind: Did Nicholas have a quadroon mistress in

New Orleans?

Having asked it, Tabitha carried it further. Did it matter if he did? She felt an intense, burning jealousy surge through her and she thought, *Damn it, he's my husband. And even if I don't love him—and he doesn't love me—he's still mine. And I will not tolerate any dusky wench sharing him with me!*

She sat for a long moment, seething inwardly at the thought of Nicholas having a faraway mistress. Then it suddenly occurred to her that Nicholas was impotent anyway. What would he do with a mistress? Nothing, unless these sexually efficient women really did have techniques that plantation women had never heard of, as Jane Manley had implied.

For a while she allowed her feeling of jealousy to dominate her, and then, unbidden, her mind bridged a great gap and the image impinged on her troubled mind dissolved and it was not Nicholas she was seeing at all but Mike Long. She felt again the burning kiss stolen in the shadowy protection of the forest, and how she had responded to it with greater fervency than any kiss ever delivered by Nicholas.

She leaped up from the escritoire and threw the quill down with a show of temper. Damn it, damn it, damn it! Why did Mike Long continue to intrude like some unwanted ghost on her mind?

9

The garden house at Bellaire was a cool inviting place during the heat of the day. Garland McRae spent many hours there in dreamy relaxation, and had equipped it with a dressing table and tester bed so that it might serve as a second bedchamber when she desired a nap during the day.

Garland sat now at the dressing table and looked critically at her image in the ornate mirror with its gold leaf frame. She was naturally aware that she was an attractive woman, and it had occurred to her on more than one occasion that her beauty was frightfully wasted in her marriage with old John McRae. John was a darling, but he was a ninety-year-old darling, and his limitations more than once had vexed the younger Garland. She looked with secret admiration at her soft and delicate features, her magnolia-white skin topped by the golden cascade of her hair, and she knew instinctively that she was one of the prettiest of all the plantation women she knew.

Of course, there was Tabitha. Tabitha was a lovely and delightful creature, and Garland liked her immensely. There was, as she had pointed out to Tabitha, a kindred spirit between them. And this likeness drew her closer to Tabitha than she had ever been to any other plantation lady. She had never liked the exquisite families of Natchez. Her rebellious nature had forced her to view them as conforming snobs who lived a particular way because others lived that way, who vied jealously with each other in the homes they built and the way they furnished them. If one plantation family imported all of its furniture from France, another had to counter with fashions from Spain or England. If one had marble fireplaces from Carrara, another must have the most beautiful Limoges china. There was competition, too, when it came to soirees and dinners, each family striving to present the most sumptuous table and thus be rated high on Natchez's much-admired social list. And the men competed with their crops, and the number of blacks they held, and ran their finest horses at the quarter track in Natchez-under-the-Hill to show the superiority of their own personal strain. It was a constant, endless and hopeless race to keep up with each other, and Garland was not particularly fond of people whose lives were spent in a feverish drive to outdo their neighbors.

Garland was not a conformist, and this was perhaps the reason she had received such a devious thrill out of marrying ancient John McRae. It had shocked the plantation wives from their empty little heads to the hems of their flowing silk skirts. The countryside and the city of Natchez had buzzed for months with frank speculation. Garland is so beautiful; why should she marry that old wretch? With all the fine single men around, looking for a woman of Garland's beauty and charm, why would she pass them all up for John McRae? And then the answers came—whispered, malicious, acrimonious. She figures, of course, to get his money. The old fool can't last much longer, and Garland is willing to sacrifice a few good years of her life to inherit his wealth. And when she does, she'll marry a man of her choice. Yes, Garland was a shrewd one, they said; she had a head on her. She was, in fact, a diabolical opportunist, as predatory as a hawk, but at least she was making old John's late years the happiest of his life, for he was unbelievably proud of her and strutted about like a bantam rooster when Garland was at his side.

Garland smiled at her recollections. They had whispered plenty about her, and most of it was true. But she did not care. Perhaps in a few years—for John could not live much longer—she would be sole owner of Bellaire and the McRae cotton fortune. She would also be her own boss, and could select a man to marry or reject all of them, as she wished. She might spend a year or two traveling—to Paris, Rome, the Orient—and, if she felt like it, she might never come back to Natchez at all. Which, she thought, would give the women of Natchez even more to speculate about.

Garland selected a tiny bottle of French perfume from her dressing table and applied it lightly to her hair. She was dressed only in a silken peignoir with low decolletage, but she had applied makeup and she knew she looked ravishing. That was her intention, for her lover would be here any moment now.

He was not the first lover she had had since marrying John McRae. She had enjoyed several. Garland had, quite early in her teens, recognized something in her makeup uncommon to many women—an imperative physical need for men. There was some fire deep inside her that burned feverishly at the sight of a virile male, a longing and desire that had first shamed her but, as she grew older, became an integral part of her personality. She remembered her first sexual experience at the age of fifteen in the sun-warmed softness of the hayloft on her father's farm. The boy had been a huge lout from a nearby farm, overcome by lust and clumsy and brutal in his eagerness. But Garland had shivered through an unimaginable ecstasy so strong that she henceforth could not look at a man without shameful notions prodding at her mind.

Since marrying John McRae, her sorties into the realm of extramarital sex had been limited to those rare times when John was absent from the plantation. McRae's absence now in New Orleans had given her this opportunity to see her present lover. He would come through the woods, approaching the garden house from the rear, careful that none of the slaves or household servants saw him. He would knock stealthily on the back door of the garden house at any moment now, and she would greet him, and that which she had been denied by her marriage to John McRae would again be hers.

Garland tingled with excitement. That her actions were adulterous hardly occurred to her. If she had any twinges of conscience, they were shoved aside rather brusquely. She could easily rationalize her actions. She was young. She had the normal desires of a passionate woman. Her marriage was unsatisfactory, except in a monetary way, and she was entitled to the kind of life meant for the young. In her restless mind, the fact that she had married feeble old McRae in a frenzy of ambition, did not make it mandatory that she forego all other forms of frenzy.

John, she realized, would be hard put to understand such obtuse reasoning. Or if he did understand, he would not approve. John was normally a mild man, but when his anger was aroused he could become dangerously violent. But Garland was prepared for him, should he ever learn about her indiscretions. She would then tell him frankly that she craved and needed the company of younger men, and that if he insisted on being stubborn about the matter she would divorce him. This, she knew, would bring him to heel. Garland was aware that she was old John's greatest pride. That he, a man of ninety, could have a wife of Garland's age and beauty, was almost incomprehensible to him—and he presented her with such chest-swelling pride everywhere he went that he could not bear being without her. John would submit to almost any arrangement to keep her, of this Garland was certain.

Her thoughts were interrupted by the expected knock on the door. Garland glanced at herself in the mirror, patted a stray strand of hair back into place, and moved lithely to the door. Her diaphanous nightdress clung to her fine body, revealing every curve and indentation, precisely as she had intended. She paused for a moment with her hand on the latch, her heart pounding furiously, her entire body feeling a glow of expectation. Then she pulled open the door and smiled seductively at her visitor.

"Come in," she said softly.

Big Sam walked into the room.

10

Winter came reluctantly to the Natchez country, as it often did. It began in November, after the cotton crop was in, with soft gentle rains that pattered delicately, like the toes of ballet dancers, on the roof of Magnolia Manor and stippled the dust in the fields. By December the rains had increased to heavy downpours that turned the land into oozing mud and washed dull gray streaks down the white sides of the manor, transforming the sunny world into one of moist dreariness.

The slaves huddled in their drafty whitewashed cabins, away from the driving rain and the chill bite of the wind that swept upward from the mudflats along the Mississippi and over the bluff, as if propelled by a cosmic broom. And in Magnolia Manor, itself, candles and whale oil lamps burned even in daytime to chase away the ever-present gloom, and the fireplaces crackled and roared to fend off the creeping cold. The rainfall—sometimes listless and at other times wildly aggressive—continued through the winter, and did not diminish until April.

It was one of the wettest and most miserable winters Tabitha had experienced in the Natchez country. Except for one thing, she would have found the weather intolerable. This was the season for parties, and Nicholas was using the interval to strengthen his and Tabitha's position at the top of Natchez society. Each month Nicholas gave an elaborate soiree and planters and their wives from miles around came through the miserable weather to attend. They were bright and elegant balls, preceded usually by a sumptuous dinner and followed by wine and brandy and dancing to a slave orchestra. Sometimes there were as many as a hundred guests, but at all of them Tabitha was the center of attraction. She made sure that this was so. She had by now lost all concern about her ability to conduct herself in an acceptable manner, and this freedom of mind permitted her to more freely use her natural coquettishness to turn the heads of the males present. The men flocked about her like fluttering birds around a feeding trough, begging to dance with her and beguiling her with their best manners and most deft approaches. And while she was the recipient of many male attentions, she was also the focal point of jealous glances from the ladies present—a fact that dismayed Tabitha not at all and pleased her much. Still, despite their reserved feelings about her, the ladies treated Tabitha with all the respect she deserved as mistress of a great house, and it seemed on the surface at least that her poor beginnings in Natchez-under were being put aside, if not entirely forgotten.

Perhaps what Tabitha liked best about the flamboyant soirees was the fact that they invariably had the effect of boosting her to great heights of popularity as a hostess while diminishing Martha Enright's influence on Magnolia Manor. For Martha Enright always fared badly at these events, due in one respect to her blindness which limited her participation and in another to the simple fact that she was a naturally dour person who disliked crowds of people and could therefore not feel at ease among them. In fact, as the months slipped by, it seemed to Tabitha that she and Nicholas had definitely won their relentless under-cover battle against the old lady. She seemed more docile now, more resigned, and those moments when she attempted to impose her authority were more widely spaced than formerly—and not as effective.

"Mother has been outclassed," Nicholas said one day, not hiding the pleasure in his voice. "She is receding into the background, against her own will to be sure, but nevertheless receding. We have won the battle, Tabitha. At last I feel of some importance in my own house."

"The soirees have helped, Nicholas."

"Yes. They have helped to establish you as mistress of Magnolia Manor, elevate you in the eyes of Natchez society, replace the image of mother which this manor has too long held. I trust you are satisfied with your victory." When Tabitha did not immediately answer, he went on. "And I hope that, having all the advan-tages of wealth and social position, you have given up your naive insistence on love as a factor."

"I am still hopeful we can learn to love each other," Tabitha said.

He walked a few feet away from her, then turned back.

"Let us not speak of love, for it only angers me," he said. "We have been getting along well lately, and I delight in your company. Let us not spoil it with a debate about love."

"As you wish, Nicholas," said Tabitha. She, too, did not want to ruffle calm waters.

"One thing, however, must continue," said Nicholas. "We will continue to sleep in separate rooms, my dear, for I would not want my inept lovemaking to ruin this little empire we have so carefully built."

During the long winter months Tabitha watched Nicholas with rapt attention. Over the past few months his strong feelings of persecution had somewhat abated. He had made no direct reference of his suspicions, and Tabitha took heart, feeling that perhaps Nicholas's success against his mother and his stronger position as a man of importance had buoyed his confidence and returned him to a degree of normality.

Mike Long was another problem. Although Tabitha saw little of him, since he was continuously busy administering to the blacks, on those occasions when the business of the plantation threw them together she always felt a curious, unexplainable yearning for him that she found impossible to control. On several occasions she had even dreamed about him — frightfully lewd dreams that mortified her when she awakened. Why this should be she did not know, except that the memory of his stolen kiss still caused her heart to pound, and the dreams seemed to be a logical extension of the kiss. It occurred to her on more than one occasion that she might actually be in love with Mike, but she tried to expunge this errant thought from her mind as not only impossible but exceedingly unwise. Still, her mind was in revolt. Mike

Long kept coming back, like an insidious intruder, constantly.

What was even worse, it seemed that Mike understood the battle that raged within her, for he would watch her with just the faintest suggestion of a smile on his lips, as if he were saying, "Fight it, Tabitha, if you wish. But you will not be able to subdue it."

Then, as the summer of 1834 arrived and the weather warmed, two incidents occurred that abruptly renewed in Nicholas the fearsome feeling of persecution. Tabitha had been riding Lady Belle around the plantation, despite the fact that a soft rain was falling. When she returned, her face flushed from contact with the rain and wind, she felt a curious exhilaration. She had ridden alone because Nicholas had been busy with his overseer, making plans for the planting of the spring cotton crop. But she found him now in the music room, and as she entered he turned from the big window with the red portieres and fixed her with almost a savage glare. His face was livid with rage and his eyes held the old fear-crazed look again that made Tabitha's heart sink.

"Nicholas! For heaven's sake, what is the matter?"

He was so beside himself with anger that words would not readily come, and Tabitha shuddered inwardly. But at last the words formed in his mouth, erupting in exploding syllables.

"Do you smell it?" he demanded.

Tabitha crinkled her nose. She had noticed a fishy odor in the room at the moment she had entered it, but Nicholas's wild appearance had driven it from her mind. Now it was back, a pungent odor that pulled at her nostrils.

"Yes. What is it?"

"Whale oil!"

Tabitha stared at him uncomprehendingly.

"The portieres are soaked with it," said Nicholas, barely able to hold back his violent anger.

"Soaked? Why on earth—"

"Look at these!" Nicholas grabbed the portiere closest to him, holding it out for Tabitha's inspection. Coming closer, she could see that the lower half of the portieres were wet with oil.

"Whale oil's very good for lamps," said Nicholas in measured tones. "It's highly inflammable. Does that suggest anything to you, Tabitha?" His voice grated harshly, like steel against steel.

"But who would—"

"Yes! Who, indeed?" Nicholas dropped the heavy curtain, turned and sat wearily in a chair. He ran his hands through his hair in a worried gesture, and when he looked up at Tabitha again his face had the drawn and haunted look she so feared.

"My dear, excuse my exasperation," he said in even tones, "but I am greatly distressed. Ten minutes ago I came into this room and found my beloved mother pouring whale oil on the draperies. Tabitha, *she was planning to burn down Magnolia Manor!*"

The words cut through Tabitha's consciousness like a sharp cleaver through meat. She walked away a few paces to settle herself, then turned back, her face still reflecting disbelief.

"Nicholas, are you sure—"

"I am damned sure!" roared Nicholas. "I sent her to her room and, by God, she went. And she'll stay there. I have instructed Sophie to sit outside her door and to inform me at once if she comes out. Sophie can be trusted. Mother cannot."

"Why should she want to burn down the house?" Tabitha's voice sounded weak, bewildered.

"It's obvious, knowing Mother. Don't you see, Tabitha? She knows that she has lost control here. She knows you have replaced her. It beats upon her and she cannot bear it. So she has decided, very simply, that if she cannot rule this house, there will be no house. Another few minutes and she would have succeeded in reducing Magnolia Manor to cinders!"

Tabitha put her hand to her forehead. The whole idea was incredible. Destroy beautiful Magnolia Manor? Impossible.

"Nicholas, she must be demented."

"I have suspected it for some years. Demented in the way all power-mad people are demented."

Tabitha sat down in a chair. Her legs felt weak. She said nothing. At last Nicholas rose. His face was set in stern lines, rigid with anger.

"She will never burn this house," he said firmly. "Mother will be under continuous guard from now on, twenty-four hours a day. Her every move will be watched. She will be a prisoner here."

Nicholas walked stiffly out of the room after these prophetic words and Tabitha sat in brooding silence. Two household servants arrived to take down the damaged portieres, but Tabitha hardly noticed them. She was stunned by the revelation that Martha Enright had attempted to put a torch to the manor. But as she tried to bring order out of the chaos of her mind, the pattern of evil emerged—and sounded logical. Martha Enright had fired what was to be her last shot in the battle with her son and daughter-in-law. Frustrated in her desire to control Magnolia Manor, she had turned to destruction as a way out. Unable to win the influence she coveted, she had decided to deprive her enemies of victory by destroying the symbol of victory.

Well, thought Tabitha, it was an admission of defeat at any rate, and this analysis pleased her. Buoyed by the thought, she strode from the room with a sudden new pride of bearing. Only one thought troubled her: the job of keeping Martha Enright a virtual prisoner in the house would be an unceasing one. But, as was her habit when matters became too weighty, she shoved this annoying thought aside, confident that Nicholas would somehow see that it was properly done.

Tabitha passed quickly into the high-ceilinged hallway. Her eyes shifted automatically to the severe portrait of Martha Enright on the wall. Fury gripped her and with a defiant gesture she ripped the offending painting from the wall. She had wanted to do this and had hesitated; today seemed like the proper time. Toby happened to pass at the moment and Tabitha handed him the portrait.

"Get it out of my sight!" she demanded.

"Yes'm." Toby accepted the painting without so much as a change of expression, as if he had expected this act for some time. Tabitha smiled grimly. So Toby had sensed the change in command at the manor too. Perhaps all the servants had. That was good.

The sun, stubbornly penetrating the rain clouds,

aimed a shaft of light through the fanlighted windows, forming a golden pool on the hallway floor. Tabitha walked to the door and opened it, letting in the sunshine with a rush. She was just in time to see Mike Long dismounting and striding purposefully across the veranda. Much to her distress her heart thumped wildly at sight of him, and she said to herself: *Don't be a damned fool, he's nothing to you.* But before her heart got into an argument with her mind, Mike confronted her with a seriousness unnatural to him. His usual light banter was missing, and into his eyes had crept a worried and perplexed look.

"Where is Mr. Enright?"

A shuffling noise came from the music room and Tabitha turned to see Nicholas moving with his curious limp toward them.

"What is it, Doctor?"

"There's a sickness among the slaves," said Mike.

Nicholas looked disturbed. As if he did not have enough trouble, now there was sickness among the slaves. His brows crowded down over his dark eyes in a suffering scowl.

"Serious?"

"It could be serious. There are four men and one woman down with the same symptoms."

"Well! What's ailing them?" Nicholas's voice was impatient.

Mike hesitated a moment while he fixed Nicholas with a level gaze. It was best to tell this man the blunt truth, he decided.

"It might be malignant fever."

Nicholas's jaw went slack. His dark eyes sharpened.

"Are you sure of your diagnosis?"

"No, I'm not sure. It's too early. But the victims have violent chills and high temperatures. Pulses are slow. In two cases there is delirium."

"Malignant fever has never touched Magnolia Manor, not even during the worst outbreaks. Could it be something else?"

"It could be. We should know definitely in a couple of days. If these symptoms are followed by bleeding at the nose, gums or bowels, and the vomiting of black matter, we shall know for sure. I'll try to purge their systems of it before these symptoms appear. I'm also keeping the sick in strict isolation."

Tabitha, her face troubled, said, "But I've heard that darkies don't get malignant fever."

"You've heard old wives' tales," said Mike. "In the Philadelphia fever plague of 1793 it was first thought that Negroes were somehow immune. But they got it, like everyone else."

Tabitha turned and walked back into the hall. Distressed, she sat down on a bench underneath the painting by Corot to think things out. She had experienced several sieges of malignant fever when Natchez-under-the-Hill was hit hard by the plague. It was a dreadful disease, and difficult to cure. Usually, when it came to the Natchez country, it stayed for the summer and departed again as the weather cooled. It was extremely virulent and it spread panic as it struck down one person after another. It seemed particularly unfair to Tabitha that this abominable problem should arise now, when things were going with reasonable smoothness for Nicholas and her. Well, maybe Mike Long was incorrect. Maybe it was something else. She would prefer to think so.

The sound of horse's hooves on the hard dirt road to the house cut her thoughts and Tabitha followed Nicholas onto the veranda. It was Faunce Manley, sweating profusely as he dismounted and walked toward them with long purposeful strides. Nicholas had on his face the expression of slight contempt with which he always greeted Faunce.

"Well, what is it?"

"I have bad news," Manley said gruffly. "There is malignant fever in Natchez-under."

BOOK IV
The Yellow Death

1

The great scourge of yellow fever came almost yearly to the Natchez country. It began, in most cases, in the filth and impurity of Natchez-under-the-Hill. Gaining a foothold there, it then crawled to the heights and draped its miasmic pall over the haughty city on the Hill. Usually the plague came stealthily, without warning, an invisible criminal stalking the streets. The first cases were mild, but they grew in deadliness as more and more people succumbed to the pestilence. The "malignant fever" as it was known to Natchez citizens, was usually a killer before the people were quite sure of its presence.

But then the dread word would spread. "The fever is here again. . . . Get away to the country. . . . It's the only safe place. . . . Those who must stay should take great precautions." And those who could leave Natchez-under-the-Hill would do so, boarding steamboats or departing by carriage or on foot. And as the disorder spread to the highlands, the people of Natchez proper would also flee, locking their doors and closing their businesses, and the streets would become empty pathways in which grass and weeds and underbrush, no longer impeded by the rough passage of men and wheels, would grow rapidly, as if they had been waiting their chance.

Those forced to stay in the city took what precautions they knew—pitifully inadequate measures but hopeful to those who did not understand the cause or the nature of yellow fever. They built huge bonfires of pine faggots and burned tar to drive the pestilence away. It was believed that chewing tobacco would filter the disease and keep a man safe, and there were those who soaked their bodies in vinegar, or wrapped themselves in blankets treated with camphor, to ward off the evil.

The people did not know what caused the noxious plague. They knew only that the affliction was a frequent visitor to whom they could bar no doors, and the people accepted this sad fact with a certain despairing apathy. No one suspected the lowly mosquito, or believed that ships from Latin America might be importing the disease. It was thought instead that the mucky soil of Natchez-under-the-Hill contained the ingredients of the fever, and the city of Natchez made it a felony at certain seasons of the year to "excavate the soil or stir up the seeds of disease."

Upon the Hill the rich planters greeted each announcement of another malignant fever epidemic with indignant resentment. They blamed Natchez-under-the-Hill and the tawdry people who lived and worked there. They placed the stigma on the tippling houses and gambling dens and brothels and grogshops, and upon the chunky shoulders of the rivermen who plied the Father of Waters and lived in stench and dissipation and were, somehow, responsible for bringing the foul miasma to decent men. "We will clean out Natchez-under when this is over," they would threaten, but after the plague subsided and the people returned to resume their normal lives again, they would forget the threats, and the gamblers and prostitutes would drift back to their lairs and the rivermen would again take the bawdy town to their hearts—and those on the bluff would return to their own haughty ways and pretend again that Natchez-under did not exist.

And the fever would lie fallow until another time, insidiously waiting its opportunity to stalk the land once again.

2

Abijah Clay became aware of the presence of the dreaded plague on the same day that Nicholas and Tabitha learned of it, but under different circumstances. Abijah was wending his way slowly along Water Street toward the wharves where the steamboat *Creole Lass* was preparing to depart. Abijah enjoyed watching the wharf hands loading and unloading freight and the draymen vying loudly for luggage. The wharf hands worked with a sort of happy rhythm, often singing ancient chanteys as they carried heavy burdens to and from the white steamboat.

The workers on the wharf were profane and vulgar as they bent to their tasks, but Abijah shut his mind to this disturbing fact. After all, the commercial area of Natchez-under-the-Hill was a veritable paradise of normality compared to the seething desert of ugliness and sin that marked most of the city. Here, at least, men did an honest day's work and earned their keep by the sweat of their brows, and this placed them an echelon higher in Abijah's opinion than the gamblers and whores who made their foul money out of the weaknesses of man.

But today, as Abijah approached the quay, he noticed a strange difference. It was so apparent, in fact, that he halted in the middle of Water Street and looked with uncertainty at the scene before him. The *Creole Lass* was at this very moment pulling away from dockside, its huge sidewheel revolving, its stacks belching smoke. But it was not leaving in the usual manner, with people on its decks shouting to those below, with a band playing on the hurricane deck. Instead, it seemed to be sneaking away, making some sort of stealthy escape. Except for the crew and a scattering of grim-visaged passengers, there were few people on the decks; nor were there many workers on the docks. The towering piles of boxes and bales remained unattended on the wharf, the draymen were not in evidence, and a curious stillness hovered over the shoreline and the river.

Abijah's brow furrowed in perplexity. Except for one old man who stood wistfully watching the *Creole Lass* pull away, the docks were deserted. Abijah turned his gaze up Water Street, the way he had come. He had been so preoccupied with his own thoughts that he had failed to notice it before, but now he observed that the street was virtually forsaken. Usually the hellish noises of Natchez-under were audible day and night. Sounds of vulgar merriment, the tinkle of an off-tune piano, the scratchy squeak of a badly played violin, the clatter of silver on roulette and faro tables, the swish-swish of the croupiers' rakes along the green felt table topping—these disturbing noises had become a part of Abijah, so that he heard them without hearing them. And because he was burdened this morning with heavy thoughts he had not noticed their absence. For a moment the gripping silence made no sense to him, and then he recalled several similar occurrences at precisely this time of the year, and the dread word gripped him.

Plague!

It came back to him suddenly, in a violent rush that numbed his soul. The Bacchanalian revelry of Natchez-under-the-Hill never ceased except for one thing—the plague. When malignant fever came, invisible and mysterious and incomparably vicious, spreading its poison in the air and over the land, the people fled in terror from their shacks and businesses. With blankets and little else, they climbed the steep hill of Silver Street and, even avoiding the heights of Natchez proper, went on to the surrounding forests to live where the air was pure. Here they stayed until the fever had run its course and it was again considered safe to return, and this device managed to keep some of them alive, although a severe epidemic would often reach even into the forests and select as many victims there.

Abijah shook his shaggy head wearily. He had spent two days at home, studying his Bible and communing with the Lord. Consequently, he had not noticed the gradual exodus from the flatlands. Now he became suddenly aware that most of the people had fled. Only a few remained—those whose businesses demanded their presence, or those too old or lame to move, or perhaps those stubborn ones who were determined to "ride it out" and not leave their homes before the onslaught of an enemy they could not see.

To his nostrils, too, for the first time, came the astringent odors that always accompanied the onset of the fever—tar burning in the streets, pine faggots crackling, the smell of garlic and camphor. Abijah had no basic knowledge of medicine, but he instinctively felt that people deluded themselves by thinking the burning of tar and faggots, or the soaking of clothing in camphor or vinegar, or the heavy eating of garlic or chewing of tobacco, would stem the fever in its relentless march through the city. His eyes scanned the muddy street, flanked by unpainted buildings that catered to the legitimate business and the illegitimate pleasures of mankind. Most of them were padlocked, or occupied only by a few foolishly brave souls who stubbornly refused to flee the pestilence.

At sight of this enforced idleness, Abijah felt almost like rejoicing. Perhaps the malignant fever was part of God's divine plan. Maybe this was His way of cleansing the sin from the city, of providing it a fresh bath now and then to rid it of its filth. If so, however, it seemed an inadequate measure—for as soon as the fever abated the gamblers and whores returned to ply their nefarious trade and all was as it had been before. Abijah could not conceive of man's wickedness continually triumphant over God's goodness. Why, if the Lord visited the fever on sinful Natchez-under, did he permit the sinners to escape to the highlands and return after the fever passed by? This was a defeat for God! It seemed to Abijah that a much better plan would be to strike the sinners of Natchez-under quickly, without warning, circumventing their escape, and thus wiping from the face of the earth this modern Gomorrah on the Mississippi!

Abijah caught his breath, amazed and frightened at his own brashness. Who was he to question the wisdom of God? The thought humbled him. Perhaps God was trying to warn the sinners, perhaps trying to save them even as he, Abijah, was so ineffectively trying to do. Yes, that would account for what seemed, on the face of it, woefully weak measures on God's part. And Abijah was certain—as certain as he was that eternal life followed death—that someday, if the sinners did not learn their lesson, God would permanently destroy Natchez-under-the-Hill and all similar places from the Memphis Gut to New Orleans' Vieux Carre with one gigantic sweep of His mighty hand. Abijah prayed that he would be alive to see the final judgment.

Abijah continued slowly down Water Street, alert now to all about him. An old woman stood in front of one disreputable shack and vigorously washed the door frame with vinegar. Just outside another building pine faggots burned noisily, spitting at the hovering disease in a vulgar gesture of defiance. Columns of white smoke curled into the air from bonfires. A man passed him, glancing up briefly without recognition. His face was heavy with despair, his eyes haunted. His clothing reeked of camphor. From a brothel a painted girl with flashing eyes and a body ripe with animalism emerged, carrying a blanket folded on her back. Another woman, older and scarred of face and body by her profession, stopped her.

"You leavin', honey?"

"I won't stay in this Goddamn hole with the fever on," said the younger one. "Besides, all my customers will be in the woods."

The two women laughed harshly and the one with the blanket moved toward the bluff towering over the batture land. A man, drunk and staggering, appeared in the doorway of a tippling house as Abijah passed.

Three others stood behind him, and the inebriated one held up a bottle to Abijah.

"Whyn't you have a drink with us, Preacher?" he shouted, and the last word held contempt. "Might as well live today—you might be dead tomorrow."

Abijah halted in his tracks. He knew he should ignore these drunken fools. But it was something Abijah had never learned to do. Every man was a challenge to him, a problem he simply had to solve.

"If I die," he said steadily, "I prefer not to enter God's Kingdom reeking of alcohol!"

The man laughed. He turned and winked at his companions.

"You figger God's gonna turn us out of His heaven if we been drinkin'?" he asked. "If so, He'll hafta turn away plenty, I'm thinkin'."

When Abijah did not immediately reply the man tried another assault.

"What's the matter with your God, Preacher? Why don't he stop the fever?"

Abijah leveled cool eyes on the man. His gnarled fingers were clenched as anger rose in him.

"Why should He stop it? Perhaps He is delivering it!"

"Yeah?" The man's eyebrows rose. "What kind of God is that, he goin' around killin' people? Why'd he bring the fever? Tell me that, preacher!"

"Only an unbeliever would ask such a blasphemous question!" Abijah shot back. "It is said in Exodus, *Let us sacrifice unto the Lord our God, lest He fall upon us with pestilence.* You are the sinners in the eyes of the Almighty. It's time all of you got down on your knees and asked His forgiveness."

"A few more swigs outa this here bottle and I'll be on my knees!" The man took a long draft from the bottle, rocking as he did so. The others laughed roughly at the joke.

Abijah trembled violently. He never grew angrier than when a vulgar unbeliever questioned his tenets or made fun of them. He could take constructive criticism and discuss the questions and doubts of an intelligent man—even an intelligent atheist—but the vulgar ones sickened him.

The man with the bottle faced his friends. "The preacher says we are all sinners," he said argumentatively. "What makes us sinners, Preacher?"

"You have violated every one of the Ten Commandments, this I can tell by looking at you!" cried Abijah rashly.

The riverman squinted at Abijah. Spittle dripped from the corner of his mouth.

"Tell me about them Ten Commandments," he said. "What are they? Name 'em to me and I'll tell you if I ever done 'em."

Abijah knew the man was chiding him, yet he drew himself up with dignity and began to recite those of the Ten Commandments he thought would fit the men.

"One is, *Thou shalt not kill!* Can you say in truth you have not?"

The man glanced at his fellows, enjoying the presence of an appreciative audience. His voice, thick with whiskey, boomed.

"Have we killed anybody lately, men? Don't recollect we have. Ain't been a good brawl in any rivertown we visited for a week. Besides," he turned and leered into the face of the minister, "you kin see we are all gentle souls that wouldn't swat a fly."

Abijah wanted to escape from the man's nonsense, but his outrage drove him on as he tried vainly to embarrass and chasten his opponent.

"Another is, *Thou shalt not commit adultery!*"

The drunk's eyes twinkled. "Now there's one for you, boys! Has any of you been cheatin' agin your wives lately?"

There was a chorus of ringing denials. The man with the bottle grinned lopsidedly.

"Ain't been committin' no adultery neither, Preacher—despite we all have a good itch in the crotch!"

"And," roared Abijah above the profane laughter of the men, "*Thou shalt not steal!* Tell me, now, that you haven't stolen in your misguided life!"

"We-ll," the drunken man drew his hand over his whiskered face, "I remember snitchin' a apple off'n a peddler oncet, if that's called stealin'. But far as stealin' anything big, hell! I ain't never had a chancet to steal nothin' worthwhile, or I'd have more money than I got now!"

It was all Abijah could stand. He dismissed them with an imperious wave of his arm.

"You are blaspheming fools!" he cried. "You are doomed to Hell as this city is! This place is evil incarnate and some day fire, storm or pestilence will wipe it away!"

Abijah stalked away in fury. He felt the anger searing the inside of him and as he walked on he was aware of a subtle pain creeping into his chest. It grew more severe and he clutched a nearby hitching post and clung desperately to it for a moment. His breath came rapidly, gasping, and he stood still and allowed the pain to gradually recede. At last his breathing became normal and he stood for a moment without the support of the post. With slow but determined steps he walked toward the quay where the old man still watched the *Creole Lass* churn foam with her sidewheel as she moved into the deeper water of the channel. As he approached the old man looked up at him. Abijah noticed that kindly blue eyes peered from his wrinkled face.

"You're the preacher, aren't you?"

"I am."

"I observed your troubles with those men. A hard job you have."

"But a rewarding one," said Abijah.

The man's brow knitted in thought. He jerked a thumb toward the deserted buildings on Water Street.

"What do you think causes these infernal plagues?"

Abijah shrugged. "One doesn't know. But one suspects it is indigenous to the soil of Natchez-under, that it lies dormant for a length of time and then manifests itself—when God decrees that it so do."

The man had a kind face, a voice softly inquiring.

"Then God is responsible, as you suggested to those men? Do you really believe that?"

"I do. For it is said in Chronicles that, *The Lord sent a pestilence upon Israel from the morning even to the time appointed; and there died of the people from Dan even to Beer-sheba seventy thousand men.*"

The old man considered this statement for some time, his prune-like face twisted in the agony of doubt. Finally he held out his hand.

"You don't have to convince me with Biblical quotations, as you did those rivermen. I'm a Godfearing man. Name's MacTavish—Angus MacTavish—and I guess from that you can judge my nationality. I'm a cotton factor. My business is here. There are some decent people in Natchez-under, you know."

"I am Abijah Clay. I agree that such people exist in the mudflats. One must sometimes search diligently to locate them, however."

"I've watched you many times," said MacTavish cautiously, weighing his words. "I've seen you stand before a brothel and berate the men who enter. I've seen you draw crowds on a corner when you preached. I've studied their faces. They don't believe a word you're saying, you know."

Abiajh nodded. "I am aware of it."

"Then why do you keep trying?"

"Christ kept trying."

"Until they crucified him," said MacTavish.

"Yes. Until then."

"Why," asked MacTavish, fingering his chin thoughtfully, "don't you go up on the Hill and preach to people who will listen to you?"

Abijah gazed at the *Creole Lass,* slowly growing smaller as it inched its way downstream, trailing a disturbed white wake behind. MacTavish, he knew, was not being critical. He was sympathetic.

"Who knows why I stay here?" he said, shrugging again. "I believe that God wants me to stay. I have felt a divine call. I have been urged by the Lord to save the souls of the sinners, to proclaim His teachings where they have not been proclaimed before. The country grows, Mr. MacTavish. New frontiers keep opening up. Some of us feel the need to establish the Kingdom on these new frontiers."

"I suppose you are right, but it seems such a useless waste of talent and effort."

"I will permit God to decide that. If I have talents, He gave them to me. I shall use them as He directs." Abijah looked at the old man curiously. "Are you going to flee the city?"

"No. My business keeps me here, or so I feel anyway."

"I understand," said Abijah. "My business keeps me here too. Where there is sickness, whether of the body or the soul, there I must stay."

"And you are not afraid of the pestilence?"

"I am not afraid. God's will must be done."

He bade goodbye to MacTavish and walked back up Water Street in the direction of his home, feeling better for his contact with the Scot. As he drew near he saw a magnificent carriage pulled by two impatiently alert horses at the door of his cabin. His heart thumped as he saw Tabitha and Nicholas Enright alight from the carriage and go inside, and he quickened his pace because he was fond of Tabitha and delighted in seeing her again. For a moment, as he hurried toward the house, he realized that he had entertained no thought this morning of Ryma. Where was she? Had she fled the city? Or was she staying in some stinking hole of a place, perhaps already ill with the fever?

The thought sickened him, but he stubbornly pretended he did not care. He felt no obligation to Ryma, but to the rest of his family he owed the best he could give in protection both spiritual and physical.

He hurried to the cabin and burst in upon the excited voices of Tabitha and Rachel as they embraced each other. In the excitement he was momentarily overlooked, and then Tabitha realized his presence and came to him, kissing him with tenderness.

"You're both well?" she inquired.

"By God's will," said Abijah.

He shook hands gravely with Nicholas, and thought how grand the man looked, dressed in his ruffled shirt and fawn-colored coat and trousers, holding the ever-present riding whip in his hand, his bearing superior to all else around him. In his presence, Abijah felt slightly uncomfortable. The vision of the great soiree he had seen when he had gone to Magnolia Manor to approve Tabitha's marriage to Nicholas intruded cruelly on his memory. He had not told Rachel that Nicholas had been drunk, and that others in the room were also inebriated, and that even Tabitha held a glass of brandy in her hand and her cheeks had looked flushed and her eyes feverish. The sight had raised fleeting doubts in his mind about the manner of life on the plantations, but in a moment of broad-mindedness he had put aside the scene as perhaps only an isolated case inspired by the joy of the occasion. Still, the doubt returned from time to time, and now it was present again, unwanted, insidious.

"Nicholas and I want you both to come to Magnolia Manor until the fever abates," Tabitha was saying, looking first at her mother and then her father.

"The fever will spread to the heights too," said Abijah.

"Yes, it is possible. In fact, we suspect a few of the blacks may have it already. But at Magnolia Manor, why—" she floundered for a moment in her explanation, then turned to Nicholas. "Tell them, please," she said, hoping Nicholas's power of persuasion was more potent than hers.

"We feel that you would be safer at Magnolia Manor than here on the mudflats where the fever is always worse," said Nicholas, his voice cool, unemotional, and devastatingly practical. "We know, of course, that the fever may spread to Natchez. I understand there are already a few cases in the city. But Magnolia Manor is several miles from the city. The air is fresh there. It cannot, of course, be guaranteed that the fever will not reach us, but we feel our location lessens the chance. Will you come with us?"

Rachel's dark eyes went to Abijah. Her face was firm.

"Whatever your father wishes, Tabitha."

Abijah strode silently to the window, then turned back to face his daughter and son-in-law.

"I appreciate the kindness of your offer. But I must stay here. My duty is to the people who remain here, to the sick and the dying."

"But, Father!" Tabitha's face showed alarm. "You'll be exposing yourself to the fever and—"

"I have exposed myself before," said Abijah, "and God has protected me. I leave my fate in His capable hands." He shrugged his gaunt shoulders and smiled wanly. "I would consider it a great blessing, however, if you took your mother up to Magnolia Manor."

Rachel shook her head stubbornly. "No. If you stay here, Abijah, I stay. My place is with you."

"But you need not expose yourself—"

411

"My fate, like yours, is in God's capable hands," said Rachel, and Abijah had no answer for that.

Nicholas looked perplexed, as if he could not understand such dedication on the part of either of them.

"Surely, my good man," he said to Abijah, "you would not risk your life and that of your wife to protect a city of—of perverts and sluts."

Abijah smiled. "Nicholas," he said softly, "you are a proud man. Perhaps too proud. You have been taught to think of yourself first, at all times, and the devil take the hindmost. I am made of different clay. I have devoted my life to thinking of others first, and the devil take *me* if I fail them!"

So it was that Abijah and Rachel stayed in Natchez-under-the-Hill while Tabitha and Nicholas returned to the relative safety of Magnolia Manor. And such was the capricious nature of the plague that it was to leave Abijah and Rachel untouched and, in its unpredictable fashion, sweep the heights and settle over elegant and breeze-swept Magnolia Manor where it was to be an unwelcome guest for many harrowing months.

3

The month of July was warm and muggy. Black, cumulonimbus clouds scudded incessantly across the lowering sky, but they brought no rain. The planters and the people who stayed in Natchez prayed for rain, for they believed that a cleansing rainfall would wash away the miasma from the air and save them from the plague. It did not come. Instead a fetid atmosphere persisted, and the fever grew in virulence and it drove the people from their homes and struck down mercilessly many who stayed.

Much ignorance about the plague existed. Doctors, haggard and worn and on the verge themselves of coming down with the dread disease, worked around the clock administering faithfully to those who fell. But they worked with pitiful tools. They knew neither how to stop the strange fever once it got started, nor how to prevent a person from contracting it. They worked mostly on the theory that the patient must be purged of the poison, that the stomach and intestines must be mightily evacuated. This drastic action, they believed, was necessary to prepare the way for other curative remedies, but often it weakened the patient so much that death resulted from dehydration caused by the harsh purgatives.

There was much difference of opinion as to the exact medication necessary to purge the patient. Many felt that a strong combination of calomel and jalap in large doses was required. Others leaned toward milder forms of medication—moderate salts, cordials, mint, cinnamon, snakeroot, herb tea and fruit punches. In cases where improvement of the patient's condition lagged, some doctors forced the sufferers to be bled by leeches to purify the blood. Once the patient's body had been purified, it was agreed that he should stay abed, drink water and eat gruel, and take an anodyne to relieve pain and discomfort.

The doctors came to know the symptoms of the disease intimately. Most cases began with high temperatures and chills. As the plague began to claim the body of the victim, his pulse slowed, his eyes became bloodshot and his skin turned a sickly yellow. At times livid spots appeared all over the patient's body, and he bled from the nose, the gums or the bowels. Delirium was almost always present, with the victim thrashing about in his bed and raving senselessly, and when the hideous, evil-smelling black vomit erupted the doctor knew that the end was near. Only rarely did a patient recover after the vomiting.

The doctors did not know—nor have a way of checking—the contents of the vomit. Some said it was putrid bile. Others insisted it was diseased blood. They knew not whether it originated in the kidneys, the spleen or the liver. But despite their handicaps and gaps in knowledge, they did a dedicated job—for no doctor left the city, but all stayed on to administer to the sick, and many of them contracted the disease and dropped as they walked in the half-deserted streets.

City officials of Natchez tried to be helpful. They distributed lime to those too poor to buy it, and this substance was used to treat stagnant pools in the city—for they suspected that the still, green-scummed ponds might contribute to the disaster, just as they felt the muddy flatlands of Natchez-under spawned the fever. People continued to take superstitious and ineffective precautions. Everywhere, below the Hill and upon it, the glare of pine faggots lighted the night, and the pungent odors of burning tar, vinegar, and camphor filled the air.

Business came to a virtual standstill in Natchez proper, as it did on the batture land. Banks closed and merchants no longer exhibited their wares on the streets. There was no reason to do so, for there were now no buyers. The moss-draped oaks stood like weary sentinels too long on duty, spreading their leafy boughs protectingly over empty and unresponsive streets, and draped over the usually bustling city was a pall of silence and inactivity. On occasion one would see a man or woman, forced by some circumstance to remain in the city, walk down the street, cautiously, peering into doorways, avoiding houses where the pestilence was known to exist. Weeds grew eagerly in the deserted streets, and the city assumed the appearance of a ghost town, left to decay by some remote civilization that had moved on to other more benevolent climes.

A few businesses did flourish. Undertakers' establishments did a thriving business. Processions wound down the dreary streets in endless numbers, giving to those who could afford it a decent burial. But as the number of casualties mounted, a funeral caravan for

415

each victim became impossible. At night wagons would rumble through the city's darkened streets, picking up corpses that had fallen unattended on the sidewalks or taking the bodies of fever victims who had died in the houses and who had been left on the front stoop for hasty disposal. These were buried in common graves and then covered with lime. And, at night when the stillness was heavy and suffocating, one could hear the rat-a-tat-tat of carpenters' hammers, for wooden coffins were a prime need.

The fever brought out the best and worst in men. Some families remained fiercely loyal to each other, as one member after another succumbed and all were dead. In other cases, men fled to the forests leaving sick wives and children behind; or women fled from their stricken husbands. And the fever respected no one, no rank, no position. It killed gamblers and whores in the shacks along the river, and rich cotton planters on the Hill. And the carpenters worked diligently on the wooden coffins until some of them dropped at their benches and ultimately filled the boxes themselves.

July and August crawled by sullenly, as if reluctant to leave, and each day brought new horrors. In Natchez-under-the-Hill, Abijah went from shack to shack, dropping to his knees beside the sickbeds and praying for each victim's recovery. The seriousness of the plague softened his feelings and moderated his prejudices, and he prayed for the decent and the indecent. There were times when he kneeled at the bedside of a harlot and prayed to God Almighty that he not only permit this wayward woman to recover but to lead her on the paths of righteousness. Gamblers and pimps and footpads and murderers received the same unstinting service, but most of the victims were so listless that they barely understood what Abijah was doing for them. The still-healthy stood by, in grudging respect, while Abijah prayed, but most of them did not believe the Lord could be relied on to cure the sick. They took more comfort in their vinegar-soaked clothing and their burning tar, and the monstrous purges given them by hurried and harassed doctors.

Abijah did not see Ryma, for she had fled to the open country at the first sign of the pestilence, but one night in the quiet of his bed he overcame the bitterness in his heart sufficiently to implore the Lord, "Save her, O God, and perhaps she will then save herself."

On the plantations the work went on. The cotton had to be tended, regardless of the fever, for some of the planters were so financially overextended that they could be completely ruined by a one-year crop failure. In most cases the blacks did not come down with the disease, at least not in large numbers, and this gave credence to the belief that the blacks were somehow immune, that the darkness of their skin, in some mysterious way, shut out the disease. At Magnolia Manor, Mike Long worked industriously to keep the blacks healthy, and his dedication pleased Nicholas. Mike reasoned that if the blacks could be kept free of the fever—and he kept all free except five—the dread plague was unlikely to spread to the house. Magnolia Manor was excellently located on a high bluff, away from the festering sore of Natchez-under and four miles from stricken Natchez proper. The manor had escaped epidemics on other occasions, and it seemed altogether likely it could do so now. And it did—until August.

Tabitha sat on the veranda, taking advantage of the shade cast by the upper gallery and the freshening breeze that had quite suddenly come up from the river. It had been extremely hot for the past week and Tabitha relished the cool breeze, for she believed that if the weather cooled the pestilence would in turn recede. Suddenly Nicholas came from the big fanlighted door and stopped in front of her.

"Mother is sick," he said. The words were cold, factual, devoid of emotion.

Tabitha looked at him wide-eyed, a sudden fear gripping her.

"The fever?"

"Likely. She has the temperature and the chills."

Tabitha came to her feet in fright. Her eyes glittered.

"Oh, Nicholas! That means—"

"That it might spread to the rest of us?" asked Nicholas with a sardonic smile. "How like you, Tabitha, to worry about the rest of us."

She was instantly stung by his words, but before she could reply he went on blandly. "I admire your never-deviating self-interest, my dear. And you're quite right, of course. Mother has outlived her usefulness, to herself and to us. We have many years before us. We must not permit her to infect us."

"I wasn't going to say it quite that bluntly," Tabitha said irritably, conscious that he had once more combed her innermost thoughts. "But the fever is highly contagious, as you know, and—"

"Mother has been isolated in her room since she attempted to fire the house," said Nicholas soothingly. "She is still there. Sophie sits outside her door with instructions to use violence, if necessary, to keep her there. Now I'm going down to get Doctor Long. It's the least we can do, don't you think?"

"What about her usual doctor?"

"He's so busy in Natchez these days he could never come out here. It's one of the penalties of living on an isolated plantation at plague time. Mike will have to do. He's kept the blacks virtually free of the fever, so he must know a thing or two."

"We must all be very careful," Tabitha warned.

"Of course, my dear." Nicholas's half-smile was all-knowing. "I should be sadly distressed if either one of us took to the plague now that we have practically won our bloodless war with Mother."

Chuckling, Nicholas limped off to find Mike Long. A chastened Tabitha sat down in her chair, her mind in turmoil. She tried to assess the situation calmly. Tabitha had made a few small inroads on Martha Enright's position since her marriage to Nicholas. The blacks recognized her as the true mistress of Magnolia Manor and so did Natchez society. But still Martha's death would remove the last obstacle in her path. The thought occurred to her that it would be a blessing if Martha should succumb—she being blind and all—but she brought these thoughts to a crashing halt. No, that was pure rationalization, and she should not be that heartless. Nicholas, damn his attitudes, had planted those thoughts in her mind. She simply would not think in such terms.

Nicholas was back within minutes with Mike Long in tow. The two men raced upstairs to Martha's room

419

and Tabitha, not wishing to intrude too obviously, followed them at a distance. She did not enter Martha's bedchamber, but stood at the open door, gazing into the ornate room where Martha Enright lay in death-like stillness on the big four-poster bed. The only thing about the old lady that suggested continuing life was the fever-bright eyes that stared sightlessly at the canopy overhead.

Nicholas stood at the foot of the bed, watching as Mike Long bent over the immobile form, feeling Martha's pulse, estimating the extent of the fever with his flattened hand against her forehead. Sophie stood obediently to one side, her tawny face fixed in awe as she waited for the doctor's verdict. At last Mike Long stood erect and, nodding slightly to Nicholas, moved out into the hall. Sophie followed and Mike closed the door softly.

"Very slow pulse, bloodshot eyes, high fever, languor," he said, his voice crisp. "All the symptoms of malignant fever."

Nicholas's eyes shifted to Tabitha, then quickly returned to the doctor.

"We must keep her isolated then," he said practically. "What about Sophie?"

"Someone must attend her," said Mike softly. "Sophie will have to do it. However, warn her to stay in the room only briefly when required. You might put a bed outside in the hall for Sophie to sleep on at night."

Nicholas nodded in agreement. "And the treatment?"

"The usual thing. I'm prescribing these powders to be taken with sugar and water every six hours." He

420

took the medication from his bag. "They contain ten grains of calomel and fifteen of jalap. They should be taken until they produce four or five evacuations of the bowels. Have her drink plenty of water and eat only gruel. The evacuations should purge her body of poisons. When that has been accomplished, liquids and perhaps an anodyne should do the rest."

"You expect recovery, then?" asked Nicholas.

"I expect nothing. Her age is against her, and the fever, as you know, is a killer. If evacuation does not cleanse her sufficiently, several things will occur. Bleeding from the gums or nose. Blood in the stools. A yellow color, usually beginning on the neck and breast, spreading to other areas of the body. If she at last vomits black matter, this can be considered the end."

"We'll start your treatment at once. I realize you can promise nothing."

"The treatment is the best known to us at this time," said Mike. "Beyond that, she is in the hands of God."

"I suspect, in that case, she'll recover," said Nicholas with an amused smirk. "I'm certain God wouldn't want her."

Tabitha winced. Nicholas's levity was much out of place. She wondered briefly if Nicholas really wanted his mother to expire, but she put the thought aside as too horrible to contemplate.

The next few days were fraught with deep anxiety. The eeriness that hung over Magnolia Manor thickened. People talked in hushed voices as they do in the presence of the dead. A few of the slaves came to the house and stood humbly at the front door until

Tabitha went to them. They inquired about Martha Enright's health, made no comment when told she was dangerously ill, and walked away in silence, having thus paid their respects at the house of the Massa. Only one visitor came to Magnolia Manor, and that was Garland. She did not go near Martha's room, but sat on the veranda and talked with Tabitha.

Nicholas would allow no one to enter the room where his mother lay except himself, Sophie, and Mike Long. All others, including Tabitha, were strictly barred. Sometimes, when she passed the closed door, Tabitha could hear the old lady moaning in what appeared to be pain, and sometimes she heard an inane babbling that sounded much like delirium. Surprisingly, Nicholas visited his mother often, and inquired of her health from Sophie at frequent intervals. And each day he went to fetch Mike Long so that the doctor might examine her. Whether this rapt attention signified sympathetic concern on Nicholas' part Tabitha did not know. More likely, she thought, Nicholas was being coldly practical about his mother's illness, as he would be if a slave took sick. She was sure he was icily calculating the results should she survive or die; but she noticed one thing about him that filled her with dread. The old stricken, haunted look had crept back into his eyes, and this she did not quite understand until he turned from the piano one night and said in a bitter tone: "They will try anything, won't they?"

"What do you mean, Nicholas?"

"My enemies. They stop at nothing."

Tabitha stared at him. She wanted to say something to divert him, lure him away from what seemed to be a destructive train of thought that had suddenly reappeared after a long absence. But she did not know what to say.

"Several times since Magnolia Manor was built the plague has come to the Natchez country," Nicholas said, his eyes shifting wildly. "But it has never come to this plantation. Doesn't it seem strange, now, that it should come here?"

"It—it just happened, " said Tabitha.

"You oversimplify it," Nicholas said, impaling her with his fierce eyes. "I am convinced, my dear, that my enemies are poisoning the atmosphere of Magnolia Manor!"

Tabitha caught her breath. Poisoning the atmosphere! My God, wasn't this one of the fears Mike Long had mentioned was common to a paranoiac person?

"Really, Nicholas, how in the world—"

"How! How! They find a way, never fear! Mother has fallen victim to poisonous vapors *meant for me!*"

Tabitha exploded to her feet, an icy horror gripping her. She caught Nicholas by the shoulders, almost shaking him to rid him of his strange, incredible fears.

"Nicholas, for God's sake! You have no such enemies!" Her voice was edged with panic. "Do you hear me? You have no enemies! The plague is a natural thing and your mother happened to catch it. That's all!"

Nicholas's lips pulled tight. He took her by the wrists and put her to one side like a child.

"You don't understand, do you? Nobody understands. But I," he said pounding his chest violently, his breath coming in spasmodic gasps, his eyes alight with a strange insanity, "I understand!" He almost fled from the room, his stiffened knee causing him to list grotesquely as he hurried away.

The vigil went on. Two days passed, then three. On the third day Mike Long came from Martha's room with a perplexed frown.

"Well?" demanded Nicholas bluntly.

"Sophie says she has not yet had an evacuation, is that right?" Mike's voice was edged with weariness.

"That is right."

"My God, man! That's hardly possible!"

Nicholas stiffened. "Are you calling us liars?"

Mike shook his head. His shoulders sagged.

"What I'm trying to say, Mr. Enright, is that ten grains of calomel and fifteen of jalap is a heavy dose. How a woman can stand to take this and not respond is a mystery. I have never heard of anyone resisting such a purgative."

"You've heard of it now," said Nicholas coldly. "Sophie has given her the medicine at the prescribed intervals. You may ask her."

"I have asked her. She says Mrs. Enright has taken the medicine as instructed." He sighed, picking up the black bag and moving toward the hall door. "As you know, she has moments of delirium now. That's to be expected. Yesterday and today there is slight bleeding from the nose and mouth. That, too, is to be expected. I have noticed also a yellowness on her neck. Also expected. What *isn't* expected is her failure to evacuate. And that is serious."

"What you are saying is that she is not recovering?" Nicholas asked.

Mike Long nodded.

"Isn't there anything else we can do?"

"I know of nothing else."

"I'll get another doctor!"

"Your privilege. But I don't think anyone can stop it now."

Nicholas's chest heaved. His eyes thinned.

"How long do you give her?"

"A day. Maybe two."

"I don't believe it! She's virtually indestructible!"

"Malignant fever is no respecter of persons, even indestructible ones," said Mike. "I'm sorry."

Nicholas sighed audibly. For the briefest instant his shoulders drooped; then, as if he sensed this to be a show of weakness, he straightened them again.

"I'm convinced you have done everything possible. If she dies,"—he turned to Tabitha—"she will have the most elaborate and spectacular funeral Natchez has ever seen!"

Martha Enright died two days later. She was listless and barely conscious at the end, her face and upper body splotched with ugly yellow. At her bedside were Nicholas, Sophie, and Mike Long, with Tabitha outside the door peering in. When the end came, Nicholas spun abruptly on his heel and walked out of the room. Tabitha followed him down the circular staircase to the main floor and out the front door to the veranda. He walked purposefully to the great terraced garden where Martha had spent hours in quiet contemplation, as if she could see the blossoming beauty around her. Tabitha drew near him.

"If she loved anything, it was this garden." said Nicholas gravely. "She used to enjoy touching the flowers, saying she could tell how they looked by the shape of them. Flowers seemed to appeal to her better nature, to some tenderness inside of her that she refused to show with people. Her grave will be decked with flowers." He gazed off into space, as if viewing the scene of her burial in his mind. "There will be a riot of color on her grave," he said tonelessly. "That's what she would have desired. She always wanted to be a queen in life, now she shall have a burial worthy of royalty."

Tabitha looked at Nicholas in wonder. She was not sure if this was a tenderness in Nicholas she had never before seen, or another display of unbelievable arrogance. She had never dreamed that he possessed any compassion or insight. Like his mother, he showed nothing of this to people. Had death revealed something in his nature that Tabitha had not known existed? Had it opened a door into his soul, where no one had trod and few had even the opportunity to peer? Or was this planning of "the most elaborate and spectacular funeral Natchez has ever seen" just another cynical gesture, with no heart behind it— perhaps just another way for Nicholas to pad his own ego? Tabitha did not know. The riddle that was Nicholas Enright was deepening.

True to his promise, Nicholas gave his mother a funeral unparalleled in Natchez. Despite the fact that undertakers were busy in the city of Natchez, Nicholas managed to secure the services of the best at a fee so attractive that the man could ill afford to ignore it. Big Sam, with the help of several other artisans on the plantation, fashioned the casket of oak and stained and burnished its sides and top until it became a deep rich brown. The casket holding the frail form of Martha Enright was placed in the great salon, and on wooden standards behind the coffin flowers of every hue and description were banked in an ascending tier. For three full days she lay in state, while Negro messengers on horseback visited other plantations to tell the people of Martha's passing. And they came—all of them—despite their fear of the plague and notwithstanding their dislike for the old blind woman, for the dead woman was an Enright and it was politically and socially important to be there.

The slaves came too, to view the body and pay their last respects, forming a long line that wound from the side of the coffin, into the hallway, and out upon the broad veranda. They shuffled slowly past the casket, stopping briefly to scan the stern uncompromising face of the old woman, and then passed on, moving sluggishly, eyes alight in their black faces as they swept the grandeur of the room.

Tabitha was unsure of her own feelings about the funeral. The tedious lying in state, the resplendent array of flowers, the passing of the slaves in review as if a President had died—all of this seemed false and pretentious. There was something about the scope of the funeral that cut across her grain; it seemed almost as if Nicholas was using the occasion of his mother's demise to hold a garish and vulgar display, as if he intended having a bigger funeral than anyone else in the Natchez country, just as he intended to always have the biggest soirees.

Martha Enright was laid to rest on the grounds of Magnolia Manor, in a small plot of ground which Nicholas had encircled with a wrought-iron fence.

The casket was transported from the manor to graveside on a two-wheeled cart decked with flowers and pulled by two chestnut mares. Behind the cart the visiting plantation families walked, followed at a discreet distance by Nicholas's slaves.

Abijah Clay officiated at the services—Tabitha recognizing this as another carefully calculated gesture of good will on the part of Nicholas toward her father—and he droned words about death being the opening of the gates of Heaven, the mysterious method by which God transferred the soul from this earthly sphere to His Kingdom where life was everlasting. Nicholas stood with properly bowed head, his eyes lidded, hardly listening to the sepulchral tones of Abijah's grave voice. Tabitha, clinging to his arm, felt uneasy and slightly dizzy as she stood before the open chasm of the grave, with the imposing casket setting along side of it, as if contemplating its own sacrifice to the earth.

Despite the severity of the plague, no one of any importance in Natchez country missed the funeral services. Except for a few who were sick with the fever, every important family was represented. The McRaes, the Manleys, the Drews, the Chamberlains, the Ansons, the d'Ubervilles, the Heppincotts, the Valances—all of them, properly showing sadness and remorse, although Tabitha was certain that none of them shed any true tears of sorrow for Martha Enright. But they had to be there, for this was not only the biggest funeral in years but a social function not to be ignored.

Tabitha, aware of the aristocratic people around her, cognizant of their transparent hypocrisy, listened to the words of her father, hearing them as if they came from afar, from some great area in space—or, perhaps, from the hollow of the grave itself.

"*The Lord is my shepherd; I shall not want,*" he said in a dull monotone, and Tabitha immediately recognized the lovely words of the Twenty-third Psalm. "*He maketh me to lie down in green pastures—he leadeth me beside the still waters.*"

. . . Tabitha, her eyes dancing over the crowd, fixing on Nicholas and wondering if his sorrow was genuine, wondering if he had any sorrow at all, wondering if he was even capable of sorrow, wondering if he was glad at heart instead, wondering if he was savoring this funeral with all its majesty as a compliment to himself. . . .

"*He restoreth my soul—he leadeth me in the paths of righteousness for his name's sake.*"

. . . Mike Long, handsome and grim-faced, standing a few discreet paces away, Tabitha feeling that curious, unexplainable surge of excitement as her eyes moved toward him, even now, with death close by, even now. . . .

"*Yea, though I walk through the valley of the shadow of death, I will fear no evil—for thou art with me, thy rod and thy staff they comfort me.*"

. . . And she lay there, cold and stiff and alone in her casket, and all these people were pretending sorrow and there was no tear among them, and Tabitha, thinking about it, felt relief that she was gone, the lifting of a weight, the easing of a pain, and then she smothered the feeling in shame and mortification. . . .

"*Thou preparest a table before me in the presence of mine enemies, thou anointest my head with oil,*" *my cup runneth over."*

. . . And Nicholas, with his seething hatred for his mother, who had told about her deliberately crippling him, who knew that she had attempted to destroy Magnolia Manor, the house he had built, and Tabitha wondering over and over again how he could sorrow at her death now, or even pretend sorrow, and thinking that this was all show, a macabre performance not spawned by sorrow but to impress his guests. . . .

"Surely goodness and mercy shall follow me all the days of my life, and I will dwell in the house of the Lord forever."

. . . Nicholas didn't believe in the Lord at all, thought Tabitha, and he was doubtful about a life after death, and she was sure that if he thought the Lord had a house at all it could not be as fine as Magnolia Manor. . . .

And, at last, the service was over, and two husky slaves lowered the coffin gently into the grave and began to shovel the moist dirt upon it. The dirt, falling into the yawning mouth of the grave, made a hollow plop-plop on the top of the casket, and the sound continued until enough dirt had been thrown in to cover the coffin and then the sound changed to a dull thud as each shovelful of dirt fell upon the moist foundation of the ones before.

And the people turned, anxious to leave now, to depart in their carriages pulled by impatient horses, to go back to their own plantations and pray to whatever deity they worshiped that they escape the dreadful plague and remain alive upon this earth.

And Tabitha, suddenly feeling a strange elation she could not deny, thought, *She is gone! At last she is*

430

gone! Now I am truly mistress of Magnolia Manor.
Now there is no doubt. Now everything will be all
right and Nicholas, freed from the evil pressure of his
mother's presence, will return to normal again, lose
his fears, relax in his victory, and what I have sought
all my life will come to fruition at last. At long, long
last.

And then the strange dizziness she had felt before
the service returned and she reeled suddenly and
caught at Nicholas's arm. Then a blackness closed
over her and she felt herself toppling forward, falling
across the wet earth that still formed a pile along side
the open grave.

Then there was nothing.

4

Tabitha's awakening was slow and difficult. She had the sensation of climbing out of a deep chasm, clawing at the slippery sides with her fingers until they ached and the nails broke and she slid back down again. Then trying again, having more success this time, painfully crawling out of something dark and wet and into a blinding light that pulled at the sockets of her eyes and dazzled her with a solar brilliance.

When Tabitha opened her eyes she found her sight was fuzzy, as if a diaphanous piece of gauze had been stretched across her face, and she was looking through it. She realized almost at once that she was in her bed, for she saw dimly the canopy of the big four-poster hovering like a giant bat over her still form. In the room were several people who came into focus only after she stared at them for a long time — Nicholas, Mike Long, Sophie, Rachel and Abijah. Her mind spun dizzily, as if it had become unhinged and dangled in a precarious limbo — and then she remembered Martha Enright, dead now, embraced in the coldness of the earth, and, before that, how she had looked as she lay on her bed, in much the same manner that Tabitha lay now, her face yellowish and wrinkled and wasted and plague-ridden. With sudden fright she started to sit up, but strong hands held her and she collapsed as a surge of weakness swept over her.

"Just remain quiet, Mrs. Enright. You are going to be all right." The voice came from a distance, a hauntingly familiar voice she could not immediately recognize. And then it came to her. Mike Long. Dr. Mike Long, looking after her. Dr. Mike Long, watching over her. Dear Dr. Mike Long.

"Stay with me, Mike," she said, and did not know fully why she said it. Nor did she see the frown flit briefly across the handsome, proud profile of Nicholas Enright.

Suddenly a wintry chill seeped through her, like the cold breath of the grave, and she pulled the covers up around her neck tightly. She felt curiously languid, not caring much what might happen to her, and the people around her became shadowy, unreal figures and their voices drifted off until they came from afar and echoed falteringly on the air. She caught snatches of conversation, unconnected words that drove through to her muddled brain, then fled again, leaving emptiness.

"Malignant fever . . . Don't worry . . . she will do fine . . . age on her side . . . healthy . . . strong. . . ."

Then someone was near her, reaching out and taking her hand under the covers, and through the haze and shimmering half-light Tabitha saw it was Nicholas, concern on his face, looking not quite as arrogant or self-sufficient as he normally appeared, as he had appeared even at his mother's funeral, and she was happy in a sort of listless way that he was concerned about her, and yet not really happy either. She wanted to say something to him, but she did not have the strength, nor would her brain produce words, and she moved her dried lips from which no sound came at all and then gave up and lay still, staring at the canopy, wondering in a sudden surge of fright whether she was going to die, and then not really caring.

Then there was Mike Long—she thought it was Mike—holding a glass, saying something about calomel and jalap in sugar water, and Nicholas holding her head up while she drank the sickening malodorous liquid from the glass; and when she had finished it she fell back on the bed again and marveled at the fact that she was so weak that even drinking was almost too much for her to stand. Then her eyes closed, even as she fought to keep them open, and she slept again.

As the disease ran its course, Tabitha lost all track of time. Hours passed, days, maybe weeks, she did not know. The fever grew worse. Tabitha's lips became dried parchment and the inside of her mouth felt as if she had been eating cotton. She felt an intense body heat and at length her lips cracked open. Her violet eyes were bright with the rising temperature, but she saw little from them. She felt her mind receding, as if it wished to escape the fever, and she found at length that she no longer recognized people in the room nor did she want to think about anything.

And then—it must have been much later—the delirium was upon her and she found herself making superhuman efforts to say words, without really knowing if she accomplished the task at all. Nicholas stood at her bedside and listened to the words laboring from her parched lips, and as he listened his jaw hardened and a shock of understanding came across his face.

". . . Mike . . . dear Mike . . . think I love you . . . help me . . . I'm falling . . . deep pit . . . no, a grave . . . no bottom to it. You are . . . in-in-insufferable cad . . . funny . . . fool to love a cad . . . and Nicholas . . . a cad too . . . my life full of cads . . . what can I do . . . God help me . . . alway loving cads . . . always. . . ."

"You must be quiet and sleep," said Nicholas sternly. His face was an immobile mask. Questions had leaped into his mind. What did she mean, saying she loved Mike Long? Did she really love him or was this the imagining of a tortured mind? Could it be possible for Tabitha to love this crude slave doctor when he, Nicholas, had made her mistress of Magnolia Manor?

Resentment smothered him. God's doublet, was there no end to what people would do to him? First his mother crippling him, then her attempt to destroy the manor, and now Tabitha loving another man? By God, he would see about it when she was well again! Perhaps he would challenge Mike Long to a duel after all, and kill him formally and with dignity. Or he might kill him as he would a rat, in ambush or in blinding rage. At any rate, he had to be on guard against everybody and everything, ready to save himself before people drove him to ruin and disgrace.

But a cold reasonableness replaced the anger, a pragmatic force dissipated it. First Mike Long had to make Tabitha well. First that. And he stayed beside the bed to catch the things she said, coldly calculating them now, storing them for future use.

". . . Mistress of Magnolia Manor . . . little Tabitha

from Natchez-under . . . no more Martha Enright . . . gone . . good and gone. And Nicholas . . . proud, he is . . . but I'll tame him . . . I'll be mistress of everything . . . more than Nicholas thinks . . . and Mike . . ."—she rocked her head from side to side as if thought was a task too difficult for her—"always there . . . always there . . . shouldn't be there at all . . . damn him, damn him, damn him. . . ."

Nicholas slept fitfully in his room at night. Sophie remained on a cot outside Tabitha's partially open door. She lay awake for hours, staring into the room, her big brown eyes fastened on the sleeping form of the new mistress of the plantation, and Sophie felt a strong resentment against the plague that had laid this lovely creature low.

A good woman, she thought, *better woman den Martha Enright, sure nuff. Good woman to run this here plantation. A real pretty woman, pretty as a bug, an' a good wife for the Massa, better'n he deserved. Domineering maybe, but nuthin' like da Massa himself, an' nuthin like his mother neither.*

Sophie hoped and prayed that Tabitha would recover, for she liked her and she hated to think of what would happen at the manor if Nicholas Enright lost his mother and his wife within a period of days. The man would be inconsolable, out of his mind. Or, maybe, he would become more ruthless than ever, driving the slaves, throwing himself into work until he dropped, or running off to Natchez-under to quench his sorrow in heavy drink or at the bulging bosom of a whore.

And Abijah Clay and Rachel stayed at the plantation now, even though Abijah knew he was needed beneath the Hill. He prayed most of the day for his daughter's recovery, and he was confident that God would answer his prayers. Once he met Nicholas in the salon and said, "I have prayed for Tabitha for two hours."

"I hope it will help," snapped Nicholas irritably.

"God will answer," said Abijah.

"Then I hope he hurries up, for if he doesn't she will be dead before he raises his almighty hand!"

Abijah felt shock at Nicholas's bold words. But after thinking about it awhile he placed the indiscretion at the door of confusion and distress, knowing that the poor man was distraught and not thinking as sanely as he would have under more normal conditions. And so Abijah forgave Nicholas his transgressions and that night he prayed for both Tabitha and Nicholas—but for different reasons.

To Tabitha the world became a milky white place with no shape or form, an indefinite panorama of indistinct furniture with no sharp edges that floated lazily in the murky air, a room of light and shadow and fuzziness. She was generally aware that the loyal Sophie was caring for her, helping her in every possible way she could, watching over her as she lay prostrate on the bed, unable and unwilling to move a muscle or even twitch a toe. At times, when she was rational, she fought bitterly against the clammy hands of the plague, her resentment high that it should strike her down at the very moment when she should be feeling the heady spice of victory, at the very hour when she should be drinking the sweet nectar of her success and planning great balls that would make her the most important and distinctive hostess in the Natchez country. The fever had cheated her of a good start in her fight for recognition, and she was determined to recover and go on to heights neither she nor Nicholas had as yet scaled.

But the insidious fever had driven the fight from her, and a suffocating languor had swept her from head to foot. In certain moments when she was barely conscious, soirees, parties, Magnolia Manor, the plantation, the slaves, even Nicholas were obscure and skulking shadows on her lethargic mind. Only one image maintained a distinct shape she could recognize. A sharp, clear vision of Mike Long.

5

Mike Long rode the gray gelding slowly through the desolate, pestilence-swept streets of Natchez. He did not look grand and important in the Spanish saddle with its high pommel and studdings of silver, as Nicholas looked atop Happy Boy. He had, instead, the austere and untidy appearance of a bucolic farmer who had somehow been misplaced on a horse too fine for him. His rugged features had been shaped by the winds and rains, his buckskin clothing was unimpressive, and his body moved almost in opposition to the smooth motion of the gelding, suggesting that a mule between his legs would have been as appropriate.

He had exhausted his supply of calomel and jalap, after giving Tabitha two doses, and he was worried. Where he could find another supply he did not know, for this popular remedy was being used by every doctor in town, and he was certain nobody had an oversupply. Yet he must find more or Tabitha would be in dire trouble.

He winced inwardly as he thought of the hideous grip the fever had on her. Two doses of calomel and jalap had not been sufficient to cleanse Tabitha's system of the poisons, and there were times when Mike looked at her hotly flushed face and despaired of her recovery. More strong purgatives were an absolute necessity if Tabitha was to be released from the fever's tenacious grip.

Tabitha! The very name caused him to tingle with a strange expectancy. Mike had never before been in love. His younger days in frontier towns had contained their quota of women, both good and bad. His first experience with physical love had been supplied by a fifteen-year-old whore with yellow hair in a riverside shack in Louisville—a sordid affair that left him feeling unclean afterward. There had been other women too, better women, but none he enjoyed without a feeling of antipathy. He was sure he had never felt for any woman as he did now for Tabitha.

Well, it was a hell of a situation. No man had a right to love another man's wife. Yet, if love came unbidden, what could be done about it? You couldn't shove it aside like an unwanted kitten. It was there, gripping you, tugging at your sensibilities, making your life both pleasant and miserable, begging for recognition and fulfillment. But there was an exquisite torture in keeping it to yourself, nurturing it, being glad it was there, and yet not able to embrace or satisfy it.

Mike thought about Nicholas. He did not like Nicholas Enright. Trying honestly to evaluate his feelings about the man, he was sure his dislike for Nicholas went deeper than simply an immature resentment of the fact that he was married to Tabitha. There was something basic in the man he detested—a monstrous, intolerable ego, a natural coldness, a smug arrogance; and Mike was also sure that he harbored a frightening streak of cruelty that could easily explode in a moment of crisis. Then, of course, there was his unhealthy feeling of persecution. Mike knew that Nicholas interpreted everything that happened to him as a threat to his well-being, and that this overbearing, remote man actually lived in mortal fear. He was equally certain that Nicholas's icy hauteur and his desire to be king among all men stemmed directly from his paranoiac personality.

This persecution complex also accounted for the man's ruthlessness, and to gain his end he would pitilessly use people as stepping stones. Mike felt that Nicholas had used Tabitha. He had recognized her ambition to live on the Hill, had perceived in her a certain relentlessness that matched his own, and had decided to use her as a foil to his mother.

This train of thought led to the obvious conclusion that Tabitha, herself, was not exactly an angel marked with starry innocence. She, too, was ambitious, and she had used Nicholas to fulfill her dreams. She had coldly married Nicholas Enright—without loving him, Mike was sure—to achieve her own personal goal. Yet Mike liked to think that Tabitha's brand of opportunism was not as unscrupulous as Nicholas's. He was certain that some day she would find herself unable to live with her husband's lack of consideration for others and for her, for it seemed obvious to him that Tabitha needed more than power and social status to satisfy her, even though she might not admit it. She needed love—and this Mike knew Nicholas would not give. Nicholas, he was sure, was incapable of loving anyone but himself.

Cursing under his breath, Mike decided that never

had two more relentless people used each other more blatantly to achieve their own selfish purposes than Tabitha and Nicholas. He was hopeful that Tabitha would someday see the folly of it.

But enough of such thinking. The plague was the problem now, the predicament that had to be conquered before it killed Tabitha and all the dreams he had about her eventual redemption. Again he thought of Tabitha lying at Magnolia Manor, the fever hot on her brow, eyes glazed, pulse feeble, and a cold sweat of fear dampened his brow. In distress he spurred the gelding, and the horse quickened its pace, angrily whipping its stern around under his insistent prodding. He emerged at length from the approaching road and turned onto Main Street where he stopped abruptly, gazing down its long length in amazement.

The city was dead.

He remembered Natchez as it normally appeared, a town of meticulously planned streets shaded by sweeping oaks dripping with Spanish moss and, in springtime, the chinaberry tree exuding its delicate fragrance over all the city. Main Street ran east from the bluff and boasted the city's greatest array of stores, mercantile houses and banks. On any normal weekday it was a bustling, busy street. Planters and their women strolled idly about, stopping in the numerous stores to examine the latest merchandise. The stores were more like bazaars, with their wares spewed out over the sidewalks so that people had to walk around these obstacles or thread their way carefully through them. The banks and business houses—all encased in fine buildings, some looking like Greek temples with their marble facades and fluted Ionic columns—did a rash of business. And the plush saloons were crowded with young bachelors whiling away their time in drink and good fellowship.

On any given weekday the planters, who took great pride in their horses and their horsemanship, could be seen riding in the streets. The plantation owners sat grandly on their steeds, their riding whips curled in their hands and white saddle blankets always in evidence. The women came in carriages, ranging from magnificent mahogany barouches to tiny cabriolets, all well-appointed and as delicate as the ladies who rode them. And often, alongside, the man rode his favorite mount, carrying the whip as he guided the coach through the churning traffic of the city.

This had been Natchez, but it was no more. Mike Long sickened at the dismal sight before him. There were few people strolling about today. Most of the stores were closed, and the few that were open did not bother to display their wares on the bleak, weed-infested sidewalks. Banks and business houses had few customers, some of them remaining open with a skeleton staff, others closed entirely. One merchant, with a macabre sense of humor, had a sign on his door which read: CLOSED—BACK WHEN THE STINK LEAVES. Others had fled in such haste they had forgotten to lock their doors, and it was obvious that looting of the unattended stores had already begun.

There were no people, no carriages, and no horses on the street. Mike had virtually an unobstructed view of the entire avenue, its empty buildings standing gray and lifeless, like hollow-eyed ghosts. Even the trees seemed to sag sadly, and the Spanish moss hung in somber dejection. In the street and along the sidewalks, Mike noticed blades of grass and weeds beginning to sprout, as if to take advantage of an opportunity rarely given them. The elegant city on the Hill was reverting to nature, and if it remained empty long enough it would become infested with undergrowth. Mike Long looked at the street and thought that this must have been the way other civilizations had perished, their cities left to the scant mercy of a nature that someday would bury them.

Mike spurred his horse forward. Despite its lifeless appearance, he knew there were still some people in Natchez. He was looking for Dr. Van Trembly, a friend he had made and one who, he hoped, would have a sufficient supply of medicines to stock his bag. As he rode along the street toward the doctor's office, located in one of the temple-like edifices, he saw a few people emerge from buildings and walk down the street, then turn again—like specters haunting a forsaken ghost town.

Mike dismounted, tethered his horse, and entered the big gray building where Dr. Trembly had his office. But he found the doctor's door closed and locked. Across the hall, however, was another doctor's office and Mike saw a thin gray-haired man with watery eyes working at his desk inside. He crossed over and introduced himself. The old man looked at him, his lips compressed in tight stubbornness as Mike explained about the illness at Magnolia Manor and how he must have a supply of calomel and jalap. The old man's face showed irritation.

"For Christ's sake," he exploded testily, "what do you think this is, a pharmaceutical house? There's a plague on, damn it! Every doctor in the city needs supplies—and can't get them! We've been working around the clock with these people, and they keep dying on us whether we give them something or not."

"But this is Mrs. Enright and—"

"Goddamn Mrs. Enright!" roared the old doctor. "She isn't a whit better than anybody else! Now get the hell out of my office, won't you? I'm a busy man."

"Do you know where Doctor Trembly is?" Mike asked doggedly.

"I haven't seen him for days. You'll find him around town somewhere, working his ass off like the rest of us!"

"Thank you." Mike left the impatient doctor's office hurriedly. The old doctor was right, of course. They were all working frightfully hard, supplies were short, and Tabitha Enright wasn't any better than anyone else. He mounted his horse and rode slowly up the street. When he saw people on the street, he would call out asking them if they knew where Dr. Trembly was—and at last a man in ragged vinegar-soaked clothing pointed fearfully to a small brick one-story building.

"There's plague in there. A man and his daughter both dead. The old lady still livin', I reckon, but near dead. Dr. Trembly's been spendin' a lot of time there. He might be inside."

Mike Long dismounted and headed for the house. The man shook his head.

"I wouldn't go in there, mister. I tole you there's plague there."

"I'm a doctor," said Mike crisply and walked through the door into the building.

He stopped shortly in the living room of the small

apartment. An emaciated woman lay on the couch, her face lifeless and waxen. The stench of death was horrifying and Mike Long caught his breath and held it. On the floor lay Dr. Trembly. Mike Long knelt down quickly and felt his pulse. His jaw tightened. The doctor was dead.

Like many, he had worked until he had dropped in his tracks. Mike went at once to the doctor's bag and opened it, his heart pounding. As his hands explored the inside of the bag a cold chill claimed him. The bag was empty. Either the doctor had exhausted his supplies or the bag had been looted. He walked out of the house in complete dejection.

Must Tabitha die because he had no way to treat her?

7

Mike Long scoured the city of Natchez for the medicine he so desperately needed but he found none. Supplies in the city were exhausted, and those few doctors who still had medicine also had patients to use it on. When he arrived again at Magnolia Manor he was met at the entrance to the palatial home by Nicholas Enright who immediately sensed his dejection.

"What happened?" he asked bluntly.

"There's not a grain of calomel and jalap in town," said Mike somberly.

"And she must have it, is that it?"

"Yes."

"Or she dies?"

"I am afraid so."

Nicholas's eyes flared angrily. "Can we get some from another city—New Orleans, Vicksburg?"

"There isn't time. Tabitha needs the purgatives now, within hours. I can't tell you how important it is. If she doesn't purge herself—"

"You've already said it." Nicholas's voice was toneless, but his face was mottled with anger. "God-damn it, man!" he burst out. "We can't just let her die because the fool doctors in Natchez have used up their medicines on—on lesser people!"

Mike Long stared at him. His insides were in turmoil at the hopelessness of the situation.

"What do you suggest?" he asked.

"*I'll* go to Natchez!" snapped Nicholas. "I have contacts. I'm sure I can get what you need."

"I don't think it's possible."

"I'm Nicholas Enright. Anything is possible."

Mike Long watched Nicholas leave the plantation a few minutes later on Happy Boy. His nerves were stretched taut. He hoped to God that Nicholas could obtain the purgatives, but he knew the chances were slim. It seemed horribly cruel and unfair that Tabitha might die because he had used all of his supplies—over-generously, perhaps—trying to save five Negro slaves and an elderly witch of a woman who was hated by everyone.

He turned quickly and went to Tabitha's room. She was asleep and he did not disturb her. He needed to do nothing but look at her to know that she was teetering on the brink of death. She lay almost like a corpse, barely breathing, her fine body ravaged by the terrible fever. As he left, Abijah Clay detained him in the hall.

"How is she, Doctor?"

"Bad," he said, choking on the word. "I'm sorry."

"She is in capable hands, yours and God's," said Abijah kindly.

"If Nicholas fails to get more medicine," replied Mike, "God will have to take over entirely."

He went to his room over the stable and sat for a long time, his head in his hands, thinking, pondering. If no calomel and jalap was forthcoming, he would have to use milder medicines—perhaps moderate salts or cordials. But he knew such treatment would be inadequate. The thought of Tabitha dying sickened him, and he paced the floor for almost an hour, his mind spinning in its hopelessness.

"Mistah Long, Doctor, suh!"

The voice came from downstairs. It sounded like the groom.

"What do you want?"

"Massa Enright wants to see you right away at de house."

Mike's heart thumped painfully. He rushed downstairs and a few moments later faced Nicholas Enright in the huge salon. Nicholas handed him two envelopes.

"Your calomel and jalap," he said simply.

Mike received them with eager fingers. His mouth felt dry.

"Where did you get this?"

"It doesn't matter. I got it."

"There's enough here for six or seven doses!"

"Exactly."

Mike could see that Nicholas would tell him no more, but it did not matter. He had medicine now, and perhaps he would yet be able to save Tabitha. He did not care where or by what means Nicholas had obtained the stuff. He would not have been surprised if Nicholas had killed for it. But that was not important now. He must see that Tabitha was given a harsh dosage immediately.

In the next three days Tabitha received six large doses of calomel and jalap. The medicine weakened her even as it purged her system. To Tabitha, the bodily weakness was the worst feature of the disease. Her temperature was uncomfortable, and there were times when her mind tossed in a sea of confusion, but the weakness brought on by the strong purgatives was almost unbearable. She had no strength even to lift her body or roll over in bed, and Sophie had to help her whenever movement was necessary. In those moments when she was rational, Tabitha felt sorry for Sophie. The faithful servant was with her constantly, exposing herself to the pestilence, yet she remained strong and free of the disease.

The slaves of Magnolia Manor showed extreme affection for Tabitha during the critical days. They would cautiously approach the big manor in the cool of the evening, after their work in the fields, and stand quietly until Nicholas emerged and announced her condition. They had not gathered in such large and insistent groups during Martha Enright's struggles with approaching death, but they thought well of Tabitha and stood idly near the house, waiting and watching.

Then, one morning, Tabitha awoke to the realization that she felt much better. The fever had abated and her mind had miraculously cleared. Shoving pillows against the headboard, Tabitha sat up in bed. A few minutes later Sophie came in, her eyes popping.

"Lawd-a-livin'!" she exclaimed. "You's sittin' up!"

"I feel a lot better," Tabitha said, smiling. "I don't know how to thank you for all you've done, Sophie."

"You don' need to thank me, Miss Tabitha," said Sophie with a wide grin. "Ah's thanked jes by you gittin' well."

"I feel like my mind has emerged from a tunnel,"

said Tabitha. "I can't remember much of what went on. How long was I sick?"

"Jes 'bout a week."

"And Nicholas has been attentive?"

"Yes'm. He's been plenty worried."

Tabitha sighed. "For the first time in a long while I feel like talking again."

Sophie chuckled. "Miss Tabitha, you been talkin' a streak since you got sick. Don' know half the time whut you was sayin'."

Tabitha looked at Sophie guardedly. She felt a sudden uneasiness. What *had* she said during her delirium? She wasn't sure. But somewhere in the recesses of her mind she remembered calling for Mike Long. The thought frightened her, but she quickly rationalized it. Mike was her doctor. Why shouldn't she ask for him? That is what she would tell Nicholas if he should bring the matter up. But deep in her mind she was beginning to suspect a terrible truth.

She was in love with Mike Long.

The thought distressed her. Sitting upright in the bed while Sophie fussed about the room, she ran this perplexing thought through her mind. Was it true? Did she really love this frontier doctor? If so, she was in a frightful mess. She had reached a pinnacle in her relationship to Nicholas and Magnolia Manor, and she was not inclined to give it up now. She thought it somehow unfair that love for Mike Long should come along at this inopportune moment. She determined that she would have to crowd thoughts of Mike Long out of her mind, banish him to some remote region of her brain so that he would not intrude on her goals—or her conscience. It might not be an easy thing to do, but she would have to do it. Her position at the top of Natchez society was too valuable to jeopardize for a backwoods doctor.

The process of thinking exhausted her and she closed her eyes. She would not worry about it now. She must get completely well first, before she could give serious thought to such meddlesome problems. True, her health was in the hands of this same backwoods doctor she wanted to put out of her mind, and if she fully recovered she would have to give Mike Long the credit. Yes, he would be a difficult person to shunt aside.

Mike Long was delighted when he examined Tabitha that morning.

"You're coming along fine now," he said. "You were a very sick lady."

"I appreciate everything you've done for me," Tabitha said gratefully. She kept her voice deliberately impersonal, but her heart was fluttering inside of her. How do you quiet a rampaging heart, Tabitha wondered. Nicholas had never aroused such excitement in her.

"It may take you several months to recover your strength," Mike said, and Tabitha noticed that he, too, was trying to maintain a strict doctor-to-patient relationship. "I'll call on you daily to see that your recovery progresses."

Mike was about to leave the room when Nicholas and Tabitha's parents appeared at the door.

"Come in," Mike invited. "Tabitha is much improved this morning. The fever has broken and she will recover now. It may take her several months to regain enough strength to take any responsibility for the house. For that same length of time, I would suggest that nothing be undertaken that would sap her strength."

Nicholas was smiling down at Tabitha, but the smile faded at Mike's pointed reference to soirees.

"Of course, Doctor," Nicholas said obediently. "It is important to me that she recovers fully." Tabitha and Mike both noticed the personal connotation in his remark. Apparently Nicholas was not glad that she was recovering for Tabitha's sake, but for his own.

"God has answered our prayers," said Abijah simply.

As the shimmering heat of August passed and cooling breezes swept in from the northwest, the malignant fever diminished. People trudged warily back into Natchez, scrubbed down their homes with vinegar and took up residence again. Within a month Natchez and its sister city beneath the bluff were active as always. Once more merchants along Natchez's Main Street permitted their produce to flood the streets, and again they were on hand to greet customers with smiles and blandishments. The banks and businesses reopened, and the streets once more echoed to the clatter of horses' hooves as the planters and other businessmen rode back into town. The burning pine faggots were quenched and the stench of vinegar and camphor gradually disappeared. In Natchez-under-the-Hill wharf hands went back to the docks and ships made port calls again as business began to revive. The gamblers and prostitutes returned to fleece the unwary and all the evil ways so deplored by Abijah Clay resumed.

As soon as Tabitha was out of danger, Abijah and

Rachel returned to their crude cabin beneath the bluff, and when he arrived Abijah regarded the rough surroundings for a moment and said, "Somehow our home seems more Godlike than Magnolia Manor. Christ, His Son, was a simple man."

For Tabitha, complete recovery was a long and painful process. She regained her strength gradually and continued to consume only liquids for several weeks. Hot steaming bouillabaisse seasoned with wine became one of her favorite dishes, and pungent cafe noir helped to settle her edgy stomach. During her convalescence Nicholas was considerate and attentive. He would personally bring food to her on an ornate tray, sit with her on the veranda and talk of small things. The crucial work in the fields he left entirely to Jed Vale, requiring the overseer to report progress each night. When her strength permitted it, Tabitha and Nicholas took short rides in the barouche, several times going to the esplanade where Nicholas mentioned their first meeting with a certain fondness of recollection that encouraged Tabitha to think that the events of his mother's death and her own brush with death had mellowed him.

Still, she could not be sure. For all his attention, she sensed a strained relationship between them. She tried to evaluate it and the attempt left her more uncertain than before. It was true that Nicholas's attention during her sickness and her recovery was beyond criticism, but the coolness with which he attended to her needs gave her the feeling that he planned it that way so that she could not accuse him of inattention. Sometimes he seemed over-polite, as an obsequious servant might be polite to his master. At times she caught him looking at her with lowered lashes and a grimness of face that she could not fathom. But at the same time he spoke grandly of a soiree he planned to give when Tabitha had sufficiently regained her health.

"It will be the greatest ever seen in Natchez," he boasted. "It will be so fabulous that no one will ever top it. There will be an orchestra from New Orleans, imported wines from Madeira and France, gifts from Paris for the ladies, food such as no one has ever before seen on a table. We shall invite at least a hundred guests, and we will astound them by dancing the daring cotillion. Yes, that's it! It will be a cotillion that I'll give, and there will be no doubt, when it is over, that you are the most desirable hostess in Natchez, and I the most important host." He looked at her and smiled. "You have come a long way, my dear. So have I. Who is there, Tabitha, more important than you and I?"

She did not answer directly. For some unaccountable reason, his words—so filled with pride and vanity and ostentation—turned her thoughts to her father.

"I have a feeling sometimes that my father does not approve of all this elegance and show," she said.

Nicholas shrugged. "Perhaps not. Your father stresses the spiritual qualities of life. We stress the material. How can one say who is wrong and who is right?"

"I was raised to believe the spiritual qualities were paramount," said Tabitha.

"And yet, you turned into a predatory female seeking material things?"

"Yes. I suppose that is right. I must admit I

sometimes rebelled against my father's way of life. And I became dreadfully tired of the Bible at times. Father used to read to us every night from the Bible, long interminable passages until I almost went out of my mind with boredom."

Nicholas looked amused. His eyebrows arched upward in mock surprise.

"Why, you little heretic, you! You speak like an atheist!"

"No. I'm not an atheist. But father did bore me to tears at times. Still, there is something inherently good about him—something so good that I look at us, sometimes, and I don't like what I see."

Nicholas slapped his thigh with high good humor. "God's blood! You sound like you're on the verge of developing a conscience! I swear, if you begin to get scruples, Tabitha, I shall find myself a better woman!"

Tabitha saw little of Mike Long during her convalescence, and when she did it was either professionally or at a discreet distance. A mild sickness had broken out among the blacks—not the fever, however—and Mike was extremely busy. He did a fine job of keeping the blacks healthy and on the job, and more than once Nicholas mentioned to her that he was the best slave doctor he had ever known.

Tabitha tried desperately to put Mike out of her mind and at the same time attempt to ingratiate herself with Nicholas. Both projects seemed hopeless. About the time she had recovered completely, Nicholas turned sullen again. His period of pleasantness was followed by one of extreme moodiness. For several days he barely spoke to Tabitha, and when she attempted to engage him in conversation he grew impatient and irritable. On one occasion Tabitha inquired gently if something was wrong.

"Something is always wrong," he said enigmatically.

"Is it something about the cotton yield that bothers you?"

"No. It is not the cotton."

"The blacks?"

"No."

"Is it something I've done?"

He looked at her for a full minute, apparently on the verge of saying something, but he did not. Instead, he got up quietly and left the room.

For several minutes Tabitha sat looking at the door through which Nicholas had vanished, feeling rejected, spurned. Then, angrily, she got up and walked toward the stable. As she often did when things went wrong, she had decided to ride Lady Belle; a horseback ride often seemed to relax tension and make her feel better. Halfway to the stable she met Mike Long coming toward the house. It was their first meeting in almost two weeks, and his initial remark indicated that he had returned to his bantering way.

"And how is milady today?" he asked.

"I'm fine," said Tabitha shortly, wondering what it was about Mike that made her answer so crisply.

"And the Master?" Mike asked.

"If you refer to Mr. Enright, he is in excellent health. The tension caused by his mother's death and my own illness seems to have dissipated and he seems quite normal."

"Very touching—the man has had his sorrows, hasn't he?" A teasing smile crept over Mike's face as he said it, then quickly vanished as he looked at Tabitha with more seriousness.

"I've been wanting to talk to you," he told her.

"What is it you want?"

"Are you going riding?"

"I had intended to."

"Allow me to accompany you to the stable. I would like to talk to you alone, unseen by your husband, if possible."

Tabitha stiffened. "Mike Long! What are you up to?"

He laughed. "Really, Tabitha, you shouldn't play the role of outraged virtue. It hardly becomes you. Besides, I have no intention of seducing you—at least for the time being."

"I refuse to go with you when you talk like that!" said Tabitha indignantly.

"Then I promise to be more discreet," conceded Mike. "Will milady come with me?"

"Milady will," said Tabitha, still trying to appear insulted but not really feeling it inside.

They entered the stable to find the groom puttering about. Mike glanced at Tabitha. In a low voice he said: "What I have to say to you is in confidence and is very important. I ask that you make a professional call—accent on professional—to my room."

Tabitha's eyes widened. "Mike, if you think I'm going to—"

"Oh, for God's sake, quit playing the innocent virgin!" snapped Mike angrily. "Come along!" He took her arm and they ascended the narrow stairway leading to his upstairs room. It was a small cubicle with a tester bed, a table, a clothes press, a couple of chairs. One wall was lined with medical books.

"Sit down," said Mike and Tabitha dropped primly onto one of the chairs, her eyes scanning him with vague suspicion. Mike Long gazed at her for a moment, with what seemed like professional interest, although Tabitha thought she saw an unbusinesslike glint in his eyes.

"I don't know quite how to say this," he began at last, feeling for proper words. "It's about Martha Enright. There are aspects of her illness that I don't understand. I don't understand, for example, why calomel and jalap did not work for her, as it did for you."

Tabitha's eyebrows raised questioningly. "You said yourself, Mike, that her age was against her."

"Yes. That's true. But even so, many elderly people have had the fever and survived. Martha Enright was a strong specimen. I would have bet money that she would recover."

Tabitha frowned. "What are you driving at, Mike?"

"I don't know exactly." Mike's tones were hushed. "I suppose the ethics of a doctor should prevent me from even saying this to you, but I have certain strong suspicions. In the first place, you know the purpose of the purgatives, don't you?"

"Of course."

"To cleanse the system," Mike said, making sure Tabitha understood. "In Mrs. Enright's case, they didn't work. Strong harsh doses of calomel and jalap did not produce the result they should have — and that is past understanding."

"Do they work in every case?"

"Definitely," said Mike. "I have never known or heard of a human being taking such powerful purgatives without a complete cleansing of the system."

Tabitha's eyes stretched thin. She was afraid to ask the next question, but it came from her automatically.

"What are you suggesting?"

"I don't know." Mike Long paced to the window, looking out pensively. "I have talked to Sophie. She says she gave the medicine as I instructed. Yet I find it hard to believe that Mrs. Enright ever took a gram of calomel and jalap."

"Why don't you say what you're thinking?" Tabitha said softly.

Mike looked at her sharply. "All right, I will. I suspect that Mrs. Enright was never given the calomel and jalap. I don't know how this came about—since Sophie insists she was given the medicine—but if it was somehow withheld from her, then I think I know who to blame."

Tabitha felt a shudder go through her. Her pulse quickened and beat rhythmically in her neck and she placed a hand to her throat to stifle it.

"Nicholas," she breathed, not quite believing it even as she said it.

Mike nodded solemnly. "It is possible," he said. "I don't want to accuse a man unless I can prove what I say, but you will recall what I told you about a paranoiac—that he might grow violent and attempt to rid himself of those he thinks are his persecutors?"

"My God! That's unbelievable!" Tabitha kept shaking her head, her eyes dull, almost unaware of Mike's presence now, the hideous knowledge that Nicholas may have killed his mother rocking her mind. Mike came closer, placing a hand on her arm.

"I need to ask you a few questions," he said.

"All right."

"I understand Nicholas barred everyone but himself and Sophie from his mother's room, is that right?"

"Yes."

"Did he control her medicine?"

"How do you mean?"

"I mean, did Sophie mix the calomel and jalap with sugar and water, or did Nicholas?"

Tabitha hesitated.

"I don't know, Mike. I really don't."

"If Nicholas did the mixing and gave the mixture to Sophie, that could account for Sophie believing she had really given Mrs. Enright the proper dosage."

"You mean—"

"I mean that Nicholas could have mixed sugar and water and nothing else, and Sophie would have known no better."

It was a diabolical thought, hardly believable, but somehow Tabitha could not help think that its very sinisterness seemed to fit Nicholas. But she found herself unable to utter such a thought, and Mike went on.

"There's another thing. Where did Nicholas get the calomel and jalap with which I treated you?"

"Nicholas told me he went into Natchez and found some," said Tabitha.

"I went to Natchez too. I swear there was none to be obtained." He ran his hand over his brow worriedly. "You know what I think, Tabitha?"

"No."

"I think Nicholas only faked a trip to Natchez. I think the calomel and jalap he found for you was the

461

same stuff he had withheld from his mother!"

"I can't believe it!"

"I can," said Mike grimly. "Anyway, talk to Sophie. Find out if she actually mixed the medicine or simply delivered it." He smiled suddenly to brighten the moment. "Anyway, I'm delighted that you're fully recovered, Tabitha. I was very distressed at your illness."

"Oh, you're just trying to be dramatic," said Tabitha, willing to have the moment lightened, not wanting to think the dark thoughts about Nicholas, not wanting to believe them. "You know, Mike," she said, her brow crinkling, "I think I do like you despite the fact that you can be most trying at times. But I want to get our relationship straight, once and for all. I am married to Nicholas and you and I live at different levels. What you did to me—the kiss—was entirely uncalled for, and both of us should forget it ever happened."

Mike smiled. "*I* didn't mention the kiss."

"I did. Because I want to settle things."

The smile turned into a low chuckle. "Tabitha, you're quite a study for a doctor. You believe only what you want to believe, don't you? You want to believe that all is well between you and Nicholas, and that you are now the most envied woman in all Natchez—the queen of the planters' social structure. Since you came here I'm sure you have seen many things that must have indicated to you that the vaunted Hill is not much different from the land below it. But you still cling to your foolish notion that this is some sort of planters' heaven, despite evidence that must have caused you some painful doubt from time to time."

"What evidence?" Tabitha was curt, on the defensive, aware that he was baiting her again.

"Tabitha, one would think you were a pup whose eyes have not yet opened. Not everything is bad in Natchez-under-the-Hill, although much of it is. Not all is good on the Hill either. You've seen some of the planters' families, and I'm not denying there are some fine ones. But it's a jungle. You've seen the cruelty of Faunce Manley. You've seen the cut-throat competition among the great ladies to outdo each other. In fact, you have engaged in this bit of warfare yourself."

"Mike, if you go on like this—"

"Oh, hell, Tabitha, stem your temper! It's only make-believe anyway, like a lot of attitudes you assume. What I am trying to say is that there is sin on the Hill as well as under it. The only difference is that sin on the Hill is conducted at a higher and more discreet level."

Tabitha arose abruptly and started for the door, her face red with anger. "I don't intend to remain here and listen to such drivel," she said haughtily.

"Like alcohol on a wound, the truth stings," said Mike in soft tones. "You're ruthlessly ambitious, Tabitha, but not as coldly ruthless as you believe yourself to be. You were determined to marry Nicholas Enright whether or not you loved him, because you believed you could get along without love or affection as long as you had high social position. But you were wrong, weren't you? You found that, as a woman, you needed love after all—and that Nicholas needs it not at all!"

She looked at him, appalled at his insight. Her embarrassment took the form of almost uncontrollable anger.

"Mike, I swear—"

"I've studied Nicholas. I'm sure he loves nobody but himself. He isn't capable of love for any other person—his mother, his wife, no one. His arrogance must drive you to distraction, and even the slaves know you don't share his bed."

"Mike!"

"Excuse my indelicacy," murmured Mike. "But it's common knowledge. The house servants know, obviously—Sophie among them—and the word gets to the slave quarters very quickly."

"Well!" exclaimed Tabitha, unable to think what else to say.

"What you are doing, Tabitha, is putting all uncomfortable facts aside and forcing yourself to believe that everything is all right. You have achieved a long cherished goal. You don't intend to let go now, no matter what happens—even if your husband is a murderer, for example—because this is still the driving ambition of your life. You have it now and you can't give it up, and so you make believe you like it."

Tabitha remained silent for some seconds. She did not know how to answer Mike. Deep inside she knew that he spoke the truth, and this fact disturbed her. For she must never admit to anyone that she was willing to put up with Nicholas's weaknesses—his arrogance, impotency, cruelty, or even a matricidal action—to maintain the position she had won. Never!

"Mike Long," she said in exasperation, "if you don't stop analyzing me, I'll have my husband dismiss you. I've threatened that before, and I shall do it if you insist on talking to me in this outrageous fashion!"

Mike shook his head. "Nicholas wouldn't dismiss me, Tabitha. I'm far too valuable to him. I can do him, personally, some good—so he won't let the whims of his wife sway him." He let the thought filter through Tabitha's mind, the preposterous thought that, in Nicholas's view, Mike Long was of more practical value to him than she was. He came closer to her, taking her by each arm, encountering no resistance. "Besides, I'm not through," he said. "You are not only burdened with matters you try to believe, but by things you are trying *not* to believe. As a prime example, you are continuously trying not to recognize the fact that you are in love with me."

Tabitha felt her face go red as she realized his meaning, and then anger came to her rescue, driving out embarrassment.

"Love you!" The words exploded from her mouth. "Mike Long, you are without a doubt the most conceited and ill-bred nincompoop that—"

"Careful, Tabitha, you'll be cussing. And cussing wouldn't become Natchez's finest lady."

"I *don't* love you!" snapped Tabitha, completely confused by the trend the conversation was taking and yet sensing that a denial was her only salvation. "Whatever made you think that I—"

"The way you look at me, for one thing," said Mike easily.

"What?"

"And a certain quite unladylike glint you have in your very lovely eyes."

"Mike, I swear—"

"And now your violent denial of what I say. One

465

always denies most determinedly that which is true. I read that somewhere."

Tabitha stopped talking. She felt absurdly limp inside, and she hung onto the post of the tester bed for support. Her thoughts were so jumbled that she hardly knew that Mike's grip on her arms had tightened, that his eyes were fixed on her now with eagerness and a new intention.

"I want to tell you something," he said softly, his voice just above a whisper. "I love you, Tabitha. I'm honest enough to admit it. I think I loved you the moment I saw you at the Silver Palace and realized you didn't belong there at all. Do you understand what I'm saying, Tabitha?"

She looked up at him, her violet eyes moist as she studied his square-jawed face—the hard lines of it, as if hewn from a solid block of granite, the backwoods ruggedness with all its strength of character, its primitiveness, its intentness.

"I'm—I'm very confused," she said, not wanting to recognize what he was saying, yet feeling within herself a warm glow at his words, a glow she should not have but could not control.

Mike drew her toward him, his deep eyes fixing her with a gaze almost hypnotic. The thought, edged with panic, slid through Tabitha's mind: *Don't let him hold you. Tell him to keep his hands off. Pull yourself up proudly, like a fine lady should, and tell this crude man that you will have nothing from him, that you will tolerate no brash advances, no liberties.*

But his hands felt good and strong on her shoulders, and the nearness of his body to hers sent an ecstatic sensation through her that was beyond anything she had ever known with Nicholas.

"I love you, Tabitha. That's what I want you to realize. I love you."

She heard the words, and they made wonderful sense even as they made no sense at all. A man doesn't tell another man's wife that he loves her. Even if it's true, one uses restraint. But now she felt herself taking a cautious step toward him, as his iron hands pulled her closer, and the thought soared through her mind: *Don't do this thing, it isn't right.*

His face was close to hers now, and she could feel his hard body pressed full-length against hers, and then one arm was around her. He was looking down at her, his mouth forming words, unbelievable words.

"You do love me, don't you, Tabitha?"

She shook her head automatically, because it was the thing to do.

"No. No. I don't know."

His jaw set rigidly and his eyes became accusing. His breath was warm on her face when he spoke.

"Damn it, Tabitha, quit playing cat and mouse! Just for once, be honest. I know you love me — and you know it."

"Mike, please—"

She tried to pull herself free of him, placing her hands against his chest and shoving him back. But her resistance crumpled as he folded his arms around her. His mouth came down on hers and smothered her protest with a kiss that was almost violent. Then his lips slid down her cheek to her neck, moist, caressing, warm with his love.

And all at once she found herself responding, not knowing why, not caring now. She returned kiss for kiss, passionately, with hot half-parted lips, and all at once she was arching her body against him wantonly, unashamed, trying to caress him with her own warmness as they stood trembling together, trying in wild desperation to please him, to satisfy his needs. And the agonizing thought spun through her mind: *It was never this way with Nicholas! Never!* Always with Nicholas she had been cold, forcing herself to give him her caresses and kisses. She had never been able to truly respond to him. She had tried and failed to arouse either herself or him. Their love-making had ended in violent frustration, perhaps because it had always been something automatic, something she knew was expected of her, and had been performed with a cruel lack of enthusiasm and was therefore dead.

And then, quite incomprehensibly, she realized they were lying together on the fresh clean bed, and that Mike's firm body was over hers. She clung desperately to him, feeling the growing hardness of his manhood as he pressed her against the bed.

"No," she breathed. "We shouldn't."

But he was aroused now with a blazing passion he could no longer control, and his hand was fumbling with the bodice of her dress. He had told her to be honest, and she thought, *Yes, I will be honest. I am telling him to stop, but if he does I will die!*

And somehow her dress fell away and with it a petticoat—how, Tabitha thought, did *that* happen?— and then there was nothing but a shimmering unreal room of love, with the feel of Mike's struggling body over her. There was the brief sweet pain of entry that brought a strangled cry to Tabitha's lips, and then he was crushing her into the bed with firm rhythmic motions that sent passion raging through her body, and she found she was giving herself to him with an eagerness and disregard which, in retrospect, would amaze and shame her, but which now seemed the most normal action in the world.

And then came the drowsy exhaustion that followed, when they lay together in silence as their raging hearts quieted and their breathing calmed, and all at once Mike became contrite and he shook his head as he looked down upon her.

"Tabitha, dear Tabitha! Should I apologize? Should I?"

"Don't apologize, Mike."

He shook his head wonderingly.

"You were a virgin, Tabitha."

"Yes."

"Nicholas never—"

"Completed the act," said Tabitha.

For a while he said nothing more. He collapsed along side of her, cradling his head in the crook of her arm. She spoke his name softly.

"Mike."

"Yes."

"You're a beast, you know."

"I guess I am."

"A marvelous beast, but a beast all the same."

"Yes."

"I should feel that I've been used."

He lifted his head and looked at her steadily. "Do you feel that way?"

"No."

It was the answer he wanted. He kissed her with a

new urgency, his hand caressing her hair.

"I don't know what to do, how to think," Tabitha said.

He kissed her again, softly, the passion gone from him now, replaced by a mystic tenderness.

"I'm Nicholas Enright's wife."

Mike's face grew taut. He drew away from her, ever so slightly. "You can't live your entire life with a man you don't love, not even if it brings you the social position and riches you think you need. It's too high a price to pay."

"I never thought it was."

"You delude yourself."

"Do I?"

"Yes."

Tabitha pushed Mike back and sat up, straightening her hair with her hands. He looked at her nude body, white and curved and soft, and the passion in him swelled again.

"You do love me, don't you?" he asked, imploring her to admit it.

Tabitha closed her eyes. Why deny it?

"If I didn't," she said, "do you think I would have permitted you to—"

She did not finish. She fell back on the bed again, as if to give substance to her answer, and he came to her again. Rain began to fall outside, beating against the window, and Tabitha closed her eyes, listening to it. A clock ticked delicately on a table, setting a cadence.

When exhaustion came again, he said, "If you love me, then in time you will forsake Nicholas. You will have to give up your position on the Hill. You will have to forsake everything. This is your decision to make — a difficult one — but you will make it."

She did not answer but busied herself with her dress and toilette, smoothing away the evidence of indiscretion. When, at last, they descended the stairs to the stable, Mike returned to his bantering ways.

"Does milady wish to ride now?"

She smiled at him, not even annoyed at his use of the word milady.

"Milady is no longer interested in riding," she said. "I must return, now, to my — husband."

6

In the accusing silence of her room, Tabitha sat before the escritoire, beset by a suffocating guilt. She had not fully realized the depth of her experience with Mike Long until she had returned to the protective walls of Magnolia Manor. Then the feeling of guilt assailed her, and the shame beat upon her like wind-driven waves upon a placid shore. And she said to herself: *I should not have done it. How did it happen? How did I fall into such disgrace?* And she answered herself: *I wanted it to happen, for a long time I wanted it to happen, even without knowing it. Great God in Heaven, I do love Mike Long!*

Fortunately she had not seen Nicholas upon her return. Had she crossed his path she was sure he would have detected guilt in her face. She had gone directly to her room, wanting above all else to be alone with her thoughts and her conscience. Now she found her mind confused and tormented. Even the sudden knowledge that she loved Mike Long did not assuage her feeling of guilt. She had allowed herself to be taken by Mike, and this in itself she recognized as a sin against her marriage to Nicholas, if not a sin against God. Yet, somehow, she felt it had not been a sin at all, but something that had happened because it had been inevitable and unstoppable.

What surprised her most about the entire affair were her own feverish emotions. She had responded to Mike in a manner that now awed her. She had never experienced completion with Nicholas, but even if she had it would not have approached the thrill of her encounter with Mike Long. Of that she was sure. Nicholas always left her cold, bereft and unfulfilled. But she had enjoyed Mike's fierce embrace and his surging passion in a way that amazed and even frightened her.

Impatiently, she tried to thrust the image of Mike Long out of her mind. She must not think of him. She must put her feelings aside, as she would unwanted clothes, hanging them out of sight in the closet of her mind, and think no more about him. That was imperative now, because if she didn't—if she found him irresistible and the event of this afternoon was ever repeated—she would be lost. And everything she had strived for in life would be lost with it.

She stood up abruptly and crossed to the full-length mirror with its goldleaf frame. For a moment she studied her reflection carefully, tracing her face with the tips of her fingers. Did she look any different? Did guilt show in her face? She had heard it said, once, that a man could always tell a woman who was not a virgin. Fie, she thought! Why should she worry herself with such nonsense? She looked the same as before, and Nicholas would not be able to tell a thing!

Irritated at the turbulence in her mind, Tabitha crossed to the portieres and pulled the bell cord. She wanted to question Sophie about Martha Enright's medicine. *That* was far more important than her silly indiscretion with Mike. She sat down again at the escritoire, where she impatiently stamped her foot and played nervously with the inkhorn and quill and sand-box. A moment later Sophie loomed in the doorway, darkening it like a cloud.

"Yes, Miss Tabitha."

"Come in, Sophie. I want to talk to you."

Sophie's eyes opened wide at Tabitha's imperious tone. She came in, standing awkwardly in the middle of the room.

"Sit down," said Tabitha crossly.

Sophie's round eyes bulged. She had never before sat in the presence of a white person. It simply was not done and she hesitated, not sure she had heard aright.

"For heaven's sake, sit down!" snapped Tabitha, taking her frustration of the moment out on the sim-ple black woman who could not fight back.

"Yes'm." Sophie eased her rounded posterior into a chair, sitting on the edge of it. "Is somethin' wrong, Miss Tabitha?"

"Everything's wrong. . . . Will you please sit back and relax?"

Sophie sank back in the chair. Her brown eyes re-mained fixed on her mistress.

"Ah'm sittin' comfor'ble," she announced.

"So you are. Sophie, I want to ask you some very important questions."

"Yes'm."

"And I want you to give me straight answers."

"Straight as a stick, Miss Tabitha," Sophie vowed.

"You are also to keep this conversation in strict con-fidence," Tabitha said severely. "You will repeat none of this to anyone."

474

Sophie smiled, regaining some of her poise.

"Miss Tabitha, Ah'm deef an' dumb an' blind when Ah's gotta be."

"Very well. It's about Martha Enright. You were the one who gave her the medicine prescribed by the doctor during her illness, weren't you?"

"Oh, yes'm. Jest like the doctah said."

"She was to receive repeated doses of calomel and jalap, as I recall.

"Yes'm. Thass right."

"And she got them?"

"Oh, yes'm!"

"And you personally gave the doses to her?"

"Yes'm."

"In sugar water?"

"Yes'm."

Tabitha tapped her foot; her brow knitted in a frown.

"Now listen carefully to me, Sophie," she said. "Did you mix the calomel, the jalap and the sugar water yourself?"

"No, ma'am. Ah didn'."

"Who did?"

"Massa Enright, ma'am."

Tabitha stood up and walked across the room nervously. She looked out over the terraced garden, brilliantly color-splashed in the afternoon sun. She turned back to Sophie.

"Now let me get this straight. The calomel and jalap were not kept in the room with Martha Enright. They were kept in the custody of Nicholas?"

"In the *whut*, Miss Tabitha?"

"Nicholas Enright kept the calomel and jalap?"

"Yes'm."

"And he mixed them at the proper time and brought the entire mixture to you to give to Martha?"

"Yes'm."

"Did you *see* them mixed?"

Sophie's eyes seemed to expand. She wet her thick lips with the tip of her tongue.

"No, Ah didn'."

Tabitha took three steps toward Sophie and peered down at her with eyes flashing.

"Then how do you know the calomel and jalap were mixed in the water and sugar?" she asked bluntly.

For the first time Sophie seemed to realize the direction the questions were going in. Her eyes became giant black marbles, and a sudden look of fear crossed her face.

"Miss Tabitha! Whatevah are you sayin'?"

"Answer me!" snapped Tabitha impatiently. "Did you *know* the calomel and jalap were actually in the water?"

Sophie shook her head slowly.

"No, Miss Tabitha," she said finally. "Ah didn' nevah ackshully know it. How could I, ma'am? Ah jest assumed that Massa Enright—"

"Very well, Sophie. You may go. And remember, don't breathe a word of this conversation to anyone, or so help me I'll have you whipped from dawn to dusk!"

The vicious threat had its effect. Sophie left the room in a state of nervous shock, vowing not to tell anyone about the conversation as long as she lived.

Tabitha sank down on the edge of the bed. She pressed her finger tips to her throbbing temples, trying to think, attempting to make sense out of what she had just heard. Had Nicholas withheld the calomel and jalap from his mother? Had he deliberately allowed her to die of malignant fever by refusing to give her the medicine prescribed by Mike Long?

Had Nicholas *murdered his mother?*

8

Tabitha spent the rest of the day in her room thinking. At first she considered accusing Nicholas directly of matricide to get his reaction, but she promptly scuttled this plan when she realized it was inimical to her own best interests. Such a plan would only provoke Nicholas and make her own situation worse. So, after a cool and deliberate study of the problem, she decided not to make an issue of the mystery surrounding Martha Enright's death. If Nicholas had truly done this terrible thing—and she could not quite believe it even now—he would pay for it with his own conscience, if he had one. And besides, there was no point in disturbing the status quo of her relationship with Nicholas now. After all, cold calculation told her that she had profited as much as Nicholas from the old lady's passing. To question the manner of Martha's death with Nicholas now would only jeopardize their relationship.

On the other hand, she owed Mike Long an answer to his question. He had asked her to quiz Sophie and since Sophie's account of what had happened corresponded with Mike's suspicions, she felt an obligation to notify him. But she had vowed to put Mike out of her mind, to destroy whatever love she had for him.

Reporting to him would only aggravate the situation, and she decided that staying away from temptation was more important than reporting to the doctor. She would settle the matter by simply ignoring it. After all, Martha Enright was dead—whether by accident or design—and Tabitha was willing to bury her suspicions rather than upset the delicate balance that existed between Nicholas and her.

During the next month Tabitha made it a point to avoid Mike Long. When she had occasion to ride Lady Belle she sent a messenger to get the horse rather than chance a meeting at the stable with Mike. She was afraid that at some moment he would confront her and ask her bluntly what she had learned, but she preferred to wait until that moment came, and then handle it. Some way out would occur to her on the spur of the moment, she was sure.

It was a lonely month, for Nicholas, busy much of the time with his land, paid little attention to Tabitha now that she had completely recovered. When, in an evening, they were together, he pored over his plantation books, sat quietly drinking Madeira while gazing thoughtfully into space, or played the piano abstractly. He was not talkative, addressing Tabitha only when necessary, and he showed petulant irritation on those occasions when Tabitha attempted to lure him into conversation against his will. The attention he had exhibited during her convalescence had vanished and his manner finally became so aloof and persisted for so long a time that Tabitha rebelled.

"I don't know what's wrong with you, Nicholas," she complained one evening. "You never speak to me. You treat me like I'm some sort of doll on a shelf."

"My dear, I've given you everything you wanted. Must I entertain you besides?"

"I'm your wife!" flared Tabitha.

"Ah, yes. You're always reminding me of the fact. And I presume other people think so too."

"What do you mean by that?"

"Simply that most men and their wives share connubial bliss on occasions. But not us."

The remark was so patently unfair that Tabitha's temper rose dangerously.

"It's not my fault if you can't—" She stopped, unwilling to encroach on such a sensitive subject.

But Nicholas caught her meaning and his face hardened. A mottled red crept into his cheeks. He looked so ugly that Tabitha was afraid he might strike her, but instead his ire subsided as suddenly as it had come and he addressed her in carefully measured words.

"My dear, if you must know, there are women on this earth capable of arousing me to extreme passion. Perhaps this is because they are more knowledgeable about such matters than you are."

Tabitha looked outraged. The thought raced through her mind, the dangerous thought: *Ryma can succeed with him while I can't!*

"You're simply making excuses for your own inadequacy," she blurted out, wanting to hurt him now. "I don't believe any woman can arouse you. You're too self-centered even for *that!*"

Nicholas stood up. His face was sliced by a wicked smile. He strode to the door, turned before he left the room.

"I suggest, my dear Tabitha, that some day you

have a heart-to-heart talk with your sister."

The conversation had infuriated Tabitha, and all that night she tossed in her bed thinking about it. By daylight, however, she had again decided not to ruffle the waters of their relationship by being as indiscreet as she had been the previous evening, and she went out of her way the next morning to be pleasant to Nicholas. If Nicholas noticed it, he gave no indication. He treated her as he had for the past month, with a shattering reserve.

One day his cool manner was broken, however, when Tabitha saw him approaching the house hastily. His face was twisted in anger, and as he saw Tabitha on the veranda he stopped abruptly.

"That damned doctor!" he grated hoarsely. "I should get rid of him!"

"Mike Long? Why?"

"If he hadn't been responsible for saving your life, I would have let him go just now!"

"It's nice to know you appreciate his efforts in my behalf," said Tabitha sarcastically.

Nicholas gazed at her bleakly. "I have an investment in you, my dear. I taught you some manners and introduced you to a new life. You are now a compliment to my teaching efforts. I should not like to have to do this all over with a new wife."

Tabitha bit her lip. She had provoked him again. She knew this was the time to withdraw, but her nature wouldn't permit it.

"You ought to realize, Nicholas, that I am a part of you now. Without me, you are nothing."

Nicholas feigned surprise. "Nothing? Don't overestimate your powers, my dear. We are a unit because we are completely alike—both of us rather despicable. I'll do anything to be top man on the Hill, and you'll do anything to be my woman. Now, about that damnable doctor."

"He's been very helpful in keeping the blacks healthy," said Tabitha, wondering slightly why she was defending him. Here was a chance to get Mike Long permanently out of her sight, to rid herself from a gnawing temptation. Why shouldn't she take it?

"It's the only reason I don't dismiss him," said Nicholas. "A few minutes ago I happened into one of the slave quarters and heard him telling an old man that some day the slaves would be free, no longer held in bondage by plantation owners. Mike Long was talking like a Goddamn abolitionist!"

"Perhaps he really didn't mean—" Tabitha began.

"He meant what he was saying! And he has no reason to talk to the blacks that way. He'll plant the seeds of revolt in their stupid skulls. They won't work as well and God knows what else they might do!"

"You're talking like Faunce Manley." said Tabitha, still wondering why she felt compelled to support Mike Long. "You always claimed that the slaves would not revolt."

"They won't unless white men give them the idea." Nicholas's anger seemed to increase with every point Tabitha made. This time he gestured to a chair on the veranda. "Sit down, Tabitha. Since you seem so inclined to defend the dear doctor, I have a few rather pertinent questions I want to ask you. They might clarify in my mind *why* you defend him."

Tabitha sat down, alarmed now, thinking rapidly, wondering. Nicholas stood before her, looking down with mockery on his face.

"I hesitated to bring this matter up until you had regained your strength, as the shock might send you into a relapse. But I think it is time now."

"What is it, Nicholas?"

"During your sickness I observed a certain phenomenon which requires explanation," said Nicholas carefully. "Frequently you called for Mike Long. At no time did you ever call for me. As a dutiful wife, perhaps you owe me an explanation."

Tabitha felt suddenly cornered. She had feared this moment, knew that it would come, hoped it wouldn't. Dimly she knew she had called for Mike during her illness, although the thought was a vague and shimmering one in her mind. She had wondered for some time if Nicholas planned to make an issue of it, and she had an excuse ready for him.

"I was delirious, Nicholas. I didn't know what I was saying."

"Really?" He smiled superciliously. "Hardly an alibi, my dear. It is well known that one in delirium often speaks truths that one would not speak consciously."

"Oh, fie! Mike Long was my doctor. Why shouldn't I call him?"

"It does seem logical, doesn't it? But allowing for all that, I still find it difficult to understand your touching expressions of love for him."

"Love!" My God, had she really said that?

"Don't you remember, dear Tabitha? You were telling him you loved him. You said he was a cad, whatever that implied, but that you loved him anyway. Oh, it was quite fetching!"

"I don't believe you!" said Tabitha. "I don't recall saying any such thing!"

"Then perhaps I can recall to your mind something you do remember. A month ago—and this was some time after your delirium—you had a very secretive meeting with your beloved doctor *in his room.*"

His words astounded her. My God, how had he known? She knew she could not deny it, so she took refuge in minimizing its importance.

"For heaven's sake, Nicholas. You're making mountains out of molehills."

"You were planning to ride Lady Belle, I believe."

"Yes."

"But you didn't did you?"

"I—I changed my mind."

Nicholas seemed amused at her discomfort. "Permit me to point out that I have certain informants on the plantation who look after my interests. One of my interests is you."

"Are you saying you have spies watching my every movement?" Tabitha said in outrage.

"I said informants, a much more comfortable word," said Nicholas. "At any rate, my informants seem to think you spent a suspicious amount of time in Mike Long's cozy little room. Perhaps you can explain to me what you did there?"

"We talked."

"Charming. About what?"

Tabitha shifted uncomfortably in her chair. This, she thought, was the right time to tell him Mike's suspicions that he had withheld calomel and jalap from his mother. Such an accusation would certainly serve to change the subject, putting him on the defensive instead of her. But she couldn't do it. It would enrage him beyond all reason, perhaps make matters even worse.

"He was inquiring about my recovery," said Tabitha. "He was quite properly concerned."

"He could not inquire here instead of in his room?"

"I happened to run into him when I was getting Lady Belle saddled."

"And he inveigled you to go to his room?"

"He didn't want the groom to hear."

Nicholas reached lazily for his snuffbox, took a dainty pinch from it and sneezed. He was assuming a calm and dignified approach but something about his face terrified Tabitha. His curiously calm demeanor seemed to predict a violent storm that might erupt at any moment. But his voice came softly, in almost dulcet tones.

"I prefer that you be completely honest with me, Tabitha. Nothing that you say will surprise me, because I am as certain as I stand here that you and Mike Long have lain together."

Raw shock seized Tabitha. Her face went scarlet. The seething memory of Mike Long's passion and her own uninhibited response flooded her mind. How had Nicholas known? He couldn't have known. He was guessing, accusing her, trying to force an admission from her.

"Nicholas Enright!" she said, as steadily as possible. "How dare you suggest that I would do such a frightful thing! Why, I—"

"Spare me the histrionics, my dear. It's been quite obvious to me for some time that you're physically attracted to him."

485

"Why, I *never*—"

"Aren't you?"

"Of course not." The lie came easily to her lips. "You're being very foolish, Nicholas."

Nicholas gazed at her for a long time, his eyebrows pinched together in a thoughtful frown.

"If you are lying and you did commit this indiscretion," he said at last, "I presume you would expect me to be uncontrollably angry."

"There was no indiscretion!"

"Persisting in it, eh? Well, assuming there *was* an indiscretion, wouldn't you expect me to be angry?"

"Of course."

He shook his head. "You don't yet know me very well, do you, my dear? If I were *in love* with you, I would naturally be angered at such a performance on your part. But as you know, I deny the existence of love. So, since I do not love you, I feel no ire at your indiscretion with Mike Long. I look upon you only as a necessary commodity to have at Magnolia Manor, rather than a wife who has, romantically speaking, taken my heart. Thus I am spared a horrid anguish at your conduct."

"You mean to say—"

He brushed her to silence. "You realize, of course, that I would be perfectly justified in defending my honor—not to mention what you have left of yours—by challenging Mike Long to a duel over this."

"Yes." Her voice was low.

"I am an excellent shot with a dueling pistol, Tabitha. I have no doubt that at ten paces with pistols I could blow his head off."

"You wouldn't do it! Dueling is so senseless."

486

"Of course it is. Particularly senseless when it's your lover I would be killing."

"Please don't refer to him as my lover."

He laughed harshly. "Very well. I shan't challenge him at any rate. He's a good doctor for the blacks and I need him. He is—like yourself, my dear—a commodity necessary to the proper running of Magnolia Manor. As such, I shall tolerate him."

Tabitha sensed an opportunity to direct the conversation away from Mike Long and place Nicholas on the defensive. But when she spoke her voice was kindly.

"Nicholas, there's something wrong with your thinking. Everything and everybody is a commodity to you. Don't you ever harbor any feelings for anyone—any human feelings? Isn't there any compassion or love in you?"

"None whatever, my dear. Any compassion I might have felt for members of the human race was destroyed by my mother. I judge people only by what good they can do me. I have yet to see a human being who, in terms of goodness and honesty and sincerity, is worth a damn. Even you, Tabitha. I married you for a practical purpose, and I've never had any illusions about you. Being the sister of a whore, one could almost predict your inclination."

"Nicholas!"

"No false surprises, please. What you did with Mike Long—and I *know* what you did—is only what I expected you to do in time, if not with him, with somebody."

"Oh, you're practically calling me a harlot!"

"Your word, not mine," said Nicholas easily.

Tabitha stared at Nicholas in amazement. His cold reasonableness about her relationship to Mike Long was beyond comprehension.

"I want to get something straight, Nicholas," she said. "Do I understand that you don't *care* if Mike and I have—have—"

"My good woman, you mean nothing to me but what I can gain from having you around. If I wish a whore, I go find one. If you wish to become a whore, I have no objection. I only ask one thing of you, Tabitha—that if you and Mike Long continue your illicit romance, you do so discreetly. It must not become common gossip or in any way reflect on me."

"And if it does?"

"Then I shall simply be forced to kill both of you."

She shook her head in wonderment. "I don't intend, Nicholas, to ever place myself in a compromising position with Doctor Long," she said firmly, believing it herself.

To her amazement he laughed outright.

"My dear, you *know* you will. But as I say, keep it quiet. And above all, don't the two of you plot against me!"

"What do you mean, plot?"

"I am not stupid, Tabitha. You are in love, as you would call it, with the dear doctor. It would be much to your benefit to rid yourself of me. As my wife, you would inherit Magnolia Manor, and Mike Long could marry the poor grieving widow and become the master of this plantation. Oh, it's a clever plot, my dear. Perhaps Mike Long's attempt to plant revolt in the minds of the blacks is a part of the overall plan. I shall watch him closely, for he is a dangerous man. You,

Tabitha, are a dangerous woman—and the two of you together could be very dangerous adversaries indeed."

Tabitha noticed again the fanatic gleam in his eyes and she shuddered. It was impossible to understand the twisting and turning of Nicholas's troubled mind. Was it possible that he truly believed that she and Mike Long were in some devious conspiracy against him? It was unbelievable.

"You always think people are persecuting you," she said.

"I am particularly cognizant of persecution," said Nicholas. "I recognize it where others don't. All I say is, don't conspire against me. I am perfectly capable of killing both of you if I deem it necessary."

Tabitha felt a cold chill at his words. Was she living with a maniac, some kind of fiend who had killed his mother and would do the same with his wife on the smallest pretext? As she watched him she saw the fierce flame fade from his eyes. He bent over and kissed her on the forehead—a mocking kiss, she thought.

"You're such a delightful creature that I should regret the need for killing you," he said, softly menacing. "Now, shall we plan our big Cotillion for one month from today?"

Her mind reeled. The Cotillion! Great God, how could Nicholas talk of plots and murders in one breath and plan a frivolous ball in the next? There was simply no comprehending the tortuous meanderings of her husband's strange mind.

The great Cotillion was held in mid-January, and there was no doubt when it was over that it had been the most elaborate social event ever seen in the Natchez country. Nicholas had allowed a respectful six months to elapse after his mother's death before daring to give the Cotillion. This lapse of time made it possible for him and other planters to get the cotton crop in, but that was not the only reason for delay. Nicholas announced his intention to hold a Cotillion far in advance, and for several months the top families in Natchez spent weary hours learning the intricate steps and maneuvers of this new and daring dance.

"Just think," Nicholas said once with a satisfied smirk, "these idiot planters will do anything to show well at a Cotillion given by a cripple and a girl from Natchez-under whose sister is a whore!"

"Nicholas, please—you make everything sound so vulgar," Tabitha pleaded.

"One of my talents," said Nicholas.

For two weeks before the Cotillion—to which every important planter family for miles around was invited, a total of more than 100 people—the house servants at Magnolia Manor were busy making ready to receive the guests. Tabitha, who practiced the Cotillion almost nightly with Nicholas, found herself growing eager as the big day drew near. With much efficiency, she supervised Sophie and the other servants in preparations for the party, thus assuming her duties as mistress of the plantation. Sophie was given the responsibility of marketing, which gave her great pride. She went into Natchez, riding sidesaddle on Lady Belle, where she had the delightful experience of shopping at the fruitmongers and greengrocers with no limitation on what she could buy. Among other things, she purchased calves' feet for gelatin. In the kitchen, the cooks cut away the tough outer layer and ground the rest into a powder which was sweetened with sugar and poured into scalding hot water and then permitted to harden—a delicacy not often found in Natchez.

Several of the women in the kitchen were put to work making fragile-stemmed candles, and some of the more artistic Negroes fashioned exquisitely shaped tapers to be placed in conspicuous locations in the salon and the dining room. On the much-awaited day of the Cotillion, the kitchen house was aglow with the warmth of cooking meats and vegetables. Dutch ovens were placed in the huge fireplace, where live coals burned red. On small trivets, pots of gumbo and bouillabaisse and creamed soups simmered hotly. Stretched across the fireplace on spits were venison, hog and wild fowl moist with oozing juices. Young children, proud to be of service in the preparation of the big soiree, carried Charlotte russes and the gelatins into the springhouse where they were kept cool until ready to be served. Cakes and cookies were made, and nougats and pralines and bonbons.

The servants, on the night of the Cotillion, were faultlessly dressed in new uniforms, and even the tiny wide-eyed black children operating the punkah in the huge dining room wore colorful, starched dresses. Nicholas had coached his house servants endlessly so that no little thing would go wrong. Each had his place and his respective duties, and woe be to the one who made a mistake after the guests had assembled.

Two hours before the arrival of the guests, Tabitha with Sophie's enthusiastic help began her toilette. She selected a gown of white French lace with bell-shaped sleeves, low decolletege and a prominent bustle, which she wore over crinolines with tiny scented sachets sewed between the folds. Sophie worked with a labor of love on Tabitha's hair, parting it in the middle and bunching it in a mass of curls over her ears—a style quite at odds with the usual chignon in back. Her face and throat and arms were powdered to a pearly whiteness and the leaves of mullein pink were rubbed on her cheeks to provide a glow of health. A French perfume, applied with just the proper touch to impart a scent provocative and luring, completed her toilette.

At last the guests began to assemble, driving up to the magnificent porte-cochere of Magnolia Manor in carriages of every description, the ladies stepping daintily to the ground as liveried servants with black faces and shining white teeth held the doors for them, the men dressed in dark cutaway coats and fine ruffled shirts, offering their arms as they strode through the ornate door, through the great hall, and into the mammoth candle-lit salon where the furniture had been set tastefully around the perimeter so that dancing could take place in the center. In one corner of the room, under banked tiers of candles, a four-piece Negro orchestra played soft music as the guests entered. And Tabitha and Nicholas stood at the door of the salon, welcoming the guests and calling them by name, Nicholas being the perfect host as he whispered flattering comments to the well-groomed women, and Tabitha assuming the manner of a charming hostess with nothing but the comfort of her guests in mind

They came in a continuous tide, moving up the broad veranda steps, those that Tabitha knew well, others she knew not. John and Garland McRae were among the first, then the Faunce Manleys, the Christophers, the Ainsleys, the Gildervans, the d'Ubervilles, the Santees, the Van Lines, and many others. And Nicholas greeted them all with a smile uncommon to him, and Tabitha could not help noticing the grand impression he made—proud and haughty, dressed in a maroon cutaway coat, the ruffles of his shirt starched stiffly, the fawn-colored trousers, the white stock fluffed beneath his firm chin. There was no doubt he was enjoying his position as the most important person in the room, for his dark eyes were alight with a fierce pride, and even while he greeted each woman with compliments and each man with a firm handshake, still he maintained a careful aloofness that set him apart from the others, that lifted him a cut above the rest, and did it in a subtle manner that forced them to recognize and bow before the pedestal on which he stood.

The servants, stiff-backed and austere, drifted like silent black ghosts among the guests, carrying trays of whiskeys and brandies for the men and imported wines for the ladies, and the hubbub of conversation as the crowd grew pressed the soft music of the orchestra into the background. And when they had all arrived, the music became louder and more persistent, and couples, one by one, took to the floor in the staid movements of the waltz. Tabitha danced first with Nicholas and found him again, as always, a graceful and accomplished dancer despite the slight limp which, in rhythm, seemed to bother him little. After the first waltz, Nicholas went from woman to woman, as if deigning to give them all a taste of his artfulness on the slick polished floor—and Tabitha noticed with a faint annoyance that most of the women seemed only too eager to dance with him.

As she stood watching the couples whirling over the dance floor, the flickering candles casting a checkered light and shadow over them, a surprising thought occurred to her. She wondered, vaguely and for no discernible reason, where Mike Long was. Out with the blacks, she supposed, administering to their woes—or in his own little room above the stables, reading and studying his medical tomes, or perhaps thinking of her. She would have given several years of her life to have him here with her, floating across the dance floor to the soft even cadence of the waltz. But it was impossible, of course, to invite a backwoods doctor to such an elegant affair. It would make the Enrights a laughing stock, and if there was anything she did not want it was to be laughed at or scorned. The whole idea was ridiculous, she told herself, and impatiently she tried to erase these vivid thoughts from her mind. This fabulous Cotillion was indicative of what she had lived and strived for. It represented the apex of her ambition, the level she had reached after a difficult climb. Mike Long was simply not at her level at all. She *must* forget him! In fact, it would be best if she learned to hate him—and certainly much safer.

Her inability to put Mike out of her mind even during the heady excitement of this grand ball irritated and even frightened Tabitha, and she quickly engaged in conversation with two women new to her, trading chitchat about the wifely duties necessary to plantation life and other boring subjects in which she had no real interest at all. Her eyes darted furtively across the floor as she talked, watching the dancers sliding gracefully to the music's rhythm. Particularly, she scanned the women. The tall statuesque beauty of Garland attracted men like a magnet . . . there was the blond and petite Mrs. Christopher with the piercing black eyes and high cheekbones . . . the dark, Spanish-looking Mrs. Santee with a comb in her hair and an almost swashbuckling air about her . . . the crude raw-boned Mrs. Manley who never looked quite civilized despite the comeliness of her attire . . . all the women, of all ages, each one gorgeously dressed, each carefully groomed, each wanting to outshine the other, each directed like an unerring arrow to the attraction of the opposite sex at whatever age level they operated. Tabitha thought there was something a little disgusting about it, for many of the women paid too much attention to Nicholas and, although she was sure she bore no real love for him, she was surprised to find it made her faintly jealous.

Just before midnight the music stopped and the crowd, now smiling and gay and in some cases slightly intoxicated, drifted into the large dining room where great mahogany tables stood in a U-shaped design to accommodate the guests. Several intricately shaped epergnes, their compartments filled with jellies and fruits and nuts, trailed flowers down the centers of the long tables. The white-clothed tables were laced with gelatins, salads and cold cuts, glistening colorfully in the candle-lighted room. Servants poured wine from cut glass decanters into dainty goblets on the tables, filling each glass as it became half empty, never allowing a single glass to be drained.

Tabitha was so excited over the obvious success of the occasion—even though the Cotillion had not yet been danced—that she could hardly eat. The soups and gumbos and bouillabaisse, the wild game and succulent domestic meats, and then the desserts of cake and gelatin passed by almost without her notice. The table was a hubbub of conversation, and Tabitha caught snatches of it as she engaged in her own prattle with d'Uberville on her left and Garland on her right.

"Your servants are excellently trained, Nicholas. . ."

"Yes. I insist on it with my household servants, my field hands and my horses."

"Speaking of horses, I have an eye out for Happy Boy. I'd give you an excellent price for him."

"He is not for sale. I'd as soon part with my wife!"

"Oh, indeed! Now you're chiding me!"

"Did you hear of the Cranbrook girl, the way she tried to run off with that steamboat captain?"

"No, really?"

"Oh, indeed! But her father caught up to her in time. If it hadn't been for a good sound thrashing administered—pardon the reference—to her bottom, she would have been pregnant by now. Oh she's a hellion!"

"Delightful, though, you'll have to admit."

"But a hellion all the same. Why, she threatened more than once to run away to Natchez-under and become a—but this is not quite an appropriate conversation for the dinner table, is it?"

"I should think," said Nicholas, "that the whims, caprices and vicissitudes of the female is a delightful subject at any time."

"Heavens, Nicholas!" objected Tabitha mildly. "I do believe you've had too much to drink."

Nicholas merely smiled at Tabitha's unoriginal remark, and the hum of conversation went on.

". . . Those two negrolings, Nicholas. Very cute. Where did you get them?"

Nicholas glanced at the children pulling the gently waving punkah over the table.

"Raised them myself. Born here at Magnolia Manor. Sired, so I am told, by Big Sam—although who can be sure?"

"Oh, a monster of a man, Big Sam! Ideal for the purpose, I must say!"

And from the distaff side:

"I really need more help in the house. My Esmerelda is a dear, but frightfully old. Besides, her superstitions drive me absolutely insane."

"Voodoo?"

"The worst form. Believes in curses, all sorts of weird things. But works very well, for her age, that is."

"That's a blessing."

"Yes, if she only wouldn't try to ward off bad spirits by spreading garlic sprigs around the house and on the doorsteps. Absolutely uncivilized."

"Perhaps," put in Nicholas, who seemed to miss no conversational gambit, "not any more uncivilized than our own methods of fighting the recent plague. People burned tar and soaked their clothes in vinegar and lit pine faggots—really all quite useless gestures, you know."

"Oh, the plague! One must do *something!*"

"And you, poor Nicholas, losing your mother. . . ."

"Yes, she was a great loss," said Nicholas somberly. And Tabitha thought, *How hypocritical!*

"And Tabitha, dear, you were so sick."

"Yes. I was quite ill."

"Thank the good Lord you recovered," said Jane Manley.

"Yes," cooed Mrs. Santee, "or we wouldn't have had this wonderful soiree!"

This brought a chuckle or two which Tabitha assumed was intended to turn a bit of bad taste into something more palatable, but Tabitha was convinced that some of the women, anyway, were secretly sorry she had recovered, for they coveted her rising position in Natchez society and the fact that she was from Natchez-under-the-Hill made the blow to their pride no easier to bear.

After the dinner the guests moved into the huge salon where they languidly sipped liquors and wines and, after a short rest from the heavy dinner, came the highlight of the evening—the much-waited-for Cotillion.

As the music drifted through the salon the couples seated themselves in chairs placed around the perimeter of the room. Tabitha stood proudly beside Nicholas in the center of the room, ready after many long practice sessions to lead the guests through the involved steps of the dance. The Cotillion was a dance of immense complexity and demanded complete concentration. It had become popular among the planters over the past few years and was rapidly replacing the staid eighteenth century minuet and the more robust contredanse. Tabitha was aware that some considered the Cotillion to be quite daring, for unlike the minuet it required a constant change of partners—a device which many looked upon as promiscuous in the extreme. It was consequently rarely seen in public places but only among people who knew each other well. Nicholas had decreed that each gentleman must start the Cotillion with a lady other than his wife—he and Tabitha as leaders being the sole exception—and this requirement added a pleasant intimacy to the dance. As the music swelled in volume, Nicholas gracefully moved into an intricate maneuver that each couple in turn tried to duplicate, and from that time on the room was a blurred kaleidoscope of whirling forms, swirling skirts with trim ankles peeking shyly from beneath, and men in cutaway coats spinning their partners.

The Cotillion was more of a game than a dance, for the difficult steps and roulades performed by the company were entirely at the whim of Nicholas, who could demand any step in his own repertoire. It was a confused combination of the waltz, the mazurka, the polka, and the galop, and it was subject to the boundless imagination of the leader. Tabitha searched her memory as she gaily swept across the shining floor in Nicholas's firm arms. Weren't there over eighty possible steps in the Cotillion? Wasn't the famous Duchesse de Berry of Paris one of its leading exponents. Hadn't there been Cotillions that lasted four and five hours, until the dancers were almost prostrate?

She tried to think of the names of the winding maneuvers as she and Nicholas performed them. There was the presentation, the trap, rounds of three, the serpent, the bridge, the Hungarian change, the graces, the double windmill, the eccentric columns, the oracle, the candle, the gliding line, thread the needle—heavens, the formations were endless! And Nicholas knew virtually all of them.

The great Cotillion lasted until three o'clock in the morning. When it was over Nicholas, warm from his exertions, downed several glasses of brandy in short order. Tabitha watched him closely for half an hour. He was slowly getting drunk, pouring down huge quantities of brandy and whiskey. His voice was growing louder and more boisterous, and he weaved slightly when he walked. By four o'clock the soiree began to break up, with guests thanking Nicholas and Tabitha for "the most wonderful evening ever." At the door Nicholas presented each lady with a vial of expensive French perfume as a gift. When, at last, the guests had departed, Tabitha sank exhausted against the door frame.

"I'm utterly spent," she said. Then she fixed her gaze on the wavering figure of Nicholas. "And you, Nicholas, are utterly drunk."

He grinned crookedly, taking an unsteady step toward her. He held a full glass of brandy in his hand.

"I'm delightfully drunk, my dear. Does a man good to get drunk occasionally. I hope I didn't insult any of the ladies."

"Fortunately, your behavior was proper."

Nicholas's eyebrows crawled upward in surprise. His smile remained lopsided.

"Didn't I even tell that son of a bitch Manley what I thought of him?"

"You didn't," said Tabitha coldly. "And I'll thank you to use milder language in the presence of a lady."

Nicholas straightened up as if he had been struck. His eyes thinned and he drained the brandy glass in one prodigious gulp.

"Lady? It's Nicholas Enright you're talking to. Your husband, you know. The guests are gone and we don't have to pretend any more. You and I know you are not—by some distance—a lady."

"Oh, you're impossible when you've been drinking!" said Tabitha in revulsion. "I'm going to bed."

She tried to pass him but he caught her by the arm and spun her around. The brandy glass crashed to the floor, splintering into tiny fragments.

"Lady!" he croaked drunkenly. "A lady whose sister is a whore! A lady who spreads herself for a backwoods doctor! A lady who plots with her lover to rid herself of her husband! My dear, who do you think you're fooling?"

She was pressed against him now, firmly, tightly, imprisoned by the iron band of his arm. She looked into his face and it was twisted and contorted, and she did not like the ugly look in his eyes or the mottled redness of his face.

"Please let me go, Nicholas," Tabitha pleaded.

"Why should I? I've got a right to you."

"Let me go!"

Nicholas laughed shortly. His breath was sour with whiskey.

"You *are* trying to act the lady, aren't you? A lady untouched by the foul hands of your husband. If it wasn't for other interlopers, you might yet be a virgin!"

"Nicholas! You're acting like a beast!"

"Perhaps. But then most women know how to handle the beast in their men. Let us see if you have learned enough by now to quiet the beast in me!"

Before she knew what was happening, Nicholas swept her up in his arms. He walked, more steadily now than she had seen him walk all evening, to the circular stairs leading to the bedrooms. Carrying her like a feather, he swept up the stairs in a dizzying whirl and took her to her bedroom. *My God,* thought Tabitha, *the man is impotent! Didn't he know that by now? Was he going to try again? Was this to be a repeat of their wedding night?*

But she did not fight him now. She was too startled by his actions to do anything. Entering her room he kicked the door shut with his heel, then set her gently down on her feet.

"Undress!" he commanded.

"Nicholas, please! You know you can't—"

"Undress, Goddamn it!"

Her eyes were wide with fear. She had never seen him quite like this. On their wedding night he had made a bold attempt and failed, becoming a savage after that failure. Tonight he was already a savage, a handsome savage with piercing eyes and an imperious manner that could not be disobeyed. Slowly, watching him warily, she slipped off the dress with its wide bombazine skirt, then the crinolines and pantaloons, and finally the silken chemise. She stood stark naked before him, fearful, yet afraid to deny him. But to her surprise he did not move toward her.

"You're beautiful," he said softly. "Lovely breasts, fine hips, and that ebony triangle of hair—enough to drive a man mad."

His words embarrassed her even as they pleased her. She watched him closely. Still he did not move. But he continued looking at her, scanning her nude body from head to toe. Finally he sighed.

"You're too damned much for any man," he said, "and as for me, I'm a useless son of a bitch."

Tabitha, not daring to reply, saw the haunted, persecuted expression creep into his eyes again.

"Even nature has cheated me," he said bitterly and walked out of the room.

10

She did not know where this room was, but it was a beautiful room, large and bright and airy, and it looked out upon a strange landscape that stretched away green and fertile to the horizon. She lay on the most wonderful bed in the world, with silken sheets beneath her nude body, and at her side her lover lay. He came to her and she felt his firm hands upon her warm body, and then the fierceness of his determination as he took her. There was a rare moment of high ecstasy, and the room spun wildly and the bed rocked and she clung to her lover in frenzy lest she tumble from the bed into the black nothingness beneath. . .

Tabitha awoke with a start. Her heart was pounding furiously and she lay for a moment catching her breath. The dream came back, like some gossamer spirit floating through murky air, and the word formed on her lips.

Mike!

She had been dreaming of Mike, and as the details filtered back into her brain from that nether world where dreams are manufactured, she felt embarrassment and shame. The dream had been one of animal passion, unfit for a lady to dream at all. It reminded her of the dreams she had endured in her early teens when she would be embarrassed all day by her nocturnal adventures with boys. Now the unnamed boys had become Mike Long.

She did not permit her mind to dwell on the dream for long. After all, it was only a dream, and one cannot help what dreams one has anyway. And the dreams were hers alone, to be shared by no one—an adventure that no one else could disrupt or impinge upon.

Tabitha rubbed her eyes and gazed at the brittle blue sky outside her window. The sun was already high and Tabitha judged the time to be about eight o'clock. She would have liked to sleep longer, ensconced cozily in the luxury of her big four-poster bed, but the dream had fully awakened her and she knew she would not be able to return to sleep. With complete disregard for the time of morning—for she was certain the household would be asleep after last night's late soiree—she pulled the bell cord and rang imperiously for Sophie. A minute later the quadroon came into the room, knuckling sleep from her round black eyes.

"Yes'm?"

"I want breakfast," said Tabitha crossly. "I want it served in my room."

Sophie cocked her head to one side, gazing at her mistress with apprehension.

"You feelin' all right, Miss Tabitha?"

"I'm feeling fine."

"You don' have no headache or nuthin'?"

Tabitha immediately resented the inference in her question. "*I* was not the one who was intoxicated last night," she said. "Now, will you bring me some breakfast?"

"Yes *ma'am!*"

Sophie departed to leave Tabitha with her restless thoughts. The events of the night before came flooding back, as if a blockade in the recesses of her mind had suddenly given way. Damn Nicholas anyway! Making her strip before him while he stood there staring at her like a slobbering simpleton! She flushed red at the very thought of it. Picking up a pillow, she threw it across the room in a fit of rage, but she quickly composed herself. At least he had had the decency not to beat her. That, at least, showed some restraint.

It took an almost physical effort to get the matter out of her mind, and by sheer willpower she directed her thoughts toward the great Cotillion. It had been superb, a scintillating coup in Natchez's social world, and for this she must give Nicholas full credit. It had, without a doubt, been the finest soiree ever given by a Natchez planter. It would be talked about for months, and it might never be equaled. Despite too much brandy, Nicholas had conducted himself in masterly fashion, and Tabitha knew that she too had been every inch the most gracious lady among those present. The Cotillion had definitely established her as the supreme hostess in Natchez country, had placed her on that elevated pedestal she had been seeking so long, and had made the Enrights the most renowned family in the planter society.

Well, that at least was a satisfying thought to savor, even though Nicholas had spoiled the evening with his boorish actions after the guests had departed. She supposed she could forgive him for that—in fact, knew she would. He had been drunk, and he would probably be contrite this morning, ashamed of what had occurred—although, knowing his haughty nature, he was not likely to admit it or apologize too abjectly. So, considering that he had given her so much in power and prestige last night, Tabitha felt that perhaps she should not feel like a martyr after all.

By the time her breakfast of a boiled egg, toasted bread, orange juice, French brioche and cafe noir was delivered on a sterling silver tray she was in a better frame of mind.

"Set it on the escritoire," she said to Sophie. "I'm sorry I got you up so early."

"Thass all right, ma'am."

"After breakfast I'm going for a ride. Have Toby bring Lady Belle to the front of the house."

"Yes'm."

Tabitha picked at her food, found she had little taste for it, and shoved it aside. She dressed quickly, surprised at her ambition so early in the morning following a late party, and went rapidly down the staircase to the hall. She was hoping she would not see Nicholas, for she felt a need to be alone. A quick glance assured her that he was not around, and she passed out the front door to the porte-cochere where Toby was already waiting with Lady Belle.

"Mornin' ma'am," Toby said.

Tabitha acknowledged the greeting with a curt nod of her head. She was developing an air of superiority lately toward the blacks—and she knew it. After all, she was the lady of the manor, wasn't she, and as such she was entitled to hold herself above the hired help. One could not get too friendly with one's underlings.

The groom helped her to mount and, sitting

sidesaddle, she spurred the horse into a trot. The esplanade was too far away for a morning ride, and she headed toward the cotton fields, now wet and muddy awaiting the spring planting. The string of whitewashed shacks that housed the slaves looked depressing in the early morning light. Feeble streaks of smoke issued from some of them, for the air was chilly. She stopped Lady Belle at the edge of the expansive fields and looked out over the muddy marsh. Despite the ugliness of the fields at this time of the year, a strange sensation she had noticed before gripped her. It was a heady feeling of power, for these fields were the source of her influence and her strength. She was convinced she was developing the same love of the earth, the same feeling for cotton, that the planters had — and Tabitha decided she liked the feeling.

Even now, looking at the desolate sight before her, she knew how beautiful the fields would become in a short time. In the spring when pink and white flowers graced the growing cotton plants there was beauty here. Later, when the bolls burst and the fields turned white, there was both beauty and power. For the white fiber meant a way of life for them, it meant cotton to be made into cloth for people all over the world to use and enjoy. Yes, cotton was the most important crop in the world, no doubt about that.

She neither saw nor heard Mike Long as he emerged from one of the cypress shacks, carrying his small black bag, and was not aware of his presence until he was beside her.

"Milady is up early this morning."

Tabitha twisted in the saddle to face him. She felt

her heart thump at his voice, but she caught herself before her startled reaction betrayed her, regarding him with coolness, as the mistress of the plantation would normally regard the help.

"The milady routine has worn itself out," she said caustically. "And I'm not in the mood for small talk this morning."

Mike looked nettled. "For God's sake, Tabitha! Try being human. You told me you loved me once. You haven't forgotten our—"

"Mike, please! I prefer to forget about that. I *must* forget about it."

He stood by the side of the horse, squinting up at Tabitha in the bright morning light.

"You look as beautiful as ever. No sign of the ravages of last evening."

"The evening was not of a ravaging nature," said Tabitha with resentment.

"I suppose you are right," Mike conceded. "But I must say that when the Enrights give a soiree, it is one that gets talked about. It was, in fact, the most beautiful party I have ever seen."

"Seen?"

"Oh, we slaves looked on from outside. Most of the blacks stood at a discreet distance from the house, gazing with great curiosity through the windows, hoping to catch a fleeting glimpse of the gentry at play."

"You put it hideously, Mike."

"But truthfully. We were all quite impressed with the vulgar lavishness of it all."

"Quit saying 'we'!" snapped Tabitha. "You put yourself on the same level as the Negroes."

Mike chuckled. "You know, Tabitha, you're getting

absolutely overbearing, like most plantation ladies."

"I hadn't noticed. . . . Mike, why do we always quarrel?"

Mike smiled. "We don't—always. I can remember distinctly one occasion when we didn't."

Tabitha flushed. "I've told you, Mike, that I prefer to forget the occasion you refer to. It will be better if we both forget it."

"I don't agree. I savor the memory of it."

Tabitha made an impatient gesture.

"What's the matter?" Mike asked. "Don't you like to be reminded of your little transgression? Get down off that damned horse, Tabitha, so we can talk face to face."

Tabitha dismounted. It occurred to her that she was being ordered about quite a bit lately, by Nicholas last night and now Mike. But it did not occur to her to deny Mike's request. She stood before him, looking up at him now, her chin tilted, her eyes frank and open.

"I love you, Tabitha," he said.

She shook her head and retreated a step. She hoped he could not hear the wild beating of her heart.

"You must not say it. The whole thing is impossible for us, so it's best if you put it out of your mind."

"I love you, Tabitha," he said again, "even if you are the most pig-headed and stubborn little hoyden I've ever known. You love me too, Tabitha, and it's about time you become honest with yourself and admit it. And while you're being honest you can admit, also, that all the glittering trappings of an Enright soiree is not really what you want in life. You've been dazzled by a way of existence you have never known, and you're letting the image of this new life get in the way of your sense of values."

"Mike, if you don't stop preaching I'll leave at once."

"Not before I ask you a question," Mike replied. "What makes you think that this vulgar display of wealth at Magnolia Manor, this elegant way of life, this frivolous approach to all problems and questions, this feudalistic system—what makes you think that it's the best possible life?"

"Really, Mike, you always confuse me. I've looked forward to living on the Hill ever since I was a little girl. I felt it was a noble ambition, not a vile compulsion. Is there anything wrong with that."

"There is, when you sacrifice principles and morality to achieve it."

"And I did this?"

"Of course. You sold yourself to Nicholas Enright."

"I didn't *sell* myself!"

"But you did. You gave yourself in marriage to a man you do not love because he could give you the way of life you sought. Now, because you do not love him and he shows no love for you, you are confused and perhaps a little disillusioned. I think you are aware of the falsity in the planter society too, although you won't admit it now. Tabitha, the planter's way of life has no moral justification for its existence. Slavery is wrong, totally wrong."

"Mike, you're talking nonsense. Slavery is a natural state for the blacks."

"Why?"

"Because they are an inferior race."

"Can you prove that?"

"I *know* it. After all, they are simple people, not much above the level of animals."

"Who told you this? Surely not your father."

"No."

"Who, then? Nicholas?"

"No one told me. I've simply always known that the blacks are an inferior race who not only serve the whites but are content to do so."

"Are you sure they're contented, Tabitha? I watched them as they stood wide-eyed last night, staring at Magnolia Manor with its dazzling lights and well-dressed people. Oh, a lot of them were impressed. I suspect that some of them were even proud, in a distorted sort of way, that they were owned by the Enrights who could give such a fabulous Cotillion. But some showed resentment too—some of them could not help draw a comparison between this way of life and their own. And they wondered."

Without an answer Tabitha put her foot in the stirrup and mounted Lady Belle.

"I hope, Mike, that Nicholas does not hear you talk in such manner."

"He has already. He knows my views."

Tabitha nodded. "Yes. He mentioned them to me. But if you keep on expressing them openly, I'm sure he will finally dismiss you. I, for one, don't intend to stay here and listen to you compare Nicholas and myself and all the gracious people who were at the Cotillion last night with these uneducated and uncultured blacks."

Mike caught the bridle and kept Tabitha from departing. He grinned up at her.

"It was Marie Antoinette who said, 'Let them eat

cake.' " His voice was low, almost menacing. "Let us hope that the Southern planter does not come to the same dubious end that Marie and her Louis did."

"You talk like an Abolitionist!" Tabitha shot at him, angered at his criticism.

"I have a feeling for all people. Perhaps that comes from being a doctor. Anyway, I dislike quarreling with you, Tabitha. I'm only trying to open your eyes. I'm praying for the day that you will see the shallowness and falsity of all this. On that day, I shall stand a better chance with you."

His words distressed her and Tabitha spurred the horse and rode away. In her fury she rode all the way to the esplanade this time and, dismounting, looked down upon the jerrybuilt shacks of Natchez-under-the-Hill and the silvery ribbon of river speckled in the morning sunlight. She had never met anyone quite as exasperating as Mike Long. It was probably true that he had a love for all people, despite the pigment in their skin. She supposed this was laudatory—at least she was sure her father would have thought so. Yet she deplored his criticism of her new way of life, for if this new way was wrong then she had misdirected all her ambitions and energies. If it was wrong, she would need to reorient her entire thinking, and this was an undertaking too colossal for Tabitha to contemplate.

She stayed on the esplanade for some time, viewing the panorama before her, trying to find comfort in its serene beauty. She often thought the view from the esplanade was like a magnificent painting done by the talented hand of God, but this morning it held no peace for her. At last, restlessly, she mounted again and rode back to Magnolia Manor. She found

Nicholas in the terraced garden, giving the wizened black gardener instructions for planting new blooms. When he saw her he approached and took the bridle of the horse, stopping it.

"You seem none the worse for wear this morning, my dear," he said, and Tabitha thought with revulsion that there was dry amusement in his statement.

"You were drunk last night," said Tabitha, "and on that basis I excuse your boorish manners."

"You are very wise. I rather thought you would not allow either my intoxication or my fumbling manners to interfere with the prize you won last night. It was considerable, you know."

"Yes."

"And I must say you were magnificent. You were all I ever hoped to have in a wife. You were the perfect counterpart to the position I have built for myself. I feel fulfilled today as I have rarely felt it before. I have shown everyone that a man with a crippled foot need not be a drudge on the human market. With my own hands and brains I built Magnolia Manor. With my own toil at first, and slaves as I was able to acquire them, I built my own cotton dominion. I shocked the society of Natchez by marrying a woman from Natchez-under—practically an unforgivable sin—and then made her the grandest lady of them all so that they must honor you and rub their proud noses in the dirt to you. And this must hurt them, my dear. It must give them great pain to realize that grand ladies are not produced solely by intermarriage among the planters, but that the qualities inherent in a grand lady can come from sources outside their ken. Tabitha, last night was yours and mine, our supreme

514

moment of triumph. No one shall ever look down on either of us again."

Tabitha was smiling now. She had dismounted and stood by Nicholas, thrilled at his complimentary words and tremendously proud. Yes, they were at the top now, the pinnacle, with all others looking up to them in admiration. And with her help, Nicholas had shored up his confidence. Perhaps, now, he would conquer his feeling of persecution, toss aside his fears that everyone was working to undermine him.

It was the beginning of a new, more satisfying existence at Magnolia Manor. For almost four months Nicholas and Tabitha lived serenely in their new world. Buoyed by his success, Nicholas gave another soiree in February and a third in March. More and more his life revolved around these magnificent events, and Tabitha rightfully judged that giving the parties satisfied Nicholas's great ego, made him feel that no man in all Natchez was more popular, more sought after, or better known than Nicholas Enright. Tabitha was delighted in the change that had come over him. He made no reference to his fears any more, and he treated Tabitha as a partner in his grand scheme to make Magnolia Manor and its occupants paramount in Natchez's snobbish society.

Aside from the soirees, things at the plantation moved with new efficiency. Tabitha learned more about her duties as a mistress of the plantation, taking a load from Nicholas's shoulders, and on a couple of occasions Nicholas complimented her on the job she was doing. Even the weather cooperated, so that the spring crop prospered almost from the moment of planting. By June the fields were splashed with white and pink blossoms, harbingers of the great bolls of cotton that would come.

The only distraction from Tabitha's new-found happiness was the mystique of Mike Long. During the euphoric four months that followed the first Cotillion, Tabitha tried hard to put him out of her mind, but she never wholly succeeded. She was successful in avoiding him, however, and that helped. Out of sight was not exactly out of mind, but at least it eased the hurt in her heart. Her decision to hate him, however, foundered. Her mind kept returning to the rendezvous in Mike's room, and when it did she became exasperated with herself and tried to deny that it was of any importance. In this attempt she failed.

Still, she was reasonably pleased with the present situation. Nicholas's demeanor had changed for the better; he had put aside sarcasm and arrogance and treated her as an equal partner in the running of the plantation. He no longer had the haunted look in his eyes and he seemed more content than ever before. It was late in June, just as Tabitha had convinced herself that the dangerous days of her marriage were over and that she had finally won her spurs as mistress of Magnolia Manor, that her newly won heaven was rudely upset by a twist of history that brought cruelty and terror to the Mississippi Valley—and ultimately, in a very personal way, to Magnolia Manor itself.

It was mid-afternoon of a steaming day when two horsemen burst from the shaded tunnel of oaks into the semicircular entrance to Magnolia Manor. One was Faunce Manley, the other a stranger wearing the broad-brimmed hat of a planter. Nicholas and Tabitha were on the veranda at the time and watched as the two riders reined in their horses, lifting dry dust off the road as they came to an abrupt halt. Tabitha noticed that both men wore grim expressions.

"Now, damn it," was Manley's rasping greeting, "maybe you'll believe what I say about the niggers! The slaves are planning a rebellion!"

Nicholas glanced from one man to the other. His face was expressionless.

"Whose blacks? Yours?"

"Yours too!" retorted Manley. "All the blacks, damn it! All up and down the Mississippi! A revolt, by God!"

"If it's true," said Nicholas coolly, "it's because men like you mistreated them, Manley."

Manley's eyes flashed. He waved his arm imperiously.

"I'm not here to argue the pros and cons of treatment! I'm here to spread an alarm. The black sons of bitches are going to revolt, I tell you!"

Tabitha frowned. She recalled briefly her conversation with Mike Long. It irritated her suddenly that what he had said might prove true. She had not yet grasped the horror of what revolt could mean, but when she glanced at Nicholas it was brought forcibly home to her. To her dismay she saw the look of fear in his eyes had returned, the haunted look that had been so long absent. His belligerence to what Manley said dissipated suddenly and he said, an anxious tone in his voice. "You think *my* blacks will revolt?"

"Of course! Every Goddamn nigger in Mississippi is involved!"

Nicholas had a faraway expression on his face. He stared out toward the long row of cypress shacks.

.

"I treated them kindly," he said, half to himself. "Why should they revolt? Unless—" his eyes brightened momentarily "—unless Mike Long has actually succeeded in—"

"No, Nicholas!" Tabitha permitted the words to slip out unimpeded, wondering as soon as she uttered them why she wanted to protect the doctor. It would be better if Nicholas fired him now, getting him out of her sight and, ultimately, out of her mind. But she went on, the words emerging almost involuntarily. "I'm sure Doctor Long has nothing to do with this. There must be some other explanation. Why don't you hear Faunce out?"

Nicholas glanced at Tabitha but said nothing. Faunce Manley took immediate advantage of the opening given him.

"Thank you," he said with strained gallantry. "No, Nicholas, this isn't only my slaves and yours. This is a gigantic plot." He jerked his thumb toward the stranger, a lean gaunt man with red-rimmed eyes and a look of weariness. "This is Jeff Gable. He's been riding all night to spread the alarm. He comes from Madison County up north. Tell them about it, Jeff."

Gable's voice was hoarse, as if he had repeated the story many times and was weary of it.

"There's a plot, all right. And it's led by white men."

"White men!"

"Yes. They've been stirrin' up the niggers for months, tellin' them that when the time comes they must rise up and kill their masters with axes and clubs. Then they're supposed to seize firearms on each plantation and circle toward the towns. Every white

518

planter up and down the Mississippi is marked for death, and when they get enough blacks together they plan to attack Natchez in force. It's the Nat Turner plan all over again. The niggers have been promised freedom and white women to rape—pardon the mention of it, ma'am."

Tabitha drew in her breath sharply. The whole idea seemed preposterous! How could such a thing happen? The blacks were inferior people with no leadership. But if the leadership came from whites—her thoughts slid to a horrified halt, and a seething anger took hold of her. Why did this have to happen *now?* It was so unfair for something like this to interfere at the exact moment that she had reached her cherished goal. Surely, now that she had gained luxury and power, it could not be taken away! Certainly not by slaves! She glanced at Nicholas again, hoping to find encouragement there, but the expression on his face appalled her. The look of fear had returned.

"What white men are behind this plot?" he asked thickly.

"John Murrell's Clan, we think," said Manley. "It's Murrell's plan all over again. You remember it, Nicholas. Murrell and his gang of outlaws planned to lead a slave revolt but a young member of the Clan betrayed him and he was arrested and put in jail for ten years."

"I remember," said Nicholas. "The conspiracy was stopped, was it not?"

"No!" said Manley. "The Clan is still alive and determined to strike without Murrell, and we have to counter it—or we're dead."

Nicholas moistened his lips nervously. His eyes

darted from side to side, as if he expected an imminent attack. The Clan! Yes, he remembered the Clan! Yes, of course, the Clan had always been opposed to him!

"And when is this revolt to take place?" he asked

"Within the week," said Manley. "On the Fourth of July."

BOOK V
The Beckoning Flatlands

1

The long and sinuous Natchez Trace offered the only wilderness road available from Nashville to Natchez, and its 550 miles were traversed by farmers, preachers, businessmen, and frontiersmen in the early nineteenth century trek to the Natchez country. Along its shadowed and forested path lurked the feared land pirates—bloodthirsty and greedy men such as the Harpe Brothers, Samuel Mason, and the cleverest of them all, John Murrell.

The bizarre plot, hatched by Murrell while he was in prison on a minor charge, envisioned a rebellion of the slaves and the eventual establishment of an outlaw empire throughout the South. It was a wildly pretentious plan. Murrell had many friends among the brigands and rogues of the rivertowns, and those who were natural leaders he planned to put in charge of regiments of men. He and his cohorts would first travel through the slave country, urging the blacks to revolt when the signal was given, promising them each freedom and a white woman to rape and ravage. He, Murrell, would be the supreme commander, and when he gave the word the slaves would attack the plantation homes, kill the owners, steal guns from the plantation, and then converge on the rivertowns where regiments of outlaws would be waiting to join them. The mob of mixed whites and blacks would then sack the towns and move south, until finally they descended on Natchez—and, at the very end, they would even take the city the British could never conquer, New Orleans itself.

The original date set for this ambitious insurrection and the establishment of Murrell's criminal empire was Christmas Day, 1835.

That such a desperate and well-laid scheme could collapse simply because Murrell liked to boast too much sounds incredible, but it happened. A young man named Virgil Stewart joined the organization—which was elaborately called the Grand Council of the Mystic Clan—and after learning of its secret plans decided he wanted no part of it and relayed the information to authorities in Madison County, Mississippi. Murrell was arrested, brought to trial in July, 1834, and sentenced to serve ten years. Murrell's arrest, however, did not end the plot. The Clansmen decided to go ahead with their nefarious plan anyway, but they changed the date of the revolt. They moved it up to July 4, 1835, hoping to strike before the planters were aware the plot still lived.

But once again the news leaked out. It fell among the planters like grapeshot from a cannon, spreading excitement and distress throughout the South. The secret emerged in late June at the plantation of a man named Latham who lived near the town of Beattie's Bluff in Madison County, Mississippi. Mrs. Latham overheard a servant girl and a fieldhand discussing the plot and alerted her husband. Immediately all Madison County was up in arms. At Livingston, the county seat, a vigilance committee calling itself the

Committee of Safety was formed with "power to bring before them any person or persons, either white or black, and try in summary manner any person brought before them, with the power to hang or whip."

Slaves and white men suspected of complicity in the plan were dragged before the already biased court. Slaves were beaten to make them talk, and those with any knowledge of the devilish plot were hanged at once. Finally, through the sweat and the blood and the agony, there emerged names of white men who were leaders in the Clan, the brains behind the coming rebellion. There was Joshua Cotton, a "steam doctor" who practiced a form of therapeutics popular at the time; his partner, William Sanders; Albe Dean, a shiftless carpenter; Lee Smith; John and William Earle; and, most surprising of all, a wealthy planter named Ruel Blake. He was the most unbelievable Clan member, because he owned many slaves and was an important man in his community—yet he had joined the movement to destroy his own class. All of these conspirators and others were quickly hanged—fifteen whites and six blacks—but Blake cheated the gallows for a while. He escaped the Committee's clutches and was not found for several days. At last they located him in a low tavern in Natchez-under-the-Hill and he, like the others, was hanged.

The shocking story of the whippings and killings in Livingston spread from town to town and county to county, sowing fear and confusion in its wake. All along the Mississippi, from Vicksburg to New Orleans, the old nagging fear of a slave rebellion quickened and terror spread. The white planters set up kangaroo courts and questioned their slaves, ready to destroy anyone—black or white—who came under even the remotest suspicion. Because the audacious plot planned to make use of rivertown criminals, Natchez and Vicksburg and Memphis looked with new suspicion at their slum-infested waterfronts, and some wanted to wipe out the rivertowns once and for all. Others cautioned against precipitous action, saying that the plot had matured in the minds of a small group of men and that it was sufficient simply to destroy the handful of conspirators, as they had at Livingston, and to eliminate any black who was approached by the plotters. There would be time later to take care of the rivertown slums, if that seemed necessary. This view prevailed because time had now become an important consideration. The Fourth of July was only a few days away, and it was essential that each planter eliminate those among his slaves who were involved in, or even aware of, the conspiracy.

And an orgy of blood and lust swept the South.

2

The night after Faunce Manley spread the alarm to Magnolia Manor, Nicholas sat near a window facing the slave quarters, a rifle across his knees. A troubled Tabitha watched him with growing concern. Manley's alarming news had brought back fear into Nicholas's eyes, and that was a sign that disturbed her.

"Now perhaps someone will realize that a plot is about to destroy me," he said. "The Clan is out to get me, and they will use my blacks to gain their ends."

Tabitha tried to reason with him. "There is no plot aimed at you personally," she said. "It's directed at all the planters—if, indeed, there is such a plot at all."

She might have saved her words, for her efforts to depersonalize the threat had no influence on her husband's wild thoughts. He sat all night at the window, his rifle in readiness, and then fell asleep as morning came and the servants in the house again stirred. He was awakened within an hour by another visit from Manley.

"We are forming a court," said Manley in his booming voice. "I suggest that we set up the court at Magnolia Manor for questioning the slaves of all the nearby planters. It is better that we work together rather than separately."

Nicholas agreed. His sleepless night had magnified his fears, and he was ready to agree to any steps necessary to counteract the terrible threat to his well being and the existence of Magnolia Manor.

"Yes," he said. "I'm anxious to get on with it, because something is becoming obvious to me that wasn't clear before. I have a white Clansman working on my plantation!"

"Who, for God's sake?"

"Mike Long has been arousing my blacks with nonsensical talk about freedom."

Manley looked startled. "Good God, Nicholas! Are you sure?"

"I'm positive."

"It sounds impossible."

"Not impossible at all," said Nicholas softly. "Many times he has talked to the blacks about freedom. He has even had the gall to make his views known to me."

"Then why have you kept him on the plantation?" snapped Manley.

"Because he's a good doctor and I needed him. But now I see the light. If he is plotting against me—if he is a member of the Clan—then it is better I find it out now!"

Faunce Manley waved his arm as if indicating there was no point in discussing the matter further. He was impatient with Nicholas. He had long recognized that Nicholas had some sort of complex involving a feeling of persecution. The slave rebellion, and his suspicion of Mike Long, fit that complex perfectly. And while Manley was not entirely convinced that Nicholas was right about the doctor, still he was not above taking advantage of Nicholas's mood.

"A man has to fight back!" he said belligerently. "We must not only execute some of our own slaves, but we must seek out any white man behind this horrible plot."

Nicholas nodded. "Yes. There are times when murder is quite justified."

Tabitha, who had been standing inside the big door leading to the veranda on which the two men stood, tiptoed away, her mind troubled by the turn of events. Obviously, Nicholas's remarks about Mike Long's possible guilt, made the previous day, had plagued his mind during his night-long vigil, and she was certain that Nicholas would hang Mike without a qualm. Despite her determination to put Mike out of her mind—and the fact that his absence would help her to reach that goal—she could not tolerate the thought of his execution at the hands of the suspicious planters. She stood for a moment in the hallway, wondering what to do. Then, suddenly, she broke into a run, leaving by the back door, crossing the flagstone patio between the house and the kitchen, and heading heedlessly for Mike Long's room above the stable. She virtually flew up the stairs and, without knocking, burst through the door. Mike was sitting at his desk, examining some papers. When he saw Tabitha he came to his feet. The next instant she was in his arms, her warm body soft against his, her head tipped back as his firm lips crushed hers. She savored the kiss for some seconds, then frantically pushed him away.

"No, Mike! Not now, please!"

An incredulous expression crossed Mike's face. "You look as if you've seen a ghost," he said. "What is wrong, Tabitha?"

"Mike, your life is in danger!" The words tumbled out.

"My life? I don't understand."

"There's a revolt brewing," Tabitha said. "The blacks are going to rise up and kill all the whites. At least they *were* going to do it, but some planters found out about it and killed a lot of niggers and a lot of white leaders. Now every plantation in the South is questioning the blacks and looking for white men who might be planning to lead them in revolt."

Without a word Mike took Tabitha by an arm and guided her to a chair. Then he sat down at the desk.

"I have heard these stories," he said calmly. "But I think the fear of revolt has outgrown the actual threat. If Nicholas believes his slaves are going to rebel, he is mistaken. I know them. I work with them. They feel a strong loyalty to him—or more directly, to you. There is no immediate danger."

"But—"

"Is Nicholas planning to question his blacks?"

"Yes."

"He will find no guilt."

Tabitha shook her head impatiently. "You don't understand. It's *you* he's after. He has an idea, now, that you are a Clan member, plotting to do him in. And I know how his mind works. He will accuse you of fomenting trouble among the blacks, and in the planters' present state of mind, they'll hang you if Nicholas can prove that you even talked of freedom to the blacks. And besides," she said, trying to clinch her argument, "he knows about us."

Mike frowned. "How?"

"He says he has spies on the plantation who inform

him of such things."

Mike stared into space for a long time as comprehension slowly crept into his reluctant mind.

"I see the pattern now," he said calmly. "I *have* told Nicholas that someday the slaves would be free. He knows my views. And if he also knows about our little tryst, then I can see why he wants to get rid of me."

"He will destroy you, Mike. I know he will." Tabitha placed a hand on his arm. "You must flee, Mike," she said. "You must get away from here. You must go into hiding."

Mike Long stood up. He walked to the small window and gazed out. The slave shacks, splashed yellow with the morning light, spread before his eyes.

"No," he said at last. "To flee would be an admission of guilt. They would send out search parties and bring me back. It would be worse than if I stayed. Besides, I have an ace in the hole. If Nicholas tries to incriminate me, I think I can switch the tables on him."

"How?"

"Would Nicholas like to be branded a murderer?" he asked.

"A murderer?"

"Yes, or more precisely, a matricide?"

She stared at him, not able to speak. He took her by the shoulders and looked into her eyes.

"Did you verify with Sophie that Nicholas mixed the calomel and jalap for his mother?" he asked.

"Yes." Her voice was weak.

"Then I am convinced that he did not mix it at all, and that it was this same calomel and jalap he gave to me when you were sick. Nicholas murdered his mother by withholding treatment from her. If he starts on me, Tabitha, I'll have him investigated by proper authorities for murder! I think that even the threat of such action will stop him!"

Tabitha shuddered. She did not like to think of Nicholas as a murderer. Yet she knew that what Mike said was undoubtedly true. She shook her head in an agony of concern.

"I can't understand him, Mike. What kind of a man is Nicholas anyway?"

"He's a monster, Tabitha. He will never be anything else, of that I'm certain. Medically certain. He's obsessed. Thinking that everyone is an enemy, he will strike out against innocent people and harm them. He will strike against me or Faunce Manley or even you — anyone he thinks is persecuting him. By all the medical knowledge I have, I can only draw one conclusion. Nicholas Enright is dangerously mad."

Tabitha closed her eyes. Mike had refrained from using the word "mad" before now. To hear Mike, a doctor with a knowledge of mind and body, say it was unbearable. Her whole life since she had met Nicholas raced through her mind. Was everything she had built with this man to be swept away because he suffered a peculiar form of madness? How in God's merciful name could such a thing happen?

Thought of God caused her to think of her father. What would he say of this? Had she been too ambitious, too determined, too willing to ignore Nicholas's peculiarities and faults, simply to reach a cherished goal? Was this God's punishment for her calloused outlook? She was sure her father would so interpret it, but she could not bring herself to that conclusion. God was merciful. He was not a God of hate, not an entity that wreaked destruction and havoc. Or was He?

She hardly realized that Mike had taken her gently into his arms and that they had reclined on the bed and that his hand was already on her exposed breast, stroking it with a sweetness that excited and overwhelmed her. And then there was the ecstasy again, as she had known it before with Mike Long but never with Nicholas, and her fears vanished as the room became a protective shield, a nest of security, which no trouble could penetrate.

3

The garden house was used as an interrogation chamber. The tools were removed and chairs and tables placed at one end of the room to accommodate the inquisitors. In the center was a heavy stout puncheon table over which the Negroes suspected of complicity in the Clan's iniquitous plot would be bound and whipped for information. At the opposite end from the judges' tables was an open area where the beaten slaves were to be administered to by Dr. Mike Long.

Since the interrogation would occur on Nicholas's property, he was honored with the center chair along the wall, which ostensibly made him the chief justice. Flanking him were Faunce Manley, John McRae, Chris d'Uberville, Terrance Ainsley, and several other local planters. All of them had asked their overseers to bring to the interrogation center any Negro he suspected of knowing about the plot, or had reason to believe harbored feelings of resentment against the white masters. If he had none who fit these two categories, he was to bring the most intelligent, since it was believed that the smarter ones would be those the Clan might more readily approach.

"We will loosen their minds, these intelligent ones,"

predicted Manley with a slight trace of anticipation in his voice.

Faunce Manley, betraying his anxiety, insisted that his blacks be first to face the grim planters, and ten stalwart fieldhands were herded into the small enclosure by Manley's bulky overseer. Manley motioned to the first one and several men grabbed the protesting black and tied him face-down across the table. Nicholas glanced at Manley and noted the cruel gleam already in the planter's eyes.

"Your pleasure," he said, "and I'm sure it will be one."

Manley walked to the center of the room, trailing a long black whip behind him. The Negro turned his head sideways, rolling his eyes up to meet the whip in the hands of his white master.

"You know anything about a slave rebellion?" asked Manley, toying suggestively with the whip.

"Nossuh. Ah don' know whut you means."

Manley's fine lips twitched. Without a warning he brought up the whip and laced it across the Negro's glossy back. The man gasped at the sudden pain, and a red streak of blood sprang to the surface of his ebony shoulders.

Nicholas rapped the table with a gavel. "You didn't give him much of a chance," he said.

Manley whirled about. "I'll handle my niggers the way I please!" he shot back. Then he turned back to the slave.

"Has any white man talked to you about a revolt?"

"Nossuh. Ah swears not."

The whip cracked again, smearing blood from the first wound, across the Negro's back as it unwound from around his trembling body.

"Name those white men!" insisted Manley.

"They wusn't no white men! Ah don' know whut you're meanin', Massa!" The black screamed out the words, his eyes rolling in pain and horror.

"Black son of a bitch!" shouted Manley. "Lying black son of a bitch!" Again he brought the whip down, and then again. The black man cried out in agony, his screams cutting the stillness of the room. Nicholas frowned. Manley, his natural lust for blood showing, was giving the slave little chance to defend himself. He watched as Manley, now in a frenzy, slashed at him anew, once, twice, three times. The room suddenly began to smell of blood and sweat, and Nicholas rapped again with the gavel.

"Enough, Faunce! Don't overdo it!"

Manley spun around, eyes glowing, mouth open and dripping saliva, the joy of torture in his face.

"He's my black! I can beat him if I like! I can beat him to death, Goddamn it, if I have a mind to!"

Mike Long, who had been brought to the room to treat the slaves after their ordeal, stepped forth.

"You *will* beat him to death, if you keep it up. Better let the boy up."

Manley wheeled to face his new tormentor. "Nigger lover! I know your feelings about these blacks! I should take the whip to you!"

Nicholas slammed his hand on the table. "As chief judge here, I will have none of that," he said, even though not altogether displeased with Manley's branding Mike Long as a lover of the Negro. He motioned to Manley's overseer. "Untie the boy," he said. "It's obvious he knows nothing about this."

The overseer loosened the ropes that held the man and Mike took the staggering black to one corner of the room to treat his lacerated body.

The next black man was tied down and, although Manley was not quite as precipitous this time, he managed to lash the Negro often enough to turn his back into bloody rawness. But the victim offered no information about the coming rebellion. The third was brought up, and the fourth. Each received brutal treatment from an almost crazed Manley, and each denied knowledge of the plot. Nicholas watched Manley in morbid fascination as the latter's rage increased with each man's denial of guilt. Manley was enjoying himself. His face was flushed and feverish with excitement, his eyes shining with expectancy.

He whipped the fifth and the sixth, and at last he had his success. The seventh victim struggled as the men attempted to tie him to the table. Because he was a big muscular young man, he was able to make their task difficult, and as they attempted to tie him down he turned his head toward Manley.

"You don' have to whip me, Massa. Ah'll tell you somethin'. Ah knows somethin'."

Manley looked at him as if disappointed at the fact that he had been cheated out of torturing the big fellow.

"Let him stand," said Manley curtly.

The men let go and the big Negro youth stood up proudly.

"Tell the court what you know," Manley ordered.

The Negro threw back his head and stared across the room at the planters who would judge him.

"Fust, Ah wants you to know Ah'm innocent," he

536

said. "Ah didn' join in with this man, lak he wanted me to. But he came to see me—this white man—an' he asked me if Ah wanted to be free, an' Ah said Ah guessed Ah did, that all of us felt that way. An' he says, 'They's a way you kin be free. On the Fourth of July they's gonna be a revolt of all the slaves, an' if you jine up with us you'll not only be free but you'll have a white woman too'."

"Go on," said Manley, as the youth paused.

"Ah tole him Ah didn' want nuthin' to do with it an' he says if Ah'd jest git together all the slaves on the plantation that wanted to be free and rose up when the signal came, it would be easy to kill all the whites on the plantation—exceptin' a woman Ah could have fer m'self."

"Is that all?" demanded Manley.

"Yassuh. Ah tole him Ah wanted no part of it."

"Did you talk to the other slaves about it?"

"Well, yassuh. Ah tole them whut happened. But Ah wasn't tryin' to git them together for no revolt."

"What was the white man's name?"

"Ah don' know. He nevah tole me."

Manley turned to his fellow planters on the bench. His mouth twitched nervously.

"This nigger knows about the plot. He's talked to others about it. He's dangerous. I say this nigger should be hanged."

There was a sullen silence. The man's broad face showed surprise and fear. The judges glanced at each other uncertainly, but none challenged Manley.

"I demand a vote from the bench," said Manley.

Nicholas nodded. "Very well. A majority vote will decide."

"I vote that he die," said old John McRae.

"Aye," said Manley.

There followed a chorus of "ayes." Every planter was for the death sentence. Although this assured the execution, Manley noticed that Nicholas had not voted.

"And you, Nicholas?" he snapped.

"I'm against hanging him."

Manley looked irritated. "You are outvoted, as you know," he said testily, "but nevertheless I resent your soft attitude. The boy has admitted receiving information from a white man about the rebellion and talking to other blacks about it."

Nicholas smiled crookedly. It was, of course, the reaction he had expected—even hoped for—from Manley. Manley was a bloodthirsty, revenge-seeking sadist. He would insist on having his pound of flesh. Nicholas's strategy was to make it difficult for Manley to satisfy his blood lust completely. He planned to compromise Mike Long and bring him before the court, where he would accuse him of arousing the blacks with antislavery propaganda, of being a member of the dreaded Clan—and it would suit his purpose to have Manley half-crazy for blood by that time.

"You overlook the fact, Manley, that this slave did not join in the white man's plan," Nicholas pointed out.

"How do you know that? I think he lies!" Manley was ferocious in his insistence. "This is too serious a matter, Nicholas, for us to make any mistakes. Any nigger at all involved in this damnable plot should be hanged."

Heads nodded along the panel of judges.

"There are degrees of guilt," delayed Nicholas. "Perhaps there should be degrees of punishment."

Manley shook his head stubbornly. "Unless we deal harshly with these plotters—make examples of them—we shall have trouble again. I say hang every last one of them!"

The lust for blood was evidently in them all, for the rest of the planters agreed. Nicholas had been sharply outvoted. In silence he followed the judges out into the yard behind the garden house where a huge gnarled oak tree stood. He watched as a rope was tied to a heavy branch and the noose fastened around the Negro's thick neck. The victim's eyes were wide with fright.

"Massa! Ah tole you all Ah knows! Ah didn' jine the white man! Ah's innocent!"

Manley said nothing.

"Ah's got two kids, Massa! They all need this ol' nigger! Please, Massa!"

"Swing him," said Manley coldly.

The noose tightened and the Negro was jerked into the air. He died slowly of strangulation, kicking frantically at first, then more feebly, until he was dead.

Nicholas looked at Manley. "Very impressive," he said coldly. "The blacks who denied everything got off with only a whipping. The one who offered information was hanged. Justice, planter style."

Manley swore violently. "For Christ's sake, Nicholas! You're as afraid of this plot as anyone. You said the Clan was out to get you. Well, they're out to get every planter here. I don't intend to stand by and let criminal white men and stupid blacks rape my wife and kill me! As far as I'm concerned, I'd just as soon hang those who kept silent too. Let's go back and resume the questioning."

The trial went on. Manley finished with his blacks. Then the stage was turned over to John McRae. Nicholas watched the black men come in, one by one, to face close questioning and the agony of the whip. There was no mercy shown by McRae or the other planters, and the stifling room became a torture chamber that echoed with the anguished cries of the misused men. In the back of the building the lacerated bodies of the lucky ones were laid like cordwood for Mike to work over. The unlucky ones—three more of them—were dangled from the oak tree behind the garden house.

As each planter took his turn Nicholas became more and more convinced the blood lust possessed them all. This fact, he knew, would work to his personal advantage. He was to be the last planter to question his slaves, and he would build upon what had happened before. His eyes drifted toward the corner of the room where Mike Long bandaged the wounds of the whipped men. He would bring Mike Long before this makeshift court, and he was certain the judges, in their present state of mind, would find him guilty. Hadn't he spoken many times of the injustice of slavery, and predicted the blacks would some day rise in revolt? It shouldn't be difficult to link him, in the suspicious minds of the planters, with the Clan and the uprising planned for the Fourth of July. The planters' vengeful and unreasoning mood would send Mike to the hanging tree.

The death of Mike Long would not only remove a

menace to his personal life, but would solve an additional problem that had nagged Nicholas for some time. Although he had no particular adoration for Tabitha, still he strongly resented the fact that Mike Long had been his wife's lover. Despite his callous statement to Tabitha that her relationship with Mike was acceptable if only she would keep it discreet, he found her disloyalty to him a blow to his pride. And since his need of Tabitha was an unalterable fact of life, getting rid of the doctor seemed the logical solution.

Sickening of the smell of blood, Nicholas called a recess and the planters stepped outside for a breath of fresh air. Nicholas walked slowly toward the manor, entered it and walked into the music room. Tabitha was there with Garland. She looked up quickly as he entered.

"What's happening out there?" she asked.

"Women need not be concerned with what's happening out there," Nicholas said bluntly.

"Is it very bad?"

"It's quite bad. We try to do justice, but it is sometimes hard to decide. We've whipped fifty or more and hanged four."

Tabitha's mouth went tight at the corners. Garland's face paled with horror.

"That's savagery," Garland said. "Isn't there a better way?"

"No better way," said Nicholas. "This is a serious matter. If we don't break this incipient revolt we may all be dead on the Fourth of July. At least we men will be. You women may be more fortunate. Your lives may be spared if you agree to submit to some brawny

Negro or perhaps several of them."

"How awful!" said Garland.

"I need a drink," said Nicholas and poured himself a large portion of brandy from a decanter. He downed it with slow deliberation. Tabitha watched him. He looked tired and disheveled and a little wild-eyed, like a savage animal fighting for its existence.

"I'd like to go out there and see what's happening," she decided suddenly.

Nicholas's jaw was set. "It's no place for you, Tabitha!"

"But I want to go!" Tabitha was insistent. She was afraid of what might happen to Mike Long while she sat idly in the house, and she reasoned that her presence might give Nicholas some pause.

"I refuse to allow it," Nicholas said angrily. "It's no place for a high-born lady."

"Oh, so now I'm high-born! You've never before considered so. You dragged me up from Natchez-under, remember? You've more than once made a point of it."

Her husband's eyes thinned. "I can return you to Natchez-under just as quickly, my dear," he threatened. But then his face softened as a new idea came to him. Maybe Tabitha *should* watch the proceedings. It would be a master stroke of justice to have Tabitha on hand when Mike was cast to the wolves. The macabre humor of such a situation suddenly appealed to him. He bowed his head to Tabitha in mock gentlemanliness. "On second thought, my dear, perhaps you are right. You might learn something about the perils of our time by attending the trials. Let us go."

Having attained her way, Tabitha now decided to be coy.

"Are we questioning our slaves yet, Nicholas?"

"Not yet."

"Call me when we begin," she said.

He smiled tolerantly. "Of course, my dear."

When Nicholas had gone, Tabitha turned to Garland. "I'm much worried about Nicholas," she said. "He's so self-centered, and he feels everyone works against him—perhaps even me."

"I noticed he didn't exactly address you in terms of great affection," said Garland wryly.

Tabitha smiled bitterly. "I might as well admit it, to you anyway. He doesn't love me. He admits it quite bluntly. But he needs me, just as I need him. Without each other we couldn't have this fine life."

"Do you love him?" asked Garland shrewdly.

Tabitha gazed at Garland steadily. Something about Garland drew the truth from her.

"No. I did at one time. Now I think I do not."

Garland chuckled. "I understand the situation. I don't love old John either. But he's useful to me. I need him—and I also have other needs he doesn't satisfy." She leaned forward, looking Tabitha in the eye. "Isn't that the way it is with you?"

The candid question startled Tabitha. Could Garland possibly know that she and Nicholas did not share the same bed? No, of course not. How could she possibly know?

"You're encroaching on a sensitive area," Tabitha said with caution.

"I thought so. That *is* the way it is with you." Garland seemed sure of herself. "If I am right, then I presume you have sought satisfaction elsewhere?"

"Garland! What *are* you implying?"

Garland's laugh was tinkling, musical. "Tabitha, you're so utterly transparent. Don't you think I know what has been going on? You've been seen at the esplanade with that frightfully handsome doctor, Mike Long. I've seen the two of you exchange glances on occasion. He's rugged and very mannish, the kind of big muscle-loaded man some women need. I have suspected for some time that he must be your secret obsession."

Tabitha felt blood crawl into her face and tug at the roots of her hair. Garland's insight amazed and frightened her.

"My God, Garland, do I reveal myself so blatantly? Does *everyone* know?"

"Oh, I think not. I pride myself on being quite a discerning person. Besides, I have a sort of diabolical talent for sorting out delicious gossip. Are you in love with this man, Tabitha?"

Tabitha got to her feet nervously. For a full minute she paced the floor, then sat down again.

"Look, Garland. I'll be frank with you, since you seem to already know so much. I believe I love Mike Long. But I'm doing my best to put him out of my mind. I am married to Nicholas. I have here at Magnolia Manor everything I have longed for all my life. I'm practical enough not to want to give that up, even for love."

"Very well, I shan't say any more. I understand this, because I have a similar problem. There's only one annoying fact: it's hard to get love out of your heart, once it's in there. It's a mean, ornery and persistent thing—love is. You may find one day—just as I may—that the things you have here in this planter's

544

paradise don't mean as much to you as love does. If that time comes, your dilemma will broaden."

"Well, I don't want to discuss it any more," said Tabitha, seeking refuge once more in closing her mind to her problems.

Two hours later Nicholas called to take them to the garden house.

4

Much to the surprise of both Tabitha and Garland, their entrance into the makeshift courtroom caused no concern on the part of the grim planters along the wall. Apparently Nicholas had discussed the matter with them and they had mutually agreed that it would be beneficial for the women to view some of the harsh realities of plantation life. Nicholas led the two women to chairs in one corner of the room near the judges' bench, so that they might view the proceedings at close quarters.

The room smelled of the raw passions that had been unleashed there, and Tabitha crinkled her nose in disgust. Blood and the sweaty odors of black and white bodies mixed with grayish smoke from choice Havana cigars assailed her nostrils and turned her stomach. Tabitha noticed that the floor and table were blood-splattered, and when she saw the suffering blacks being helped by Mike Long she almost retched. Mike looked up from his work and caught Tabitha's eye, holding it for a significant moment. Tabitha forcibly turned her attention to Nicholas who was now the center of attraction. He stood near the table, a coiled whip in his hand, his bearing as magnificent as a Grecian statue.

"Bring in Tommy," he said to Jed Vale.

A young black man about twenty years old was ushered into the room. Rumors of what was happening in the garden house had reached the slave quarters, and the man was obviously in great fear. Tabitha looked at him with pity.

Jed Vale and two other men started to tie the black man to the puncheon table.

"Let him stand," said Nicholas.

Manley jerked his head toward Nicholas. "What's going on? Tie him down like all the rest."

Nicholas merely smiled. "I do not intend to follow your example by beating my slaves. If they refuse to cooperate, or if they lie to me, I shall take proper measures. But each will have an opportunity to talk freely."

Manley threw up his hands in resignation and disgust at Nicholas's softness. "Well then, make the bastards talk, damn it!" he said angrily.

Nicholas nodded. He had watched the reactions of the planters, and particularly Manley, to the beatings for long tedious hours. They had grown more calloused, more pitiless with each whipping. An unquenchable lust for blood and death had seized them, turning them into ferocious animals delighting in the torture. Too, their patience had grown short. The least admission on the part of a slave that he knew anything whatsoever about the proposed Fourth of July uprising brought an instant condemnation to flagellation or the hanging tree. Nicholas was prepared now to play strongly upon this lust for blood and vengeance. Instead of satisfying the planters' inordinate appetite for revenge, he planned deliberately to deny them the cruelty they craved. Once he had deprived them of the bloodshed they desired, he would build a careful case against Mike Long, deftly turning the planters against him. What his blacks said would incite the vulnerable planters and, in their frenzied hate, they would send Mike Long to the hanging tree without a qualm.

Nicholas's eyes shifted momentarily to Tabitha. Yes, it had been a stroke of genius to let her view the trial. He would show her that he was capable of reducing Mike Long to nothing, by condemning him to death.

When he had delayed questioning Tommy long enough to play on the planters' impatience, Nicholas said in almost a fatherly tone: "Tell us what you know about the rebellion."

The boy's eyes bulged in fright. "Ah don't know nuthin' about no rebellion."

Nicholas smiled indulgently. "I have been told, Tommy, that you and others are going to try to kill me on the Fourth of July. Is that true?"

"No! No, Massa!"

"And you're going to rape my wife, too?"

"Nossuh! Ah swears—"

"And all over the state of Mississippi the blacks will be doing the same thing. Is that the plan?"

"Ah don' know nuthin' about it, Massa!"

"And then after you kill all the planters and rape their wives, then you will attack the towns, right?"

A croaking sound issued from the boy's throat. He could not seem to utter words of denial.

"And Natchez will fall to your black hordes, too, and you will plunder the town. Is that it?"

"Massa, Ah's tellin' you Ah don' know nuthin' about no plan like that. Ah's happy heah, Massa. Ah's real happy. Dancin' happy."

"You never heard that there would be a rebellion? You never heard that the blacks were going to do these things to their masters and mistresses?"

"Nossuh. Ah nevah heard."

"Have you ever talked to other slaves about being free?"

Tommy swallowed with difficulty. His eyes rolled toward the two women, as if imploring them to intercede in his behalf. Tabitha closed her eyes and bit her lip.

"Ah guess Ah has, Massa." The boy's voice was resigned. "Evahbody's talked time or two about bein' free. Ain' nuthin' wrong wid dat, Massa, wantin' to be a free nigger. Evahbody figgers he do a good job for the Massa, maybe some day he be a free man. Ain' a thing wrong wid dat—"

"Has a white man ever talked to you about being free?"

"A white man, Massa?"

"Yes. Tell the truth now!"

"Well, yassuh. One white man did once."

"Who?"

"Doctah Long, suh. We talked once. Wusn't nuthin' wrong about it, Massa. We jest talked about it, how nice it would be."

Nicholas straightened up. He had forced an admission from Tommy that he had intended to get at all costs. He was glad that Tommy had talked without the necessity of a beating. Nicholas's gaze traveled to Mike Long. Tabitha felt her heart pound. She saw

Mike rise slowly to his feet. He had apparently expected something like this, had been waiting for it. He would be called forth now, and Nicholas would accuse him of being a member of the Clan, of inciting the slaves, of preparing the way for revolt. And the blood-drunk fools who sat in judgment would be so overcome with suspicion and the lust for revenge that they would believe the lies flowing from Nicholas Enright's lips.

But Nicholas did not press his advantage yet. He returned to the frightened Tommy, ignoring Mike.

"What did Doctor Long tell you?"

"Ah don' want to git the doctah in trouble—"

"Never mind! What did he tell you?"

"He jest said he thought some day all slaves would be free, thass all."

"Did he say how this would happen?"

"Nossuh. Ah don' think so. He jest said it would happen. That it was inev—inev—"

"Inevitable?"

"Yassuh."

Nicholas nodded to Jed Vale. "Take him away," he said.

Manley reacted as expected. He slammed his fist down on the table with a resounding noise.

"Don't be so damned lenient, Nicholas! We've got to make examples of some of these boys. That slave should at least be whipped!"

Nicholas glared at each planter in turn, his face defiant and his voice challenging when he spoke.

"Does anyone else want this slave whipped?"

They cowered beneath his stare, shrugging or shaking their heads.

"You've been outvoted, Manley," Nicholas said shortly.

Nicholas noticed that Manley's baleful eyes shifted to Mike Long. Several other planters were also gazing in his direction. Nicholas liked what he saw. There was suspicion in their eyes. They were in a mood to condemn any white man who showed any inclination to be a "nigger lover." They could take no chances. Their lives and their way of life was at stake, and they did not intend to relinquish either without a fight.

"I think we'd better talk to your doctor," Manley said malevolently.

Nicholas merely smiled; he was not ready yet to put Mike on the stand.

"Bring Old Matt in," he said to Jed Vale.

The overseer ushered the ancient Negro preacher into the room. There was dignity in this man. Even the planters, with their closed minds, recognized it. He stood erect, an old man with a face scarred by time, his gray hair close-cropped over his rounded head, and he surveyed his inquisitors with just a trace of aversion. Tabitha leaned toward Garland.

"If Nicholas whips this old man," she whispered. "I'll stop him myself!"

But Nicholas had no intention of whipping Old Matt. He looked at the preacher and smiled.

"Matt, you're a man of God, aren't you?"

"Ah tries to walk in His footsteps."

"You are opposed to all sin."

"Ah is."

"Would you say it was a sin for the slaves to rise against their masters and slay them?"

Old Matt scanned his grim audience. Then he

looked directly at Nicholas.

"Ah say that all killin' is sinful in the eyes of the Lawd. Ah say that for the blacks to rise against the plantation owners would be a great sin, almost as great a sin as planters now puhform by whippin' their slaves and mistreatin' them."

A rumble of discontent came from the planters. Manley mumbled something about Old Matt being an impertinent son of a bitch. Nicholas, however, was pleased.

"In your estimation, slavery is wrong?"

"Yassuh. It is wrong. It is morally wrong. No man should own another."

Manley's fist came crashing down on the table again. His face was purple with rage. "I don't tolerate impertinence from slaves!" he roared. "We should string that old bastard up!"

"One moment, Manley," said Nicholas severely. "A man is entitled to his opinion."

"Not a slave, by God! You start letting them have opinions and you've got real trouble on your hands!"

Nicholas ignored him, turning again to Old Matt. It was obvious that Manley was in an agitated state, and this was ideal for Nicholas's purpose. Nicholas intended to prolong the questioning until Manley was in a mood to send *anyone* to the hanging tree, confident that the other planters would go along with him, since Manley was considered a ring leader.

"You have preached the gospel of the Lord to your people?" asked Nicholas.

"Ah have."

"You have preached against slavery?"

"Ah have, suh!" There was a note of prideful defiance in Old Matt's gravelly voice.

"Have you preached rebellion?"

"No Ah have not."

"What's the difference?"

"Oh, for Jesus Christ's sake!" exploded Manley. "Do you intend to stand there, Nicholas, and have a philosophical discussion of the slave culture with this old black fool? We have work to do. Let's get on with it!"

Nicholas rewarded him only with a sidelong glance. He fixed his gaze on the preacher.

"I repeat, what's the difference?"

Old Matt stared at the wall above the heads of the judges. His voice came clear and strong, without a waver.

"Ah preaches that slavery is wrong," he said. "Ah tells my people that some day this will change, that white men will see the light and heed the words of the Lord. Ah tells them to pray for that day. But Ah tells them they must wait for deliverance—in God's own time. Ah do not tells them to rebel."

"He talks like an Abolitionist!" snarled Manley.

"Hardly," drawled Nicholas. "He talks like a preacher."

"Nevertheless, he's agitating among the blacks. By God, I'll bet the old fool is in league with the Clan."

Nicholas smiled. Manley had blood in his eyes. Good.

"Old Matt," Nicholas said, deftly denying Manley his moment, "has been a trusted black of mine for many years. I respect his opinion—in this case, considerably more than I respect yours."

"You speak nonsense, Nicholas! This man is dangerous."

Nicholas ignored him again, looking back at Old Matt. "Have you ever talked to Doctor Mike Long about slavery?"

Old Matt's marble eyes rolled toward the doctor. He seemed to sense that it would not be right to involve the doctor in this. His answer was cautious.

"Ah suppose Ah have. Ah've talked to most evahbody about it. Most evahbody."

"Would you say that Doctor Long is opposed to slavery, Matt?"

"Yassuh, Ah would. But he's a good man."

"Is he an Abolitionist?"

"Ah don' think Ah'd say it that way. He's jest a sincere man an' believes certain things."

"Like the fact that slavery will some day cease to exist?"

"Yassuh."

"Take him away," said Nicholas abruptly to Jed Vale.

Manley was on his feet at the words. His face was livid.

"Take him away? Hang him, I say!"

Nicholas raised his eyebrows. The bloodlust in Manley was so strong it was impinging on his ability to reason. He would be a hard one to deal with now. By the time he finally questioned Mike Long, there would be no containing Manley. His plan was working well. He must tease Manley and his cohorts now by depriving them once more of the brutality for which they hungered. He wanted their lust for revenge to reach a peak from which they could not retreat by the time Mike Long was called.

"I don't intend to punish Old Matt for his

opinions," Nicholas said firmly. "He is a loyal man. Anyone voting to hang him will have to fight me first."

Manley glanced down the table for support. He found none.

"By God, get Mike Long up here now!" he growled.

Nicholas merely smiled. He turned to Jed Vale.

"Bring in Big Sam," he said easily.

5

Jed Vale ushered the giant man into the evil-smelling room. He stood before the court, naked to the waist, his big black chest rising and falling slowly, his arm muscles bulging, the great head erect, his eyes fastened at some spot on the wall directly before him and over the heads of those who would judge him. In his proud bearing there was a slight arrogance, an unmistakable disdain.

Tabitha felt a gnawing sickness inside of her. She saw plainly, now, Nicholas's diabolical plan to incriminate Mike Long. She had listened to his deft questioning of the slaves as he milked from them the subtle information that Mike opposed slavery and had even told the blacks they would some day be free. She realized the condemning nature of all this, and she wondered what fuel to the fire Big Sam would offer.

Against her arm she felt Garland tremble.

"You're shaking," Tabitha whispered.

"Yes."

But Nicholas was talking and they had no opportunity to explore Garland's nervousness.

"You all know Big Sam," said Nicholas, addressing the planters. "He's one of the most loyal and best artisans in the Mississippi Valley. He is not a freeman, although he enjoys some of the benefits of a freeman. I would trust him to carry out any assignment I might give him."

The big chest swelled with pride. But Sam did not turn his massive head. He looked straight ahead, over the heads of the judges.

"Sam, this whip is not for you," Nicholas said, tossing the weapon aside. "I want you to talk freely and tell me again what you told me yesterday."

"Yassuh."

Out of the corner of his eyes Nicholas saw Manley sink back in his chair, obviously disappointed that Nicholas had thrown the whip away.

"You overheard a conversation, I believe," Nicholas prodded.

"Yassuh. Ah did. Down in Natchez-under."

"Tell the court first what you were doing in Natchez-under-the-Hill."

Big Sam licked his thick lips. His eyes remained fixed on the wall.

"It was yesterday mornin'. Ah was down there to meet the *Mississippi Belle*. She was bringin' supplies for our kitchen. Ah went down to the dock to pick 'em up."

"And what happened?"

Sam squared his mammoth shoulders, the muscles rippling under ebony skin.

"Well, suh—Ah was standin' there waitin' while the *Mississippi Belle* tied up. They was a lot of stuff piled up on the wharf that was gonna be shipped, bales an' boxes an' stuff. Ah heerd the voices of a couple men talkin' behind a pile of bales."

"Did you see these men?"

"Not right then, suh."

"Go ahead."

"Well, suh, they was arguin' like. Ah heerd one man say, 'They's killin' niggahs right an' left in Madison County, an' they's killin' white men too.' "

"Is that all you heard, Sam?"

"Nossuh. Ah heerd the other man say, 'Who'd they kill?' An' then the fust man he said a lot of names—seems like Cotton an' Sanders an' Ah don' remember whut others."

Nicholas interrupted the testimony to address the planters. His voice was low, subdued.

"As you will observe, this conversation has reference to the action of the Committee of Safety in Livingston in Madison County," he said. "I think you are all familiar with the action taken by this Committee by now. . . . Go on, Sam. What then?"

"Well, suh, Ah don' rightly know. They got talkin' in lower voices then, an' Ah couldn't hear. But finally Ah heerd one of the men say, 'Ah don' care what they're doin' in Livingston, the Fourth of July rebellion must take place!' An' the other said, "Ah'm in hidin' an' if they catch me in Natchez-under they'll hang me sure. Ah don' intend to take any action in the revolt—not now.' So the fust man said that he was agoin' to take action *ir*regardless of anything."

"That was the end of the conversation?"

"Yassuh. Thass all Ah heerd."

"Tell the court what happened then."

"Well," said Sam, still staring straight ahead, "the *Mississippi Belle*, she was in by this time an' Ah started over to where they'd be unloadin' her an' these two men that'd been talkin' they walked out from behind the bales."

"And you recognized them?"

"Jest one of 'em, suh."

"And who was that?"

"He was—" an uneasy hesitation "—Doctah Long, suh."

Tabitha felt her throat constrict and her head pound as blood rushed to her tortured brain. A thick silence spread across the room. Only small sounds were heard—the heavy breathing of Big Sam, the slight movement of Mike Long as he rose to his feet, the shuffling of shoes on the bare wooden floor. Nicholas Enright looked at Mike with a trace of satisfaction on his face. Mike was staring at the huge Negro in disbelief.

"That," he said, "is a damned lie. I was not in Natchez-under-the-Hill yesterday morning!"

Nicholas smiled indulgently. "You shall have your chance to speak," he said softly. Then, turning again to Big Sam he asked: "The other man that Doctor Long was with—you did not know him?"

"Nossuh. Ah nevah seed him befo'. But I heard Doctah Long call him Blake."

"Blake!" The word shot from Faunce Manley's mouth like an explosive bullet. "Ruel Blake, by God!"

Nicholas nodded. "Exactly, Faunce. You'll recall that the renegade planter, Ruel Blake, escaped from the Livingston Committee. Their posses have been looking for him—in fact, I heard just this morning that they found him in a bawdy house in Natchez-under. Ruel Blake is a recognized leader of the Clan—and he and Mike were talking about the plot on the dock yesterday morning!"

Tabitha sat in helpless silence, listening to the careful case being built against Mike. This was exactly what she had feared, that Nicholas would succeed in compromising Mike. She had an impulse to rush into the blood-soaked arena to tell the planters that Big Sam was lying, but she caught Mike's eye and something in his expression stopped her. He was saying, as clearly as if he were speaking to her, that she must stay out of this, that she must not show her concern for him by rushing to his aid.

Her glance shifted to Nicholas and she shuddered. In his triumph his dark eyes were ablaze with a fanatic light. He was glaring across the room at Mike Long, who stood stiffly still, towering over the abused bodies of the blacks on the floor at his feet, staring back. Faunce Manley slapped the top of his table with his hand for attention.

"I'd like to hear Doctor Long's side of the story," he said.

"You shall!" Nicholas said, not able to conceal the note of triumph in his voice. "Step forward, Doctor Long—and if you are a man, tell us about your well-contrived conspiracy."

Mike Long moved slowly to the center of the room. Big Sam stepped to one side, still staring at the wall ahead, not looking at the man he had accused.

Mike's eyes were leveled on Nicholas. "Do you wish to strap me over the table so you can make me talk with the whip?" he asked sarcastically.

Nicholas smiled smugly. "I doubt that such action will be necessary." He paused for a moment, milking as much drama out of the situation as possible, permitting the eyes of the suspicious planters to play over the rugged backwoodsman who stood before them. "Now then," he said at last, "you have heard the testimony of Big Sam?"

"I have."

"What have you to say to the charges leveled against you?"

"I say they are all lies. Complete falsehoods. I was not on the Natchez-under docks yesterday morning, never had such a conversation with any man, and never in my life until this moment ever heard of Ruel Blake."

"Where were you yesterday morning?"

"I was attending the slaves."

"And I presume," Nicholas rolled the words in his mouth, "a slave or two would vouch for the fact that you were with them?"

"I believe so."

"And do you really believe that this court, in its present temper, would attach much weight to the testimony of such a slave?"

Mike Long looked directly at the bench. "Judging from the makeup of this court, I'd say they would not."

Nicholas brushed aside the gentle rebuke. He pointed with the whip to Big Sam.

"This man said he saw and heard you talking with Ruel Blake in Natchez-under."

"I've already said he's lying."

"Why should he lie?"

"I don't know."

"What would he gain by lying?"

"I don't know."

Nicholas's eyebrows raised to indicate his doubts

about Mike's logic.

"Permit me to digress, Doctor," he said finally. "Do you think that this simple man—" he motioned to Big Sam with the whip again "—is capable of *creating* such a story as he just told us? Do you think he has the imagination necessary to create such an elaborate story?"

"No, I don't."

"Well, then—if he does not have the capability of creating this unusual story, then he must be telling the truth. Isn't that so?"

"No, it is not so."

Nicholas turned to his cohorts, an amused smile on his fine lips which said eloquently but without words that, after all, the man's testimony made little sense.

"Will you explain, Doctor Long, how this man can be lying when he lacks the ability to think up the lie?"

"Very easily," said Mike. "Someone else thought up the lie for him!"

Nicholas's face slid into a frown. By God's own doublet, there had been a loophole in his logic! The best weapon left to cover up this faulty reasoning was ridicule.

"Come, now, Doctor. You are accusing a third party. Surely you must have the identity of this third party in mind. Would you name him?"

Mike Long's eyes flickered briefly toward Tabitha, and Tabitha was sure he was again warning her to silence. The question was one that Mike had feared. He was convinced that Nicholas Enright had planted the story in Big Sam's mind, had perhaps bribed the big Negro with a promise to free him if he would so testify. But if he named Nicholas, the next questions would be damning. If not Nicholas himself, then Faunce Manley would ask him why Nicholas would want to falsify charges against him. And Mike could not say, "Because I love his wife and he wishes to rid himself of me." In Tabitha's interest, he could not embroil her in this thing, could not label her an adulteress—all of which would come out under relentless questioning. Yet, by withholding Nicholas's name, he realized he was performing a disservice to himself, perhaps jeopardizing his very life. Nicholas, in asking him to name a third party, had apparently figured all of this out in advance and had decided that Mike would refrain from answering him.

"I won't name him," said Mike softly.

Nicholas shrugged. "In other words, Doctor, you do not *know* who could have planted in this Negro's mind the fantastic story he told."

"That's right. I do not know."

"Therefore, if nobody planted the story—and if he was incapable of creating it—then Sam must have told the truth?"

"I would not say that necessarily follows."

Nicholas's eyes flared. He faced the tribunal at the table.

"The doctor talks nonsense. He can talk nothing else, because he is trapped. . . . Big Sam, do you swear by the good Lord that you heard this man and Ruel Blake speak as you testified?"

"Yassuh."

"Naturally, the good doctor would deny it," said Nicholas pointedly, with a truculent gesture toward Mike. Mike glared at him. Between the two men was complete understanding. Mike knew that

563

Nicholas was responsible for the fabrication about his meeting with Ruel Blake, and Nicholas knew that Mike could not accuse him without tarnishing Tabitha's name. Tabitha, her heart fluttering in her chest, sensed too what was happening. She caught again the warning look from Mike, but with sudden rashness she decided to throw caution to the winds—anything to rescue Mike Long from this devilish plot against him. As she moved forward in her chair, it was Garland who held her back.

"Don't do it, Tabitha."

"I must!" Her voice was a hoarse whisper. "They're accusing him falsely!"

Garland looked at her with pity. Then, impulsively, she said to Tabitha, "Just stay where you are. I think I can settle this little matter."

"You?"

"Yes."

Suddenly Garland McRae was standing, moving lithely into the center of the room. All eyes turned toward her. The pale yellow illumination from the whale oil lamps flickered over her, casting a patchwork of light and shadow across her. A muttering went up from the planters, for such beauty as Garland's seemed strangely out of place in this room of blood and torture. McRae, his rheumy eyes wide in astonishment, leaped to his feet.

"Garland! What is the meaning of this?"

"I have testimony to give," said Garland simply.

"What about?"

"About the dispute between these two men," she said, indicating Mike Long and Big Sam. "I might be able to clear up the matter, if you will allow me."

Tabitha stared at Garland in amazement. Had the girl lost her mind? What possible information could she have to clarify the dispute between Mike and Big Sam? It was old John McRae who found his voice in the hushed silence of the room.

"Garland!" he roared, shaking with anger. "I forbid you to appear here! Now get out or I'll—"

"Wait a minute!" Manley was on his feet. "If the lady has any pertinent information relative to these two men, I for one want to hear it."

Nicholas was staring at Garland in fascinated awe, his eyes puzzled, even frightened. He had not figured on this interruption, and he was not sure what Garland's testimony might do to his case.

"I hardly think this is the proper place for a lady—" he began.

"Damn it, Nicholas! Let's hear what she has to say!" growled Manley.

The other planters nodded in agreement. Nicholas quieted and McRae sat down slowly, his anger subsiding by degrees, the blood going out of his face. But he was looking at Garland intensely.

"Speak up, Garland," said Manley bluntly.

Garland smiled. It was a radiant smile, and in this room of grim madness it was like a ray of light.

"I will speak freely," she said, turning to Nicholas, "and you won't need to use the whip."

Nicholas felt his face go hot under this second taunt about the whip. But he said nothing, glowering at Garland as if she were some monstrous apparition intruding where she did not belong.

"Will you please say what you have to say," said Manley with weariness.

"What I have to say is very simple." Garland let her dark eyes fasten upon the huge ebony form of Big Sam. "This man is lying."

Nicholas leaped upon the statement. "Oh, come now, Garland," he said suavely. "Doctor Long has already said that but has been unable to prove it. If you have nothing further to offer—"

"I have something to offer," Garland cut in. "Proof that he's lying."

John McRae's mouth dropped open in surprise. Manley's eyes thinned. Nicholas shifted the coiled whip from one hand to the other nervously. What possible proof could Garland have in this dispute between a backwoods doctor and a Negro artisan? He had not planned on this intervention and he was worried about what Garland might say. McRae was coming to his feet again and Nicholas heard Manley's booming voice. "Sit down, John! Let your wife have her say. . . . Cite your proof, Garland!"

Garland's face was pale in the yellow glow of the lamps. Her nostrils flared slightly at the offensive odors of the room.

"I happen to know that Big Sam was not in Natchez-under-the-Hill at the time he says he overheard Mike Long and Ruel Blake," she said firmly.

"And where was he?" Manley asked sharply.

Nicholas looked at Faunce Manley. He had a feeling that Manley was taking the interrogation away from him. He glanced briefly at Tabitha, who was looking fearful, then returned to Garland. Garland fortified herself with a deep breath.

"He was with me," she said softly.

Her words brought John McRae to his feet again.

Now his face was ashen. Of all those in the room, he alone sensed the true meaning of Garland's words. As he saw Manley about to speak, he cut in, his voice edgy.

"Permit me to question my own wife, Faunce," he snapped. "I think I understand this better than you."

Garland's eyes shifted to the old man. Tense lines pulled at her face, giving her features a hardness that was unnatural to her, that marred the beauty she possessed.

"What do you mean, Garland, when you say that Big Sam was with you?" McRae said ominously.

Nicholas shifted the whip again, uncertain, fearful. Mike Long's face was one of open wonder. Tabitha was holding her breath, not wanting even to disturb the silence of the room by her breathing.

"I mean exactly what I say, John," Garland answered her husband. "It's nothing unusual, you know. You have often borrowed Big Sam from Nicholas to do handiwork around the plantation. He's quite talented."

"I did *not* borrow him yesterday," said McRae grimly. "I was in Louisiana yesterday, tending my land there." His voice took on a note of weariness, as though this matter was something he had been concerned about for some time. "I do not intend to permit you to explain this to me privately, Garland, because it affects, I think, the future of this doctor. Therefore, I ask you to explain how Big Sam came to be in your company yesterday."

"I had need of his services."

"What services?"

Garland drew herself up, the tall beauty of her

dominating the unhealthy atmosphere of the room.

"You remember the escritoire with the broken leg that we've been intending to fix? I had him work on it."

McRae's eyes clouded. He stroked his tapered chin. "He was there all morning?"

"Yes."

"So that he could not have overheard Ruel Blake and Doctor Long on the docks of Natchez-under—is that your contention?"

"Yes."

McRae turned to the big Negro. His eyes were pale and frosty.

"Is this true?"

Big Sam's mouth had fallen open in astonishment at Garland's revelation. He cast an almost pleading glance at her. Then he straightened, drawing up his huge shoulders, his head still turned toward the wall behind the row of planters.

"Nossuh. It ain' true. I weren't at Miss Garland's place. I was in Natchez-under."

"He *was* at my place!" Garland cried.

Nicholas's eyes shifted from Garland to Big Sam to John McRae. God's doublet, but he had been stupid to permit Tabitha and Garland to witness this trial! If Garland had not interfered, he might by now have Mike Long swinging from the hanging tree! While these conjectures raced through his mind, Faunce Manley took the inquisition away from him again.

"There seems to be an important difference of opinion between Mrs. McRae and Big Sam," he said heavily. "On this difference of opinion rests the whole story of Doctor Long's supposed conversation with

Ruel Blake. Garland, did anyone else on your plantation see Big Sam yesterday morning—anyone who will support your testimony?"

She shook her head. "No."

"Not *anyone?*"

"No,"

Manley's eyes were suspicious. He turned to Big Sam.

"And did anyone in Natchez-under who knows you see you at the time you claim to be there?" he asked the slave.

"Uh—nossuh."

"You must be an invisible phantom, for Chrissakes!" Manley exploded; then, calming, he said, "So our problem is to find out which one of you two is lying?"

John McRae was leaning across the table intently, his old body shaking with emotion, his eyes glowing with a terrible hatred.

"*I* know who is lying!" he half screamed. "It's my wife who tells the truth, I swear it! *He was with her!*"

"How do you know this?" Manley asked.

"Because I know *her!*"

Without warning he was on his feet, striding toward the center of the room. In his hand was a whip which he sent hissing in the direction of Big Sam. The big Negro retreated hastily as it wrapped itself like a vengeful snake around his shoulders, biting into his glossy skin. Sam fell to the floor and McRae loomed over him.

"You black son of a bitch!" he roared, shaking violently. "You were with my wife, weren't you?"

"Boss, please!"

The whip sang again. It whined and cut, opening a

wound on the slave's cheek that bled freely. Nicholas, suddenly recovering from his surprise at McRae's violent action, leaped toward the old man.

"You can't whip that boy of mine!"

McRae turned savagely on Nicholas. "Stand back, or I'll have your hide too! This black bastard of yours has it coming. *He's been lying with my wife!*"

A shocked silence gripped the room. The small noises, the inconsequential noises, sounded louder now—Sam's pathetic moaning, a soft sob from Garland, groans from the wounded blacks, the uneasy scraping of a shoe.

"That's a hell of a thing to say, McRae," said Manley tightly. "You'd better be sure."

"I'm sure." McRae's voice was high-pitched with anger. With a quick movement he laced the big Negro artisan with the whip again, and Big Sam rolled along the floor, trying to escape. Garland covered her face with her hands and stood in the center of the room sobbing. "Confess, you black bastard!" McRae was shouting. "You've been to bed with my wife, haven't you? And more than once too! You think I haven't suspected it?"

Tabitha stared at the scene in stunned astonishment. She saw that Nicholas looked confused and puzzled and unsure of himself. Impulsively she leaped to her feet and ran to Garland's side.

"She must be lying!" Tabitha cried. "This can't be true!" And even as she said it she knew she was undermining the only defense Mike Long had, the defense Garland had voluntarily built for him with her dangerous confession.

"She's not lying," said McRae, trying to harness his

rage, keeping his voice under strained control. "I've known about her infidelity for some time. She's a common whore. She's tried to get into bed with every young man that's come along. She's not satisfied with an old codger like me. Every time I go to New Orleans or Louisiana she finds herself a lover. I've known it and I've put up with it, because I wanted to keep her. But now—now—" his voice shook with the bitterness inside of him "—now she's consorting with a goddamn black slave and I won't stand for it!"

His own accusing words angered him all over again and he lashed out with the whip once more, bringing it down on the cowering figure of Sam, sitting on the floor now, trying to ward off the savage blows with his hands and arms.

"It's true, isn't it, nigger? You were in bed with my wife yesterday morning!"

"Boss, please. Ah don' know how to answer!"

"I'll coach you," said McRae maliciously. "What do you remember about yesterday morning? The conversation between Mike Long and Ruel Blake—or the delights of Garland's body?"

"Massa—"

"It was pretty good, wasn't it?"

"Chris' Awmighty!" moaned the black.

Once more the whip tore at his hide and Big Sam gritted his fine teeth as the agony surged through him.

"Must be quite a thing for a big black nigger slave to have the soft curves of a white woman," McRae went on maliciously. "I bet it makes you feel mighty proud. Isn't that right?"

Big Sam started blubbering unintelligibly, but a few words seeped through. "So help me God . . . didn' rape your wife . . . she was willin' . . . willin'."

McRae's eyes shifted to his wife, and Garland wilted under his implacable stare.

"You whore!" McRae said coldly. "In front of everyone I call you what you are—a low whore, worse than the harlots of Natchez-under! I shall settle with you at home."

He turned away, his lean shoulders drooping as the anger abruptly left him, leaving him a beaten and mortified man. With a stifled sob Garland broke for the door, and before anyone could summon the presence of mind to stop her she had raced toward the manor and reached the haven of her carriage. McRae walked slowly to the door and watched the carriage disappear into the black of the night. Then he turned, just as slowly, and his hand held a gleaming pistol.

The shot was like a dynamite blast in the tiny close-packed room. Sam emitted one sharp scream and threw his hands up protectively, but not in time to hide the blood that splashed from a hole in his forehead and dripped down over his twisted face. He died without another sound.

The suddenness of McRae's action stunned the men in the room. Nicholas was the first to react. He spun on McRae, his face a mask of fury.

"You've killed my nigger!"

"He deserved killing."

"He's my property. By God, you'll pay for this, McRae!"

"Name your price," said McRae resignedly. "It was a pleasure to kill the bastard."

"I'll have you arrested!" snarled Nicholas, not at all mollified by McRae's offer of financial restitution. He was so beside himself with rage that he did not hear Manley pounding with his heavy fists on the table to bring order between the two antagonists. But at last Manley made himself heard by shouting for silence.

"For God's sake, Nicholas," Manley roared, "no court would convict a man for shooting a nigger who had raped his wife!"

"From what I understand," retorted Nicholas, "it wasn't rape."

"Impossible to prove," said Manley, "especially in a white court. With the temper of the times, no court would condemn McRae for his action. I suggest you bring no charges, Nicholas. The important thing for us to decide is the validity of Big Sam's testimony against Long. There seems no doubt now that his story of Long's meeting with Ruel Blake is pure fiction—therefore I would say there is no reason to detain the doctor longer."

"You're wrong!" Nicholas was like a madman now. His eyes were haunted, his face contorted and flushed. "You must hold him! His innocence hasn't been proved. I vote that he be held for further questioning."

Tabitha looked at him in horror. He was glowering at the planters like a wild animal at bay, a beast trapped. And as he stood there, hair disheveled, the familiar wild look in his eyes, Mike Long's voice came softly.

"Gentlemen, I ask you to look at Nicholas Enright. He is an animal stricken with fear. He is a man who has taken leave of his senses."

They looked, fascinated, unable to tear their eyes away. They saw him, as voracious as a wolf, a strange madness in his agonized eyes.

"Big Sam was doing this man's bidding when he told the story of my meeting with Ruel Blake," Mike went on. "There was no such meeting; it was a complete lie. I don't doubt for a moment that Enright promised him his freedom if he would so testify."

"Lies! Lies! Lies!" Nicholas screamed the words, his voice harsh and out of control. "Are you going to believe this nigger lover? Are you going to believe this man who plots to kill us all? This man is a member of the Clan."

"There is no proof, Nicholas," Manley said calmly.

"He has talked freedom to the blacks. He has talked with Ruel Blake. What other proof do you need?"

"Nothing has been proved, Nicholas," Manley said levelly. "I will be frank with you. I believe that you attempted to build a case against Doctor Long by bribing Big Sam to testify against him. I would like to know why."

Nicholas's feverish eyes swept the room, in the way that an animal's eyes seek a way of escape from entrapment. He retreated under the steadfast gaze of the other planters, shaking his head from side to side, and his voice was hoarse when he spoke.

"You don't understand! Nobody understands!" He reached the door, staggering drunkenly against the jamb. "He's a Clansman. He's plotting against all of us—especially against me. He plans to destroy me. Everybody plans to destroy me!" His voice teetered on the edge of hysteria. "Everybody! Everybody! You hear me!"

"There is no plot to destroy you," said Mike Long easily.

"Yes! Yes! There is! All my life there have been plots!" His face was contorted, purplish; his terror-stricken eyes shifted from side to side, sweeping the room suspiciously.

The planters stared in awe at this man who had suddenly gone berserk before their eyes, had lost reason and sense and become a raving lunatic. He stood there, his entire body trembling with anger and fear, clutching now at the doorjamb for support, his fingers clawing.

"Nicholas, listen to us a moment—" Manley began.

"No!" He shook his head, screaming out the word, his strained voice reaching a falsetto pitch, a demented expression on his face. "Everyone wants me dead. You too, Manley—all of you. Long, my wife, everyone! Goddamn your souls to hell, I want no more of you!"

He spun around and fled from the room, disappearing into the gathering blackness toward the manor. The men in the room sat in horrified silence. At last, in a hushed voice, Manley said: "You are right, Doctor. He has gone completely mad."

"Perhaps," said Mike, "he has always been mad."

6

The Fourth of July came bright and hot to Mississippi, and the much-feared revolt of the blacks did not occur. The back of the smoldering rebellion had been broken at Livingston in Madison County by the ruthless whipping and killing of its leaders, and by the cleansing brutality of planters up and down the Father of Waters. Without leadership, the blacks were helpless to act, and those who had looked forward to widespread insurrection sulked in their whitewashed shacks and forgot there was ever any hope of freedom.

The day passed slowly for most planters, many of whom stood at strategic posts in their homes, gun in hand, tense and ready to fire upon any black approaching the premises. Women, knowing the horrible fate in store for them, trembled in their rooms, keeping out of sight so that no black approaching the house would gaze upon their charms and become aroused.

Tabitha, however, was not one of those who kept to her room. Her mind was in turmoil and she paced the floor of the huge salon most of the day. On one hand, she felt she should rush to Garland's side and thank her for the terrible sacrifice she had made to extricate Mike Long from the trap set by Nicholas. But

Nicholas's actions made it impossible for her to leave. After bolting the trial, he had fled to his room and had not reappeared all night. It was now two o'clock in the afternoon of the Fourth of July and he was still locked in his room. All day there had been muffled sounds, uncertain footsteps, that suggested to Tabitha that Nicholas was drinking heavily. Tabitha recalled now what Mike Long had told her when Nicholas closeted himself.

"I am afraid for your safety," he said. "Nicholas is definitely unbalanced. He is retreating now, as I mentioned he might do, trying to escape his imagined persecutors. His next move might be to run away completely, or he might turn on those he feels are persecuting him. There is no assurance, Tabitha, that he won't become violent."

"What should I do, Mike?"

"Nicholas should be placed in an asylum. You will have to face up to that."

She shook her head stubbornly. She could not accept that. What would she do if she did not have Nicholas Enright? Everything she had gained by marrying him would be destroyed if he were institutionalized. She could not tolerate the thought of such a thing happening just because Nicholas might be temporarily insane. That was it—temporarily! She clung desperately to the idea.

"He might get better," she said hopefully. "I can't remove him from Magnolia Manor. Not yet."

"You're rationalizing, Tabitha," said Mike. "I'm sure it will come to that, if he doesn't run away himself and never return. In any case, I will sleep tonight on a cot downstairs. I am a light sleeper and will hear you if you call. At any sign that he is coming out of his room, call for me at once."

Tabitha nodded. But there had been no need to call Mike. Tabitha had taken the precaution of bolting her bedroom door, but she slept little that night. When she finally arose she asked Sophie if Nicholas had been up at all during the night.

"Never seed nor heerd him," she said.

About mid-morning she had gone to Nicholas's door and asked if he wanted breakfast. She had been answered by a surly growl like that of a snarling beast. When she had tried to persuade him, he had shouted in anger. "For Christ's sake, Tabitha, let me be! How do I know you won't poison my food?"

The words stunned Tabitha. Poison his food? My God, did he really believe she would do that?

She sat now, in the salon, caressing the brocaded gold covering on the arm of the rosewood chair with the palm of her hand as her mind spun with numbing thoughts. The more she considered the difficult problem facing her, the more she realized that her concerns were selfish ones. Although Nicholas's distressing condition disheartened her because it portended an end to her ambitions, she found that it caused her no personal bereavement. She had absolutely no sympathetic feeling for Nicholas in his plight, which convinced her all the more—if, indeed, she needed such conviction—that she bore no real love for him. What he had become only annoyed her. She saw in his debilitation a great obstacle in her path, and that was what irritated her the most. If Nicholas, with the help of medication or by some God-given miracle, could be returned to normality she could hold her coveted position and make her life secure. But there would be no place for her, no homage paid her, if Nicholas was foolish enough to become insane. Her mind was suddenly flooded with a deep-seated resentment at the fate that was making her life a shambles. Why, she thought, does Nicholas have to lose his mind now, if that is what he's done? It was frightfully inconsiderate of him, and untimely as well. A man who couldn't control his emotions was a millstone around a woman's neck. It was necessary, Tabitha decided, to consider ways to escape such an unwanted fate.

Faced with an insoluble riddle, Tabitha permitted her mind to wander to other situations she could more easily control. Perhaps she *should* visit Garland. She would let Nicholas rot in his room for all she cared! Sympathy for Garland welled up in her. What she must be going through now! She had been wonderful, unselfishly risking her own reputation to right a wrong Nicholas was committing. What other woman in all the Natchez country would have done so much? Garland had had no reason for revealing Big Sam as a liar, except that she knew Tabitha loved Mike Long and did not want to see him hanged when he was innocent. It was typical of Garland to act so magnanimously. She was the most considerate person Tabitha had ever known.

But copulation with a Negro slave? Tabitha shuddered. Garland in bed with Big Sam seemed incredible; yet Big Sam had finally admitted it, and Garland had not denied it. It was not that Tabitha was surprised at Garland's baser instincts. Garland, she had thought from some of the young woman's remarks, was perfectly capable of adultery—especially since her

579

aged husband had long passed his period of usefulness. But with a slave? Tabitha shivered again at the thought. It was thoroughly disgusting. God only knew what perverse craving had prompted Garland to accept Big Sam.

Perhaps Garland needed to talk to an understanding person, Tabitha thought. Maybe her presence might help to salve the wrath of old John McRae, might even bring about a reconciliation. Anyway, she was sure Garland desperately needed someone now, and because she was tired of sitting alone and waiting for the emergence of her husband from his locked room, she decided at once to go to her.

Quickly she got up and crossed the flagstone patio to the kitchen. Mike Long was there, sitting at a table sipping a cold lemonade.

"Mike, will you keep an eye on Nicholas? I'm going to see Garland."

Mike nodded. "It was a tremendous thing Garland did for me—for us. I will be thanking her in due time, but I don't think this is the proper moment. It's good that you go, though—and please thank her for me."

"I will."

Tabitha went to the stable and had Lady Belle saddled. It was a half-hour ride to Bellaire at a brisk trot. She would take it slowly, though, for riding at a slower pace would give her time to think—and God knows she had plenty to think about now. She dreaded to think of the scene that must have occurred when old John McRae returned last night to Bellaire. He had been furious, and for the first time it occurred to Tabitha that Garland might even be in physical danger. She had been too engrossed in her own troubles to think of it before, and the thought of it now spurred Tabitha to heel Lady Belle until the mare broke into a trot.

She was halfway to the plantation when Tabitha saw another horseman approaching from the opposite direction. The horseman was riding at a fast gallop, and drew up quickly as he approached Tabitha. She recognized the rider as Jethro, an old Negro handyman from the McRae plantation. His eyes were wide with excitement.

"Miss Tabitha! Ah come to git Massa Enright!"

"Mister Enright is indisposed, Jethro. What has happened?"

The old Negro gasped for breath, his eyes bulging. "Ah don' really know, Miss Tabitha. Ah found them jest fifteen minutes ago—both of 'em."

"For heaven's sake, Jethro! What happened?"

"Massa McRae an' Miss Garland, both of 'em, in the garden house," the old Negro chattered on. "Ah don' know how to explain. You come with me, Miss Tabitha!"

He wheeled his horse about and headed back to Bellaire. Tabitha, uncertain about what Jethro had found, heeled Lady Belle and started off at a gallop. A few minutes later both horses thundered up the long bridlepath leading from the Bellaire mansion to the garden house.

Tabitha slipped from Lady Belle and Jethro swung down from his stallion. Tabitha made directly for the door leading into the long rectangular building and pushed it in. She stopped in frozen horror at the sight before her, throwing her hand to her mouth to stifle a scream.

Old John McRae was closest to the door. He lay in a crumpled ragdoll heap on the floor, his legs drawn up underneath him. In his right hand he held the same pistol with which he had killed Big Sam. He had obviously taken his own life, for the right side of his head above the ear was blown away, revealing an ugly red cavern and a sickening trail of brains on the floor. A large pool of blood had formed—and dried to a brownish crust—next to his head.

And then there was Garland—and this was so terrible that Tabitha could not believe it. Garland lay on her back. She wore only the lower portion of her dress, the upper part having been savagely ripped to her waist. Great ugly red cuts striped her body where the whip had fallen, slicing the soft skin of her belly and almost amputating the smooth roundness of her breasts. Even her face had not been spared. She had obviously been beaten with fists, for her nose was crooked and broken, her lips bulging and thick, both cheeks discolored and swollen. Her beauty—the great beauty that had attracted so many admirers—had been completely destroyed, and her face was now that of an ugly gargoyle that sickened Tabitha and made her turn away.

For several agonizing minutes Tabitha thought she would faint, but she steeled herself and walked to Garland's side. She felt for a pulse and heartbeat, but there was none. The body was already cold, indicating that she had been dead for some time. She stood helplessly for a moment, looking about her, horror seizing and twisting her until she almost screamed.

Then she noticed a note on a nearby table. It was written in John McRae's pinched hand:

I have killed her, and now I will take my own life. Her great beauty was a terrible curse, for it led all men to desire her. She was never true to me, and for bringing shame and disgrace to my name and my house, I have destroyed that beauty even as I have destroyed her. I beat her to death with whips and my fists, for I do not want her to look desirable to anyone, not even in death. God forgive me, but the shame was too much to bear.
                                                    John McRae

Jethro stood in the doorway, his lean frame shaking, afraid to come into the gruesome room of death. Tabitha, feeling a sudden nausea rising, walked unsteadily toward the door. Outside she gulped at the fresh air and the sickness slowly dissipated.

Her mind, saturated with an indescribable horror, refused to work for several moments. Then a terrible thought came to her: *Nicholas had really killed these people! Nicholas and his fantastic attempt to hang Mike Long had precipitated this carnage. It was really Nicholas who had killed Big Sam and John McRae and Garland—yes, and he had even killed his own mother.* She saw him quite suddenly as an inhuman monster, a beast incapable of any sympathetic feelings, any softness. His actions had destroyed four people, and he had intended to destroy Mike Long. And her sudden perception of Nicholas's murderous capabilities was followed in natural order by another: *If Nicholas was capable of murder, then she was no safer than anyone else in his merciless hands!*

Such a horrendous thought was not one that Tabitha could endure for long. She tried to shove the terrifying thought of her own demise back into the far recesses of her mind, thinking that, after all, Nicholas *did* need her. And when he recovered from his present mood, which she convinced herself was only temporary, he would be shrewd enough to realize her importance. Without her he was only a shell of a man, a fumbling bachelor with no hold on the society he wanted so fiercely to dominate. He needed her as a foil to the vicious infighting of snobbish Natchez. Without her he would be nothing. It was a comforting thought, and Tabitha grasped at it with desperation.

She turned to Jethro. "You'll have to ride to Natchez and notify the authorities there," she told him. "I'll go back and tell Mr. Enright."

She mounted Lady Belle and dug her heel viciously into the startled mare's flank. A cloud of dust trailed her as she headed for Magnolia Manor.

7

"Nicholas! Come out!"

She stood at his bedroom door, beating with her fists upon the hardwood paneling. She could hear him inside, moving about, but he would not answer.

"Nicholas!" she raged. "John McRae and Garland are dead! Do you hear me—*dead!*"

The movement inside the room stopped. A moment's wait, then the big door swung open. Tabitha was shocked at the sight of Nicholas. He stood swaying uncertainly in the doorway, his eyes bleary and laced with pink threadlike lines, his mouth drooping at the corners, his fine black hair, normally so well-groomed, disheveled and hanging down over his forehead. The odor of whiskey almost sickened her as the door opened. He held a glass in his trembling hand, and when he spoke his voice was hoarse with drink.

"What did you say?"

"John McRae and Garland are dead!" repeated Tabitha irritably, trying with those six blunt words to shock him out of his stupor.

No expression crossed Nicholas's face. He looked at her uncomprehendingly, then pushed her rudely aside, moving in a weaving line into the hallway. Looking at him, she was glad for the protection that the presence of Mike Long nearby afforded. She had told Mike about the McRaes, and had insisted on rousing Nicholas with the news.

"It might bring him back to sanity," she had said.

"Or push him over the edge," Mike had replied dubiously. "I'll be nearby if you need help."

How Nicholas managed to negotiate the spiral staircase Tabitha could not understand, but he did. She followed him down the stairs and into the music room. He walked directly to the piano and sat down before the instrument. His fingers traveled expertly over the keys, despite his drunkenness, and he played beautifully. It seemed that creating music beneath his fingertips was a soothing balm to Nicholas, and he was using it now to reduce the shock of Tabitha's news. He played a selection Tabitha had not before heard, a sweet, beguiling melody which he produced with a purring softness. As the last notes fled from his fingertips, he stood up abruptly.

"So John McRae is dead," he said heavily. "Old son of a bitch was living beyond his time anyway."

"Garland is dead too!" Tabitha almost shouted, trying again to impress him with the tragedy of what she was telling him.

He looked at her uncertainly, vague suspicion in his eyes, then waved her to a chair.

"You are not lying to me? This is not some kind of trick?"

"I tell you they're dead!" said Tabitha sharply. "I saw them!"

He sat down slowly, feeling for the chair behind him. He groaned with the effort.

"How did Garland die?" he asked.

"John beat her to death. . . . Oh, Nicholas, it was horrible! I rode out there and found them both in the garden house. Garland had been whipped and pummeled. John had ended his own life with a pistol. He left a note saying she had disgraced his name and his house."

Nicholas stood up again, walked to a small table and selected a brandy decanter. He poured himself a generous portion.

"Have some?"

"No."

"It would do you good to get drunk once in a while," he said. "Fine feeling. Like looking at your troubles through the wrong end of a spyglass—they become smaller. Strange, but I can't bring myself to the point of grief over the deaths of old John and Garland. Maybe they both deserved it."

"You're a beast!" said Tabitha with loathing.

"All men are beasts. Didn't I prove that to you in our bedroom?" He chuckled at his own mirth. "Down in Natchez-under, you know, the beast in man is close to the surface. He fights and he brawls and he kills, like the savage he is—and like the savage he is, he has no compunction afterward. Up here on the Hill, we try to hide our bestial qualities, but we're animals nonetheless. We've just added a little polish to cover it up, so it isn't as readily apparent."

Tabitha was surprised that his speech was so articulate and his reasoning unflawed, for he looked as if he had been drunk for weeks. She watched him as he drained the brandy glass, shuddered a little, and then set the glass down on a table unsteadily. She did not like the way he looked; he was still wild-eyed, half-crazed. She was, in fact, afraid of him. She knew from her bedroom experience that Nicholas was capable of violence, and liquor seemed to spark his ferocity. Yet, when he began talking again, his voice was temperate and what he said made surprising sense.

"So old John McRae got up on his hind legs and whipped his lovely wife to death because she had disgraced his good name, eh?" Nicholas seemed to derive a perverse amusement from the situation. "Very interesting, considering that old John himself was never any paragon of virtue. I've heard him tell stories of his younger days that would make a keelboatman blush. And I'd like to have an acre of cotton for every time he tumbled some wench in the hay!"

Tabitha did not answer, but her expression indicated her disgust with Nicholas's comment.

"It's true," Nicholas insisted. "He was a lecher. Like most of us, I guess."

"Well, that's beside the point now," said Tabitha stiffly. "What's important is what to do about John and Garland."

"Do?" He poured more brandy, spilling some of it on the table. "We're not going to do a damned thing. They're dead. Gone. So we toss them aside. They are of no further use to us, so we go on."

Revulsion seized Tabitha and anger rose sharply. She could not temper the agitation in her reply, and her words got away from her.

"Don't you have a conscience? Don't you realize that you were responsible for—" She stopped short, unable to finish.

Nicholas downed the brandy in a gulp. "You were

going to say that I'm responsible for their deaths, is that it? That I murdered them?"

She drew in her breath sharply. With all the brandy and whiskey he had consumed, how could he be so distressingly discerning? She decided to bluff it through.

"Yes. I was going to say that."

Nicholas's eyes thinned. Tabitha watched him warily.

"My dear, it was not my fault that Garland decided to lay with a big Goddamned nigger."

"Nevertheless, you forced her into that confession by your—your ill-considered attempt to convict Mike Long of something he never did!" Tabitha flared.

"Ah, now we come to the crux of the situation!" Nicholas sat down again, bending forward, resting his forearms on his knees and looking up into Tabitha's eyes. "You are not, after all, so much concerned over Garland's plight as you are over Mike Long's. . . . Incidentally, has he fled?"

Tabitha decided it was best to give him no definite information.

"I really don't know. I haven't seen him."

"Not even while I was in my room?"

"Of course not."

"You missed an excellent opportunity. It's not like you."

He saw anger light her eyes and he laughed harshly. Then his mood changed to one of complete solemnity.

"Mike Long was a very foolish man to cross me. I shall have to hunt him down and kill him."

The threat frightened Tabitha, and she sought to allay his suspicions. Her voice was almost pleading.

"Why, Nicholas? You're wrong about him. He never tried to do you any harm."

"My dear, dear Tabitha. I'm not a fool, you know. Your beloved doctor has been recruiting the blacks for months. He is a member of the Clan. As such I can no longer tolerate him. He must die because he was a leader in the slave rebellion."

"There was no rebellion!" Tabitha shot back. "The Fourth of July has come and gone."

"Of course. We planters succeeded in thwarting the ambitions of the unscrupulous whites who were to lead the revolt by our own brand of cruelty—the whip and the gallows. But men like Mike Long are dangerous. They will work toward the day when they will foster another rebellion. I don't intend to let him live that long."

Tabitha shook her head helplessly. There was no point in trying to reason with Nicholas. He was beyond it. Yet she had to try.

"I tell you Mike Long is not a Clansman!" she said, emphasizing her words. "*You* tried to convince the planters that Mike was a member. You deliberately tried to involve him. You made up that fantastic story about Mike meeting with Ruel Blake. You got Big Sam to lie for you. You had a chance to see Mike Long hang, and you made the most of it. I dare you to tell me I'm right!"

A crooked smile sliced Nicholas's face.

"Very well, I'll admit you are right," he said easily. "The testimony of Big Sam was faked, but only to make sure that Mike Long was convicted. Because he *is* guilty of arousing the slaves with his talk of freedom, and for this he no longer deserves the right to live."

Blocked by his refusal to believe that Mike was innocent of fomenting a slave revolt, Tabitha decided impulsively to put Nicholas on the defensive with some accusations of her own.

"You're lying, Nicholas." Her voice was chilling. "You didn't want Mike out of the way because you thought he was a Clansman. You had another more important reason. You wanted him out of the way because he was your wife's lover! Admit it, Nicholas! You *do* love me, don't you? And you're jealous—plain jealous!"

She knew she was gambling and she held her breath for his reaction. He simply shook his head.

"Poor, poor Tabitha. You still don't understand, do you? I *don't* love you, my dear—not one iota. And to prove my point, I would never try to do away with a man as valuable to me as Mike Long simply because he possessed you. I decided to get rid of him only because he became dangerous to me—and for that reason only."

"But you failed!" said Tabitha, stung by his words.

"Not completely. I will get him yet, my own way."

"You're utterly ruthless," snapped Tabitha.

Nicholas laughed aloud this time. It was one of the few times Tabitha had ever heard him laugh outright.

"There is some old bromide that occurs to me at this moment about the pot calling the kettle black," he said suavely. "Of course I'm ruthless, as much so as you, my dear. I've said it before, neither of us is a very nice person."

"I haven't stooped to murder yet!"

Nicholas shrugged. "Does one stoop to murder, or rise to it? Murder takes a great deal of courage.

591

Perhaps that is why women don't as readily employ it. Women prefer to fight in more subtle ways, while men often use the shortest route to victory."

She did not answer. She watched as his face clouded over, and his eyes assumed that fanaticism she had come to fear.

"I will murder anyone who stands in my way, Tabitha," he said in icy tones. "I'll whip to death any black that revolts against me. I'll finish off any planter that crosses me. I will get Mike Long, that you can be sure of. And if sometime you force me to it, Tabitha, *I will finish you too!*"

She sat there, her mind numbed by Nicholas's direct and deadly threat. A great revulsion surged through her and for a brief instant she wanted to throw away everything that had happened to her in the last few years and start all over again, to go back to Natchez-under, to the strict sanctimoniousness of her father and the staunch common sense of her mother. Suddenly her parents' security seemed preferable to living with an elegant madman on a hill. But she knew instinctively that she would not be able to do that. She wanted the affluent life so much that she was imprisoned by her own desires. And the horrifying thought came to her: *she was as much a slave at Magnolia Manor as the blacks in the field, and Nicholas Enright was the slave master.*

Damn Nicholas anyway!

8

With the Fourth of July gone, the planters breathed easier. For a few blissful days they relaxed, savoring their heady victory, content that they had saved from destruction their own lives, their properties, and their women. They had dealt so drastically with the conspirators, both black and white, that they felt certain another attempt would never be made.

But when the initial euphoria of victory passed they realized that their triumph had been a hollow one. It had not eliminated forever the blacks' longing for freedom, and there were always white men who would try once more to mastermind the kind of revolt that had failed. Despite the paralyzing blow they had dealt to their blacks and their white leaders, the underworld still existed and festered in every river town along the Mississippi. The gamblers and prostitutes, the pimps and murderers, the footpads and thugs—people from which the original plotter, Murrell, had emerged— still held sway. It occurred to them that these outlaws were a constant threat to the civilized life the planters had tried to build, and it was becoming more and more apparent to the thinking people of the time that the river towns would have to be cleaned up.

In Vicksburg, Mississippi, a mass meeting was held

and a Vigilante Committee established. A resolution was taken and notices posted in the river area, giving outlaws, gamblers, prostitutes, and other people of ill reputation twenty-four hours to leave. But the outlaw element refused to forsake the area, for profits from the river trade were too tempting to forego without a fight.

One day later the townsmen swept down on the shacks at the river's edge. Five gamblers were caught and hanged in the street, their dead bodies left dangling as a warning to others. The ploy was effective. Frightened prostitutes, pimps, and footpads fled the area, and the Vigilantes put the torch to the ramshackle buildings that spawned the evil they deplored.

The news swept the Mississippi Valley. A flame of righteousness gripped each river community. Vigilante Committees were formed in every town, up and down the river, and notices posted that all underworld characters must leave within twenty-four hours. And the burnings and hangings continued.

Nicholas Enright knew nothing of this development because he spent the long warm days of July in virtual seclusion. After his conversation with Tabitha about the McRaes, he went into the kitchen, gathered some food, and again retired to his room, also taking with him several decanters of brandy and whiskey. For three more days he remained in his room, pacing the floor like a caged animal.

Even in his seclusion he grew more frightening to Tabitha. On several occasions she heard him thrashing about in a manner she feared would reduce his room to a shambles. At other times he talked to himself in a loud, whiskey-raw voice, remarking that "they" would never get him as long as he had breath with which to fight. On three different nights Tabitha awoke with cold sweat on her brow, listening in terror as Nicholas screamed his way through a horrible nightmare. But no one could reach him to comfort him, for he was suspicious of everyone, even Sophie, and he kept his door bolted.

Mike Long remained close to the house, afraid that Nicholas might emerge from his room with some maniacal violence planned. Tabitha felt more comfortable knowing he was close.

"We'll have to wait it out," he had told her. "Right now he's retreating from reality, and I frankly don't know how it will all end. He may snap out of it temporarily, he may flee, he may turn to violence. He belongs in an asylum, Tabitha."

"I can't take that step, Mike," Tabitha said.

Mike nodded. He knew Tabitha was not prepared to make such a drastic move. It would take time.

Mike's closeness—and Nicholas's absence—posed a critical problem for Tabitha. She made a serious effort to avoid any social or physical contact with the doctor. Her heart constantly warred with her mind. She knew that with Nicholas she had everything; with Mike, nothing. Except, of course, a love she was finding it more and more difficult to deny.

On one occasion, however, Mike came to her in the big salon where Tabitha was sitting in a sort of grand loneliness. She saw him approaching in one of the huge gilt-framed floor-to-ceiling mirrors, and she rose to meet him, wanting desperately to fly into his arms but fighting off the feeling, greeting him with a defensive coolness.

"How is our patient today?" he asked.

"Still in his room. He's acting like a spoiled child, Mike."

"Perhaps that's what he is, Tabitha. There's so much about the human mind we don't understand."

Tabitha shuddered. It was impossible to believe that Nicholas's fine mind was being destroyed by some hideous demon inside him that she could not comprehend.

"Can't something be done to cure this awful sickness?" she asked, knowing the answer.

Mike shook his head. "We have no medicine to cure a sick mind. We can mend bones and sew up cuts and attend the miseries of the intestines, but the mind is beyond us. I know, as a doctor, that Nicholas is mentally ill. He will have moments when he is completely rational, and you will think that perhaps the sickness has gone away. But the tiniest thing can arouse his suspicion, cause him to go mad with fear. This is what you must live with the rest of your life, Tabitha—this, or divorce."

"Divorce?"

"Yes. I've been thinking deeply about the problem, Tabitha. It is your way out. You love me, Tabitha—not Nicholas. If you loved Nicholas you would spend the rest of your life tending him here or in an asylum. But doing this would destroy your life, and you don't love Nicholas enough to do that. True, I can't give you the comforts Nicholas can, but I can give you something he can't—love. It counts for something, Tabitha."

"Please, Mike."

"You need love, Tabitha, more than you want to

admit," he went on. "Marriage has given you a great mansion, gilded mirrors, French rosewood furniture, fine liquors, rare perfumes, a place in society, but it has failed to give you the one thing you need more than anything else—love. Love doesn't have the purchasing power of money. In fact, it's a rather cheap commodity, because there is so much of it in the world. But when you have it, you have something precious, something all the jewels and spangles and glitter in the world can't duplicate."

"Mike, I just don't know—"

He reached out and took her around the waist. She said to herself, *No, I must not do this thing.* And even as she said it, she came willingly into his arms and he crushed her body to his. His lips came down hard on hers, warm and moist and questing, and she felt again the insistently demanding desire to caress him with every inch of her body, from head to toe. She artfully twisted her body against his, and her lips parted so that Mike felt the tip of her warm tongue on his lips, and the room shimmered and rocked gently and became a thing apart.

At last she pushed him gently away, feeling faintly ashamed of her actions.

"I wish you wouldn't do that, Mike."

"You know you want me to."

"Yes. That's the worst part. And we shouldn't."

He tried to take her again, but she held him at bay. Her voice was hushed, trembling.

"Please don't."

He gazed at her a long time. Then, finally, he smiled and left. Tabitha sat down on one of the rosewood chairs and wept softly. At length she stood up again, dabbing at her eyes, angry with herself. *You're a fool, Tabitha,* she upbraided herself mentally. *Forget Mike Long. Keep what you have. Hang onto what you've built. Maybe Nicholas will get better. That's right, maybe he will get better!*

The sudden clatter of horses' hooves outside the house cut through her thoughts like a sickle. Tabitha scurried to the veranda in time to see a dozen planters, in their wide-brimmed hats, thundering to a stop before the front door. At their head was Faunce Manley, who ascended the three steps to the veranda with long firm strides.

"Where's Nicholas?"

"Upstairs in his room."

"Fetch him," said Manley abruptly. "We have important news for him."

"I'm afraid he is in no condition to be fetched," retorted Tabitha, annoyed at his peremptory command. "May I give him a message?"

"What's the matter with him?" asked Manley irritably.

"He's quite drunk," said Tabitha with bluntness. "He's been drunk since the Fourth of July. He won't come out."

"The damned fool! Has he lost his mind?"

She did not answer. There was a scraping noise on the veranda behind her, and she saw Manley's mouth drop slack and his eyes open wide. Nicholas Enright stood at the door, swaying, a decanter of whiskey in his hand, a lopsided smile on his unshaven face.

"What in the hell do you want of me, Manley?" he demanded shortly. "Tell me what you want and then get the hell off my property!"

Manley's face turned red. He wiped sweat from his forehead on the sleeve of his shirt.

"Still sore because we didn't hang your doctor?"

"Tell me what you want, Goddamn it!" snarled Nicholas, not answering the question.

"All right. We're going to destroy Natchez-under-the-Hill!"

Nicholas squinted at him, as if trying to bring him into focus by straining his eyes.

"*What* did you say?"

"You heard me, Nicholas. We've posted twenty-four-hour notices for gamblers and thieves and murderers and whores to get out. Tomorrow morning, when the time is up, we ride into town and string up every last bastard that doesn't leave."

Nicholas took a long pull at the decanter, tipping it up and swallowing in huge ravenous gulps. He wiped his lips with the back of his hand, then rubbed the hand on his trousers. His dark eyes never left Manley.

"You're crazy, Faunce," he said deliberately. "You haven't got a chance."

"No? Vicksburg cleaned out its river town. All up and down the Mississippi River they're forming Vigilante Committees and cleaning out the shacks. We figure to do the same, and we want you to join us."

"Join you? By God, you *are* crazy!"

Manley took off his broad-brimmed hat. He looked at Nicholas closely.

"You don't seem to understand. For years we've lived with this festering sore at our feet. We've tried to ignore it, tried to make believe it wasn't there, while our sons were sampling the whorehouses and our daughters were in dire jeopardy every time they went down on the flats to meet a steamboat. It's in the rivertowns that outlaws like Murrell exist. In our own defense, it's time we cleaned them out, once and for all."

A smirk crept over Nicholas's face. "You talk like a crusader. Why, all of a sudden? You've never thought Natchez-under was a festering sore before. In fact, I'd hate to have to give you a hundred dollars for every time you walked into a bawdy house down there."

"You've said enough, Nicholas," warned Manley, his face crimson with embarrassment and anger.

But Nicholas went on. "You say we planters have tried to ignore it. What sanctimonious piety! I never did. I enjoyed the place on occasions when I sought its delights. And you did too. Now, all at once, you want to destroy it!"

"Yes." Manley's voice was clipped. "And I'm asking you only one thing, Nicholas—are you with us or not?"

Nicholas walked unsteadily toward Manley. He brandished the decanter in Manley's scowling face.

"No. I'm not with you."

"Why not?"

"Various reasons," Nicholas said vaguely. "But mostly because I don't think you can clean out Natchez-under. It isn't possible. As long as a river-front town exists, as long as steamboats and flatboats ply the river, as long as there are rivermen, there will be a Natchez-under. The rivermen want their fun raw—raw liquor, raw fights, raw women. There's going to always be a Natchez-under to serve them. You can't change it, Manley."

"You're drunk," said Manley gruffly. "We'll come back when we ride into town tomorrow afternoon. Maybe you will have changed your mind by then."

He strode away with the other planters, and as they mounted their horses Nicholas came to the edge of the steps and shouted in a maniacal voice.

"Don't come back, Manley! Stay out of my sight!"

The men rode away. Nicholas watched them disappear into the forest, then turned to Tabitha.

"So that son of a bitch has found a new place to satisfy his lust for violence—Natchez-under. He's the type who would like to burn down a town and hang its citizens. He would have made a good righthand man to Attila the Hun. A dangerous man, but I'll see to it that he doesn't hurt me!" He swiveled around precariously and limped slowly into the house. Tabitha followed him cautiously, watching him as he carefully climbed the circular stairway to disappear once again into his room. The bolt on the door slid into place with a clatter of finality.

Nicholas did not reappear that evening. Sophie tried to lure him to dinner but he would not leave his room or accept food through the door. When Tabitha retired later in the evening, he was still there, and she stirred restlessly in her bed as she listened to his incessant pacing of the floor. Unable to sleep, Tabitha arose and unlocked her door, leaving it ajar to catch a breeze from the hallway. She was sure there was no danger from a man who insisted on living like a recluse. It was not until four o'clock in the morning that Tabitha slept, and at eight she was suddenly awakened by a frightening sound close at hand. She sat bolt upright in the bed as she saw Nicholas standing in the doorway. He had the decanter in his hand again, and his hair was disarranged, his eyes red-rimmed and watery, the corner of his mouth sagging drunkenly.

"Lovely," Nicholas said. "Absolutely lovely. Haven't seen you in bed for a long time, Tabitha. You look as pretty as a harlot!"

His words chilled Tabitha. In his drunken stupor, was he going to try once again to become amorous? She tried to calm him down by answering angrily.

"Comparing me to a harlot isn't very flattering," she said.

"On the contrary, my dear, it's extremely flattering." He came forward, sat on the edge of the bed, and surveyed Tabitha with moist, bloodshot eyes. She watched him warily. "That's the trouble with these high-toned, goody-goody plantation wives," he went on. "They don't really understand what appeals to a man. They don't understand his drives and his needs — and if they do, they resent them. But a whore understands. A whore accepts men as they are. I've always been convinced that the average plantation wife could learn a lot from a good whore."

"Nicholas, I deplore being compared with a—a strumpet!" Tabitha's lavender-tinged eyes flashed angrily.

Nicholas grinned. "You should be highly pleased," he said; then his face grew sober. "I'm leaving, Tabitha."

"Leaving? Where?"

"I'm going to Natchez-under-the-Hill. Thought I ought to let you know this time."

"What are you going there for?"

Nicholas smiled slyly. "Perhaps to find a woman whose favors have a special allure for me," he said, and his voice had a taunting diablerie in it. But then his mood changed again and his face became etched in hard lines. "Actually, my dear, I go to warn some of my friends in Natchez-under to get away before Manley and his gang ride into town. By God, the man means to do it!"

"What friends?" Tabitha demanded.

Nicholas's hand traveled down Tabitha's shoulder and cupped itself around her breast. Tabitha stiffened at the bold caress, but she did not dare to deny him.

"Some of my best friends live in the flatlands," he said. "I had my beginning there, you know. You remember me telling you that I ran a saloon and bawdy house to get my start? Well, I still run it."

"Nicholas! Do you still *own* some of these horrible places?" Tabitha said it in surprise, pretending not to know.

"Of course, my dear. And very profitable they are too. I never lose interest in anything that makes money."

"But that's filthy money!"

"Filthy." His mouth twisted bitterly. "It's filthy money that built this house. It's filthy money that bought your clothes and everything you've got. It's filthy money that gave you soirees and the Cotillion. Bless that filthy money, my dear, for without it you would be nothing!"

She looked askance at Nicholas as his voice escalated in a weird crescendo. A sudden fear clutched at her heart. He was peering at her in that fanatical way he had, and his hand, creeping again to her shoulder, had tightened painfully.

"They'll try to take that money away from me, won't they?" he said, babbling almost incoherently now. "But I won't let them! The damned jealous planters want to ruin me, because I'm top dog now and they resent it. They'll do anything to destroy me, and Faunce Manley is their leader. He knows I own the Silver Palace. That's what's behind his scheme to burn and wreck the shacks. I'm not going to let Manley set a torch to my place. I'll see him in hell first!"

He retreated from her, backing away several steps as he surveyed her with his wild, haunted eyes. Then, nervously, he looked about the room.

"I hate this place!" he shouted suddenly.

Tabitha struggled to her feet. She grasped his arm, trying to restrain him. But he broke free.

"I hate Magnolia Manor! Every Goddamn stick and stone of it! I hate it! I built it to impress people, and it hasn't!"

"It has, Nicholas!"

"No!" He shook his head like a wild man, hair dancing over his forehead. "It has only created jealousy. It has made me more enemies than before. Now they are all out to ruin me, to bring me tumbling down, to trample me and exult when they do! I'm going to Natchez-under, Tabitha. I'm going to warn my people to get out. But I'm staying, and when Faunce Manley rides into town, I'm going to shoot him down in cold blood!"

"You wouldn't do that, Nicholas!"

His face hardened, the lines deepening. He took her by the shoulders again. She caught at her night garments as he bodily lifted her and carried her across the room. But he did not take her to the bed, as she feared. Instead he stopped before a closet and hooked the door open with his foot.

"You'd try to stop me, wouldn't you?" he said. "But I won't brook any interference with my plans." He shoved her into the dark closet and slammed the door, sliding the bolt shut on the outside. Tabitha screamed.

"Let me out of here, Nicholas! How dare you!"

"It will do you no good to scream," came Nicholas's muffled voice from without. "I sent Sophie shopping in Natchez. I found Mike Long in the house and told him to get out and tend to the slaves. One of them will return and let you out, no doubt, but not in time for you to interfere with my plans for Manley's vigilantes. When I'm finished with Manley and his gang I'll be back to deal permanently with Mike Long. Manley's blood on my hands will undoubtedly make me thirst for more."

"Nicholas! You've lost your mind!" Her voice echoed in the narrow confines of the closet. "Do you think you can kill Manley and get away with it?"

Apparently he was not listening. She heard his footsteps as he left the room. And in the still darkness of the closet her thoughts became frightfully clear. Mike Long was right. Nicholas Enright was an implacable monster—a monster that must be either caged or destroyed.

9

Abijah Clay was breathless when he reached his cabin door. The excitement that fired his soul had driven him to a faster pace than his normal gait as he practically ran from the center of Natchez-under-the-Hill to his log home on the outskirts. He was aware that such haste was not good for him. In the last hundred yard approaching the cabin, sharp needle-like pains in his chest slowed him down. When he slackened his pace the pains diminished, but the shortness of breath remained even as his excitement did.

"Rachel!" he cried as he burst into the cabin. "I have the greatest news!"

Rachel looked up, placing the long thin knitting needles and the ball of gray yarn to one side. She was momentarily alarmed at Abijah's excitement-flushed face, but he gave her no time to dwell on the matter. Abijah sat down in a chair and leaned forward in tense agitation.

"The day has finally come—the Reckoning! God is prepared to destroy Natchez-under-the-Hill!" He announced it bluntly, with a fervent flair for the dramatic.

Rachel greeted this startling news with something less than unbounded elation.

"It is bad for you to hurry so, Abijah," she scolded firmly. "Please try to relax before you continue. I am sure the good Lord has no intention of hurrying you."

Abijah gazed at his wife with wild resentment, then finally hunched down in his chair.

"Rachel, you are a sedative to me," he admitted. "But how you can possible retain your New England stoicism in the face of one of God's miraculous acts I do not know."

"I am probably one of His most relaxed disciples," said Rachel, picking up the needles and yarn again, "not to mention His severest critic."

"Rachel! Don't be blasphemous!" cried Abijah, who was sometimes shaken by his wife's light-hearted attitude toward heavy-hearted matters. She was a devout person, Rachel was, but Abijah felt sometimes that her wry sense of humor left the degree of her dedication somewhat in doubt.

"Now what is it you are tying to tell me?" she asked.

"I tell you the end of Natchez-under-the-Hill is nearing just as it came to Sodom and Gomorrah," he replied. "In Genesis, it is said, *Then the Lord rained upon Sodom and upon Gomorrah brimstone and fire. . . . And he overthrew those cities, and all the plain, and all the inhabitants of the cities.* And it is said again in Jude, *Sodom and Gomorrah, giving themselves over to fornication, and going after strange flesh, are set forth for an example, suffering the vengeance of eternal fire.* This is now about to come to Natchez-under, as it did to those ancient cities of the Bible."

Rachel's eyebrows raised quizzically. She continued knitting in what Abijah considered a disgraceful display of calmness and unconcern under God's wrath.

"You mean the good Lord is about to rain brimstone and eternal fire on Natchez-under, Abijah?" she asked.

"Yes! That would be it, of course—fire!" Abijah's eyes danced like fluttering blackbirds in his head. "Natchez-under and its sin is about to be erased, Rachel!"

"How do you know this, Abijah?" asked Rachel practically.

"There are signs posted all over the city," said Abijah with mounting excitement. "They give all gamblers and women of the night and other criminals twenty-four hours to get out."

"Signs, Abijah?"

"Yes. Many signs. And if the criminals don't leave, they will be driven out and their hovels destroyed and their lives taken—so say the signs."

Rachel put down her knitting again. She looked Abijah squarely in the eye, impatience in her manner.

"Abijah, tell me something. Who posted the signs in the city—God?"

"By God's hand they were placed," said Abijah.

"You mean God came down here and placed those signs in the streets of Natchez-under?" demanded Rachel incredulously.

"He *caused* them to be placed," amended Abijah carefully.

"And who placed them?"

"The planters."

"I see. If the criminals do not leave, the planters intend to attack Natchez-under and destroy the shacks?"

"Yes."

"Then it is men who plan this."

"No, Rachel! It is God's way. *He* is behind this. He is using the planters as His agency for destroying Natchez-under!" Abijah's voice rose, striking a fevered pitch, for he was fearful that his practical-minded wife did not believe his interpretation and it irritated him that she should have such little understanding.

"The good Lord must be mellowing with age," said Rachel with a soft smile. "He rained brimstone and fire on Sodom and Gomorrah and gave the people no chance to escape. Here, in Natchez-under, he mercifully provides them with twenty-four hours notice!"

"Rachel!" Abijah's voice was filled with dismay. "Who are you to question God's methods?"

"I don't question them, Abijah. I only think that the Lord could save Himself a lot of trouble by merely sending a cyclone or some other natural cataclysm to destroy Natchez-under, instead of using unpredictable human beings as His pawns."

"Shame on you!" cried Abijah, appalled. "That you should even mouth doubts is unbecoming of you, Rachel. Neither of us can question God's ways. The Lord plainly says, *Neither are your ways my ways. For as the heavens are higher than the earth, so are my ways higher than your ways.*"

"I am sorry, Abijah," said Rachel, feeling suddenly contrite at having doubted a belief he apparently held so strongly. "But this is a most serious matter. What about—Ryma?"

Abijah's face became rigid. "She must bow to the Lord's wrath as do the others!"

"She might be killed, Abijah! Don't you have any compassion for her?"

"I have none. She has strayed from the ways of the Lord, so shall she suffer."

"When is this—attack due to begin?" asked Rachel.

"Tomorrow."

"If you have no compassion for Ryma, then perhaps you should for us. I think we should leave for safety's sake."

Her practical words had an amazing influence on Abijah. He stared in perplexed wonderment at his wife for a long time, and when he finally spoke his voice was hoarse with emotion.

"You would leave?"

"Of course."

Abijah came to his feet in sudden anger. He crashed his gnarled fist on the puncheon table top, rattling dishes that sat there.

"By God's holy word!" he roared. "I shall stay! I do not flee from the Lord's doings!"

"Abijah! We endanger ourselves if we stay!"

"No. You do not understand, woman. Comprehension has left you as fear has come to replace it. I have been preaching for years that the Lord's wrath would one day descend on this vile place. I have been laughed and jeered at and insulted, but I have warned all of them. Now that it is to happen, I intend to see it. It is what I have waited patiently for, what I have prayed for, what I have worked toward. And I intend to stand in the midst of it, and watch those who laughed at me flee for their lives or die in the dirt of the streets. This I shall have!"

"Abijah, there is one thing that makes no sense.

You have always been opposed to violence. You have abhorred it. Now, because violence is on the Lord's side, you not only condone it but want to stand and revel in it. Is this not hypocritical?"

"No! Does it not say in Matthew, *All they that take the sword shall perish with the sword?* So it is that those who rob and steal and kill and fornicate in Natchez-under must perish in like fashion."

"Then violence," said Rachel quietly, "if directed by the hand of God, is excusable?"

"It is not only excusable, it is laudatory!" cried Abijah. He was waving his hands, clenched into great fists, over his head, and his face was fiery with zeal. Rachel felt immediate concern for him and attempted to placate him—for she knew now that he would stay, that he must stay, that the destruction of Natchez-under, if it was to occur, was a part of his own triumph.

"I question you only because I do not have your deep understanding," she soothed. "Please sit down and relax, Abijah. We must enjoy what peace we have before the holocaust."

Abijah sat. The familiar pain was in his chest again and he permitted his fluttering heart to calm. When at last the pain subsided he stood up, walked into the bedroom and emerged again with a pistol in his hand. Rachel looked startled.

"What are you doing, Abijah?"

He placed the gun on the table, gazing down at it with some dubiousness.

"I have not used this gun since that awful day when I killed the bandit on the Natchez Trace," he said solemnly. "But I think perhaps I should take it with me when the time of the Lord's wrath descends."

"Won't God's armor protect you?" Rachel could not help ask.

Abijah reacted coldly to his wife's latest blasphemy. "I am certain it will," he said. "But the Lord is going to be very busy. Whatever attention he deems me worthy of might be distracted. I therefore think I shall arm myself against that moment when the Lord's attention may be directed elsewhere."

Rachel smiled and went back to her knitting.

10

Tabitha sat in the stale darkness of the closet like a wayward child banished to his room. The minutes dragged into several hours and the time seemed endless. Fortunately, enough air crept beneath the door to permit her to breathe, but Tabitha wondered vaguely if Nicholas had given any thought to the possibility of her suffocating. From time to time she beat upon the floor and walls to attract attention, but the room was so secluded from the main section of the house that no one could hear her. She grew impatient at her imprisonment and with impatience came seething anger. By the time Sophie returned and, hearing Tabitha knock as she went about her work on the second floor of the house, released her, Tabitha was almost insanely violent.

"Let me out of this damned place!" she screamed.

The bolt scraped and the door swung open. Sophie stared in wide-eyed amazement.

"Lawd-a-livin', Miss Tabitha, how'd you git in there?"

"Don't ask stupid questions!" Tabitha snapped. "Go to the stable and bring up Lady Belle while I dress. I'm going to Natchez-under!"

"You're goin' to Natchez-*whut?*"

"Natchez-under, damn it! Have you never heard of it?"

"Yes'm. Ah sure has."

"Well, get going! Hurry now!"

"Yes, *ma'am!*"

Sophie scurried off, quite aware that when the mistress of Magnolia Manor was in short temper it was best to move quickly and ask no questions. A few minutes later Lady Belle was delivered by the groom to the front of the house and Tabitha came out to mount. To her surprise she saw Mike Long mounted on a gray gelding, standing by. She did not know whether or not she welcomed his presence.

"I'm going with you," he said simply.

Something in his determined tone irritated her. She turned to Sophie.

"Did you tell Doctor Long where I was going?" she asked peevishly.

"Yes'm. Ah thought you was actin' a little odd, ma'am — beggin' your pahdon — an' Ah fetched the doctah."

"I'm not half as crazy as most of the people around here!" snapped Tabitha. "Go back to your slaves, Mike. I'm sure there must be a baby ready to be born or something. I'm riding alone."

"No decent woman goes to Natchez-under alone," said Mike.

"Oh, fie!" Tabitha permitted the groom to help her into the saddle. A thought crossed her mind and she looked at Mike with renewed interest.

"Maybe it would be just as well to have you along, in case of an emergency," she conceded. "Do you have a pistol?"

"Yes. What do you have in mind?"

"Nothing. Except that I intend to bring Nicholas back with me, if I have to wound him to do it."

Mike Long smiled. "Still the completely ruthless lady of the manor, aren't you? Still clinging to the myth that life on the Hill with Nicholas is worth saving."

"I don't intend to argue," said Tabitha petulantly. She heeled her horse and Lady Belle set off down the road at a gentle trot. Mike brought the gelding up at her side.

"Now tell me the whole story," he said. "Has Nicholas fled to Natchez-under?"

"Yes." She unfolded the entire story of Nicholas's holdings in the flatlands and his determination to protect them against the Vigilantes. Mike Long thought about it in silence as they rode through the canopy of moss-draped oaks shredding the sunlight.

"It's not unheard of for a planter to have interests in Natchez-under," he said musingly. "It's part of the hypocrisy of the planters' snobbishness. Those who live on the Hill look down their classic noses at those underneath, but they are not above reaping a tidy fortune from the rivermen. Those who treat women with elaborate courtesy and respect on the Hill do not hesitate to run a house in the flatlands with a bevy of whores. Those who drink the finest whiskey and imported brandy and Madeira wine at their elegant soirees don't object to selling the rawest rotgut to those on the mudflats. Outwardly, those on the Hill never mix with those under it, but there is often a strong, if hidden, thread that connects them."

"Oh, stop your damned preaching!" said Tabitha

crossly. "I'm in trouble, Mike, I don't know what to do about Nicholas, even if I get him back. He seems to be such a beast."

"Where do you think he is?"

"At the Silver Palace."

"With your sister?"

Tabitha felt a faint annoyance at the question, a twinge of dismay that Nicholas would run to Ryma in his moment of distress.

"I suppose he's with her, " she admitted. "When a man's in trouble doesn't he always run to the security of a woman's arms?"

"That's the accepted routine," said Mike easily, "but often the woman he runs to is his wife."

Tabitha looked at him with irritation. "I hate you, Mike Long," she said simply.

Tabitha's obvious vexation caused Mike to discard his bantering style. They rode, then, in silence, emerging finally at the esplanade. They did not stop but took the descending slope that led to the bawdy polyglot world of Natchez-under-the-Hill. Tabitha noticed at once that a hushed silence had gripped the rivertown.

A few people moved like grim specters in the streets, but for the most part they were deserted. It was impossible to say whether most had fled or were hiding away in the shacks awaiting the arrival of the Vigilantes. But the discordant noise of pianos and laughter, which had marked the streets of Natchez-under-the-Hill ever since Tabitha could recall, was now stilled. A few of the assignation houses appeared to be open for business, but even in those only a scattering of shadowy figures could be seen through the open doorways, and there was no blatant attempt to lure business, no sibilant shuffling of chips, no profane voices.

Tabitha saw the Vigilante notices posted on trees and on the jerrybuilt shacks themselves, and she knew this was the cause of the strange and ominous quiet. Glancing toward the quay, she saw a group of gamblers and a few women huddled on the dock, preparing to board the *Creole Miss* which nestled against the wharf. She decided, then, that only the fearless had remained, and by the time Manley's men rode in to town it would be virtually cleaned out, except for token resistance from those diehards who would not be frightened away. And she was sure, too, that when the Vigilantes rode out again, the gamblers and whores would return, rebuild their wrecked hovels and reopen for business.

They rode along Silver Street, somewhat awed by the silence of this normally roaring avenue. When the street made its turn toward the river's edge, the Silver Palace, standing precariously on its stiff stilts over the water, came into view. Tabitha bridled again at the thought of Nicholas being inside. She wondered if, having warned his "people," he might also have decided to leave. She thought it unlikely. Nicholas was too fiercely proud to flee before Faunce Manley's riders, any more than he would flee before his mother's dominance, the supposed plotting of Mike and herself, or the threat of an uprising by the slaves. His towering arrogance would force him to fight against his persecutors.

Mike and Tabitha dismounted in front of the Silver Palace and tethered their horses.

"I'm going in alone, Mike," she said.

Mike hedged. "I thought I came along to help. Besides, you shouldn't go in there alone."

"Oh, fie! I've already done so, remember? It's where I met you."

"I'd better go with you," Mike insisted. "There's no telling what condition Nicholas is in."

Tabitha shook her head stubbornly. "I must talk to Nicholas alone. If he sees you, he'll harden his resistance. Wait outside. If I don't come out in half an hour, with or without Nicholas, you may come looking for me."

"He could be dangerous, Tabitha."

"I know. But he's my husband. It's a chance I'll have to take."

Reluctantly he let her go, watching her as she ran up the ramp to the door, entering this time without hesitation. Tabitha remembered with some pain her first visit to the Silver Palace. Her embarrassment had been almost unbearable. She was surprised to find, now, that she had none whatever. She walked boldly through the open door and entered the dark confines of the bar room. The oak bar stretched before her, like an elongated coffin, and behind it was the same porcine bartender she remembered from her first visit. He looked at her with his marble-like eyes, and several men at the bar turned slightly to behold this exquisite lady who had suddenly appeared in a house of sin.

"I'm a ring-tailed screamer, if'n that don't look like a lady from the Hill," said one riverman loudly.

"Prettiest bitch I seen in a coon's age," said another. "But I hear tell them plantation women is as cold as a well digger's ass."

Tabitha set her jaw. A painted woman at the bar looked at Tabitha with disdain and then possessively threw an arm around one of the men at the bar.

"You don't want no prissy woman from the Hill, mister, when you got me," she told him.

The door leading to the parlor and thence to the anteroom where she had found Nicholas before opened suddenly and Ryma burst into view.

"I saw you ride up, Tabby," she said.

Again Tabitha found herself shocked at the hard lines in her sister's face, the carmined mouth, the gaudy dress with its low decolletage which revealed the upper bulges of her conspicuous breasts in a manner that transcended any dress worn by the women on the Hill.

"Where's Nicholas?" Tabitha demanded.

Ryma's eyes clouded. Her lips set firmly.

"You'd better go home."

"I said, where's Nicholas?"

"Look, honey," Ryma said softly. "It's best if you don't see him now."

"Why not? Because he's having some wench and his wife oughtn't cast eyes on his unfaithfulness? Fie!"

"It's not that way," said Ryma. "He's in the anteroom, facing Silver Street. He's got practically an armed camp in there. He's got rifles, pistols, ammunition. He says he's going to stand off the Vigilantes all by himself."

"He can't do that!"

"Of course not. But he doesn't know it. He's crazy, Tabitha. He has a wild look in his eyes. Oh, Tabby!"

"I know all about it. His mind is going. I'm not quite sure what is wrong. But I've got to help him if I can. I've got to take him home."

Ryma sighed deeply. It was obvious that Tabitha was not to be dissuaded. She had been a stubborn young lady all her life, Ryma remembered. Headstrong. Determined.

"I'll go in with you," said Ryma.

Tabitha did not object. In fact, she was a bit dubious about how she would handle Nicholas and the moral support offered by Ryma might be extremely helpful. She followed as Ryma once again led her through the parlor where couples were lounging in various stages of undress and through the rickety door into the anteroom.

Nicholas sat at a small table, a bottle of whiskey in front of him, a glass in his hand. The room had only one other straight-backed chair and was illuminated by a single whale oil lamp in one corner. That and a saffron ray of sun from one of two windows gave the room a crimson glow that reminded Tabitha — horrifying thought! — of blood. Near the second window, facing Silver Street, two long-barreled Kentucky rifles stood as if at attention. A pistol lay on the table.

Nicholas looked up slowly as the two women entered, and Tabitha saw his face become mottled with anger as he recognized her. He started to get up, swayed perilously, and fell back into the chair. His eyes were glazed, his mouth drooping at one corner, his hair in wild disarray. A sudden thought flashed through Tabitha's mind: *Get him drunker, so drunk that he cannot handle a rifle, get him to pass out. That is the solution.* But his voice was surprisingly steady as he spoke, erasing this notion from her mind.

"Damn it to hell, Tabitha! You shouldn't have come here!"

"I'm here to take you home," Tabitha said boldly, though she felt anything but courageous.

He laughed derisively, drained the glass of whiskey, and added more from the bottle. His eyes wavered between the two women, then settled on Tabitha.

"Get out of here, Tabitha!" His voice was husky with drink. "Get out before all hell breaks loose. There's going to be a fight, a damned big fight. I'm going to stand there at that window and cut those Vigilantes down, one by one, as they ride down the street. They can't get me in here, but I'm an excellent shot and I'll pick them off so fast that those that remain will run for cover. They're not going to get me, Tabitha, and they're not going to get my place!"

"They won't run, Nicholas," Tabitha warned. "They're in no mood to run. Half the gamblers have already cleared out of Natchez-under. The planters will fire the shacks and hang anybody they can catch. They'll get you, Nicholas, if you insist on resisting them. They'll get you!"

"I'll kill Manley!" said Nicholas, his voice rising dangerously. "I'll kill him first. He's their leader and without him they'll run."

Tabitha kept shaking her head, her eyes wide with the comprehension that Nicholas was truly mad.

"Why are you doing this, Nicholas? Even if you do own a few places down here, they are nothing to what you have on the Hill. It's on the Hill you belong. Not down here, protecting these filthy shacks!"

But reason was not going to work. "I started here," Nicholas said, "and I have returned here. Ashes to ashes and dust to dust, isn't that what your preacher father would say?"

"Nicholas, you've got to listen to me!"

His lips twisted spasmodically. He swallowed more of the whiskey, shaking his head as it went down.

"I have already listened to too many people in my life. Now I intend to listen only to myself. Get back to Magnolia Manor, Tabitha. That's what you've wanted all along, Magnolia Manor—not me. Well, I give it to you. Lock, stock and barrel—every last stick and stone of it. Yours! Do you hear me, Tabitha?"

"You're crazy," she said softly.

"Not crazy. Waking up, maybe. After I have done with the Vigilantes I shall go to New Orleans, maybe Europe. But never back to Magnolia Manor. I hate it now."

"You don't mean that."

"Yes. It has meant nothing but defeat to me. Defeat in those years when my pernicious mother ruled it. Defeat when Mike Long and my niggers planned rebellion. Defeat again if I let Manley have his way. Nothing I dreamed of ever came true."

Burning anger assailed Tabitha. How can he use a word like pernicious when he's so damned drunk, she thought querulously.

"All your dreams have come true," Tabitha said, trying to turn his argument around. "You're the most important planter in Natchez. You have the finest house. You and I give the most celebrated soirees. On the Hill you are something; here you are nothing. Don't you see, Nicholas?"

"Yes," he said bitterly. "I am something on the Hill. Top dog in a social order of mongrels!"

Tabitha's mind whirled. What could she say to him? Nothing got through, nothing penetrated, nothing made sense to his wavering mind. He was unreasonable, illogical, emotionally inept. His obsessions had conquered him—the old feeling of being persecuted, run out of his home, tormented—and now his whole being had revolted and he was ready to do murder to avenge himself against those he felt were wronging him.

And she could not make him understand!

A raucous noise came from the street outside and Nicholas stirred restlessly and walked to the window. It was a distant noise, growing louder, the thudding of horses' hooves, the muffled shouts of men in anger. Nicholas's hand reached for one of the rifles, his fingers curling around the barrel. Ryma and Tabitha edged toward the window and peered out. Nicholas made no effort to stop them.

"That's it, look out," he said. "Since you're here, you may now view the slaughter."

Fully a hundred men on horseback were coming down the steep incline from the top of the bluff, the vanguard of them heading for the shacks along Silver Street. From the window Tabitha saw them halt and dismount quickly, forming two bands, one for each side of the street. They were like soldiers taking positions in preparation for battle.

But they were not to take the shacks without opposition. From the black interiors men spilled out, armed with clubs, knives and guns. The two opposing forces faced each other over a space of a dozen yards.

Tabitha noticed that Nicholas was gripping the rifle tightly, the knuckles of his hands pinched white. But he did not raise the gun. Although the shouting voices of the antagonists could be heard, they were too far away for accurate shooting. Plainly, Tabitha heard the booming voice of Faunce Manley. He was standing in the street, gazing balefully at the opposing army of men before him.

"We bear no ill will except for the criminals among you!" he roared. "I see there are rivermen here. We do not wish to shed your blood. You may return to your boats unmolested. It's the criminal element with which we now quarrel."

There was a sullen rumble from the defenders. The rivermen made no move to escape. One among them hurled a challenge.

"We ain't standin' by to see our places wrecked by no dandies from the Hill!"

The Vigilantes answered with a headlong charge into the ranks of the defenders, and a moment later half of the planters were locked in a whirling melee with some fifty opponents while the other half remained on the perimeter of the battle ready to rush in if the tide turned against them. At the window Tabitha watched the senseless battle with mounting horror, as clubs, axes, knives, and guns came into play. Shots rang out and two men crumpled to the ground. One riverman stabbed a Vigilante in the back, and was immediately cut down by a planter who swung an axe at the man's head, cleaving it like a melon. Tabitha closed her eyes, unable to watch the merciless killing. When she opened them again she was appalled to see a man standing in the very center of the swirling battle, his arms raised to the heavens, his eyes searching the skies. And the stentorian voice of her father rose like a great roll of thunder above the clatter of battle.

"God has his revenge! Drive the sinners into the river! Destroy their monuments to sin! Do God's work!"

"It's Father!" cried Tabitha. "He'll be killed!"

"Men of the cloth are often fools," said Nicholas, his breath coming now in excited gasps. "He, too, is on the side of the planters—on God's side, so he believes. I may have to personally disabuse him of that idea some day."

He stared fixedly at the pitched battle taking place on the street, and he held the rifle in readiness. His dark eyes were ablaze, his nerves stretched taut.

"The Vigilantes outnumber us, which is good," he said in a measured, calculating tone. "They will force the defenders back along the street. And when they come within range of my rifle they will get their surprise. I'll pick them off, one by one, until they flee in disorder."

Nicholas's evaluation of the fortunes of battle proved correct. Little by little the Vigilantes began to drive the defenders back along the street. The fighting was fierce and several bodies already lay still on the ground. Tabitha eyed the rifle in Nicholas's hand, the other standing near the window. If only she could get her hands on one of them. . . .

But no. She would never reach either of them. Besides, she did not know how to use a rifle. There was no chance of stopping her husband's plan.

Suddenly one of the saloons burst into flames, the dry lumber crackling and the flames licking at the sky. A great roar went up from Manley's men.

"They mean business, don't they?" said Nicholas mildly. "They fired one of the buildings."

"They'll fire this one too," put in Ryma, trying to make him see the reality of what he faced.

"They will not get close enough," said Nicholas calmly.

As the battle ebbed and flowed, Nicholas watched it with strained eagerness. Particularly, he kept his eye on Manley. The man was in the forefront of the battle, fighting savagely, wielding a huge curved knife and cutting a path into the defending fighters. The Vigilantes' superiority in numbers permitted them to press on, just as Nicholas had foreseen. Even though more rivermen and hoodlums joined the fray, the Vigilantes continued to drive them back, closer and closer to the Silver Palace. A frame structure suddenly went up in flames and screaming women poured from the doorway into the street; another shack was actually torn from its moorings by the frenzied planters, crashing in splintered debris. And in the center of the raging conflict was Abijah, walking like some protected ghost, unmolested by either side, imploring God to wreak His wrath on the sinners of the flatlands.

"Strike them down, O Lord, strike them down!" he prayed in a high-pitched, shrieking voice. His face was red, his entire body trembling with the sweet ecstasy of his greatest moment.

The battle inched closer to the Silver Palace. At last, under relentless pressure, the defenders dispersed, some of them fleeing toward the docks to dash aboard the *Creole Miss,* others disappearing into nooks and crannies of the street where they could hide from the planters' wrath. Some made a precipitous dash for the last refuge on the street—the Silver

Palace sitting on its wooden pylons over the Mississippi. Nicholas lifted the rifle in expectation.

"Please, Nicholas!" Tabitha made one last attempt. "You haven't a chance. Don't try it!"

But he took no notice of her plea. "Any minute now, any minute," he said. "They'll be marching on the Silver Palace now, but they don't reckon on confronting me. One by one I'll take them. Manley will have the honor of being first."

But the group of victorious planters did not immediately attack the Silver Palace. With the defenders in flight, they stopped to regroup their forces, attend their wounded—and make an example of one of the gamblers who had fallen into their hands. He was an emaciated hawk-faced croupier from one of the gambling dens, dressed in a cutaway coat and ruffled shirt. His slick pomaded hair glistened in the sun, but his face was pale and drawn with fear. The men held him as Manley threw a rope over the limb of an ancient oak tree, and now a less militant group of citizens gathered around, their curiosity piqued, as the planters prepared to hang the gambler.

"This man is hanged publicly," cried Manley, "as a warning to all criminals who may decide to come back to Natchez-under when we are finished!"

From the window Tabitha saw her father approach the doomed man. He gazed at the wretch for a long time, then turned to face the crowd of onlookers.

"Thus shall the wrath of God descend!" he shouted. "Destroy this sinner. It is God's will!"

Tabitha could not believe what she was seeing. Her father, who had always deplored violence, was urging the planters to destroy the gambler. For a moment she could not understand, until she realized in horror that this was her father's supreme moment, the moment he had waited for, when all the sinners of Natchez-under would be struck down and laid waste. And this was why he was condoning murder without even thinking of it as such.

The noose was fastened around the man's neck and several men pulled the rope tight. The gambler's body shot upward. He kicked frantically at the end of the rope, and his face turned from white to red to blue. He died in an agony of choking, his tongue lolling from the corner of his mouth, his eyes protruding, his kicks diminishing as life ebbed from him. Abijah Clay stood during this long moment of suffering with bowed head, deep in prayer. Manley stood proudly before the hideous spectacle, staring with belligerence at the sullen crowd.

And then, before Tabitha knew he was about to do it, Nicholas raised the rifle to his shoulder, took brief aim, and fired. The noise of the gun filled the room and the acrid odor of burnt gunpowder assailed her. Manley staggered uncertainly. Blood gushed from his forehead as the bullet crashed into his brain, and even before he crumpled to the ground his face was already placid in death.

11

The Vigilantes stood motionless for several seconds, shocked by the unexpected shot fired during the solemn moment of the hanging. For a moment they stared uncomprehendingly at their fallen leader; then several men kneeled next to him, turning him over. They looked up at their companions and shook their heads.

"I got the son of a bitch," said Nicholas, pleased at his accomplishment. "I've wanted to do that for a long time."

From the planters there arose a hoarse growl of anger and all eyes leveled on the Silver Palace. The sound of the shot had come from that direction. To pick a man off in a crowd of people meant that it had to come from an elevation, probably from a window in the old building. The notorious Silver Palace had been a major target in their plans, and Manley had intended to make a spectacle of demolishing it. Slowly, with great caution, the Vigilantes began to walk toward their target. Tabitha saw that a new leader had emerged to captain the Vigilantes in their cautious advance toward the Silver Palace. It was Chris d'Uberville.

Again Nicholas raised the rifle. Tabitha dared to

grab at his arm.

"My God, Nicholas, don't fire again!"

He shook her off angrily; then he squeezed the trigger. The shot came sharply and d'Uberville stopped in his tracks, stiffened, and fell forward.

"Stand back, all of you!" Nicholas screamed from the window. "I can pick you off one by one. This is Nicholas Enright talking!"

He stood well back in the shadows of the room, so that he was not visible to the planters. The mob, having seen two men killed, halted its advance. The planters were uncertain about the actual location of Nicholas, and until they could determine his exact whereabouts he could cut them down mercilessly. They stood for a moment, uncertain as to their next move, and then another man forced his way to the front. It was Mike Long.

"Mike!" Tabitha's voice cut the eerie silence that hovered in the room. Nicholas swore and struck her, and Tabitha reeled under the blow.

"Stay out of this, Tabitha! I warn you! I can finish off you too if you interfere!"

Ryma went to Tabitha's side, restraining her impulse to ignore Nicholas's warning. Outside, Tabitha heard Mike's voice.

"Come out, Nicholas! There's no reason for you to fight against your own people."

"They're not my people," shouted Nicholas.

"Have you got Tabitha in there?"

"Yes."

"Send her out!"

A crafty expression crossed Nicholas's face. "I'm keeping her. And if you attack this building, I'll kill her!"

A cold horror seized Tabitha. She knew, without any doubt, that Nicholas meant exactly what he said. She glanced at the door to the room. She would have to pass Nicholas to get to it. It was ten paces away. The door stood slightly ajar. A quick dash and maybe—but no. She would never make it. Nicholas would whirl about and drop her in her tracks. He was such an excellent shot she would have no chance to escape.

"I'm not leaving, Nicholas," she assured him, edging closer to him as his attention was fixed on Mike Long in the street below. Ryma stayed close at her side. Tabitha's mind buzzed. Should she attack Nicholas suddenly? Try to disarm him? It would never work. She and Ryma were simply trapped. Trapped with a madman while those outside threatened to rush the building.

Through the window she caught a glimpse of Mike as he conferred with the Vigilantes. At last he stepped a few paces closer to the Silver Palace. Nicholas's eyes narrowed.

"One more step and I'll drill you!" he warned shrilly.

"These are your friends, Nicholas!" Mike shouted. "Everybody you know. They're trying to clean up Natchez-under-the-Hill. They have no quarrel with you. Go back to Magnolia Manor and live the kind of life you were made to live."

The plea fell on deaf ears. Nicholas was beyond all reasoning. His eyes blazed with blind, fanatic hatred. His mouth twitched spasmodically.

On the street the crowd grew suddenly restless. A

surge from the rear pushed Mike Long and the front line forward. With a scream of rage, Nicholas brought the rifle to his shoulder. It was then that Tabitha acted. Whether she was acting in defense of Mike or herself never occurred to her at the moment. But before Nicholas could fire she leaped forward, grasping the rifle barrel and forcing it upward. The shot echoed in the room as the bullet tore into the ceiling.

"You bitch!" snarled Nicholas, shoving Tabitha violently to one side. He turned again to the window, but he had lost his chance. Mike Long was no longer in his gunsights. Apparently the surge of the angry crowd had pushed him toward the ramp leading to the building, and out of Nicholas's aim.

"Burn the place! Burn the rats out!"

The noise welled up from below. Others thought of a more spectacular way to end the Silver Palace.

"Push it off its moorings! Knock it into the river!"

Nicholas, thwarted, spun toward Tabitha. His eyes were fierce, filled with hate. He tossed the rifle to one side and picked up the pistol on the table. He pointed it directly at Tabitha.

"To get me, they'll have to sacrifice you first," he said, almost calmly. "Come here, Tabitha."

Tabitha did not move.

"Come here, Goddamn it!" Nicholas raged. "I have a gun on you and I can blow your brains out. Come here!"

Tabitha, frightened, nevertheless edged cautiously toward Nicholas.

"What are you going to do?"

"Come here!"

He waited until she had come within arm's length

and then he reached out quickly, like a striking snake, and grasped her wrist. Ryma took a step toward Nicholas and he turned the pistol in her direction.

"Get back, Ryma. It's Tabitha I want. She's my darling wife, and she'll be my shield."

He pulled Tabitha toward him, twisting her wrist painfully. Suddenly his left arm was around her waist, and he held her in a vice-like grip before him. Tabitha dared not struggle. He was too dangerous. With one arm encircling her and the other holding the gun, Nicholas moved slowly to one side of the room—directly over the trap door that she had first seen when she had rescued Nicholas from drunkenness at the Silver Palace. Tabitha felt her flesh creep with horror. They were directly over the muddy waters of the Mississippi River! He was holding her there, on the flimsy trap door, his eyes fixed in a maniacal stare at the door of the room.

"Nicholas, for God's sake!" cried Ryma. "You wouldn't!"

His shining eyes flicked toward her and a weird smile cut his lips.

"Wouldn't I?"

Suddenly the building shuddered under their feet, moving as if activated by an earthquake.

"They're trying to shove the building into the river!" cried Tabitha. "Nicholas, we've got to get out of here!"

He didn't reply. The obscene noise of the crowd below rose in undulating waves, pouring through the window, cascading from the bare walls. The noise of angry, unthinking men. Mob rule. Men satisfied only with violence. They had fired some of the shacks, they had run the gamblers out. They had hanged one. And this—the Silver Palace—was the focal point, the ending, the victory. And then came the pounding sound of hurrying feet inside the building, not of many men but of one, coming closer, closer.

Tabitha struggled in Nicholas's tenacious grip, but she was no match for him. His strength had always been superb, like an animal's. She heard the footsteps approaching and knew it must be Mike. In final desperation she cried out.

"Mike! Don't come in here!"

Nicholas cursed and his arm tightened around her viciously, squeezing the breath from her. But her warning either was too late or went unheeded, for all at once Mike stood in the doorway, pistol in hand.

"Drop it!" snapped Nicholas

Mike Long blanched. He knew this place. The trap door, the lever on the wall, the waters of the river below, waiting. Seeing Tabitha's position, he had no choice. He dropped the pistol to the floor with a clatter.

"You look somewhat afraid, Doctor," said Nicholas with an edge of glee in his voice. "Why? Why should you care what happens to me—or my wife?"

"What are you going to do, Nicholas?" Mike asked slowly, playing for time.

A contemptuous smile crossed Nicholas's face. "Look at him, Tabitha. Look at the man you gave yourself to. He stands alone and unarmed. His mob is about to tear down this building. Look at him, my dear, for it may be your last look."

Mike's voice came urgently. "This building will collapse any minute, Nicholas. Let's talk sense and get out of here."

"I intend to get out," said Nicholas blandly. "I intend to walk from this room, down the ramp to the steamboat. And I expect that you will give both Tabitha and me safe conduct."

"Go on," said Mike impatiently.

"You have no choice. If you refuse to call off the planters I will drop Tabitha through this trap door into the river! With a bullet through her head for good measure!"

"You wouldn't do that."

"Why wouldn't I? She was useful to me once, but she is no longer."

"Without her you're nothing, Nicholas," said Mike cooly. "You have no future without her."

"On the contrary, I do have a future but Tabitha does not figure in it."

Mike Long took a deep breath. The situation was intolerable. Nicholas held all the trumps. At gun point, there was nothing Mike could do. The only possible avenue to eventual escape was to keep Nicholas talking. Stall for time and hope that some of the planters would burst into the room and overwhelm him with sheer numbers, or that the Silver Palace would rock sickeningly and throw him off-balance for that split-second Mike needed to close with him.

There was only one way to gain the precious time he needed, and that was to take away Nicholas's advantage by placing him on the defensive. He had to strike fear into that suspicious mind, play on the devastating paranoia that gripped him. If he could do that, Nicholas's wavering mind might shift from the immediate situation for a brief instant and give Mike the opening he needed.

"Because you believe you do not need Tabitha," Mike said carefully, "you would murder her in cold blood?"

"Without a qualm."

"The same way you murdered at least six people?"

The question startled Nicholas. His dark eyes shifted from side to side, and into them crept once more the haunted look of a frightened animal.

"You don't know what you're talking about," he said uncertainly.

Mike realized that he was now on the defensive and he pushed his advantage.

"Six people, Nicholas! You've murdered six people. And I have enough evidence to send you to the gallows."

"You're crazy!" The words came out in a snarl.

"Not nearly as crazy as you." Mike's voice was soft but firm. "All your life you have been slightly mad. All your life you have suffered from delusions."

"Delusions!"

"Yes. You believe that people are persecuting you, and you have twisted every fact to fit this theory. You have even committed acts to prove—to others and perhaps to yourself—that you were really persecuted."

The restless clamor of the crowd outside penetrated the room like the buzz of giant insects. The floor rocked slightly and the old structure groaned. But Nicholas clung to Tabitha, the pistol still directed at Mike Long.

"I don't have to listen to this drivel," he said, his voice now on the brink of hysteria.

"But you will," said Mike. "You have said that your

636

mother was a domineering despot who ruled everyone's life, and that she tried to rule yours. Is that right?"

"Yes! Yes, damn it!"

"But you were wrong, Nicholas—or lying. She was the dominant personality in your household only because she *had to control you!*"

Tabitha uttered a silent prayer. She knew Mike was guessing now, trying anything to distract Nicholas. Her life—everyone's life—depended on the outcome.

"Your leg," said Mike. "You've claimed your mother crippled you by withholding treatment. But that isn't true, is it?"

"It's true! It's true!" There was fear in Nicholas's voice. Panicking under Mike's questioning, the fact that he could end the inquisition with three shots from his pistol had fled his mind.

"You manufactured that story," said Mike easily. "You created that fiction to prove to others that you were persecuted. Perhaps you actually grew to believe it after a while."

Nicholas's eyes swept the room. Mike knew his words were having a disintegrating influence on the man's frightened mind. He knew Nicholas did not want to hear these words, yet he was so intrigued that he could not help himself.

"And that business about the attempted fire at Magnolia Manor," Mike went on relentlessly. "You accused your mother of that too. But she wasn't the one who poured whale oil on the draperies at all. You did it, didn't you?"

"No! For Christ's sake, no! What are you trying to do to me?"

Tabitha struggled helplessly in her husband's grip. The building swayed underfoot. The movement was slight, and Tabitha hoped the rickety shack would stand at least until Mike had turned the tables on Nicholas—if that was possible.

"You faked the attempted firing on the manor, Nicholas, to prove to people that didn't believe you that you were really persecuted. Paranoiac people have been known to do such things."

"No! I tell you, no!"

"It would be a difficult task for your blind mother to obtain whale oil, carry it to the manor, pour it on the draperies, and set fire to the place. You did it, Nicholas."

Nicholas's eyes grew fearful under Mike's taunting.

"Stop it! Stop it!" He was almost pleading now, consternation and fright in his voice.

"I've only begun," said Mike. "The plague. Remember the plague? It arrived at a convenient time for you, Nicholas. When you mother came down with it, you withheld medicine from her. You killed your own mother, Nicholas."

He did not answer. His fearful eyes glared at his accuser.

"That was your first murder, Nicholas. Your own mother."

Nicholas trembled violently. "You're a liar—a damned liar!" he raged. "You can't prove that!"

"Yes, I can. The calomel and jalap you gave me for Tabitha's treatment was the same you withheld from your mother. This I know." Mike's "proof" was questionable, but Nicholas was now too distraught to recognize the fact, and Mike rushed on. "You killed your mother and then you tried to get me hanged. You bribed Big Sam to testify falsely against me, but your plan was disrupted by Garland. Her confession resulted in the death of Big Sam, Garland and John McRae. You are responsible for all of those deaths, and today you've murdered Manley and d'Uberville — six killings in all!"

A tense silence descended upon the room, marred only by the noise of the mob outside. Mike had used all of his ammunition. He had nothing else to fight with, except the hope that what he had said would be so unnerving to Nicholas that he would make a mistake, leave an opening, for Mike to use to his advantage. But all at once Nicholas seemed more in control of his emotions than ever.

"You seem to know everything, don't you?" he said coldly.

"Enough to get you hanged," Mike replied.

"Then I have no alternative," said Nicholas. "Six murders, you say? Then how about making it nine? You can only die on the gallows once anyway, so why not nine?"

Mike remained silent. His ploy had failed. His attempt to drive Nicholas out of his mind, to destroy his ability to reason, had seemed on the verge of success. But now his power to reason was back — an insane kind of wisdom that told him that he would have to kill Mike, Tabitha, and Ryma to settle his problem.

Suddenly, with a violent oath, Nicholas hurled Tabitha from him, sending her reeling into a corner where Ryma caught her and kept her from falling. His voice came evilly, with a certain lift to it.

"One by one," he said, "I'm going to kill all of you."

"Don't be a fool, Nicholas," Mike warned.

"I've been a fool long enough," Nicholas said, calmer now. "But no longer. I've changed my mind about escaping. I'm going to put a bullet into each of you, and then I'm going to kill myself—the tenth on my list. That should put a pretty end to the show, don't you think?"

The building swayed and groaned again, and Mike said, "let's get out of here before the building collapses."

"Afraid of death?" Nicholas said mockingly. "Don't worry. You won't die in the rubble of this building. You will die before it falls, because I won't let the Vigilantes cheat me out of the pleasure of personally destroying you. The three of you, all dead by my hand! That will be my revenge. My revenge on the whole world for what it has done to me. My final act, my legacy to the future!"

He had lost all semblance of sanity now, but he was calm and poised in his madness. His breath was heavy, swishing in and out of his lungs as if some huge bellows was at work inside of him. The ugly barrel of the pistol lifted slightly in his hand.

"You first, Tabitha!" he grated. "To my lovely wife I offer the privilege of dying first!"

Mike's jaw pinched tight. This was the moment—the final moment—that he had to counter. He could not stand idly by and permit Nicholas to shoot Tabitha down in cold blood. He had no choice now but to rush Nicholas, to distract him, to reach him before he could squeeze that trigger. He tensed as the barrel of the pistol leveled on its target, but before he could leap forward there was the deafening explosion.

The barrel of the pistol wavered, pointing to the floor. Pain streaked the features of Nicholas Enright. He stood for a moment in the middle of the floor, like a graven image, and then a spurt of blood emerged from his chest, soaking through his ruffled shirt, spreading with surprising rapidity. He staggered a step or two, and his free hand went out to catch himself, fastening on the lever that operated the trap door. And then the floor opened beneath his feet and, as if by magic, his body disappeared, and there was a soft, dull smack as he struck the muddy waters below.

And then they saw him standing in the doorway. Abijah Clay, a pistol in his hand, smoke curling upward from the barrel. The preacher's head moved slightly, and he looked at them. There was a dazed expression on his face.

"God forgive me!" he said.

"Father!" Tabitha ran to him, clinging to him, sobbing. She felt his body shake in a giant upheaval.

"I have killed your husband," he said.

Tabitha glanced with horror at the opening in the floor through which Nicholas had fallen. Her mind reeled. Nicholas gone! Everything gone with him! Nicholas, Magnolia Manor, the plantation way of life, the lavish soirees, the prestige—all gone. And, strangely, for she could not understand it yet, another feeling emerged. She was rid of him. She was rid of it all, everything she had thought was important was gone—and, somehow, the thought failed to distress her. Instead, there was a gentle feeling of relief.

She looked at her father. His face was ashen, a pasty gray with sickness in it. He stumbled forward and Mike raced to catch him. The pistol clattered to the floor, and Abijah's body went limp in Mike's arms.

Tabitha stared at her father, dread reflected in her eyes. She heard Ryma say, "My God!"

"We've got to get him out of here," said Mike.

He lifted Abijah in his arms, cradling him as if he were a child, and the three of them left the room. The structure was groaning again, as if in its death throes, and the floor lurched under their feet. They fled the building, bursting out into the blessed sunshine at last. Mike spied a horse and wagon standing nearby and he ran, still carrying Abijah, and placed him gently down in the wagon bed.

"Let's get him home," said Mike firmly.

"What's the matter with him?" asked Tabitha.

"Don't know. Heart, maybe."

Abijah suddenly opened his eyes. His voice came hoarsely, with a note of command.

"No! Don't take me home. Not now! This I must see!"

He raised up on one elbow, his eyes riveted on the Silver Palace. The mob of men were straining against the building. Horses had been tied by ropes and were pulling at the pilings. At any moment the building would tumble into the river.

"Bring down the walls, O Lord!" Abijah's voice was raised in a rhapsody of passion. "Like the walls of Jericho, destroy the walls of Natchez-under! Destroy this festering place of sin and kill all those who are children of the Devil!"

"Father, you must calm yourself!"

Abijah seemed aware of Tabitha's presence for the first time since leaving the building. A fleeting smile crossed his face.

"I am in the presence of the Lord's work," he said. "I respond to it with proper passion." He raised his voice again, the rich, full quality it had always possessed still present despite his weakness. "Tear down this wicked house while the Lord watches!"

As the mob attempting to overturn the building struggled and strained to do the Lord's bidding, the shrill voice of Abijah urged them on.

Mike moved around to the driver's seat and spurred the horse with a crack of the whip. As the wagon rattled over the rough road, Abijah Clay saw the end of the Silver Palace. For a tense moment the building leaned crookedly to one side, and then with an angry splitting and cracking of wood it slid with a resounding splash into the river.

"God's will be done," said Abijah contentedly and relaxed for the first time.

In the wagon they wheeled Abijah back to his log home, where a distraught Rachel greeted him. Mike carried the preacher into the house and placed him on a bed. Abijah's hand clutched at his chest and his face was contorted with pain.

"There is a great pressure on my chest," he moaned. "I believe the Lord is calling me."

Mike worked furiously. He asked if there was a sedative in the house and he administered it. But he had no medication and no way to fight this harrowing illness, except by rest.

"Do not overly concern yourself," said Abijah, smiling wanly. "The Lord has called me and I do not flinch. He has, in His great wisdom, allowed me to live long enough to witness two very great and satisfying events today."

"Don't talk now," said Rachel. "You must rest."

"The Lord will grant me much time to rest," said Abijah. "I speak now, while I can."

Rachel muffled a sob in her handkerchief. Tabitha and Ryma stood quietly, looking down with sympathy at the suffering man who looked much older than he was. He was breathing with difficulty, in short painful gasps, his hand resting on his rising and falling breast.

"Two great things have happened today," Abijah went on. "First, my daughter has come home, and I think she will now return to the ways of Christ." His pale eyes fastened on Ryma.

Ryma dropped to her knees next to the bed and Abijah reached out and stroked her head.

"I once said that you could never enter my house again," he said softly. "I was wrong to say that. It shut the door on you and made it impossible for you to again walk with God. The Lord is forgiving, and so too should his disciples be forgiving. You are welcomed back, my dear."

Tears welled up in Ryma's eyes but she fought them off, her rouged mouth twisting with the pain of her feelings.

"Father! I was so wrong. If you forgive me, I'll never go back to the shacks."

"You are forgiven, my daughter."

She bowed her head, kissing the rugged misshapen hand and letting her head rest on the edge of the bed where he lay. Soft sobs coursed through her.

"One other great event I have beheld today," said Abijah. He stopped, his face tortured by pain as he fought for breath. His eyes clouded over, but he battled back from the brink and they cleared again. "Natchez-under-the-Hill has been destroyed. The Lord has at last wiped it from the face of His earth. As Sodom and Gomorrah disappeared, so has the flatlands of Natchez!"

Tabitha glanced warily at Mike. His face was drawn tight, and as he observed the rising emotion in Abijah's voice, he said, "You had better rest now."

"I shall have an eternity to rest," said Abijah, smiling weakly. "But I shall rest in peace, knowing that Natchez-under-the-Hill is gone, destroyed by God through the implementation of decent people. It is good."

He closed his eyes, and for a frightening moment Tabitha thought he was gone. Rachel took an anxious step forward, but he opened his eyes again.

"I say goodbye now—"

"No, Abijah!" There was pain and dread in Rachel's voice.

"Yes, I say goodbye," Abijah repeated. "To you, Ryma, whom I have wronged. And to you, Tabitha, whose only fault was an ambition greater than your judgment. And last of all, to my dear wife, Rachel, who knew the hardship of being married to a wandering preacher but who never once wavered in her support and understanding. I say goodbye to all things I have treasured—my family and my work.

God bless you."

It was as if he had timed his death in connivance with the Almighty, for as he breathed the last word he closed his eyes again and was gone.

12

They stood for many minutes at the bedside, and no one spoke until Rachel, squaring her shoulders, walked out into the main room of the cabin. She sat down at the puncheon table where Abijah had so often done his writing, and she looked at the book-lined walls and the pen and quill set and the dog-eared Bible and everything in the cabin that was so full of Abijah Clay.

Her eyes were dry with a hard inner grief that needed no outward expression, and as Tabitha and Ryma and Mike followed her into the room, she said stonily: "And now? What now?"

There was no answer and Rachel stood up again and walked to the front door of the cabin, gazing out at the mudflats and the rows of shacks which, despite Abijah's proclamation, had not been totally destroyed.

"You, Tabitha, will return to Magnolia Manor?" she asked.

Tabitha shook her head. She told her mother of the death of Nicholas Enright and her mother listened in grave silence.

"For two husbands in the same family to die on the same day is almost too much to bear, isn't it? What will you do, Tabitha?"

"I won't go back to Magnolia Manor. I assume the property passes into my hands now—that's for a lawyer to decide—but if it does I will dispose of it. It's a hard decision to make, but I do not want to return to the life on the Hill." She looked at Mike Long, a remote expression in her eyes. "Father was right. My ambition was greater than my judgment. I thought the life of the planter was the highest form of human achievement. But life there is not much different from right here. Despite its elegance, it has its cruelties and injustices, just as Natchez-under has them. Refined cruelties, I suppose you would say, but cruelties all the same. I can't think of a word to describe plantation life, exactly, but it is—"

"Artificial?" suggested Mike.

"Yes. Artificial." She said no more, for Mike's word seemed to fit. The whole structure of life on the Hill was artificial. The pretense and showmanship, the jealousy and backbiting—and the hatred. That was it. The people on the Hill, despite their polished politeness, hated each other, and hatred drove them to build a greater mansion, to furnish it more lavishly, to give the biggest parties, all in an unreasoning scramble for dominance, very much like ants fighting each other to be king of an anthill.

Nicholas had realized this. Mike had, from the beginning. And she was sure her father sensed it. Now she knew, and was willing to admit it for the first time.

"So what will you do?" asked Rachel practically.

There was an uncertain silence. Mike broke it.

"She'll marry me," he said.

Tabitha's eyes swept toward him. For a moment she was confused; she didn't know whether to be angry at his presumptuous remark or to fly into his arms with unashamed gratitude. To take for granted that she would marry him was indiscreet to say the least, but there had always been an annoying impudence about Mike. Still, it was different, somehow, from Nicholas Enright's devastating arrogance. Softer, more amiable; not as haughty or as contemptuous. She answered mildly.

"You have not yet asked me," was her gentle rebuke.

"Beside the point," said Rachel, her eyes wise with understanding. "Do you love him, Tabitha?"

"She hasn't got around to admitting it yet," said Mike, "but of course she does."

"Oh, how dare you, Mike!" cried Tabitha with a pretense of outrage.

"Do you?" asked Rachel.

"Yes!" snapped Tabitha, looking angry at having been forced into the admission.

"That is good. And you, Ryma—what will you do?"

"Where you go I'll go, Mother."

Rachel nodded. "That, too, is good."

Later that evening Tabitha and Mike stood on the esplanade, looking out over the broad crescent of the Mississippi. The waning sun dappled the water with amber; the foliage on trees and shrubbery was a darker green; the breeze had died to an almost undetectable softness. A white steamboat with filigreed superstructure had departed the quay and was moving with majestic slowness down the spangled ribbon of water, its paddlewheel churning, the stacks belching puffs of smoke.

"We'll live on the Hill, but not on a plantation," Mike said. "Just a few rooms in Natchez where I can build a practice."

Tabitha looked up at him. She did not try to conceal her love for him now, for she knew that she would be far happier with this man than she had ever been with the grand and complicated Nicholas Enright. He slipped his arm around her shoulders and squeezed her gently.

"The great river," he mused, as he gazed out across the water, "is also a shoddy thing, isn't it? It is great and magnificent because it plays an important role in man's history. It helps to move him from place to place, and it handles his commerce and his trade. But it's shoddy because of what it spawns—a human scum that feeds upon it. As long as the river exists and men ply it, there will be such places as Natchez-under-the-Hill."

"Father thought it had been destroyed," said Tabitha.

"Which was a blessing for him," said Mike. "But it hasn't been destroyed. As long as there are men to patronize gambling houses and brothels, there will be other men—and women—to provide them pleasure. And so Natchez-under-the-Hill will survive the feeble blow the planters delivered to it, and the gamblers and prostitutes will return. And the gentry will go back to the Hill and forget about this inconclusive episode and once more ignore the existence of the sore festering on its river's edge—and this little incident today will be swallowed up in history and lost in its more important pages." He reflected for a long moment, then went on. "It is nice that your father died believing that sin had been cast out of Natchez-under. It gave him peace in his last moments. But he was wrong, Tabitha."

"Do you suppose his whole life was wrong?" she asked. "He spent a lifetime trying to reach the unattainable."

"He did," said Mike. "But it wasn't wrong. The world needs men like your father. Perhaps some day they will triumph. Perhaps some day there will be a better world, one free of crime and corruption, slavery and arrogance and too much pride. Maybe, on some great day, the meek will truly inherit the earth. But it will not be in our time."

They stood for a long interval, watching the river change color as the sun dropped toward the horizon and draped a blanket of purple over the earth. And for the first time in a long time, Tabitha knew complete contentment. The sun, moving down upon the horizon, became a radiant half-disc on the edge of the world, and then no sun at all. The sky changed from pink and orange to deep purple with cirrus clouds of black that signaled the coming of night.

"It seems as if the sun doesn't want to leave," said Tabitha. "As if it wants to paint the world with a variety of colors, indelibly, so that night will never be able to erase them."

"But it will lose its fight too, and night will come," said Mike.

And night came, casting its darkening shadows over the earth, blotting out the landscape and the river and destroying the artful work of the sun. Mike and Tabitha descended the steep hill of Silver Street and walked toward the cabin, where a single candle flickered bravely in the window.

FICTION FOR TODAY'S WOMAN

WHISPERS (675, $2.50)
by Dorothy Fletcher
Her husband too involved in his career, her children too old to be children, Christine was restless and bored—until coincidence brought a young man into her life. And that's when the WHISPERS began. . . .

SEASONS (578, $2.50)
by Ellin Ronee Pollachek
No one knew the real Paige Berg—not even Paige. But when she begins managing one of the most exclusive department stores in the world, people begin to find out!

EMBRACES (666, $2.50)
by Sharon Wagner
Dr. Shelby Cole was pregnant. She was also dedicated to her career in medicine—a career her lover couldn't accept. Somewhere along the line, something had to go. And it wouldn't be the baby. . . .

THE VOW (653, $2.50)
by Maria B. Fogelin
On the verge of marriage, a young woman is tragically blinded and mangled in a car accident. Struggling against tremendous odds to survive, she finds the courage to live, but will she ever find the courage to love?

FACADES (500, $2.50)
by Stanley Levine & Bud Knight
The glamourous, glittering world of Seventh Avenue unfolds around famous fashion designer Stephen Rich, who dresses and undresses the most beautiful people in the world.

BE CAPTIVATED BY THESE HISTORICAL ROMANCES

READ THESE MEDICAL BLOCKBUSTERS!